THE SUNDOWNER'S DANCE

THE SUNDOWNER'S DANCE

TODD KEISLING

Content warnings can be found at the back of this book.

◉

The Sundowners Dance is a work of fiction. The characters, incidents, and dialogue are creations of the author's imagination or are used fictitiously. Any resemblance to actual events or persons, living or dead, is entirely coincidental.

Copyright © 2025 by Todd Keisling

All rights reserved. No part of this book may be reproduced in any form or by any electronic or mechanical means, including information storage and retrieval systems, without written permission from the author, except for the use of brief quotations in a book review.

Without in any way limiting the authors' and publisher's exclusive rights under copyright, any use of this publication to "train" generative artificial intelligence (AI) technologies to generate text is expressly prohibited. The author reserves all rights to license use of their work for generative AI training and development of machine learning language models.

Cover and interior design by Alan Lastufka.

First Edition published April 2025.

10 9 8 7 6 5 4 3 2 1

ISBN 978-1-959565-51-2 (Hardcover)
ISBN 978-1-959565-52-9 (Paperback)
ISBN 978-1-959565-53-6 (eBook)

For my elders, earthly and cosmic alike.

Howdy, neighbor!

PART ONE
FAIRVIEW

1

The realtor opened the door and Jerry Campbell stepped inside. "It's a relatively new construction," Stewart Taylor said. "This one's about a year old, give or take. Never been lived in." He paused, gave Jerry a quick once-over, and smiled. "Hell, the development is barely thirty years old, so I guess it's all new in the grand scheme of things."

Jerry ignored him, walked ahead into the living room, hands in pockets, and pretended to be interested in the finer details. This was his eighth visit to a prospective home, and the first that hadn't been occupied at one point or another. All the others were either too small, too big, or too expensive.

He hadn't considered Fairview before, had only driven through the place a couple of times when he was younger and still working in corporate. A tiny blip on the map between Stroudsburg and Scranton. Hardly a town. More like a village where everything there was to see lay on either side of Main Street.

This place was twenty miles outside Fairview's city limits, nestled in a round valley between the mountains. One of those gated retirement communities, a fact which initially gave him pause. When Stewart recommended it the first time, Jerry had waved away the notion of living in such a place. *Retirement communities are where people go to die,* he'd said with some indignation, refusing to accept that his seventy-third birthday was fast approaching. Stewart had persisted, broaching the subject after every other showing, and after seven houses, after Jerry had a long talk with himself about his age, after his broken heart refused to mend, he finally acquiesced to Stewart's suggestion.

"See? Not so bad, is it?" Stewart's voice echoed across the empty space.

Jerry nodded and directed his attention to the living room window. The neighborhood, or at least this part of it, seemed quiet enough. A man in a straw hat tended to his azaleas across the street. An American flag protruded from the adjacent house, waving lazily in the breeze, and birds sang from somewhere overhead. Well-manicured lawns. No kids. Not a cloud in the sky. A perfect spring day in the Poconos.

Now that he was here, the place looked just right. So did the price tag.

It doesn't get more Americana than this. Abby would hate it. Ten years ago, I probably would've hated it too.

"—you think, Mr. Campbell?"

"Huh? Oh, I'm sorry, Stewart." He twirled his finger next to his ear. "This old mind wanders. What were you saying?"

"That's quite all right. I was just remarking on the space. It's in the range of square footage you've been looking for."

Jerry made a show of sizing up the room. "Yes, you're right about that. My house is just too big now. Too many memories." He offered the realtor a wounded smile. "You understand."

"Indeed, Mr. Campbell, I do. Many of my clients are in the market for the same thing and for the same reasons. I believe you'll find this home suitable to your needs. It's got a great open floor plan."

Jerry allowed the young man to give a guided tour. He followed Stewart from room to room and took in the bells and whistles: new appliances, hardwood flooring, crown molding, a modern kitchen, and basement storage. All the living space on a single floor. Everything about the house was what he'd been looking for, something with more reliability, more efficiency to keep the bills down, and a place free of memories from a past life.

Stewart's phone rang when they reached the master bedroom, and he excused himself to take the call. Being shadowed throughout a strange house had set Jerry's mind on edge, so he took some relief in the realtor's sudden absence and relished the silence. He studied the empty room, making mental notes for where to position his bedroom furniture, and half-turned to ask his wife her opinion before catching himself. Warmth flooded his face. He rubbed his eyes and blinked away the tears.

Men my age shouldn't have to start over.

Jerry stared absently out the bedroom window to the neighborhood beyond. From here he could see the solitary neighbor in the straw hat, still watering his azaleas. The man saw him and waved. Jerry waved back.

But I guess if I have to, maybe this is the place to do it.

He thought of his home for the last twenty years. The closets to be cleaned out, their contents donated. The furniture to be sold or discarded. The framed photographs and the urn on the mantel.

"You're getting ahead of yourself," he said to the empty room. The sound of his voice unnerved him. God, since when did he sound so weak?

Stewart's voice echoed down the hallway. "Did you say something, Mr. Campbell?"

Jerry sighed, shook his head. "I said I'll be right there."

When they returned to the living room, Jerry gestured to the window. "I like the place well enough, but how's the neighborhood? Seems pretty quiet."

"Oh yes," Stewart said, "Fairview Acres is a wonderful community, one of the highest rated retirement communities in the county. And I hear the HOA is quite agreeable as well."

"Homeowners Association? I don't remember that from the listing."

"It's. . ." Stewart faltered, searching for the right words. Jerry studied his face, amused, waiting for the lie to cross the young man's lips. Here we go. Finally, here comes the bullshit.

Stewart cleared his throat. "The Fairview HOA isn't on the listing because it isn't a formal association. I only call it that for lack of something better. Consider it more like a. . . community association. No monthly dues, no penalty fees, no by-laws. Nothing like that."

"A community association?"

"Think of it as a club. Living in Fairview Acres makes you an automatic member. And this club is, well, quite exclusive."

Jerry smirked. "I'm not a fan of hippie-dippie bullshit, Stewart."

"Certainly, Mr. Campbell. Look, it's nothing like that. More like. . . a support group. A way for everyone to get to know each other. Weekly activities. A huge barbecue every month. Neighbor taking care of neighbor. You know. Like an exclusive club."

"You said that already," Jerry said, enjoying watching the young man sweat. The scent of fear over losing a commission was palpable. "But sure, why not. I like this place well enough. Let's meet tomorrow and discuss further."

Outside, after Stewart locked up the house, they shook hands and parted ways. Jerry remained a moment longer to survey what he expected would be his new start. The rancher was smaller than his current home, and devoid of personality with all that white siding, but he supposed he could make it a comfortable place to live.

Or a comfy place to die. He grinned. Even now he could hear Abby scolding him for his cynicism.

On his way back to the car, he spotted the man in the straw hat. He was still where he'd been ten minutes earlier, perched behind his azaleas with a watering can. Jerry wasn't a green thumb—that was Abby's specialty—but he wondered if all that water was drowning the flowers.

Their eyes met. Jerry raised his hand and waved again.

The man waved back. "Howdy, neighbor!"

"Hi," Jerry said. "Just window shopping."

"They all say that," the man said. "I bet we'll be seeing you soon, though. By the moon's eye."

He waved again, but Jerry only offered a nervous smile in reply before climbing into his car. As he drove away, he looked in the mirror and saw the man in the hat was still watering the same patch of flowers. He was still waving in Jerry's direction, too.

Of course, Jerry thought, *the neighborhood weirdo would live across the street.* He chuckled to himself as he navigated through the neighborhood's winding streets. He'd seen his share of planned neighborhoods, the same cookie cutter floor plan spaced evenly in a perfect grid, but Fairview Acres was far more organic. The houses were similar models, ranchers with the occasional split-level here and there, but the streets snaked their way through the valley and reminded him of old farm roads from his youth, twisting and without order.

As he followed signs for the security gate, a curious observation wound its way into the back of his mind. Where were all the neighbors? He expected to see others outside on such a beautiful day, but the sidewalks and yards were empty. No one was out walking their dog, mowing their lawn, or washing their car, and an absurd notion struck him in that moment. *What if I'm alone out here, twenty miles from anywhere?*

His late wife spoke up in the back of his mind: *Isn't that what you wanted, love?*

He couldn't argue. Silence and solitude were all he'd wanted for months now, a quiet place to grieve and age and die, the way a dog might crawl under a porch when it senses its time has come.

Jerry pumped the brakes as he neared the security gate. What was it the weirdo in the straw hat had said to him?

"By the moon's eye," he muttered, waiting for the crossbar to rise. This place might as well have been on the moon, and so what if the neighborhood was empty? Maybe it would just be him and the weird man in the straw hat, living alone in Fairview Acres on the dark side of the lunar surface.

As Jerry neared the crossbar, he spotted a symbol embedded in a bronze plate above the entrance archway: a crescent moon eclipsing an eye.

"Huh," he muttered, shrugging off the chill creeping across his shoulders. He turned down the air conditioning and went on his way.

2

The next morning, Jerry second-guessed himself all the way back to Stewart's office. What if he was making a rash decision? He hadn't gone through the mortgage process in more than twenty years, and when he and Abby had closed on their forever home, Jerry swore he'd never do it again. She had just laughed and told him everything would be fine.

He missed those gentle reassurances.

Today, as he traveled up the highway to the village of Fairview, he could only conjure doubts from the chaos roiling in his brain. Wouldn't he be better off just staying put? Shouldn't he wait another couple of years to see if the home-buying market improves? And what if he saved his pennies and remodeled his old home instead? It's what Abby would've wanted.

There it is, he told himself. *What Abby wanted. She wouldn't give a hill of beans about remodeling the house. All she wanted was for you to be happy and functional.*

Jerry mustered a weak smile. Functional. Abby was fond of saying that when he was on the verge of a panic attack. A little remark spoken in jest to make him smile, focus, and stay grounded. But the longer he lived without her, the more he realized that her desire for him to be functional wasn't so much a joke at his expense as it was an endearing wish. The sad truth was that Jerry wasn't functional, not really, and he was utterly terrified of facing the world. Abby had made him feel strong and capable, had cheered him on when the chemicals in his brain were hellbent on destroying him from the inside.

She was patient. She possessed a knack for cutting through his panic to reach the core of what troubled him. For thirty-five years she'd been his rock, holding him down when the world threatened to pull him away, urging him to seek help for the demons in his head. Without her, he wouldn't have considered that he had a mental illness. Things like anxiety weren't understood when he was younger, especially with men who were expected to be strong, calm, and collected at all times.

Abby didn't believe in that bullshit, though. She knew when he was struggling with the daily drudgery of his accounting job. She held him at night when he was so worried about going to work the next morning that he couldn't stop shaking. And she took his hand when she asked that he go see a doctor.

I love you, Jerry, but I hate seeing you like this, and it's just getting worse.

A week after they moved into their forever home, Jerry made an appointment with a psychiatrist and began his journey to better living through chemicals. Abby stood by him every step of the way, from one medication to the next, until he found the right cocktail of drugs. *Through sickness and health,* she used to say with a smile, and he remembered feeling immortal when she looked at him like that.

Now she was gone, and he was getting older. Facing the world without Abigail Campbell was scary enough, but facing each day burdened with anxiety in the shadow of her absence terrified the hell out of him.

Jerry slowed the car as he drove into Fairview. Stewart's office was less than a block away, and when he flipped the turn signal, he realized his hand was shaking. He parked the car along the curb and took a deep breath, waited for his nerves to settle.

He looked at his reflection in the rearview and listened to the emptiness of the car, the tick of its cooling engine, and the rush of passing traffic.

He said, "Who am I without you?"

No answer but the beating of his racing heart and the quickness of his breath. He tapped the steering wheel, focused on the sensory input, and counted. His breathing and heart rate slowed by the time he reached nine.

A moment later, he collected his paperwork from the passenger seat and climbed out of the car. He was ten minutes early for his meeting.

◉

"All right, Mr. Campbell, I think that's everything for now."

Jerry watched Stewart collect his check for the down payment. A pit had opened up in his gut at the start of their meeting. Sliding the check across the table widened that pit into a chasm. Any further and he might collapse into himself.

Stewart glanced at his watch. "Do you have any questions for me?"

"I do." Jerry's mouth was dry like he'd swallowed a handful of salt. He licked his lips, wishing he'd rationed the bottle of water Stewart's receptionist had given him. Only a few drops left. "Have there been any other offers? I know we're aiming low with the bid—"

"You're the first. I happen to know the developer and suspect he won't have a problem accepting your terms. They're eager to fill those homes, after all, especially in this market."

"I'm sure they are. . ." Jerry relented and reached for the empty bottle. Those few drops were better than nothing. "And this homeowners association—"

"Right, the Fairview Acres Community Association."

"That's it. Do you have any more information about that? A list of provided services, that sort of thing?"

"Ah, I almost forgot. I have this for you." Stewart reached into his suit coat and produced a slender envelope. Jerry's name was scrawled across the linen surface. "It's early days, of course, but the association likes me to give this out to prospective buyers. Think of it as a welcome letter."

Jerry took the envelope and looked inside. A colorful brochure printed on glossy stock depicted a smiling elderly couple sharing a laugh. Whatever had preceded the photo must have been so goddamn funny. They wore matching pastel jumpers. *Looks like Heaven's Gate*, Jerry thought. *They probably have matching sneakers too.* A message below the laughing couple read: *HOWDY, NEIGHBOR!*

A memory flashed through his mind. The man in the straw hat watering his azaleas. Hadn't he said the same damn thing?

"That should answer any questions you might have."

Jerry unfolded the brochure and skimmed its contents. Lawn care and landscaping by request, a community-owned internet service called "FairviewNet," community pool, gymnasium, on-site emergency services, monthly summer barbecues in the park—the image revealed another smiling couple in what he assumed was the park, with a massive boulder in the background—and no mention of dues. He folded the page and returned it to the envelope. "Sounds too good to be true," he said under his breath.

Stewart shook his head and smirked. The expression drove a hot spike through Jerry's gut. He knew that look. It was the same patronizing smile the kid at the gas station sometimes gave him when the pump wouldn't read his credit card. The same dismissive attitude of "okay, boomer" personified in a glance and festering with the same assumptions: that he was too old to understand and too proud to learn. Thick pockets of heat filled his cheeks as he clenched his jaw. Ten years earlier and he would've given this condescending prick a piece of his mind.

But then he remembered the empty house waiting for his return. The one haunted by the absence of his late wife. A void of life ready to embrace him and return him to dust. And he remembered how badly he wanted to escape the claustrophobic emptiness that held him in the dark, whispering of better and healthier times.

Jerry took a breath, smiled through his resignation, and pocketed the envelope. He followed Stewart out of the conference room and back into the office lobby. They shook hands. Jerry gave Stewart's a good squeeze.

"I think you'll like it in Fairview, Mr. Campbell. What our little town doesn't have, the community surely does."

"I'm sure I will," Jerry said. "What about a bookstore? Or a good place to get coffee? Anything like that here?"

"No bookstore," Stewart said, "but we have a nice library at the edge of town, and a wonderful coffee shop just around the corner. Common Grounds. Can't miss it."

Outside, the sky was overcast, and the mountain air nipped at his ears as he walked to the end of the block. He didn't mind the cold, however; he was still fuming on the inside, imagining all the ways he'd rip that cocky son of a bitch a new one if only he could go back and do it again. Oh, the ways he'd make Stewart feel two inches tall. If only he'd said this, done this, reacted this way—

"Staircase wit," he said to the sidewalk. "Damned if I could say it in French, though."

L'esprit de l'escalier.

The spirit of the staircase, only the French version sounded so profound and eloquent. Of course, Abby knew how to pronounce it—she'd taken those French courses in college—and delighted in making him laugh. *You're a master of the staircase, darling.* Then she'd say something else in French that he couldn't understand and laugh some more at his annoyance. He'd take that annoyance a thousand times more if it meant hearing her voice again.

Jerry paused when he reached the next corner and shook his head. "You old fool."

He'd walked right by the coffee shop, lost in his own head, a master of nothing but regret and panic and heartache. He turned back, eager for something bitter besides the bile teasing the back of his throat.

The village of Fairview stretched out in a straight line, its Main Street a two-lane detour off I-380 that stretched from one highway ramp to the next. Jerry saw all the town had to offer in the span of five minutes, three of which were spent sitting at the single traffic light, sipping his coffee, while downtown traffic crawled through the intersection. There was one gas station, one library, one volunteer fire company. A town of singles trapped in the heyday of the 1960s and barely hanging on to what remained of Poconos tourism. Rowhomes filled out the side streets before giving way to the state game lands that made up most of the wilderness between here and Stroudsburg. A billboard near the highway ramp read "Visit Jim Thorpe!" in faded blue letters. He wondered if anyone these days even knew who Jim Thorpe was.

Satisfied that he'd seen all there was to see of Fairview, he merged onto the entrance ramp and began his journey home. *I think you'd like this place, Abby. There's no bookstore, but at least it's got a library. You always had something clever to say about small towns and libraries. Christ, what was it?*

He opened his mouth expecting the words to tumble out, but none came. She was there in his mind, already laughing because she knew how he'd react, but her words were gone. No sound, her voice silenced by time and his piss-poor memory. Was this how he'd spend the rest of his life? Clutching at the memories of his best friend, fearful they might fade like old photographs?

The swell of grief was as instant as it was heavy. A sucker punch of reality, time, and gravity. Getting older would mean losing her again in the most insidious of ways.

His memories of her would disappear with time, beginning with the little details he hadn't considered savoring in the moment. What she had for breakfast the day after their wedding, or what she wore on a random Wednesday ten years ago—all the fractured minutiae of a life in forgotten moments, cracked and chipped and flaking away like an old painting. She would become the suggestion of a person distinguished by his most intimate and dear memories, less a person and more of a concept, a slippage from present to past tense, here and gone. A face out of focus. Forgotten.

Jerry wrestled with this new reality for the duration of his drive back to Stroudsburg. The overcast sky made good on its promise of rain, with the first warning droplets pelting his windshield as he pulled into the driveway. Their house—just his house now—looked as exhausted as he felt. One of the gutters sagged along the eave over the garage, and the siding needed a good wash. He'd been so caught up in house hunting that he'd neglected to take care of the lawn. Weeds sprouted from the flower beds Abby had taken pride in maintaining over the years.

I'll fix it, he told himself and closed the garage door.

His cell phone rang as soon as he stepped inside. The screen lit up. "Fairview Realty," it read.

Stewart was talking before Jerry had time to say hello. "—ood to see you this morning. I just wanted to let you know

I've already heard back from the property manager. They've accepted your offer."

Jerry stared blankly around his kitchen, at the fingerprints on his refrigerator, the stack of unwashed dishes in the sink. A hint of pressure bulged in the back of his skull. Stress headache, maybe. Or pressure from the storm.

"Mr. Campbell?"

"Yes, sorry. They accepted the offer? Already?"

"Correct."

"And they didn't even negotiate?"

Stewart laughed. "I told you they're eager to fill those homes. We've also got a buyer for your current home."

"Really? Already? Who made the offer?"

"A land developer. Offering you ten percent above the asking price."

"Wow. That's... perfect timing, I guess."

"It certainly is! Can you drop by again tomorrow? Just to sign off on some more paperwork."

"Uh... sure—"

"That's great. See you tomorrow!"

The call disconnected before Jerry could respond. He stared at the screen for a moment and frowned.

Prick.

He spent the rest of his day cleaning the house, something he'd put off for the better part of a week. His daily routine had been in disarray ever since Abby's passing. The ensuing depression had destroyed whatever drive he'd had beforehand. But with Stewart's news and the sudden interest from a developer, he found the drive to begin—even if he didn't want to.

That evening after he'd prepared for bed, he picked up the book Abby had been reading in the hospital. A crime thriller by S.A. Cosby. Her bookmark protruded from the center. He flipped the book open to the marked page. The bookmark was decorated with swirls of color and a single statement in white letters: "A town without a library is like a skull without a brain."

Jerry closed his eyes and laughed.

3

Two months later on a fine May afternoon, Jerry closed on his new home with little fanfare. He had no children, no close friends, or extended family left with which to celebrate. The friends he did have were made on account of working for the same company, and he hadn't heard from any of them since Abby's funeral. He supposed he'd make new friends in Fairview Acres. That was the point of moving into a retirement community, wasn't it? To be among peers? He told himself as much every day leading up to close. Positivity—for as forced and unnatural as it felt—was what made those last few weeks bearable as he sorted through Abby's things.

Now, with everything packed in boxes in the back of a moving truck, Jerry thought he might be ready to begin again. He wanted to be ready, even if that meant masking his anxieties the way he used to in his accounting days by being social and outgoing, laughing at stupid jokes, and feigning interest in sports. But didn't he retire to escape all of that pandering fake bullshit? Hadn't he already served his time by putting on the suit, masking up, and going to work for thirty thankless years?

Abby would've told him to quit bellyaching and take it in stride.

I'm trying, he thought. *But it's all so goddamn heavy to carry.*

His phone alarm chimed. The movers were scheduled to meet him in an hour. Jerry gave his old Stroudsburg home a final tour, said goodbye to its ghosts, and closed the door behind him.

◉

Given everything Stewart had told him about the community, Jerry half-expected there to be a welcoming committee when he rolled up to his new home. Instead, he found his side of the neighborhood to be much like he'd left it a few days before, during his final walkthrough: empty sidewalks, freshly cut lawns, and not a soul in sight. Not even his green thumb neighbor across the street was out this morning.

Just as well. Last thing he needed was an audience while those boys unloaded his things. He glanced at his watch and frowned. *If they ever get here.*

Jerry parked along the curb so the movers could have the driveway and popped the trunk. He'd packed some of his personal effects separately—the essentials like toiletries, a few changes of clothes, another one of Abby's books—in case he lost steam unpacking everything over the next couple of days. And he expected he would, given how much his muscles and joints ached from the last week of lugging boxes.

Once everything was unloaded on the front porch, he unlocked the front door and stepped inside. When he'd first walked through the place with Stewart, he'd possessed an element of detachment; now he found the atmosphere stuffy, oppressive, and the space too intimate. There were hairline cracks in the paint where wall met ceiling, faint cobwebs, and a lazy *plink* of water dripping from the kitchen tap. Regret bubbled up in his gut, filling his head with that nagging voice which often accompanied big decisions. The one that said, *This is a mistake. It's too small. Too empty. Too new.*

"But it's home," he whispered to the emptiness. "Whether I like it or not."

Underneath the pangs of regret and anxiety, he *did* like the place. It just didn't feel like home yet, and that would come in time. If the movers ever arrived.

He pulled out his phone and was about to dial the moving company when the truck came barreling down the street. Jerry stepped outside and waved to the driver, whose window was already down.

"Sorry, boss. Got hung up in traffic."

"All good," Jerry said, making a mental note of the time. He'd check it against their invoice just to be sure.

An hour later, while watching two young men maneuver his sofa through the front door, Jerry heard someone call his name from the street. His green thumb neighbor drove up in a white golf cart. He still wore the straw hat and friendly grin. A basket of assorted vegetables sat at his side.

"I knew you'd be back, neighbor!"

Jerry couldn't help but crack a smile at the man's earnestness. He crossed the lawn to meet his first neighbor of Fairview. They shook hands.

"I'm Jer—"

"Jerry Campbell, yes, I heard. Arthur told me you'd be moving in. I'm Gary Olson. Here, these are for you." He heaved the basket from the golf cart into Jerry's hands. Cucumbers, zucchini, squash, and ripe tomatoes. "Fresh from my garden."

"This is mighty kind of you, Gary. Thanks."

"Don't mention it. My garden is your garden." Gary took off his hat and wiped the sweat from his bald head. "Has anyone else stopped by to say hello?"

"No, you're the first."

"Give it time. Brad and Matilda live next door to the right of you. You probably won't see them for another hour or two. They like to sleep in."

Jerry gave their home a once-over. He'd think the place empty if not for their car parked in the driveway. "I'll be sure to say hello when I see them."

"You do that. They've been looking forward to meeting you. Arthur said you're recently retired. Accounting, was it?"

"I'm sorry—Arthur?"

"Oh, forgive me. Arthur Peterson. He's the chairman of the Fairview Acres Community Association. Think of him like everybody's hippie big brother. Great guy. Keeps everything running like clockwork around here."

Jerry forced a smile. "I'll be on the lookout for him too, I guess. And you're right. Retired accountant here."

"Yeah, I bet you couldn't wait to get out of that rat race, huh? I used to work in security. Been retired for ten years now and living here in Fairview for almost as long. I tell ya, Jerry, you're gonna love it here. By the moon's eye."

"By the what?"

Gary's face blossomed rosy pink. He cut a grin and said, "Just a little something we say around here. I'll let Arthur fill you in."

"All right. Well, I'm gonna get back to supervising—"

"I won't keep ya. Nice to meet you officially, neighbor. By the moon's eye."

Jerry didn't know how to respond to that, so he simply offered the odd man a smile and a nod. *By the moon's eye*, he thought, recalling what he'd said to Stewart months earlier. *Hippie-dippie bullshit.*

◉

Morning bled into afternoon and offered a brief respite from the suffocating Pennsylvania humidity. Jerry tried to help the trio of young men with the boxes, partially to hurry them along (they were being paid by the hour) and partially because he hated feeling useless. It was a short-lived gesture—he pulled a muscle in his back while carrying a box of Abby's books and spent the rest of the afternoon on his sofa like an upturned turtle. One of the young men offered him an edible, which Jerry politely declined out of sheer pride, and later regretted being so damn foolish. Instead, he popped some ibuprofen from his overnight bag and waited for the pain to subside.

He'd almost dozed off when one of the movers said, "You gonna make it, sir?"

Jerry opened his eyes and feigned a smile. "I've had worse. How're things coming along?"

"We're just about done. Only a few boxes left. We can go ahead and settle up if you want."

After the movers left, Jerry lingered on his porch and arranged the few pieces of patio furniture he'd kept from the old house. His rocking chair, a birthday gift from Abby a few years back, and a pair of restored chairs she'd purchased from an antique shop, were charged with good memories, and he couldn't bear to part with them.

Their evening routine had seen them enjoying each other's company in silence while lounging on their old porch. Those days, she'd usually be nose-deep in a book, and Jerry would have one or two beer bottles lined up next to his chair. The only thing he'd had to look forward to was retirement and more days like those, relaxing with his love, watching the sunset and stars.

Those days. Funny how so much can happen in two years. Feels like a fucking decade.

He yearned for a beer, if only to numb the pain in his back for a while, and wrestled with whether or not to head into town. When he moved, however, every muscle sang in protest.

"Guess I'll order pizza."

While he sat and scrolled his phone, a gaunt fellow in a pink polo shirt and jeans emerged from the house next door. Jerry arched his brow and watched.

The neighbor—what did Gary say his name was? Brad? Brett?—seemed oblivious to the world, and when he stepped into the waning light, Jerry saw his clothes were covered with dark stains. Dirt or grease, he couldn't tell. The gaunt man shuffled down his driveway to check his mail. Only when he turned back did he notice Jerry staring.

"Howdy, neighbor!"

Jerry raised his hand. "Evening."

"It is a nice one, isn't it?" The man approached, stuck out his hand, but quickly second-guessed himself. "Sorry, I'd shake your hand, but I've been. . ." He met Jerry's gaze, one corner of his smile faltering for an instant, the gears turning in his head.

Jerry said nothing, opting to let this man finish his lie, whatever it might be. There was an odor to this odd man. Something he couldn't place. Metallic.

"...working on my lawnmower. Changing the oil. You know how it is."

"I guess I do."

"Anyway, I'm Bradley Scott. Nice to meet you."

Silence filled the gap between them. Jerry held his breath, tried to quiet the anxiety racing through his mind, wondered if he was being too awkward, too standoffish. He slipped on the mask of a jovial retiree, forced a smile. Abby was always the one to handle matters such as introductions. She understood his shyness and anxiety better than anyone, and while he'd felt her absence more every day, nothing compared to today—so far.

She's not here to protect you, old man.

Every ring of the doorbell, when he felt the weight of her name on his tongue; every interaction with an unfamiliar face, without her to catch his nervous glances; all harsh reminders of this fact. Burying the hurt in his heart only made the agony worse.

"Jerry?"

"Huh? Oh, sorry. It's been a long day, Bradley. I'm afraid you caught me at my worst."

"Not at all, my friend."

Jerry smiled, but inside he was screaming. *Are we, though? Are we friends? We just met.*

"So, what do you think of Fairview Acres so far? Great place, isn't it?"

"It's... quiet. Is it just us and Gary across the street?"

"Oh, no. There's my wife Matilda, and that's Bethany..." He pointed to the house next to Gary's, and then the next. "Grace and Roland—guy used to be in the Marines—and then there's Sal and his partner Fabio. It's a full block. There's just a couple of empty properties on the other side of you."

Jerry followed his finger, tried to make a note of all the names so he wouldn't be at a loss when he inevitably met them. He was about to ask where they all were today when the front door of Bradley's house opened. A thin brunette walked outside and made a beeline for Jerry's porch.

"Hey, honey. This is Jerry Campbell. Moved here from Stroudsburg. Jerry, this is my wife, Matilda."

"Oh, Stroudsburg, I love that little town. Nice to meet you, Jerry." She gave her husband a once-over. "Brad Scott, you are filthy. Why didn't you change after you finished all that landscaping?"

Bradley squeaked out a nervous laugh, and Matilda joined him.

Jerry watched the pair play off one another, wondering which story they'd stick to, wondering if he was asleep and trapped in this awkward fever dream.

"Well, Jerry, we won't keep you." Matilda took Bradley's hand and slowly pulled him back toward their house. She didn't seem to mind his filth now. "Have a lovely evening."

Jerry's smile faded as they retreated to their home. When they were gone, he exhaled and buried his face in his hands. "I don't know if I can do this, Abby. I really don't."

He listened, absently hoping for her to reply, but there was only the whisper of a breeze in his ears. Birds sang from somewhere overhead. The rest of Fairview Acres was still.

His stomach rumbled. He patted his gut and slowly climbed to his feet. As he stepped inside and dialed the local pizza joint, a nagging thought bubbled to the surface of his mind.

I didn't tell them I moved from Stroudsburg. And that smell on Brad. Was that copper?

Someone answered his call, and Jerry forgot all about his visit with the Scotts.

◉

Jerry awoke later that night to a scream.

Figments of a dream he'd been having lurked just below the surface of consciousness, eager to draw him back down into darkened waters, but the scream pulled him free of such depths. He opened his eyes and stared at the ceiling. His heart raced. Where the hell was he? This wasn't—

Footsteps. Or what sounded like footsteps, at least. Two pairs, tramping across the roof right above his head.

He sat up, kicked off the sheets, and fumbled for his watch. 1:08 in the morning. Fog clouded his head as he scanned the room. Towers of boxes, furniture askew, and Abby was nowhere to be seen. He placed his hand on her side of the bed. A cold pillow.

He sighed, wiped the sleep from his eyes, and tried to ignore the heartache flooding the hollow spaces of his chest. Of course Abby wasn't there. And this was his new home.

But the scream and footsteps—had he dreamed them?

"She went this way!"

"I see her. Over there in the new guy's yard!"

"Someone call Arthur. She's seizing again."

"Already did. He's on his way."

He didn't recognize the voices. They were panicked, fearful. Desperate.

Another series of footsteps pounded across the roof and gave him a start. Visions of marathon runners filled his head. What the hell was going on? He crossed the room and peered out the window.

Outside, a group of men and women approached his yard, forming a semi-circle around a thrashing figure. He wiped his eyes again. A woman's features slipped into focus. Her curly silver hair shimmered in the streetlight as she clutched her face. She turned toward his house. Her face screwed up, frozen in a rictus of pain as her eyes fluttered open, and Jerry thought he saw something bulging from her forehead. He blinked and it was gone.

A man Jerry didn't know took a step toward her, one hand held out in offering.

"Kat, honey, you just need to breathe through this. It'll be over—"

She gripped a fistful of her hair, yanked her head back, and let loose with a scream that made Jerry's blood run cold.

"Christ. . ." He turned away, snatched his phone from the nightstand, but hesitated when he saw headlights cast the onlookers as silhouettes. An ambulance slowed in front of his house, and two paramedics climbed out. *Huh,* Jerry thought. *That was fast.*

A moment later, another vehicle approached from the other end of the street. The pickup truck made a sharp turn and parked in his driveway.

"Everyone stay clear." One of the paramedics jogged across the lawn toward the woman. "Katherine, everything is going to be all right."

She hissed back, *"Get. . . them. . . out."*

The second paramedic joined his partner. He held a syringe in his hand.

The driver climbed out of the pickup. "Hold on a moment, boys." He was short, clad in shorts and a tie-dyed T-shirt. His flip-flops clapped across the pavement.

The woman's knees buckled, and she collapsed in a shivering heap, but when Mr. Tie-Dye approached her, she mustered enough clarity to shrink away from him.

"Kat, please, we're only trying to help. If you fight this, it's just going to get worse."

"Stay away... from me..."

Mr. Tie-Dye frowned, shrugged his shoulders. He nodded to the paramedics. "Take her." And to Katherine: "It doesn't have to be this way. We can talk about this when you're not so hysterical."

While she struggled to speak through her convulsions, one of the paramedics took hold of her arm and plunged the syringe into her bicep. Whatever medication he'd injected began to take effect immediately. Her convulsions slowed enough for the paramedics to lift her to her feet. Jerry watched helplessly as they led the poor lady to the ambulance.

A moment later, the ambulance pulled away. No lights or sirens. It turned the corner and slowly drove out of sight. The onlookers lingered for a few more minutes, chatting with Mr. Tie-Dye. Someone said something, and the others erupted in laughter. From his bedroom, Jerry thought they all looked like gossiping children.

Finally, Mr. Tie-Dye clapped his hands in a gesture of dismissal, something Jerry's old manager loved to do at the end of a meeting. He climbed back into his truck, but before he put the vehicle into reverse, he poked his head out the open window and waved at Jerry.

Jerry didn't return the gesture. He closed the curtain and crawled back into bed.

Sleep eluded him, and in the twilight hours before he finally began to drift off, he thought he heard more footsteps across the roof.

Footsteps and a dry, rattling croak.

4

The following morning, Jerry dragged his ladder out of the garage and climbed up to the roof. He found new shingles, an air pipe for the plumbing, and fluffy clouds painted against a beautiful summer sky. He wasn't sure what else he'd expected to find. Footprints, maybe, as foolish as that seemed. The noise from above hadn't relented until dawn, and by then he was wide awake, irritable, and confused.

He hadn't dreamed it. The noise was as real as the screaming woman last night—concerning, but at least that sound could be explained. Footsteps on the roof were something else entirely.

What the hell could make that kind of racket?

Nothing that he could see from here. Not so much as a splatter of bird shit, though avian visitors were the only thing that made sense. Squirrels were too small to make that kind of noise.

Then again, it would take something huge like a wild turkey or plump goose to distress the beams, make the timbers creak—and more than one.

"So what was it then?"

No answer, but the breeze kissed with a remnant of spring chill.

He lingered a moment longer, scanned the roof one more time, before muttering "Fuck it" under his breath and going about his day.

Whatever had trespassed across his roof did not return that night. Nor did his rest remain undisturbed. Sometime after midnight, he opened his eyes to a dark room split with faint beams of light. Laughter echoed across the street.

"Give me a break," he whispered. Laughter, lights, a big fucking party—he stumbled across the room to the window and pulled back the curtain. A couple dozen people loitered on the sidewalk in front of Gary's house, drinks in hand, laughing and chatting the night away without a care. A fluffy brown Pomeranian trotted across the street into his yard to squat.

Goddammit, I don't want to be that guy. Please don't make me be that guy.

He'd never had to be that guy in his old neighborhood. Even if he'd tried, Abby would've put a stop to it right away.

No one likes that guy, love. Remember that old Tom Hanks movie? It had Bruce Dern, too. He was always at war with a neighbor over a little dog shitting on his lawn.

Jerry remembered. *The 'Burbs.* It had that creepy family from the Old Country, with the one guy who took the trash out at night. What was their name? It was right there on the tip of his tongue—

Music drifted from Gary's party. An '80s pop song, heavy with piano and bass. Someone cranked the volume, and the crowd cheered.

He sighed, turned on his bedside lamp. "Guess I'm gonna have to be that guy."

Jerry tied off his robe and walked to the end of his driveway. Charcoal smoke and cooking meat tickled his nostrils.

He stared in disbelief, afraid to admit that he wasn't upset anymore, just perplexed.

"Hey, Jerry! Over here!"

Gary emerged from the crowd. He wore an apron printed with the muscular torso of a bodybuilder. Jerry shook his head, couldn't resist the laugh rising up his gullet.

"You should join us, neighbor. Got some burgers and dogs on the grill."

Jerry glanced at his watch. "I would, but. . . Gary, it's almost one in the morning."

"Ah hell, I'm sorry, Jerry. Did we wake you?" Gary didn't wait for a reply. He spun around, shouted to the crowd, "Guys, turn that shit down!"

The music grew louder in protest.

"I'll make 'em turn it down. Really, I'm sorry about this. You're so new here, I forgot to tell you—I mean, it's an open invitation. . ."

"Thanks, but I'm beat from unpacking. I'm gonna head back to bed." He made to turn but stopped short and said, "Go easy on the music, yeah?"

"Absolutely."

He watched Gary retreat to his yard and disappear into the crowd. A moment later, the volume dropped to a reasonable level. Abby whispered in his head, *You should join them.*

"Maybe when I get some sleep," he whispered, shuffling back to his house. When he reached the door, a name drifted up from the murk of his memories: *Klopek.*

The weird neighbors in that movie were named Klopek. He'd moved into a goddamn neighborhood full of them.

👁

Another party happened the next night at the Scott residence next door.

The night after, another party—this time at the house next door to Gary. Someone named Bethany lived there, but he hadn't met her yet. Jerry sat on his porch watching twin strings of lights pulse and blink to reggae music, contemplating going over and introducing himself as That Guy. His only solace was the hope that these parties would eventually migrate further down the block. At least they kept the music at a decent volume.

Not that it mattered much. There were so many people congregating at these parties that their incessant chatter transformed into a continuous drone of background noise.

On the fourth night, Jerry lay on his side, staring at the window and waiting for the nightly festivities to begin once again. Always after midnight, and always in the open air. The clock ticked past twelve, and within minutes, he heard muffled chatter echoing from further down the street. Grace and Roland's house, Bradley had told him, but they were just names to him, another couple of faces he'd yet to meet.

A few weeks after Abby died, Jerry saw his doctor about insomnia and walked away with a prescription for Ambien. He'd flushed them after a week of usage, when he'd awakened one morning with the side of his face covered in peanut butter and a loaf of bread at his side. Sleepwalking and sleep-eating were a common side effect, he'd learned afterward. Those pills had worked, though, and he found himself wishing he'd held on to them for nights like this.

Assuming this is temporary, he thought. He'd read stories of retirement homes being places of rampant debauchery, with cases of STDs highest among the elderly interred in those places, but an entire neighborhood? Parties every night in celebration of what? Getting older? Dancing in the streets to mark another day closer to the grave, drinking to commiserate another week lost to fatigue, or smoking up another year around the sun until the inevitable nothing awaiting us all arrived—he could do without it, would rather wallow alone in his misery, thank you very much.

He realized he'd been tapping his foot to the beat of the music and rolled away from the window.

Wouldn't hurt you to go meet them, you know.

Just like Abby to try and push him out of his shell. He might've acquiesced if she were there, if he were still in his twenties or thirties. Hell, even his forties. Now the thought of joining them out there seemed like a waste of time—his and theirs. He drifted off to sleep sometime after one, humming to an ethereal tune that might have been Pink Floyd.

He awoke the next morning with a mission in mind: ear plugs. Maybe a set of blackout curtains and a white noise machine, too. He didn't know if such things could be purchased in town, but he also needed coffee so he'd have to make the trip anyway. He gave himself a once-over in the bathroom mirror and frowned. Dark circles rounded his eyes. Abby would've said he looked like a raccoon.

Common Grounds was bustling this time of morning, filled with patrons on their way to work and a few younger folks who could've been students. ESU, maybe. Possibly Northampton Community. Then again, he mused, they all looked like kids to him; the barista behind the counter was practically fetal. Jerry supposed his age afforded him one positive thing: anonymity. None of the others paid him any mind, their eyes skipping over him like stones on water, and he was fine with that. He relaxed in his seat, opened the local newspaper, and the bustling shop slowly faded into the background.

"Jerry Campbell?"

He looked up to find a short fellow in a green Hawaiian shirt, checkered board shorts, and flip-flops standing before him. Red aviators sat atop a mop of thinning gray hair, accenting the cool baby blues and patch of white stubble.

Jerry smiled out of politeness, wondering why this man looked familiar. "Yes, sir. And you are?"

The man stuck out his hand and flashed a smile that was all teeth. "Name's Arthur Peterson. I'm the chairman of the Fairview Acres Community Association. It's a pleasure to meet you."

"You as well."

They shook, and that should've been the end of it—a polite "hello, nice to meet you, now back to my business" greeting, but Arthur hovered by the table, staring. Jerry forced a smile, unsure of what to say, gripping the newspaper until the paper crinkled.

"I try to welcome new residents in person, but I've not had a chance to drop by your place this week. Been busy with administrative things. You know how it is. Anyway, I understand there was a disturbance at your—"

"Cold brew for Mr. Peterson!"

"Ah, that's me." He glanced at his watch. "Sorry, Jerry, I'm afraid I've got a meeting to get to. Are you free for lunch today? I'd really like to talk to you."

Jerry's initial impulse was to say no—he was too tired, too busy, too cranky—and he might have declined, if not for the last few nights of disturbances. He'd considered making a complaint with the association, and now the opportunity had presented itself.

"Sure," he said. "I've been meaning to reach out, too. What's good for lunch around here?"

Arthur told him about a nice sandwich shop a few blocks away, and they agreed on a time.

On his way past the picture window where Jerry sat, Arthur paused to tap on the glass, offering a goofy grin and a wave.

Jerry lifted his hand to return the gesture, and paused as a memory drifted to the surface of his sleep-deprived mind. The wave and the smile. He'd seen this man before, just a few nights ago when that poor woman collapsed in his front yard.

The man in the truck.

He returned to his newspaper but found he couldn't focus any longer. Maybe this Mr. Peterson could explain what the hell had happened to that woman.

Then again, he might be inviting more trouble by sticking his nose where it doesn't belong.

But then again, he thought, *they were on my property. I have a right to know.*

He looked back to the window. "You're making this into something it's not," he said in a low voice, staring at his reflection in the glass. This was where Abby would tell him he was being silly, to let sleeping dogs lie, and she'd be right about that.

"But then again. . ." He finished off his coffee. "Then again. . ."

👁

Bailey Bros., Fairview's lone sandwich shop, stood wedged between an antique store and an abandoned Laundromat. It was what some of those reality TV shows might call a "hidden gem" but was really the living corpse of a business that refused to die, kept afloat by the simple fact it was the only place for miles to get a bite to eat. Lots of "character," they might say. Jerry thought it looked like a shithole, but he'd been wrong before; sometimes the worst dives offered the best food.

Arthur was already seated inside and waved him over. "Jerry! Over here, brother."

The shop was laid out like a diner from the '50s, all chrome and bright colors—at least, it had been at one point in time. Years of grease and nicotine coated the walls with a thick, yellowing film. All the chrome accents were either hazy or cracked. A small sign reading "out of order" hung from a jukebox full of old 45s. Nestled in the corner booth was Arthur, beaming like they'd been friends for years, with two menus already on the table.

"Any trouble finding the place?"

Jerry slid into the booth and shook his head. "Hard to get lost in this tiny town."

"Ain't that a fact? Lived here my whole life and watched the place ebb and flow. It's a good village. Lots of privacy."

A bubbly young waitress approached the booth and took their orders. Jerry ordered a Diet Coke with his lunch. One coffee a day was enough.

When she was gone, Arthur said, "So, how're you liking Fairview Acres?"

"It's... nice. Very friendly."

"Ah, but you hesitated there, man. It is friendly, but that's not what you were going to say, was it?"

Jerry's face flushed. Clouds of heat clung to his face. He held up his hands. "You got me there, man. Guilty as charged."

The waitress returned with their drinks. Arthur thanked her, gave her a wink, and sipped his coffee.

"Listen, Arthur, I don't want to cause any trouble..." He trailed off, trying to gauge the chairman's sincerity, but if Arthur was bluffing, Jerry couldn't tell.

"Look, you're sitting across from the man who can fix whatever the problem is. Lay it on me."

"All right, then." Jerry did as he was asked, telling him about the parties and the hours at which they occurred every night. As he talked, he wished he could sink into himself somehow and vanish. *This is what That Guy sounds like,* he told himself. *You're the angry old man on the block who yells at kids who get too close to his house—except they aren't kids, and you're just an asshole.* He took a drink of his Diet Coke and wished it had a splash of bourbon. "So, if I seem cranky, it's because I haven't had that much sleep these last few nights, Arthur. I'm sorry if—"

"All right, Jerry, let me stop you there."

Oh boy, here we go.

Arthur shook his head. "I'm the one who should apologize here. See, this is why I like to visit newcomers to our community and see how they're settling in. Fairview isn't your average retirement community. Something I tell everyone is to leave their expectations and inhibitions at the door. Think of it as less like a gated neighborhood and more like. . ."

"An exclusive party?"

"Exactly, yes! We like to let things hang loose in the evenings—hell, we have a big party in the park once a month, with music and barbecue and a little grass if that's your thing. All medicinal, of course." He winked.

Jerry couldn't help but smile.

"But I'll have a chat with everyone at the next FACA meeting and let them know to keep it down for you."

"I appreciate that."

"Now, I won't bullshit you, man. Sometimes, things get out of hand. They did just the other night, in fact."

Jerry's smile slipped away. "The woman in my yard on Sunday night."

"Mrs. Dunnally. Katherine."

"Is she all right? She was. . ." *Screaming, Arthur. She was fucking screaming for help, and you shot her up with a giant syringe.*

"She's going to be just fine. An absolute miracle, really. Straight from the goddess above." He swiped a finger across his temple and pointed to the ceiling in reverence. "By the moon's eye."

Jerry nodded, pretending like he knew what the hell that meant, and prayed to the universe that he hadn't moved into a religious commune by mistake.

"Katherine suffers from a form of dementia. Sundown syndrome, they call it. Gets worse for her at night, especially when she doesn't take her meds—which happens from time to time, I'm sorry to say. She'll go wandering all over Fairview when things are really bad. Hell, one time she tried to take a bath in the community swimming pool. It's common, I'm afraid. A few of our residents suffer from it."

"Dementia," Jerry said. "My grandma suffered from that in her later years. Horrible disease."

"But the good thing is, Katherine is feeling much better. I checked on her just this morning, in fact, and she's her old self again. Good as new!"

"Must've been one hell of a cocktail your guys gave her."

Arthur smiled. All teeth. "Only the best for our residents."

The waitress brought their meals, and as they ate, Arthur asked Jerry questions about what brought him to the area, his former life in Stroudsburg and accounting, and even Abby. Jerry kept his story light on the details—"hitting the bullet points," an old manager was fond of saying—but found himself easing into the conversation as time went on.

By the time their meal came to an end, Jerry still hadn't decided what to make of Arthur Peterson. The worst people always came dressed in suits and smiles. Arthur dressed like an aging hippie, but smiled like a shark. Abby would roll her eyes at his sense of caution, but this was one time Jerry wouldn't relent. He'd dealt with this kind of person in the past—the kind who was your best friend because they needed something from you—and knew enough to keep him at arm's reach.

In another time and place, maybe he would've warmed up to Arthur's camaraderie, but now he wasn't interested in making friends. Not this fast, not while he was still grieving for Abby. Everyone else could party on without him.

"Well, my friend, I hate to eat and run, but a chairman's job is never done." Arthur made a show of looking at his watch. He pulled out his wallet and left three twenties on the table. "Lunch is on me, man. Welcome to Fairview!"

"I appreciate that," Jerry said, mirroring Arthur's smile. "I guess I'll see you around."

"Count on it. Maybe sooner than later."

They said their goodbyes and went their separate ways. A thought struck Jerry as he walked to his car: He'd spent the entire meal talking about himself. Arthur had asked the right questions to keep him going, but he hadn't said a thing about himself.

5

Jerry stepped outside to savor the cool evening air. After spending the afternoon cooped up inside unpacking boxes, watching the sunset with a beer in his hand seemed like a great way to wind down. The neighborhood was mostly quiet except for a yapping dog somewhere down the street. *If only it could stay like this all the time,* he thought. Fairview Acres seemed peaceful enough when its residents weren't behaving like college kids. Then again, all they were doing was enjoying the rest of their years. If only Abby were here, maybe he could learn to let loose himself and party with them.

He drank the beer in four deep gulps and went inside to retrieve the rest of the six-pack. Maybe he would let loose in his own way and have a pity party for himself on the porch. He popped the cap from another bottle and drank, soaking up the suds, preparing to drown in a rising tide of maudlin thoughts. Had he acted too quickly, moving out of the home they'd made together? He'd told himself the place was much too big for him, but in hindsight, growing older and dying alone wasn't the way he'd expected to spend his retirement.

"Somehow moving here was supposed to make it all better?" He belched and promptly laughed at himself. Moving away from that tomb of a house *was* supposed to make it better, or at least a little easier. He knew loneliness, had never had many friends growing up, but he'd never felt so lost before. Surrounding himself with people seemed like a good idea on the surface, something his grief counselor had suggested to break through his shell of depression, but deep down Jerry knew it was bullshit. Surrounding himself with others, subjecting himself to their happiness, was just another reminder of how alone he felt.

Now that the ink was dry on his mortgage, cold pangs of regret stirred in his gut.

Stop it, you old fool. This place is just fine, and you'll be fine. Make it your home and be happy. Give yourself time.

He smiled. Abby occupied his mind as much as his heart. Her ashes had been the first thing he'd unpacked, and the urn now adorned the fireplace mantle along with a photograph from their twenty-fifth wedding anniversary. God, she'd looked so beautiful in that emerald dress. The photo captured everything he loved about her, exuded the essence of her personality in a single moment. A light that not even cancer could extinguish. Even when she drew her final breaths, she'd still whispered for him to be happy, to keep smiling. But she hadn't told him how hard it would be, and in the following months, the weight of a smile was something he didn't have the strength to bear.

"This ain't the same without you, Abby."

His raspy words were overwhelmed by a chorus of crickets. Jerry wiped his eyes and drained the last of his beer. He lined up the bottle with the rest of his empties and retired indoors to the living room.

With his head buzzing and heart aching, he reclined on the old plush sofa and watched the last of the daylight slip away. Long shadows took their place, drawn forth from secret places only the night knew, and Jerry closed his eyes to join them.

◉

A loud crash woke him some time later. He sat up with a start, gasping, his heart thudding away like a snare drum. He wiped sweat from his brow and found his bearings. *Did I dream that noise? The empty bottles. I forgot to toss the empty bottles. Probably an animal, a raccoon or a stray cat—*

Another crash erupted outside as glass shattered, accompanied by a short yelp. Bottles clinked together. Glass cracked under pressure, and another cry pierced the gloom. Jerry staggered into the living room. He flipped on the porch light and pulled back the front door's portiere.

"What the hell?"

A thin silver-haired woman in a blue bathrobe stood in the corner of his front porch where he'd lined up his empty bottles. She lifted her leg and smashed another bottle beneath her bare foot. Jerry winced as blood gushed from between her toes. She lifted her foot to pluck a thick shard of glass from the sole. A crimson stream splattered across the shattered fragments.

Jerry stared in shock, held hostage by the woman's bizarre act of self-mutilation. A single word squirmed its way to the forefront of his mind—*Why?*—and he found the will to act, stepping into his slippers and walking outside.

"Ma'am? Ma'am, please don't—"

The woman turned and forced a pained smile. Her cheeks glistened with tears.

Oh shit. The lady from the other night. What the hell was her name? Kate? Katherine?

"Leave," she gasped, reaching for him.

Jerry took her hand and ushered her away from the broken glass.

"The moon watches. It sees. It sees."

"I'm sure it does. Just walk with me, okay? We're going to get you fixed right up."

He led her to a chair, but she resisted sitting. "Can't when it's watching. And it is watching. Always watching. So many eyes." She clutched his sleeve. "A head full of eyes. To see us, you understand? You need to leave before it sees you too."

Her words faded into whispers, the energy draining from her as quickly as the blood from her wounded feet. Jerry finally coaxed her to sit down.

"I'm just going to go call for help, and then I'm going to get something for your feet. You just sit tight, okay? Can you do that for me, Kat?"

She looked into his face with clarity for the first time, the glassy look gone from her eyes. Her confusion stirred a cold memory from the depths of his mind, something he wished he could forget once and for all. *Abby had looked like that,* he thought, *just days before...*

"Who..." she began.

Jerry shook his head, gave her hand a squeeze. "Call me Jerry, ma'am. Just—you just sit tight. I'll be right back."

He went inside and raided his medicine cabinet for what little was in there. On his way back through the house, he unplugged his cell phone from its charger and dialed 911.

She was still in her seat when he returned, hunched forward with the robe pulled tight around her. A puddle of blood had formed beneath her feet and spread slowly across the porch. Jerry knelt before her, cradling the phone between ear and shoulder as he went to work on her feet. He hadn't found much in the way of supplies—just a few bandages and some peroxide—but he did the best he could.

An operator asked about his emergency, and he relayed the facts. He looked up into the woman's exhausted face, noting the smile lines and crow's feet, the dark circles beneath her eyes, the skin pulled tight across her cheeks and forehead. Her flesh was a sickly yellow, the color of infection.

Arthur's words flashed through his mind: *Sundown syndrome, they call it. Gets worse for her at night, especially when she doesn't take her meds.* Jerry remembered his grandma, God rest her soul; she might've been disoriented, didn't know who people were half the time, but she'd never hurt herself. He gave the poor woman another once-over, glanced at the bloody fragments of glass, and shook his head. This was something else.

"This'll have to do," he said, slipping a small hand towel beneath her feet. "Step down on that for me, okay? Good, just like that."

"Thank you, Jerry." A shadow drifted across her eye like a faint ripple in a dark pond. Shivering, she placed a hand on his shoulder and squeezed.

"You're welcome, Katherine." He climbed to his feet, wincing as his knees popped, and took a seat beside her. "What're you doing out here at this hour? Why did you hurt yourself, huh?" *And why did you have to do it on my porch?*

Katherine shivered, pulling the robe tight around her. "Came... to warn you."

"Warn me? I don't—"

She clapped a hand on his knee and squeezed so hard that he gasped in pain. He looked at her, wide-eyed and confused and scared, unsure of what to say or how to say it.

"Listen," she hissed, moving closer to his face. "You need to leave. The worms... they dance at nightfall..."

Arthur's words again: *Gets worse for her at night.*

He looked in her bloodshot eyes, trying to puzzle out the meaning of her gibberish, when she pulled away from him, shivering violently as though in seizure.

"The worms... are dancing."

Katherine went limp, slumped to one side of the chair, and bowed forward as if in prayer. A hiss of breath rattled from her chest, and she fell still.

Jerry put his hand on her shoulder and gasped. Her body radiated cold even through the bathrobe. He put his fingers to her neck and found no pulse. Her skin was like cold wax, all its heat leeched away in seconds.

Oh God, it's just like Abby was that morning.

A soft moan escaped his lips as he reached for the phone. He dialed 911 again but didn't give the operator time to speak, screaming for someone to come and help this poor woman because she was either dying or already dead.

The calm operator remained on the phone with him until the paramedics arrived twenty minutes later. No siren, only lights, and when the same two men from the other night climbed out of the vehicle, he wondered if calling for them had been a bad idea. They checked her pulse, muttered something to each other, and nodded in agreement. No syringe this time, no miracle cure.

Jerry watched in stunned silence as they loaded her onto a gurney. He couldn't bear to watch someone else slip away like this. When they wheeled her toward the ambulance, he noticed her ear was caked with blood.

"What happened?" he asked.

But the paramedics said nothing. He might as well have been a ghost.

6

Katherine's bloody footprints stained the length of the porch, marking her journey from one end to the other, where her wounds had left a dark patch on the concrete. Jerry stood over it, chewing his bottom lip. He didn't have any bleach or stronger chemicals on hand, and cleaning blood stains on concrete would be a bitch no matter how he approached it. Hints of a stress headache pulsed in his forehead. *I'll deal with this later.*

Once he'd swept up the glass, he returned to his chore of unpacking boxes. There wasn't much left from his old home. Most of his and Abby's belongings had been donated or sold at one of his many garage sales. Her wardrobe, her costume jewelry, all those handbags and pairs of shoes had gone in a matter of weeks. He'd sifted through her things like a ghoul, weighing what to keep and what to discard, resisting the urge to throw out everything in a selfish act of emotional preservation. What little he'd kept fit in just a few boxes. These little tokens of her existence were pieces of a greater whole that had shattered the day she died. Keeping them all was like holding on to a jigsaw puzzle where only the outer border remained, its image forever incomplete. He couldn't bear to look at them, and he couldn't bear to part with them.

His thoughts drifted, caught in a stream of memories both pleasant and painful, and an hour had passed before he realized he was still sitting on the floor, staring at an unopened box of Abby's things. *You're going to have to do it sooner or later,* she whispered. *They're just things, hon. It's the memories you keep that matter.*

Those memories were poignant enough to remain tethered to his heart would torture him until his final breath. Every good memory of Abby—of their first date, their wedding day, their twenty-fifth anniversary—was paralleled by an equally grim and harrowing memory: her glassy stare, her cracked lips thin and drawn, the way she'd gripped her blanket in her last moments. The stillness of the room after it was all over, suddenly empty without her wheezing breath choked with phlegm. The acrid smell from her bedpan and sterile citrus of disinfectant.

Those memories he couldn't wipe from his mind no matter how hard he tried, and in a masochistic way, he didn't want to. *Through sickness and in health*, he thought, and pushed himself off the floor. He looked at the box and shook his head. Not yet. One thing, one memory, one regret at a time.

His phone rang later that morning. A local area code, but not a number he recognized. He answered.

"Hey, Jerry. It's Arthur."

Jerry frowned, sank back into his sofa, and closed his eyes. "Hi, Arthur. How are things?" The words felt like sharp stones grating across his tongue.

"Can't complain, man. I wanted to call you about what happened at your place last night."

"Yeah, I'm sorry. It happened so fast—"

"I know, and I wanted to tell you that she's going to be just fine."

His eyes snapped open. "I'm sorry, what?"

"Mrs. Dunnally," Arthur went on. "She's going to be just fine."

"I don't understand. . ." Jerry leaned forward in his seat, stared across the room at the wall he'd decorated yesterday. One of the framed photographs was crooked. "She was dead when they took her away last night. How—"

"A miracle! Isn't that something? A miracle from the goddess above."

A feeling of déjà vu swept over him. He pictured Arthur from their lunch yesterday. Grinning, saying she was just fine while swiping a finger across his temple. *Christ, how many times has he used this line?*

Jerry cleared his throat. "A miracle. Right."

"The paramedics told me there was a lot of blood on your porch. You'll have a hell of a time getting that out of the concrete. I can loan you my pressure washer if you want. . ."

"So, she's alive? I'm sorry, I just. . . I was certain she'd passed away last night." He remembered the feel of her skin. Cold. So cold.

"I know, it's a confusing thing, but the truth of the matter is that Kat's still alive and kicking. They released her from the hospital this morning, and she's back at home, resting."

Home. Resting. The words did not fit with the image of the dead woman frozen in his mind. Had he imagined her death? But she'd had no pulse. The way she'd seized and clutched at life with a final breath rattling in her throat was clear in his mind. She had been there, rambling incoherently

(the worms are dancing)

and then nothing. The lights had gone out of her eyes. *Oh God, her eyes, there was something* in *her eyes—*

"Jerry?"

"Yes, sorry. My mind wanders. Are you *sure*—"

"I hope the party didn't wake you. I asked everyone to keep it down for you."

If there had been a party, he hadn't heard it. "No," he said. "I slept like a rock."

But about Katherine, he wanted to say. *None of this adds up.*

"Well, that's great! I'm glad to hear it."

I bet you are. Instead, Jerry said, "Would you mind giving me Katherine's address? I'd like to drop by and check on her, see if she needs anything."

"I'm sure that won't be necessary," Arthur said, but quickly backpedaled when he realized his tone of voice. "I mean, no visitors are allowed. Her nurse is quite strict. But she'll be good as new tonight, just in time for the monthly gathering at the Moon Pool."

"Monthly gathering? Oh, the barbecue thing?"

"That's one of the perks of being chairman—I get to organize the monthly fellowship, and what better way to get to know your neighbors than by breaking bread together?"

"Of course," Jerry said, swallowing back the bile in his throat. He'd not been to church since he was a boy, had grown to resent it in his later years. If he'd known Fairview was a religious community, he would've reconsidered his purchase. The thought of suffering through a spiel about salvation every month for the rest of his life turned his stomach.

"We meet at the Moon Pool in the park, just a few blocks from your house. You can't miss it."

He remembered seeing something in the brochure his realtor gave him. A small pool with a huge stone in the center, surrounded by manicured landscaping and obelisks. At a glance, he'd thought it looked like a cemetery without the graves. A memorial of some kind.

"Well..." Jerry began, trying desperately to think of an excuse, something that would make sense—*"Thanks but no thanks, Mr. Peterson. There's still so much unpacking to be done!"*—but something Abby used to say piped up from a dusty corner in his mind.

Jerry Campbell, you'd be a hermit if I'd let you—but you're not, and I won't.

He smiled. She'd always been the one with faith, always the one trying to drag him along to church, but he'd never relented. Now he wished he could've spent that time with her. The idea of joining his neighbors stirred a bittersweet agony in his belly, the sort of swift sucker punch only stark reality could deliver. He'd rather close himself away and pretend Abby was still alive.

But you can't, and I'm not.

"—it's fine if you can't make it. I'm sure you've got plenty of unpacking left to do."

Jerry pushed away his wife's ghost. "No, no, it's okay, I just. . ." He glanced over his shoulder, gave the stack of boxes in his living room a stern eye. "Tell me more about this Moon Pool."

"Well, it's the center of our community. Whole neighborhood is built around it. The reflecting pool there. . . well, you'll understand when you see it."

"Sure," Jerry said, his curiosity piqued. "I'll think about it."

"Excellent! I'll drop by around eight o'clock. If you're up to it, we can walk over together, and I'll introduce you to everyone."

A cloud of heat swept over Jerry's face, and suddenly he was eight years old again, terrified on the first day of school. *You can't hide forever,* he told himself, trying—and failing—to be brave.

"Sounds good to me." He swallowed air and nearly gagged.

"By the moon's eye, my friend. See you tonight."

"Sure," Jerry said and ended the call. He walked across the room and straightened the picture frame. "By the moon's eye. Whatever the hell that means."

◉

The afternoon sun poked through a net of clouds, offering a mild reprieve from the morning's humidity, and Jerry welcomed the cool breeze sweeping over him. He was carrying a stack of cardboard toward the recycling bin, preoccupied with making a mental grocery list, when a voice broke his concentration.

"Hey, neighbor!"

He looked up, startled. Matilda Scott was halfway across her yard, clad in a sun hat and sunglasses, smiling a little too wide, her stride a little too eager.

You must want something, he thought.

You're in a mood, Abby whispered, and he couldn't argue. Instead, he offered a short nod and smile to his neighbor and began cramming the cardboard into the bin.

"Jerry! I'm glad I caught you."

"Hello, Matilda." He pushed the last sheet of cardboard into the bin and winced. A thin paper cut trailed along the tip of this thumb.

"I wanted to stop by earlier, but. . ." She held up a pair of gardening gloves and a trowel. "Chores pulled me away. You know how it is."

"I sure do." A drop of blood seeped from the wound. He tried to staunch the flow with his forefinger. "What can I do for you?"

She lifted the brim of her hat. "We heard the commotion last night, saw the ambulance in your driveway. Is everything all right?"

Jerry nodded. "Yeah, we had a little scare. Katherine showed up on my porch, and. . ." He looked at his reflection in her shades and wondered if she already knew all about the incident. He couldn't imagine a scenario where she didn't. "You know what? It doesn't matter. Mr. Peterson said she's recovering and will be okay."

"Did she say anything to you?"

"Pardon?"

"Katherine. Did she *say* anything to you?"

Jerry studied her face while a dozen rude comments crossed his tongue, but they would only prolong this conversation. After working in an office for decades, he'd dealt with his share of gossip. He'd hoped to leave that bullshit behind when he retired. A silly expectation, he realized, looking at his neighbor and the way she could almost taste the drama in the air. Better to let her starve.

He shook his head. "Not really. She mumbled a lot, but I couldn't understand it."

"Huh. You're sure about that?" Her demeanor changed, her mask slipping for a moment, just long enough for him to glimpse the person underneath. God, he hated people sometimes.

"Yeah," he said flatly. "I'm sure."

And then she was all smiles again, like nothing had changed and everything was right in the world. "Well, at least she's all right now. We try to look after our own as much as we can. That's what good neighbors do!"

"One hundred percent, honey!" Bradley appeared from the side of their house, pushing a wheelbarrow full of mulch and wearing a droopy white hat. Jerry thought he looked like Bob Denver from the set of *Gilligan's Island*.

"Hey, hon. We were just talking about Katherine's episode last night."

Bradley set down the wheelbarrow and grimaced, bracing his lower back. "Terrible thing, what happened. Did she say anything to you?"

"No." Jerry smiled. "Was she supposed to?"

Silence settled between them. Matilda and Bradley exchanged looks for a moment before breaking into unsettled laughter. Jerry kept smiling, even offered a hearty chuckle to match their faux camaraderie. When their laughter finally faded, he saw his chance for escape. "Well, I was about to go for a walk, so I suppose I'll see you two later."

He was three steps further down his driveway when Matilda said, "We hope so!"

Jerry looked back over his shoulder. She had joined her husband on their side of the property line, and together they were watching him leave.

Bradley removed his hat and fanned himself. "Tonight, at the Moon Pool?"

"Maybe," Jerry called back. "Thinking about it."

"Well don't think too hard, neighbor!"

Bradley's canned laughter followed him down the sidewalk. Jerry glanced back again when he reached the corner of the street. The Scotts were still watching him, holding hands. Matilda raised her hand to wave.

A cold finger slid down the back of Jerry's neck. He waved in return.

Did she say anything to you?

He shook his head, told himself not to read into it too much, but as he walked on down the block, he found himself returning to their confrontation. What had been the point of all that? Probing for gossip? Everything that Katherine said

(you need to leave)

was gibberish anyway.

There you go again, Abby whispered. *Mountains out of mole hills. You moved here to relax, love. Try to enjoy it.*

"You know that's easier said than done," he mumbled to himself. "This is me we're talking about."

Abby said nothing in reply.

7

Jerry hadn't given much thought to exploring the neighborhood since moving in. It wasn't much of a priority compared to turning his new house into a proper home. But now that he was out here, he found himself strangely at peace, and wished he'd taken a walk sooner.

In her last years, before the big C disrupted their lives, Abby had taken to walking in the early evenings during sunset, and Jerry had joined her. Abby did it because she enjoyed the scenery and peace it brought her, but Jerry's motives were purely health related. Years of sitting at a desk had wreaked havoc on his body. Weak muscles, a slight hunch in his posture, high cholesterol, an A1C teetering on the edge of Type 2—he had a multitude of reasons to keep active. And it didn't hurt to have great company while he counted his steps.

Those evening walks had ceased when Abby died, and he'd packed on some weight in the time since. Now was as good a time as any to get back into the habit. He journeyed to the end of the street, and then down the next, until he reached the gated entrance to the development. There was no gate attendant. Every resident here had a four-digit keycode. He'd used Abby's birthdate, 3348, something he'd never forget. He hoped not, at least.

Katherine's condition lingered on his mind. *Christ, what a terrible way to go.*

He tried to imagine everything around him slowly slipping into an all-encompassing fog, even the most familiar of things. Faces, people, a lifetime of memories, all stolen—but not all at once. Dementia was an insidious thief. Sometimes it returned what it had taken and stole something else. And sometimes it stole more than a long-held memory or short-term recognition; it stole a personality, a soul, and left a stranger in its place.

Sundown syndrome they called it.

She'd been confused, afraid, in and out of the present, but something about Arthur's explanation of her condition didn't sit right with him. He could still feel her cold, lifeless skin on his fingertips.

But she hadn't died after all, if Arthur was to be believed. A dubious claim that Jerry couldn't quite reconcile, not after what he'd witnessed. The feel of her cold skin was burned into his fingertips.

A crow cawed overhead, stirring him from his thoughts, and he shuffled to a stop. The neighborhood no longer looked familiar at all...

Up ahead he spotted the entrance to a park. He smiled and set off again, feeling foolish at the sudden relief that he wasn't losing his sense of awareness. Arthur had mentioned the park was just a few blocks away. He could find his way home from there.

The street circled the perimeter of the community, marking the edge of the park like the rim of a bowl. From the road, the park grounds sloped down toward the Moon Pool at its center. On the opposite side, just below a dense thicket of trees, a group of people were bustling around a large bandstand, setting up for the evening's festivities. A rooftop peeked out just above the tree line behind them.

A trail of scattered flagstones led from the bandstand down to the park's center, and there he saw the community's beloved Moon Pool. Two rows of granite obelisks decorated the immediate path toward the pool, where a massive stone rose from the water. The photos in the brochure hadn't done it justice; the stone was huge even from this distance, and a bizarre inclusion to such an otherwise normal place.

Even though his feet and ankles ached from his walk, his curiosity was piqued. He took the slope carefully, angling his feet to the side in case he lost his footing. A dull ache in his hips and knees announced its presence when he reached the bottom, suggesting that his descent wasn't the best idea after all, but he was undeterred. He'd come this far, and that was half the battle. The scent of fresh cut grass and citronella lingered in the air. He relished the aroma as he caught his breath.

The giant stone was pockmarked and porous like lava rock but glistened like limestone. It was imperfect in its formation. Jagged ridges rose in uneven segments, marking off patterns of small canyons across the surface. It reminded him of a giant stone walnut and looked even stranger up close, with ridges like the bars of a cage and a bulbous, glittery surface. In bright light, it appeared almost organic. Staring at it for too long filled him with unease, and he shrugged off a chill before turning away.

He examined the nearest obelisk, which stood six feet tall, easily. Seemed like a waste of good granite, especially when there were cheaper alternatives. Just below it, a small plaque had been affixed beside the stone walkway, facing the Moon Pool. It read:

EST. 1903 – TO COMMEMORATE WHEN
OUR GODDESS TOUCHED THE EARTH.

"Huh." The stone gave him the creeps, but he was also curious now. He found himself almost looking forward to this evening.

His ascent back to the street was a brutal reminder that he was not getting any younger, and his lungs were full of smoke and flame. *Haven't had a walk like this since. . .*

Since Abby. Their walks had been sacred to him.

Tears welled in his eyes. He stopped, placed his hands on his knees, and breathed deep. "Gotta stop doing this to yourself, man. It's time to move on."

He righted himself, shook off the sorrow, and kept on down the street. Half a block later, he saw a familiar figure standing on her porch and waved to her. If Katherine saw him, she made no sign, and she was quickly ushered inside by another woman whose face he could not see.

The second woman wore a mask of some kind, one that obscured most of her face, and was clad in white scrubs—an in-home caregiver, he supposed. He slowed, hoping to have a word with the nurse if she emerged again, but the door remained closed.

When he finally made it home, Jerry found a small envelope tucked inside the screen door. Plain white, with his name written in elegant cursive across one side, smelling faintly of perfume. He opened the flap and removed a small thank-you card adorned with a floral design.

Inside, the card read: *Thanks for being there!* And below it, in the same swirly cursive handwriting:

Jerry,

I came by to say thank you for helping me last night. ~~You're kinder than most around here~~ *You're very kind. Little cards like this always seem so disposable and empty. Will you be at the Moon Pool tonight?*

I'd love to see you and say thanks in person.
—Kat
P.S. Here's my number if you ever want to reach me...

He slipped the card back into its envelope, checked his watch, and frowned. He'd been gone almost two hours and had just enough time to get cleaned up before Arthur arrived. He re-read the card and smiled. It *would* be nice to see her again. Checking on her seemed like the least he could do. The right thing to do.

◉

The doorbell rang at eight on the dot. Jerry opened the door, freshly shaven and bare skin stinging with aftershave.

Arthur took one look at him and chuckled. "You're dressed like a retiree, grandpa."

Stunned, Jerry searched for the right words with which to reply but managed little more than a confused stammer.

Arthur clapped a hand on his shoulder and erupted in laughter. "I'm teasing! You're dressed just fine. Come as you are."

"If you say so." Jerry forced a smile through the sting of mild embarrassment. He gave himself a once-over in the hallway mirror. Blue polo shirt and khaki shorts. He *did* look like a retiree. At least his socks weren't pulled up to his knees. "Let me lock up and then we can go."

Arthur led the way down the sidewalk. The sky was on fire with evening light, the warm air kissed with a cool breeze, and the sound of crickets and jubilation carried on the wind. Fireflies blinked lazily in the grass. *A perfect summer evening,* Jerry thought.

When they turned at the corner of his street, he saw others leaving their homes with coolers and lawn chairs in tow. Music blared from up ahead, the words too muffled to make out. The distant sound filled him with melancholy. Abby loved music, loved to dance, and had tried teaching him a few times but he was too awkward, too stiff. A few years before she fell ill, she'd surprised him with a refurbished turntable and made a habit of playing an album every evening after their walks. Elvis, Johnny Cash, Pink Floyd, The Church, and Joy Division were among her favorites. An eclectic mix, just like her. He'd loved watching her dance in their living room, even when she tried coaxing him out of his armchair to join her.

Hearing the music now reminded him of how much silence he'd endured since losing her.

Try to have a good time, hon. Dance for me, or try to. For both of us.

He smiled and breathed in the evening air. Maybe he would try. Maybe this sort of thing was exactly what he needed. Something to get him away from the isolation of his own head for a while.

"Ah, there she is!" Arthur trotted ahead. "You're a bit overdressed!"

A lively platinum-haired lady walked down her porch steps, the hem of her indigo evening gown trailing behind with a soft hiss. Katherine Dunnally. She smiled, her bright blue eyes lighting up the dusky gloom. "I wanted to wear something nice tonight. I feel like a million bucks!"

Can't be, Jerry thought, staring. He tried not to gape but found he couldn't keep his mouth shut. She looked radiant, a far cry from the fragile specter he'd glimpsed earlier that afternoon, and from the woman he'd met on his porch the night before. They might as well have been different people.

His mind flooded with images of her eyes like cloudy marbles, her bloody feet, the ghostly sensation of cold, waxen skin. *You died,* he wanted to say but was too stunned to speak.

"Oh, Mr. Campbell!" She crossed her lawn and took him in a tight embrace. Her curly hair smelled of lavender. "You got my card?"

Jerry returned the hug while his mind screamed *(You're dead, I watched you die, how are you even here)* this was impossible. He swallowed back the disbelief and forced a smile. "Yes, thank you. I'm... glad you're okay, Mrs. Dunnally."

"Please, call me Kat. And I'm just fine, thanks to you."

"I'm just glad you're okay." He glanced at Arthur, who was staring at them with an intensity that unsettled him. "You *are* okay, yes? Do you remember—"

"Of course." She gave Arthur a big smile. "A bad reaction to new medication. All better now."

"Good," Jerry whispered. "Real good. How about those feet?"

Katherine tapped her toes on the sidewalk. "Right as rain. I'm even wearing my dancing shoes."

He looked down at her feet and thought of all the blood she'd left on his porch.

She took his hand and pulled him forward. "Come on, you two. It's a beautiful evening."

"Indeed," Arthur said, trailing close behind them. "Let's rejoice with the goddess."

Jerry remained silent as an unsettling thought occurred to him: *Her skin's cold. So cold.*

◉

A joyous atmosphere settled over the residents of Fairview Acres as the evening gave way to night. Stars twinkled through a bruised sky, while below the residents chattered and danced with one another in celebration of life and good health. Walkways were lined with torches filling the air with a haze of citronella, and strings of tiki lights hung between lampposts coating the park in a warm, friendly glow.

Katherine had rushed away to greet some friends when they'd arrived and was soon lost to the crowd; Arthur had excused himself not long after, promising to return and make introductions once he'd attended to some "committee matters," whatever that meant.

A steady mix of music featuring Jimmy Buffet, the Grateful Dead, and the Beach Boys was projected from a pair of loudspeakers on the bandstand. The DJ's table stood between the speakers, operated by a lone fellow hunched over a turntable. His white mane draped over his shoulders, held out of his face by a headband. Near the entrance, a series of tables offered a spread of finger foods and drinks, and at the far end a pair of men in aprons and chef's hats conducted an orchestra of flames over open grills.

Jerry walked through the crowd, hiding a perpetual sensation of puzzlement behind his smile. He hadn't seen partying like this since college and was in awe of the energy on display. Men and women at least fifteen years his senior danced with abandon, arthritis and swollen joints be damned. They danced barefoot across the manicured grass and down the gentle slope, smiling and laughing and, in some cases, kissing their way around the park, circling the stones and pool at the center with hypnotic sway.

He found a quiet spot near the entrance and soaked in the evening. He wasn't eager to call attention to himself. Abby had always handled introductions, just as she was always the one to send the Christmas cards and keep up with their acquaintances.

But you need to get out of your shell, she whispered. *Meet new people. Maybe fall in love again.*

Jerry shook away the notion. That ship had sailed long ago.

Deep down in the hidden folds of his mind, a tiny part of him knew better, had felt a weight lifted ever so slightly when he saw Katherine emerge from her home, refreshed, glowing, and alive. There had been a bounce in his step ever since.

He spotted her now, laughing and dancing with her girlfriends as Chuck Berry sang "Johnny B. Goode" from the loudspeakers. *Don't stare,* he told himself and averted his gaze—but even feigning disinterest only lasted so long, and within a minute his eyes found her again. This time she looked up, saw him watching, and grinned. His face flushed with heated embarrassment. Looking away would just seem silly now. She'd trapped him in her stare.

"Johnny B. Goode" faded into the opening strum of Elvis's "Suspicious Minds." Abby's favorite by the King.

And there was Katherine, indigo dress aglow in the warmth of the evening, working her way through the crowd toward him, and for a moment Jerry felt like the only man on the planet, staring down the face of the infinite. Embarrassed, elated, excited—and terrified—he'd been transformed into a teenager with a mere glance. There was only one other soul who'd ever made him feel like this.

"Penny for your thoughts?" Her blue eyes shone like stars amid the party's chaos.

He smiled and stuck out his hand to collect. "One penny per thought, ma'am."

Katherine laughed. "I left my coin purse at home. I'll have to take it on credit."

"Sure. Your credit's always good with me."

"You got it, Mr. Campbell. So, lay it on me."

"I was a million miles away, caught up in the music. No thoughts in particular."

"Just vibing, huh?"

He gave her a puzzled look. "Vibing?"

"It's what the kids say these days. Like you're caught up in a moment. Vibing."

"Hang out with many kids these days, lady?"

"Only my daughter, Lisa, and she's hardly a kid. Just turned forty this year."

"Still a kid, then."

"She'll always be my baby girl." Katherine glanced at the partygoers around them. "Got any kids?"

"No," he said. "That wasn't in the cards for us."

Her expression fell. "Oh, I'm sorry, Jerry. That was rude of me. Forget I asked—"

"Not at all! I- We- That is, my wife and I. . ." He stumbled over his words, righted himself. "You know what? It doesn't matter. Lovely night tonight, isn't it?" Warmth settled over his face, thick and suffocating, burning his cheeks. *Really, old man? You're gonna talk about the weather now?*

"Sorry," he said. "I guess I'm not very good at vibing."

Katherine laughed. A big, hearty, braying laugh pulled straight from her toes. The pleasant sound of an avalanche, as startling as it was beautiful, with the power to crush the world.

He smiled ear to ear. "Thank you," he said, and bowed. "I'll be here all weekend. Tip your bartender."

More laughter. The sound filled his heart in a way he didn't know he needed until that moment. It had been so long he'd forgotten what this kind of joy felt like.

"You're a funny man, Jerry Campbell."

"And you're an easy mark, Kat Dunnally. I'm only half as funny as you think I am."

She glanced over her shoulder, and when she returned her attention to him, the smile remained but without the joy and playful innocence. Wide eyes stricken with fear held his focus now. She stood on her toes as if to give him a kiss, but her lips only grazed his cheek, moved closer to his ear.

"This is all a big show," she whispered. Her hot breath made the hairs on his neck stand at attention. "You don't have to do anything you don't want to do. Remember that."

Her words were there and gone again, a tickle of air on his earlobe, and before he could ask what she meant, she gave him a peck on the cheek.

Louder, she said, "You're *such* a kind soul."

"Indeed he is!" Arthur emerged from the crowd with a Solo cup in his hand. "I want to give a toast to the new guy. Care to join us, Kat?"

"Oh, I think I'm good for now." She gave Jerry's hand a light squeeze before slipping away from him. "Thanks again, Jerry, for the sound advice." Then to Arthur: "Go easy on the new guy, Mr. Chairman."

She drifted back into the crowd before either man could say anything in reply. Ghosts of her words, her breath, hovered just inside Jerry's ear. A pervasive chill crept over him despite the humid evening air.

Arthur tilted his head, and said, "My grandpa used to say there's no greater riddle in life than the workings of a woman's mind."

For once, Jerry agreed.

8

Jerry followed Arthur to the bandstand, where he climbed up the wooden steps and gave the DJ a short nod. The music faded to a stop. Arthur plucked a microphone from its stand. Feedback whined from the loudspeakers, and the crowd jeered.

"All right, all right, that's enough out of y'all." Arthur tugged on his collar, wiped a hand across his forehead. "No respect, I tell ya."

Everyone laughed except for Jerry. It was the worst Rodney Dangerfield impression he'd ever heard.

"I won't take but a moment of your time, people, and then we can all get back to the celebration. We've got a newbie among us tonight. Jerry Campbell, come on up here!"

Everyone applauded, and those closest to Jerry took a step back, leaving him on a solitary island of attention. He froze, wanted to crawl inside himself and disappear. Someone began chanting his name, and soon that was all he could hear, a steady susurration building into a syllabic crescendo.

Jer-ry! Jer-ry!

The last time he'd heard his name cheered like this was on a stupid daytime talk show. He'd had the benefit of separation then, the ability to change a channel, but this was happening all around him right now. He looked up at Arthur, made a face that was less a smile and more of a grimace, and shook his head.

"Come on, don't be a cranky old man. Get on up here!"

Hands on his shoulders gently pushed him forward. He looked left and right, hoping to find Katherine somewhere, someone to whom he could anchor himself, but she was nowhere to be seen.

You don't have to do anything you don't want to do.

Is this what she'd meant? Had she known?

But the decision was made for him as more hands urged him forward, and he found himself at the foot of the bandstand steps. His heart thudded away in its chamber, a piston driven with the steam of panic, terror. Thank God he'd taken his anxiety meds that morning, or he might've melted into a pile of quivering goo.

Go on, let's get this over with.

He took a breath and climbed the steps to join Fairview's chairman in the spotlight.

"That's more like it," Arthur said. "John, can you get Jerry a drink for the toast?"

The long-haired DJ emerged from behind his setup with a plastic Solo cup filled to the brim with a thick, gray froth. Jerry took it with some trepidation and eyed the contents. He detected the scent of ripe fruit—maybe overripe—and something metallic, coppery.

Arthur raised his own cup. Jerry looked across the crowd of his neighbors. Hands raised, red Solo cups in hand, glittering eyes and toothy smiles. All except one.

Katherine stood at the edge of the crowd wearing an expression he couldn't read. A moment later she turned and made her way down the path toward the Moon Pool.

"To our new neighbor," Arthur said. "Welcome to the Fairview family!"

Jerry raised his cup in return but hesitated to drink. "Thanks," he said. "What is it, though?"

Arthur sipped his drink and winked. "Love. Pure love, brother."

Love. Brother. Jerry resisted the urge to roll his eyes, focusing on the bubbling foam in the cup.

To the crowd, Arthur said, "Am I right, folks?"

More cheers and drinks. The Fairview horde reveled in Arthur's bravado, driving nervous pangs through Jerry's gut, fanning a cloying heat over his face.

"I don't know, Arthur. I have medications and this might—"

"Come on!" Arthur slapped him on the back and turned to the crowd. "*Drink! Drink! Drink!*"

All eyes were upon him, and Jerry felt the immeasurable weight of every single one. He was twelve years old again, cornered in the playground after school and dared to do something stupid. He pulled his gaze from the cup long enough to glimpse the crowd of eager faces and wide smiles cheering him on. From the back of his mind, Abby joined them. *Drink it, hon. Enjoy yourself. You deserve it.*

He closed his eyes and took a drink. What crossed his tongue was cold and thick, almost like a milkshake but with something gritty in the froth, something not quite ground up. Ice, maybe, but when he crunched down he tasted dirt. Dirt, metal, and something ripe. Sweet and bitter. Fruit and old coins. Copper. Blood.

The sensations did not last. All that remained was an aftertaste of sweetness, and he found himself yearning for another gulp while the first was already warming his gut.

"*Drink! Drink! Drink!*"

Jerry finished the cup, wiped his mouth, and coughed. His tongue tingled with a thousand prickly needles, and though every breath felt like fire, his whole chest grew cold. Arthur said something, but the words were muted against a backdrop of ringing in his ears and an ominous drone seeping through him. The sound was so loud and rumbling that his vision dissolved into a sudden darkness. In that instant, he was alone and small. *An engine,* he thought. *A machine. The engine of the cosmos. A heartbeat.*

And then the noise was gone, and he was back on the bandstand, his senses heightened in stark clarity. He heard the tap of every foot against the earth, the sway of every blade of grass in the breeze, the leaves whispering their secrets among themselves, the chattering of a hundred voices speaking in different tongues, and the slow hum of the stars above. He knew which would burn out and which would burn on forever. He knew which ones weren't stars at all, but eyes.

"Hell of a kick, huh?"

Jerry blinked. The crowd chattered and danced, their attention no longer poised upon him. He looked around the park, up into the sky. Full dark, with a scattering of diamonds across a black canvas. A gibbous moon hung low and bloated. The Grateful Dead sang "Row, Jimmy, Row." And beside him, there was Arthur wearing a shit-eating grin like he'd just delivered the secrets of the universe in liquid form. Maybe he had.

"Yeah," Jerry said, swallowing back the aftertaste. His head swam, the world trailing after itself in waves wherever he looked. "What the hell was that?"

"I told you, brother. It's pure love. Want another?"

"Hell yes."

Arthur smiled and spoke into the microphone, "By the moon's eye!"

The crowd reciprocated: *"By the moon's eye!"*

Jerry shifted his weight and nearly lost his balance. He chuckled with embarrassment as he righted himself. "You know, I've been meaning to ask what that means."

"It's a little saying we have around here, but if I tell you now, it'll spoil the surprise." Arthur clapped a hand on Jerry's shoulder, gave him a firm squeeze. "Go on and mingle, brother. I'll find you."

It'll spoil the surprise.

Jerry watched Fairview's chairman descend the stairs and vanish into the crowd. Any trepidation he might have felt had slowly dissolved in the span of one drink, and for the first time in his life, he felt unchained from the anxiety. He staggered down from the bandstand and into the crowd, where his neighbors greeted him as one of their own. Hands clapped his back and lips stole kisses from his cheeks.

Matilda Scott draped a fiery orange lei over him. She planted her lips on his forehead and vanished into the crowd like a cackling banshee in the night. Bradley anointed Jerry with a can of beer. Others in the crowd joined him, a never-ending chain of greetings and praise, each face melting into the next. Someone—he wasn't sure who—crowned his head with a ridiculous party hat wrapped in tinfoil, and Jerry brayed with amusement.

Time crawled onward as his head swam with sensation, every breath from every lung like an airhorn, splitting the night to signal his passage. He felt alive, invincible, and part of something bigger, older than he could fathom—and it felt *right*, like he'd always been part of this undefinable thing. The world and his place in it had grown infinitely smaller, a minuscule grain of sand on an alien shore, and with this knowledge he felt free of himself, free of the worries and anxieties of daily toil.

Abby was here among them, in the air and in the earth and floating freely through the ether, in every dividing cell and every breath in his lungs. She'd always been here with him, he saw that now, and he no longer felt alone. If he held his breath, peered into the night with enough focus, maybe he could see her still.

He drifted to the edge of the crowd and peered across the park. Somewhere down the slope, near the Moon Pool, a woman stood upon the shore. Jerry rubbed his eyes.

Abby?

Everything else faded into the background. He set off down the hill toward her.

◐

Jerry called out, "Abby?"

When Katherine turned toward him, a mixture of relief and disappointment bubbled up inside him. He'd never felt so conflicted before.

Katherine looked up at him with a forlorn smile. Torchlight shimmered in thin rivulets of tears streaking down her face. "Welcome to the neighborhood," she said quietly. "I hope you're having a great time."

"I'm sorry, I thought— Hey, are you all right?"

She wiped her face, shook her head. "I always get emotional at gatherings like this. Ever feel alone in a crowd of strangers?"

"Most days," he said.

"Something we have in common, I guess. You called out a name just now. Was Abby your wife?"

"Yeah. . ." He scraped a few pebbles loose with his foot. The drink had dulled his nerves, but old anxieties fought hard against its effects. "I thought. . . nah, never mind."

"No, tell me. Finish your thought."

"I looked down here and thought I saw her. But it was you, and. . . I'm glad you're here. I'm glad it's you. I just. . . for a minute, everything seemed different, like I could feel her all around me." He laughed through the sting of tears. "Am I dreaming? This all feels so surreal, like the air is fuzzy."

Katherine smiled. "The potion has that effect the first time. Try to enjoy it."

"I will, but I can't deal with all the noise back there. Too many people. Can I stay here?"

"Of course," she said, tossing a handful of pebbles into the water. "But only if you'll dance with me. I love this song."

He'd been so focused on her that he'd lost track of the music. He'd heard this song before from one of Abby's records—guitar, a steady beat, a rather droll and sullen singer to contrast the pop—but he couldn't place the name. Katherine closed the gap between them, and when she offered her hand, he took it without hesitation, pulled her close.

She rested her head against his chest as they swayed to the music, and his old feet found their rhythm. His joints grated with the exertion. He'd pay for this kind of activity come the morning, but for now he felt at peace. He held her, his head spinning with questions as a warm dampness spread across his chest. She was crying still.

He was well-acquainted with this kind of melancholy, the feeling of invasive otherness among one's peers. Sometimes holding on to someone and venting your tears was the only medicine. He'd learned this with Abby, had yearned for this kind of human contact since she'd passed, and if he could impart even a moment of comfort to this woman then the evening would be worth it.

They danced on the pool's shore, sandaled feet scraping along a bed of damp stones and earth, two lost souls locked in embrace.

They danced, swaying to the rhythm of the cosmos beneath a diamond canopy of the infinite.

They danced in silence until the song was over.

Katherine looked up and smiled. "You smell nice, Mr. Campbell. My husband used the same aftershave."

"Thanks, I..." Jerry let go of her hand, aware of how frigid her fingers were. Everything swam in trails of color, and he saw the vibrations of air from the buffeting of firefly wings. Arthur's drink had hit him harder than he'd thought. He looked away in embarrassment. "I haven't danced like that in a long time. Not since... It doesn't matter."

"It's good for the soul. I try to do it as much as I can. Want to do it again?"

He teetered on his feet, caught his balance, and smiled impishly. "Maybe not right away. Rain check?"

Katherine laughed. "I'll hold you to that, Mr. Campbell."

She took his hand and led him toward the arrangement of granite obelisks along the pool's edge, where smooth pebbles formed a pale ring around the rim.

"Sometimes I come here when I can't sleep," she said, peering into the water. "It's serene. A nice, quiet place to think about things."

The stone glistened in the moonlight and reflected on the water's surface like a natural mirror ball. "It's pretty," he said, "but I don't..."

Understand, he'd wanted to say, but Katherine put her finger to his lips and shook her head. Her tears caught the moon's reflection, and he glimpsed the frail, worried thing he'd met on his porch.

"I know, and I want so badly to tell you, but..." She nodded to the crowd. "Maybe it's better said in private."

Her words were thick in his ears and none of this made sense to him. He smiled out of confusion, for lack of a better response. He wanted to ask her if she still meant to warn him to leave, if she even remembered saying so that night on the porch, but his head swam in a drunken current. Dark splotches burst in the corners of his vision, coating the world in ink and shadow.

Katherine tip-toed along the water's edge. "Tonight isn't the night, but maybe soon."

"I'll take your word for it." He squinted, forcing back the tide of unconsciousness threatening to pull him from shore. When the moment passed, Jerry swallowed back the lump of cotton in his throat, and time slowed. He heard the crushing gears of an enormous engine grinding away in his head, in the sky, vibrating across every bone. His whole body seemed to be screaming.

Where was this coming from? He could handle his booze, even with the slate of medications he consumed every morning and night, but this was something else.

"Jerry? What's wrong?"

"It's nothing," he grunted. "Kat, I've had a great time, but I think I need to head home. That drink hit me harder than I thought."

He didn't wait for her reply, turned on his heels to stagger back up the hill. She called after him, but he didn't respond. Home was his only focus now, and with each step, a leaden weight cemented itself deeper into his gut. Jerry briefly suspected this was a joke, part of a friendly hazing planned by his neighbors to welcome the new guy. Perhaps it was the drink, then. Yes, that had to be it.

The party was still lively, his neighbors still dancing and having a gay old time. And still laughing, probably at his expense. Of course it was a sick prank. Get the new guy to the party, slip him some hallucinogenic drugs, and watch the shenanigans. Real fucking funny, ha-ha.

The DJ switched records, and Big Maybelle began singing "Whole Lotta Shakin' Going On."

Jerry neared the park entrance, trying not to panic or succumb to the onslaught of sensations ripping through his body, when he stumbled over something on the ground. He staggered forward, righted himself, and looked back. A mound of wadded clothing, shorts and shirts and what might've been a sundress. Underwear. An unused adult diaper.

The items trailed back toward the party of retirees—except they weren't retirees at all, but pale-skinned monstrosities with massive worm-like tendrils in place of their heads. They frolicked and slithered in the starlight. No eyes, no mouths, just flesh stretched and unending and swaying, every figure a writhing cilium trying to taste the sky. The stench of earth and blood filled the night.

He blinked, rubbed his face, and tried to make sense of the horror unfolding before him. He was hallucinating this. Just like the trailing colors and booming roar of the stars above. He was drunk. Worse, he was drugged.

There were normal faces among the crowd, those who hadn't changed, and they didn't seem to notice the abominations dancing beside them. Others were mid-transformation, their bare skin like Play-Doh and heads elongated beyond their necks, arms slowly fusing to their torsos.

"Hey, neighbor!" One of them broke free of the chaos—a half-human, half-worm thing. It inched toward him with a red Solo cup clutched in a free appendage. "I've been looking for you—wait, where you goin'?" Its voice was familiar but unbearably dry, the punctuation of each vowel a dull clack of wood struck against wood. Its head stretched into an impossible tendril of skin and eyes, each arm slowly mutating below the elbow.

Christ, what is this?

It raised the Solo cup in his direction. "The party's just starting, my man. I brought you that drink."

Arthur?

Jerry pretended he didn't hear and kept on walking. The thing that spoke with Arthur's voice kept calling out, following him as far as the street corner before giving up.

Head swimming, the world upside down and the universe breathing down his neck, Jerry staggered all the way home, telling himself over and over that he was having a waking nightmare, that this was just a bad acid trip.

Katherine's words crept into his head as he stumbled into his bathroom.

Came to warn you. You need to leave before it sees you too.

Starbursts of color exploded across his vision. Arthur spoke from a tumult of ringing bells, his smug voice a bitter reminder as Jerry fell to his knees: *It'll spoil the surprise.*

Jerry promptly vomited into the toilet and passed out on the floor.

9

Jerry dreamed.

He was back at the park, and the party was over. Evidence of the festivities lay strewn about his feet—piles of empty cups and plates, discarded food, pieces of clothing—and an array of holes had been dug into the slope. But he wasn't alone.

Abby was there, and so was Katherine. Both were standing at the edge of the Moon Pool. They appeared younger, their hands held out in reverence to something above. When Jerry looked up, he saw not the moon but a massive eye staring down at them. A dilated pupil divided in two, and then four. The yellow-white surface of what should have been a cratered moon rippled like water, disturbed by something lurking just beneath the surface.

The goddess sees you, Abby said.

There is love in the glory of the eye, Katherine said. *Bow to the goddess and let her heal your broken heart.*

"But it's just an eye," Jerry said. Not even an eye now, but a broken egg yolk dripping between the stars.

Katherine's face began to shift and distort, her jaw drooping as the rest of her head slowly elongated. *One of many,* she groaned.

He turned toward Abby, whose familiar face would be a respite in this nightmare. Her eyes were gone, replaced by segmented limbs wriggling free of her face, and a clipped voice spoke through her contorted mouth: *Peek-a-boo.*

Jerry awoke with a scream, his voice echoing against the bathroom's bare walls. He stared up at the ceiling in confusion, trying to piece together how he came to be on the floor. As the phantoms of his nightmare faded back into reality's shadow, memories of his evening in the park took their place, and he couldn't distinguish between them at first.

He checked his watch. After midnight now. Would the party still be going on?

Something heavy struck the roof, a vibration that resonated down through the walls and along the floor. He sat up with a start, puzzled.

"The hell?"

He pushed off the floor, steadied himself against the door, and listened.

Another impact—lighter this time but still heavy enough to shake this side of the house. A muffled sound of something clacking together. The noise brought to mind kindling crackling in a campfire. Familiar, too. The voice of that thing in the park that sounded like Arthur.

But that had been a hallucination. He was sober now, the effects of his drink all but gone save for a light headache, and this noise was definitely real.

A heavy knock on the roof followed. Then another. He followed the sounds out of the bathroom and down the hall to the living room. Two more sets of knocks, irregular and heavy, and more of the dry clacking sounds.

Those birds are back. Gotta be.

The knocks broke apart and moved in opposite directions, one toward the front of the house, the other toward the back.

Big ones, too.

But what birds would be active at this hour, and big enough to make this kind of racket?

The clattering footfalls rejoined somewhere on the center of the roof; a moment later, and they were gone.

Confused, he planted himself on the couch, stretched out, and tried to make sense of the disturbance—but his thoughts drifted back to the park.

Did Arthur drug me tonight? And why?

He closed his eyes, and sleep claimed him before he could find the answer. Thankfully, there were no dreams this time.

◉

He spent the morning occupied with unpacking and rearranging, satisfied one hour and changing his mind the next. How much of Abby's things to leave out on display, how much to leave packed, a decision which swung like a pendulum in his heart. Too much was a painful reminder of her absence; too little, and he felt like he was trying to erase her.

He finally decided on a handful of framed photographs to display—their wedding photo, a few from their college days, more from their silver anniversary—and left the rest packed in their boxes at the back of the closet. He put her engagement ring on a chain and hung it around his neck. A memorial, maybe, or perhaps it would serve as a shield of some kind.

Maybe it'll keep me safe from those weird birds, he mused.

After a lunch of leftovers, Jerry reclined on his sofa and thought about Katherine. All evening she'd looked as if there was something on the tip of her tongue, words begging to be spilled. Had it been another ominous warning to leave?

She was an odd lady who spoke in riddles. He liked riddles.

Moreover, he couldn't stop thinking about her. What she'd said, the bizarre incident that had unfolded on his porch, their quiet dance by the Moon Pool last night—all these memories had circled his head since morning, the sweet punctuations of a dull hangover hammer pounding away at the forefront of his skull. Who was Katherine Dunnally, really? What was she trying to tell him?

Jerry wandered over to the refrigerator where he'd pinned her note and dialed her number.

Three rings later, a soothing voice filled his ear. "Hello?"

"Hey. It's Jerry."

"I had a feeling I'd hear from you today. How's your head?"

"I've had worse hangovers. Sorry I barged out of the party last night. The drink went to my head, I think. How are you, though?"

"I'm okay, just. . ." A big yawn filled the line. "Still sleepy. I didn't come home until dawn."

"Holy crow. Did the party go that late?"

"Uh huh. Always does."

He leaned against the kitchen island, staring out the window at his backyard. "I don't get it."

"What's to get?"

"All the partying. Every night, seems like."

She laughed. "I guess we're all just night people."

Night people. He thought of the lawn parties every night that week. The whole damn neighborhood seemed to come to life at sundown. Birds included.

"I guess so," he said. "Arthur told me in a roundabout way that this is the way things are here."

"Arthur's hard to resist, isn't he?"

An odd question, but apropos. He thought about the night before, standing in front of all those people, and wondered what might have happened if he'd not taken the drink. "He's got a knack for commanding a crowd."

"He built this whole neighborhood. The whole town, really. Got his hands in every pie you can think of."

"More of a king than a chairman, huh?"

"He'd probably like to think so."

"Let me ask you something, Kat. And you can be honest and tell me to go to hell if this is none of my business, but. . ."

"Spit it out, Mr. Campbell." He could see her smiling with those words.

"Is this a religious commune or something? I mean, with talk of this 'goddess' stuff. . ."

Static hissed from the receiver as she burst into laughter. "What do *you* think it is?"

Why are you deflecting? The words were there on the tip of his tongue, but he knew where that path would lead him, and the last thing he wanted was to alienate the only friend he'd made here. "I. . . haven't made up my mind."

"Let me know when you do. Maybe then I'll have an answer."

Silence fell over the line. Her non-answer didn't surprise him. Given everything else she'd said over the past week, he wondered if he'd ever get a straight answer from her. Hell, even a simple explanation would suffice, but he didn't want to push his luck.

Another yawn filled his ear. "I'm going to let you go, Jerry. My nurse will be here any minute. She doesn't like it when I take phone calls. Thanks for checking up on me, hon."

She was gone before he could reply. He stared at the phone screen for a time, weighing the device in his hand as more questions arose from the ether. *Her nurse doesn't like it when she takes calls? What the hell?* Perhaps he was reading too much into this, and everything she'd said was just the ramblings of an aging mind sick with a terrible disease.

But if that were true, how did it explain last night? She'd been positively vibrant, smiling, brimming with happiness from the moment he saw her. He couldn't reconcile last night's Katherine with the one who'd thrashed and seized on his lawn, or the one who'd died on his porch just two nights ago, and the more he tried, the more his head pounded away.

Jerry chose to do what he'd always done when faced with an unsolvable problem: mow his lawn.

When he ventured outside, the street was quiet except for a dog barking somewhere in the distance. He held his breath, listened for the dull roar of distant traffic, but there was nothing. In his old neighborhood, Sundays were always bustling with activity, families going to and from church, kids playing in their yards.

Fairview Acres—or his slice of it—appeared to be in hibernation. Though if the party in the park truly had concluded at dawn, then he supposed the silence was to be expected.

They're probably all hungover. Or I've moved into 'Salem's Lot. Fuck, maybe both.

He fired up his lawnmower and went to work. The whole time, he didn't see a single soul.

👁

Jerry stepped outside after a shower, and by then, the sky had mellowed to an orange glow. His muscles ached from a day of labor, but he wasn't too old to take care of his own lawn. Not yet. When he reached that point, the community association had him covered.

Having the day to work outside left him tired but refreshed, allowing him a dedicated moment to process the last two years. He'd been living on autopilot, merely existing in the moments between life-altering events which, in hindsight, had only numbed him further from the shock.

And then there was the matter of his new neighborhood, its mysteries, and the woman at the center of it all. No matter how far back he pushed recent events into his mind, no matter how hard he dwelled on the past, the riddle of Fairview Acres and Katherine Dunnally always resurfaced. It was ever-present, a small kernel of unchewed experience wedged between his teeth. He couldn't stop tonguing it, couldn't break it free. His mind always won out, holding him hostage until he could make sense of the uncanny.

Arthur's drink and its effects were one thing, but the subject of his hallucinations was the true source of his disturbance, and he wondered what part of his mind those awful monstrosities had come from. Abby might have joked and suggested indigestion, that those creatures were "more gravy than grave" as she was fond of quoting, and Jerry might have agreed with her—but she wasn't here now, and he was alone with his troubling thoughts. He could forget about the effects and how they transformed his neighbors into horrific monstrosities—they were somewhat explainable—but his ingestion of the drug in the first place? What did Arthur stand to gain by drugging Fairview's newest resident?

"Penny for your thoughts?"

Jerry blinked, torn away from his reverie by the friendly voice. Katherine walked up his driveway clad in a sundress, her curly hair pulled back in a bun. She held a pitcher in her hands. Lemon slices floated inside.

"You'd need an awful lot of pennies," Jerry said, smiling. "What've you got there?"

"Some sweet tea. You've been on my mind all afternoon, ever since you called. Thought you might need a pick-me-up after last night. Care to get us some glasses?"

"Not at all."

They sat side by side on the porch, enjoying the tea and watching the sunset. Silence slipped between them, and Jerry found himself staring at the melting ice cubes in his glass, wrestling with what to say.

"I'll have to start a tab with you, Mr. Campbell."

He smirked. "Like I said, your credit's always good here."

"I'm gonna owe you a lot of pennies."

He blushed, took a sip of his drink. "Got a lot on my mind this evening." He looked at her from the corner of his eye. "A lot to do with last night. This neighborhood. Arthur. You."

"I had the drink, too. Didn't want to, but. . ." Katherine stared ahead at Gary's house across the street, and when she spoke, her mouth barely moved. "Anyway, this is a nice place, once you get used to it. Fairview has its charm if you're willing to look for it."

"How are you feeling? After your episode, I mean?"

"Still feel like a million bucks." She looked him in the eye. He saw that same melancholy, full of unshed tears and trepidation. "How about you? The drink packs a punch your first time. It gets easier the more you drink it. You didn't. . ." She lowered her voice, glanced toward the street. "You didn't drink any more of it, did you?"

Jerry shook his head. "Arthur went to get me another, but then I saw you, and after we danced, it all started to hit me pretty hard. You wouldn't believe some of the strange shit I saw last night. I've never hallucinated before, but last night. . . whew."

"Hallucinated," she said flatly. "It's something, all right."

"I figure it was a bad reaction to my medication. Don't expect I'll be having any more of it."

Katherine patted his hand, smiled. "Good. That's good. Maybe you'll get lucky, and one's not enough."

Across the street, Gary Olson's front door opened, and he stepped outside.

Katherine drank deeply from her glass, gulping down the rest of her tea. "Well, I don't want to keep you, Jerry. I'm glad you're feeling okay, and—"

He took her hand out of reflex. It was something he'd always done with Abby whenever she got up to leave, a private joke between the two of them—only when he looked up, it wasn't Abby looking back. Katherine blushed and mustered a shy smile.

"Sorry," he whispered. "Old habit."

"It's okay," she said. "Was there something you wanted to say?"

"Last night, *you* said you had more to say."

She glanced toward the street. Gary stepped off the curb and headed toward Jerry's front yard. "I do," she whispered, "but keep that between us. I'll visit you again." Her words came in quick succession, almost a single sentence she spoke so fast. She glanced down at the pitcher, gave his hand a squeeze, and said loudly, "You enjoy the rest of the tea, Jerry. I made it special just for you."

"Howdy," Gary said, plodding across the freshly cut lawn. He wasn't wearing his sun hat, and his bald dome reflected a hint of the fading sun. "Don't get up on my account, Kat. I just came to say hello."

"Not at all. I was just leaving. Brought Jerry here some of my sweet tea to welcome him to Fairview."

"Mighty kind of ya." Gary's gaze lingered on her a moment longer than Jerry liked. The tension between them was palpable, for reasons he could not discern. Not a romantic history gone sour. No, something else. Based on her body language, she was afraid of their neighbor, but why? The old man seemed like nothing more than a big teddy bear.

Jerry poured himself another glass from the pitcher. "It's really good. Want some, Gary?"

"No, that's quite all right." He grinned at Katherine. "Why don't you sit back down and visit with us a spell?"

"No, really, I need to be getting back. Lisa's going to call any minute, and I left my phone at home. I'm so forgetful!" She shuffled down the porch steps.

She looked back when she reached the sidewalk. "Have a good night, Mr. Campbell."

Jerry raised his hand. "You too, Mrs. Dunnally."

Both men watched until she was gone. Jerry took another drink of his tea, more confused now than he'd been before she'd arrived, but he chose to say nothing. He suspected Gary would say plenty.

"Odd bird, that one." Gary rubbed absently at his five o'clock shadow. "Ain't been right since her husband died. A case of the big D."

"Big D?"

"Dementia. The kind that gets weird around sundown."

"Yeah, I heard something about that." Jerry set down his glass. "What can I do for you, Gary?"

"Oh, nothing much. Meant to pay you a visit earlier, see how you're doing after last night." He leaned closer to the porch railing, like someone might hear them talking. "Did she, uh, say anything weird to you just now?"

"Weird how?"

"I don't know. Weird. Anything that might set off alarm bells. After her episode the other night, we've all been worried about her, you see."

Uh huh, Jerry thought. *Worried, my ass.*

He shook his head. "No, nothing like that. She just brought me some tea, and we talked about the weather, how quiet it is around here, who's her favorite neighbor, that sort of thing."

Gary gave him a stare he couldn't decipher, and Jerry did all he could to resist smiling. A full minute passed before Gary's face broke into a smirk.

"Favorite neighbor. That's funny."

"Sure is," Jerry said, slapping his knee. He climbed to his feet. "Well, I need to wind down for the night. But I appreciate you coming to check on me."

"Not a problem, neighbor. You need anything, you know where to find me. And hey, there's a party happening at Bob Ottone's place just a block over, if you wanna join. Guy makes a hell of a cosmo."

"Nah, think I'm partied out. Thanks, though."

Jerry picked up the pitcher and was about to retreat inside when something crossed his mind. He turned back, called out, "Hey, wait a sec."

"Yeah?"

"Wanted to ask you. It's the weirdest thing, but you ever see any large birds around here?"

Gary scrunched up his face, puzzled. "Like, what? Eagles?"

"Something like that, yeah. Really big. Active late at night."

"Are you pullin' my leg?" Gary chuckled quietly to himself. "Didn't take you for a kidder, Jerry. Or a bird watcher, neither."

Jerry's face flushed, and he forced a chuckle to play it off like a joke. "Yeah, I guess it does sound silly."

"Why do you ask?"

"No reason. Thought I heard something walking around on my roof last night."

Gary's smile faded. "You're right. That does sound silly." He turned back toward the street. "Have a good night, neighbor."

10

A huge knock startled Jerry from his slumber. He kicked back damp bed sheets soaked with sweat and stared at the ceiling. Overhead, a series of heavy footsteps plodded across the roof toward the center of the house.

He waited for his heart to calm. He'd been having nightmares again—vivid but disorienting. He'd been floating in space, nude and impervious to the vacuum, while a nest of leeches suckled at his body. In the distance, a pair of roiling stars burned away in a dangerous orbit, destined to collide at some point in the distant future. Mere minutes on a cosmic scale. Perhaps the end of time, or the start of something else.

Where the hell did all that come from? He'd stopped reading science fiction in college.

He wiped sweat from his forehead and listened as another set of footsteps rattled the roof from the opposite end of the house. He switched on the bedside lamp and looked at his watch. 2:08 a.m. Would he ever get a good night's sleep again?

"Goddamn birds," he mumbled. He went to the kitchen, retrieved a flashlight from a junk drawer, and stepped outside. Moonlight bathed the backyard in a pallid sheen, illuminating Abby's birdbath near the back corner, along with his wheelbarrow and other tools he'd forgotten to put away. The early summer air was cool against his damp skin, and the night was still, quiet. Not even a breeze.

He walked down the porch steps, winced as wet grass brushed against his ankles, and clicked on the flashlight.

Movement. A sharp pop of wood. Behind, above.

He spun around, panned the flashlight across the roof's edge. Nothing.

He walked further into the yard, hoping he might glimpse something at a different angle. "All right, bird..."

The circle of light crawled along the lower portion of the A-frame, left to right. He raised the light closer to the peak—

A shape darted below the edge, disappearing to the other side. It was there and gone again so fast, he wasn't sure what he'd just witnessed. But he heard it: heavy steps, one after the other, all the way down the opposite incline.

He blinked, realized he was holding his breath, and exhaled in a rush. *What the hell was that?*

He refocused the beam, panning across the rest of the rooftop. Something glistened across the shingling, but at this distance he couldn't make it out. Wet, maybe. Slimy. But he wasn't about to pull his ladder out of the garage to go investigate. No reason to go to all that trouble over damn birds.

But was it really a bird, Jerry? Whatever he'd seen darting away, it sure as hell didn't have any feathers, and was gone so fast that he wasn't sure what he'd seen. *But if you think about it, hadn't it looked like a pair of slender legs?*

A person on his roof at two in the morning? Ridiculous. He clicked off the flashlight and set off for his house.

Clouds rolled past the moon, and the yard grew darker. A hollow croak rattled through the night. He spun around, heart in throat, and fumbled for the flashlight. The beam clicked on, shuffled wildly about the yard until he got control of his shaking hands.

Flash: the birdbath in the corner.

Flash: his garden shed with its uneven doors.

Flash: thick hedges and a pair of evergreens on the property line.

Ghosts of the scenery lingered in his vision after he moved the beam. A low breeze swept over him, prompting a chill of spider legs to crawl down the length of his back.

Something rustled in the hedges. He gasped, dropped the flashlight. The beam shuddered from the impact, flickered once, and settled on the hedgerow.

Leaves whispered in the wind, the branches voicing their disturbance. Jerry stood like a deer on the highway, transfixed by the only source of light, too terrified to move, to breathe.

Because there was something beyond the hedgerow, lurking just outside the tenuous circle of light, and he could only see it if he didn't look at it. It was there in the corner of his vision, standing chest high with the hedge, but that's where the shape stopped making sense. It distorted, narrowed into a thick, wriggling branch that moved freely in the air.

Behind, above, the rattling call echoed into the night. In the distance, another. And then one more just across the yard. The shape croaked again, louder this time, an aggressive *uhk-uhk-uhk* leveled in his direction.

His blood ran cold.

Moonlight filtered through the clouds, lifting back the veil of shadows, and he caught a glimpse of the thing but it made no sense to him. A pair of legs—were those *jeans?*—and something like a long, thick neck or trunk. It rattled off another warning cry and lunged over the hedge toward him.

Jerry turned and ran, nearly losing his balance on the wet grass, and clambered back up the porch steps. The croaking grew louder, right on his heels. He cried out in terror as he threw himself inside and slammed the door behind him.

Heart pounding, his mind locked in horror, he stood with his back braced against the door. He expected the thing to try to force its way inside, but it never did. Slowly, his panic subsided, and he finally turned and peeked out the window.

The moonlit yard was empty. His abandoned flashlight laid on the grass, its beam still illuminating the hedgerow. *No way I'm going back out there with those...*

Those what? Definitely not birds. Definitely not people.

He locked the back door.

If it wasn't birds, and it wasn't people, what the hell had been walking on his roof for these last two nights? *And why was it wearing jeans?*

◐

In the morning, the backyard was as he'd left it the night before, a dead flashlight the only sign he'd been out there in the dark. He found no footprints, nothing disturbed, and he began to wonder if he'd dreamed the encounter. He wasn't a sleepwalker, but with all the stress he'd been under lately, he couldn't rule it out.

Stress. Yeah, sure. After working in accounting for decades—dealing with monthly profit-and-loss statements, quarterly audits, inept managers, two corporate mergers—he was no stranger to stress, and not once had he ever walked in his sleep.

So if I didn't dream them, what the hell were they?

Not birds. A silly idea, in hindsight, but that was the only possibility which seemed probable at the time. Then again, "probable" had flown out the window, grown a pair of legs, and strutted its way off the roof into the great unknown. Which was where Jerry currently found himself, staring into the middle distance of his backyard, sipping coffee and trying to unravel yet another knot.

Everything was so dark, and it happened so fast... there must be a logical explanation here.

He saw quick flashes of the thing running straight for him. An impossible shape carved out of the dark. The way it leapt over the hedgerow without hesitation, its thick trunk protruding from its waist like a living tree branch, drove a chill down the back of his neck. He gulped the last of his warm coffee, but a pit of ice remained in his gut.

Jerry took out his phone and typed out a quick message to Arthur: *Been hearing strange things on my roof at night. Any nocturnal critters I should know about?*

He sent the message before he could second-guess himself, tightened his robe, and wandered into the yard. *Nocturnal critters,* he thought. *Understatement.*

He could deal with raccoons and opossums, but this other thing left him questioning his sanity. Even in the sunlight, he felt exposed, vulnerable. Watched. He looked over his shoulder at the Scotts' home. All their curtains were drawn. And to his left, the empty house for sale had no curtains, every window a wide lidless eye observing his every move. Anyone could be in there—

"This is stupid." The sound of his own voice recharged his wits somewhat, despite the trepidation buried just a few decibels down. "Just check things out and put this to rest. Got more important shit to do today."

Groceries. A bag of coffee from the coffee shop. The last fifty pages of the new Cosby novel. Tasks that could be completed any time on any other day, and all of them hinged upon this one thing, this seemingly innocent and diligent act of home security which, in that moment, felt insurmountable.

He marched to the shed before he could talk himself out of it, opened its uneven doors, and took stock of the musty contents within. No jean-clad bipedal animals there.

Perhaps the perimeter, then. He walked his property line, behind the shed—nothing there but an old, fallen bird's nest—and around to the hedgerow. Nothing there, either.

"I've lost my fucking mind, Abby." He'd gone outside last night and been chased off by the conjurations of a failing mind. "Maybe this is how I wind down."

But then movement in the hedgerow caught his eye: something stuck to the leaves, flapping in the breeze. Dark, with a hint of blue. He slowly approached the hedge and squinted for a better look.

"No way..."

He plucked the torn piece of denim from the branch, held it between his fingers as sour bile rose in his gorge. "No goddamn way in hell."

◐

Jerry dialed Katherine's number and waited for her to answer.

One ring. Two.

Come on, Kat. Please pick up.

He tried to think of anyone else he could call to help him make sense of this. Anyone who wouldn't laugh in his face or dismiss this as a senile episode. As the trilling ring counted three-four-five in his ear, a heavy weight settled into his gut: he had no one else.

There were only two people he could call: Arthur, who was on his shit list for the stunt he'd pulled on Saturday night; and Katherine, who wasn't answering the phone.

Six rings. Seven.

Jerry sighed and canceled the call. He looked around his empty house and watched the walls turn glassy with tears.

Alone. You're alone.

He buried his face in his trembling hands and cried.

PART TWO
ACHE

11

He woke up screaming most mornings for the next three weeks, drenched in panic sweat, with his chest aching from a racing heart and a terrible crawling sensation moving over and through his skin. Beginning the day with an anxiety attack took its toll, and he spent the hours in a haze, groggy and irritable and aloof. He tried calling Katherine every day that first week to no avail. She didn't have voicemail set up, and even if she did, he had no idea what to say. *Hi, it's Jerry, and I think I've lost my mind. Seen any two-legged monsters with ripped jeans lately?*

Jerry was no stranger to depression. He'd suffered from it his whole life, long before it was understood as an illness, and only in recent years had he come to truly grasp how deeply it affected his life. Abby had played a big part in his healing, helped him identify his triggers so he could learn to avoid them—and how to deal with them when he couldn't.

He had medication, of course, but the pills only worked to level out his brain chemistry. Certain situations could still drive a spike of anxiety straight through his skull. With an anxiety attack, depression wasn't far behind. This time felt different, his medications somehow rendered impotent, and the world felt a little darker, the shadows a little longer.

Anxiety opens the door, Abby used to say.

His panic attack hadn't just opened the door, it had blown everything wide open. Finding that strip of denim had driven him to the brink of insanity, but the following epiphany that he was completely alone had torn a hole through his reason and shown him the hopelessness that lay beyond. He hadn't suffered an attack like that since the morning after Abby's funeral. Heart palpitations, cold sweats, weakness, racing thoughts.

He was alone, facing something he didn't understand, and wasn't even sure if it was real.

Not quite alone, he thought, lying awake during the twilight hours. Those things came back every night, marching across his roof with heavy footfalls and the telltale slap of something like skin. His mind held him hostage as he attempted to make sense of what they were and what they were doing, while memories of that night in the park flitted at the back of his mind like a moth.

Whenever sleep did finally arrive, something dragged him beneath the waves of his subconscious, where a bestiary of slithering nightmares waited.

When he wasn't floating through space and beset by leeches, he found himself back at the park and staring into the Moon Pool. Abby and Katherine were both there, twin supplicants to their goddess above. There was no moon, only a single glaring eye bearing down upon them all, and whenever he looked toward it, he felt an overwhelming tightness in his chest. The gravity of an unseen force held them all in its grip, slowly crushing them into nothing.

Depression cradled him in the nest he'd built for it, whispered its sweet lies in his ear and told him no one would understand, to not even bother reaching out. They'd all think him crazy; better to just cut himself off from the outside world for good. Besides, what could he say to Katherine or Arthur or any other neighbors? Telling them the truth was out of the question. That kind of honesty always made people uncomfortable. It was an aspect of social interaction that Jerry disliked most.

Arthur called him every afternoon. Jerry let the calls go to voicemail, and when he listened, they all began the same way: *"Hey, buddy! Arthur here. Just calling to check on you, see how you're doing, see if you need anything..."*

Spoken with precision, clarity, and an even cadence, like he'd rehearsed it dozens of times. For the first few days, Jerry almost felt a kinship and mild appreciation for Arthur's concern, but over time he convinced himself the chairman was just checking off a box from his daily duties. Depression lied about this, too, and Jerry accepted it without question.

The fallout from his anxiety attack had deteriorated his desire to talk to anyone, and he supposed it was just as well. He didn't want anyone to see him like this, a beaten-down old man questioning his faculties. Better to await the rising tide to drown.

He remained indoors, locked away from his neighbors and people in general, resorting to an online delivery service for his groceries and other necessities. Not that it did a lot of good—he lacked the energy and motivation to cook for himself and ordered takeout most days. When he'd gone through this after Abby's death, Jerry still had a job he could cling to for routine and structure. Now his routine consisted of hours in bed, the curtains drawn closed, watching daytime TV and sleeping far too much.

His inactivity invited a wealth of aches and pains. One morning, he awoke to swollen joints in his ankles and knees. Just enough low-level pain to be annoying. He was used to the usual achiness, but not when it was this constant, this tenacious. His coffee intake had doubled, a failing effort to limit his sleep as much as possible, and he suspected that might have exacerbated his joint flares. Gout did run in his family, after all. He popped some ibuprofen and forgot about it.

Katherine remained on his mind, the one bright point in an otherwise gray haze, but he'd convinced himself that she was better off if he didn't trouble her. When she did finally call him back, he sent her to voicemail, and listened to the message a few minutes later: *"Just calling to check on you, hon. I'm sorry I didn't call you back right away, I was. . . I had another spell—but I'm okay now. I hope you're not upset with me, Jerry. Please call me when you're able."*

He frowned, worried by the news of another incident, and hoped she was better. At least she sounded like her chipper self. He coveted that kind of positivity and made to call her back, but that nagging voice in his mind told him not to bother. *She doesn't need to hear about your problems,* it said. *She's got enough problems of her own.*

He put down the phone and buried himself in another one of Abby's books.

Gary stopped by one evening and left a basket of zucchini and squash on his doorstep. No note, just gourds. Jerry brought them inside and left them on the counter. Maybe he'd cut them up and fry them, or maybe he'd just order pizza again and add to the impressive stack of cardboard atop the waste bin.

Another day, Matilda Scott left a batch of cookies with a note to return the dish "whenever he felt up to it."

Oatmeal raisin. The worst.

He placed them on the counter beside the gourds.

Katherine called again, left another message. And another.

Jerry clung to her voicemails like a lifeline, caught in a cycle he couldn't break on his own, made worse by the knowledge that he was too deep this time, too far from shore. He didn't have Abby to send out a lifeboat. With enough time, he feared he might convince himself it was better just to drown in his misery, to sink and die and release himself from this horrid existence.

So when the doorbell rang one Wednesday afternoon, Jerry didn't bother moving from his bed, merely rolled over and closed his eyes. *They'll go away,* he told himself. *They always do.*

But they didn't go away. Two rings. A third, followed by knocks on the door. His phone lit up with another call: Katherine.

He worked up the strength to crawl out of bed and hobble to the living room. He slowly opened the door to Katherine's worried face. She gripped a walker, its metal frame trembling in her hands, and sweat dappled her forehead. He looked her over and his annoyance gave way to concern. She looked almost as bad as he felt.

"Kat?"

"Jerry Campbell, I ought to kick your ass." She took a step with the walker toward the opening. "Are you gonna invite me in or not?"

◉

Katherine sat at his kitchen table, watching him pick away at the meager meal she'd scrounged from his refrigerator, and he felt her judgment with every bite. Worse was his embarrassment—he'd let his new home fall into disarray, with half-unpacked boxes shoved into corners, stacks of unopened mail, and a pile of dirty clothes that had spilled from the hamper on its way to the laundry. A fine layer of dust coated the table and kitchen counters, and a swarm of fruit flies danced above the sink full of dishes.

"Are you all right?" he asked, gesturing to her walker.

"Bad knees. I'll be fine." She looked him over. "But you look terrible, hon."

He finished off a sandwich and washed it down with a beer. "I know I do. It's why I stayed away. You weren't supposed to see me like this."

She reached over, took the bottle of beer from his hand. "That's not helping."

"Now you sound like my wife."

"A woman wise beyond her years. You talk like this isn't the first time."

"It's not." He sighed, leaned back in his chair, and let loose a small belch. "I've got meds that are supposed to keep this from happening too often, but. . ." He rubbed absently at his wrist, winced. "They haven't worked too well lately."

"Did you call your doctor?"

Jerry nodded but said nothing. He had called, and the good Dr. Rapino had increased the dosage of his prescription, but Jerry was too ashamed to tell her he'd been afraid to leave his house to go pick it up from the pharmacy.

"You should've called me back," Katherine said. "I would've helped you. Somehow." She ran her fingertip along the edge of the table and frowned at the dust. "At the very least I could've helped you clean up this pigsty."

"I know. I appreciate that, and I'm sorry I didn't, but. . ."

(But I didn't want to have to explain what led me to this.)

(I didn't know how to tell you what I saw that night, didn't want you to think I'd lost my mind.)

(I didn't want you to see an old man start to deteriorate.)

(I was too shy to tell you how much those voicemails meant to me.)

". . . I didn't want to bother you."

Katherine smiled, placed her hand on his. Her skin was still cold, but he welcomed the sensation, the touch of another. "You're the only friend I've got here besides my daughter," she said, "and I only see her a few times a week. The nurse who visits me every day isn't much of a talker. And Arthur—" She caught herself. "My point is, you're one of two people I trust right now, and that means you'll never be a bother."

Jerry didn't know what to say to that and allowed the silence to speak for him. He couldn't recall becoming such fast friends with anyone else in his life—except for Abby, of course. Most people who came into his life were too eager to make him conform to their standards, too eager to shake hands and pat him on the back like they'd been best friends for decades. It made a person more malleable, susceptible to their whims when the time came to reveal their ulterior motive.

And there was always a motive. He'd learned to keep those people at arm's length as a rule.

But not Abby—and not Katherine. They met him halfway on his own terms, or in this case, met him the whole way when he didn't know he needed it, and this realization made his heart swell. This rare type of person was someone to pull close, hold tight, and never let go.

Jerry squeezed her hand and finally spoke. "Thank you."

"You're welcome." She braced herself against the table and rose to her feet. He stood and held out a hand to help steady her, but she waved him away. "I'm fine. Promise."

"You're sure?"

Katherine grinned. "Sure enough. Now, let's get this place cleaned up."

◐

They cleaned his house all afternoon. Jerry was grateful for the company, even if a plague of questions buzzed through his head the whole time, and he couldn't bring himself to spoil their time together by asking Katherine about her episodes, her warnings, or her disease. Nor did he want to bring up his hallucinations in the park, or the nightly visitations he'd experienced since. There would come a time for such discussions, and he hoped he'd be in a better state of mind then.

He walked her home after they'd finished. Her range of motion had slowly improved as the day wore on, and her reliance on a rollator had diminished. Now, as the sky burned away at sunset, he trailed behind her with the walker in tow, silently marveling over the improvement she'd made while struggling to keep up with her.

When they reached her house, Katherine said, "You can leave the walker on the porch."

He set it down beside the front door. "Won't you need it?"

"Not always."

"You're the boss."

"So I've been told." A smile spread across her face. "Thanks for walking me home, Jerry."

"Thanks for helping me out."

"Any time, my friend. Do you feel any better?"

He breathed in the evening air. It was his first time outside in days. "Yeah, I think so."

"Good. Next time the black dog starts howling in your head, give me a call, okay?" She stood on her toes and planted a kiss on his cheek. "Have a good night, hon."

Jerry waited until she closed the front door before he set off for home. He felt lighter every step of the way, and when the night brought its uninvited visitors, he slept soundly through their arrival.

12

Thursday afternoon.

Jerry had just come in from mowing the lawn, something he'd put off for weeks, and was in the process of undressing for a much-needed shower when the doorbell rang. *Let it ring,* he told himself. *If it's important, they'll come back.*

His joints were inflamed again. More than an annoyance today. Flexing his toes shot jolts of lightning straight up his legs. He peeled off his shoes with surgical precision, moving slowly to lessen the pressure, and cried out as he slid the first one over his heel. Stars burst before his eyes and sweat dotted his forehead. He'd not had a flare like this in years.

Must've been all that pizza.

His big toe was swollen. Gout. No doubt about it. He'd been on his feet for over an hour with the lawnmower, and all that walking must have irritated the joint enough to trigger the flare. Where was his cane? If this persisted, he'd need it to get around. The thought of hobbling around his home aged him ten years.

The doorbell rang again.

He huffed, eased himself off the bed, and limped to the bathroom. The hot water would do his joints some good.

After he'd showered and dressed, Jerry found his old cane in the hallway closet, an artifact from a less enlightened time in his life. He'd thought he could manage his uric acid levels with diet alone, but Abby had told him that wouldn't cut it, everything he liked to eat was rich in purines. The cane was his idea of compromise, hoping to avoid another mandatory pill, but there was only so much pain he could stand.

Cane in hand, Jerry slowly walked out the front door to check his mail—and saw a pressure washer sitting on his driveway in front of the garage. A white envelope stuck out from between the coil of hose.

"The hell?"

He hobbled over to it, opened the envelope, and pulled out a small piece of stationery.

The note read:

FROM THE DESK OF ARTHUR PETERSON

Been trying to reach you for a while, man. I wanted to say sorry about the gathering last month. I'm sure you're upset with me, but I can explain everything if you'll give me a chance.

Dinner at my place tomorrow night, 'round 8-ish. Address is below. I hope you'll drop by. And here's the pressure washer. You can keep it as long as you need. Consider it a peace offering.

—A

P.S. Got your text. I'll have pest control drop by and do a sweep of your property.

Jerry rolled his eyes. Now he wished he'd answered his door. He'd almost put that awful evening behind him, but reading Arthur's words dredged every nightmarish moment from the silt of his mind. The impulse to confront Arthur was great, but a part of him was also afraid to do so. What could he say? And how? *Hey, you drugged me at the party, and I didn't appreciate it.* The words didn't ring true in his head, and he felt foolish for even thinking of them. Maybe Arthur hadn't known what was in the drink. Maybe everything had been another bad dream. Maybe

(came to warn you)

this was all a big misunderstanding. And maybe there was more to Jerry's fear than he realized. A fear so powerful it kept his hand at bay in an effort of self-preservation. Something didn't feel right here, but now he was locked into a mortgage that he would never live to pay off. Moving out wasn't an option. These were his neighbors, whether he liked it or not.

Perhaps the fear he felt was just a projection of his own insecurities. Wasn't it always?

And this is how you deal with it, old man—by not dealing with it. The only one you're harming is yourself. You promised yourself—promised me—a fresh start here. These people are reaching out to you, and you're locking yourself away. You can do better, Jerry.

Abby, always the voice of reason even in death. She was right, and he knew it. "She'd hate to see you like this," he whispered.

Deep down, despite his physical fatigue, the grotesque memories, and the plague of unsettling dreams, he wanted to believe that night was an honest mistake. "Just a big misunderstanding. Has to be."

Admitting this to himself felt like he'd finally broken the surface, risen above the tide to take that first precious gasp of air. Anxiety always opened the door, but perseverance and reason could close it—if only for a while.

Long enough.

Arthur's pressure washer made quick work of the bloodstains, splotches that had long since darkened to the color of old rust, but the trio of streaks at the end of his porch were harder to clear. They were more than just blood. Thick, almost gelatinous. The water jet only did so much, leaving behind thin pink slivers. Looking at them, Jerry thought of the way fat drips from meat on a grill, congealing in the trap. His gut churned. He told himself he'd pick up stronger cleaner on his next trip to the store.

When he was finished, Jerry reclined on his bench and watched life in the neighborhood carry on in the late afternoon light. Gary had emerged while Jerry cleaned his porch and was busying himself with his flowerbeds on the corner across the street, weeding and watering and draining a six-pack of beer. He waved to Jerry, and Jerry returned the gesture, but not without some trepidation. He couldn't help but see the man as a worm with humanoid features, and the thought twisted his guts. Still, he supposed he should thank the man for sharing his garden's bounty, even if the gourds sat at the bottom of his trash bin, soft and rotting.

Two women in jogging suits trotted past and greeted him in unison. "Afternoon, Jerry!" The way they slowed and smiled made him uncomfortable. There were secrets in those smiles, the punchline to a joke everyone knew except him.

He didn't recognize them but raised his hand anyway. They clearly knew him. Probably from the park.

You're the new neighbor. Everyone loves the new guy.

Abby again, speaking in his thoughts. He smiled and shook his head, feeling foolish at his vanity. He could move beyond the feeling of being targeted—he'd wanted to live the life of a recluse ever since Abby's passing, had moved out here where he didn't know anyone for that very reason—but the assortment of puzzle pieces strewn about his feet was something he couldn't ignore. Arthur's drink, those things walking across his roof every night, the hallucinations at the park—assuming they *were* hallucinations—and the strange obsession with the moon.

(It'll spoil the surprise.)

And then there was Katherine. Dead on his porch one day, alive and dancing the next, with a secret she wanted to share when the time was right. He wondered if that time would ever arrive, or if this was a symptom of her dementia.

Maybe you're just looking for shadows in a bright room.

One of Abby's sayings, a playful jab at his incessant need to suspect everything and everyone. In his mind, if someone's too nice, they're hoping to gain something; if they're too quiet, they're hiding something. Everyone had an angle to play, secrets to conceal, other sides to themselves. She couldn't complain too much about his mistrust; they'd been a boon at his job, especially when it came to tracking down money from clients, and he'd received several promotions due in part to his efficiency. It had built him a career and a comfortable retirement, but the cost was great. He hadn't realized to what extent, until Abby's death had forced him to interact and take others at their word. Would the funeral director *really* organize things according to Jerry's instructions? Could the mortician *really* be trusted to make Abby look her best?

What choice did he have now? Abby wasn't here to be his buffer anymore. Sooner or later, he'd have to adapt.

And maybe now was the time.

Maybe that night in the park was just alcohol, mixed too strong for his liking, and he'd always been a lightweight anyway. The hallucinations were just a bad interaction with his daily medications. Everything he saw that night was just a skewed interpretation of reality courtesy of his drunken brain. Come to think of it, he'd had worse nights back in college. But what of those things walking across his roof every night? What the hell was that thing that had chased him through his yard? He didn't have an easy answer for that yet, but wanted so badly to believe it was a prank of some kind. A stupid hazing of the new guy, just kidding, bro, don't take it so seriously, ha-ha. At the very least, he hoped Arthur would have an answer that made sense. One that didn't reek of bullshit, like his explanation of Katherine's episode.

Was he certain she'd died at his doorstep, though? He had no medical training and wasn't equipped to make that kind of determination. Even if Arthur's claim of sundown's syndrome and dementia didn't ring true, there was plenty about it Jerry didn't understand, enough to make him doubt his assertions. Besides, what did it matter if she was okay now?

The juxtaposition of the woman he'd met a month ago with the one he knew now was something he couldn't easily reconcile. If she'd been so ill, why was she so vibrant and lucid? They'd danced, had conversations. *Flirted,* for God's sake. Even if she hadn't died, how could a woman her age and in her condition be so *alive?*

Look at you, the good doctor Jerry Campbell. Not a real doctor, of course, but you could play one on TV, dear.

Abby had said that to him once before she received her official diagnosis. He'd been pacing the waiting room, mumbling possibilities to himself, trying to find another cause for her symptoms. Abby had remained in good spirits through treatment, and even all through hospice. Jerry was the one who'd fallen apart at the eleventh hour, who forgot to clean or feed himself or get enough rest. Even at her end, Abby was the stronger of the two, and now he was adrift in the twilight years of his life. How had he managed to keep himself composed and survive this long?

Because of Abby. Always Abby.

And Katherine reminded him of her. Her strength and light that evening in the park had awakened something in him he'd not felt in years. Not in a primal way, but deeper, a resonance felt in the heart. Her visit yesterday had sealed the deal.

Jerry shook his head, annoyed with himself. These were all good people. Everyone here was kind, friendly. *The only weird thing happening is* me. *God, Abby, I wish you were here to tell me how ridiculous I am.*

"You're ridiculous, old man." Her words on his lips. The feeling brought a smile to his face, even if his heart ached with yet another reminder of her absence. "You've taken the step and started over. Now just let yourself enjoy it."

He sighed, promised himself that he'd try, and this was more than he would've said at the start of his day. Abby would've called that a win.

Jerry watched the sunset until Gary, the Scotts, and several others gathered their coolers and chairs and made their way to another street, another party. When he stood to go inside, he put pressure on his bad foot out of habit—and paused when he realized the pain wasn't there. Nor did his foot feel as swollen. He tapped his foot, bracing himself for a sudden jolt of agony, but nothing happened.

He smiled. Another win.

◉

The following day, Jerry found himself full of nervous energy and decided to go for an afternoon walk around the neighborhood. The usual low-grade ache in his knees and ankles had eased off since the morning. Movement would do him some good.

He took a similar route as before, journeying out to the entrance and then circling back to the park's rim. After a brief rest, he wiped the sweat from his brow and turned back. His knees were swelling again, and every step brought a sharp twinge of pain shooting through his legs. Abby used to call him a human barometer, said she could chart the weather patterns based on the pressure in his joints on any given day.

The forecast hadn't called for rain, but the way his joints were singing right now suggested something was on the horizon. He looked skyward. Overcast.

He already regretted leaving his cane behind. He was imagining the relief of propping his feet up on the couch when Katherine's house fell into view.

His feet wanted to keep walking straight, his joints eager for medicinal relief, but his heart had other intentions. Being here and not saying hello seemed rude. And he did want to make sure she was doing all right. He hadn't seen her since Wednesday. Maybe now they could speak openly, free of interruption.

He swallowed back the lump of cotton in his throat and climbed her porch steps. Rang the bell. The chimes echoed through her house. There was no other noise, no movement. *Maybe she's not home,* he thought, but gave the doorbell a second ring anyway. He waited, listening, and was about to give up when the floor creaked inside. Footsteps. A moment later, the door opened an inch, and a face appeared from the shadows inside.

She was young, early forties by his estimation, and not at all the woman he'd expected to see. The brass chain strung taut across the opening told him everything he needed to know.

"Help you?"

Jerry fumbled for words, embarrassed by his intrusion, and barely managed a hello before the young woman cut him off.

"Mrs. Dunnally isn't seeing anyone right now."

"I-I didn't mean to intrude. I'm her friend, Jerry, from down the street. I—"

"I'll tell her you stopped by." She stepped away and slammed the door. Her words hung in the air, accusatory, painting him as the stranger he really was.

Jerry lingered only a moment longer before shuffling off the porch toward the street. He wondered if she was the nurse he'd seen the other day.

Or her daughter? Hell, maybe both.

But the exchange left him feeling empty and cold and alienated. He was an outsider here, and so far, he'd done all he could to preserve that title. Abby was right, as always. He'd be a hermit if she'd let him.

13

Arthur's home sat at the end of a hillside cul-de-sac along the rim of the park. It was a large white farmhouse with a stone foundation, completely out of style from the rest of the community, and Jerry supposed it had been here for much longer, probably as long as the village proper. A huge maple tree, easily a hundred years old, clawed its way to the sky from the center of the yard. He'd had visions of a McMansion, something lavish and modern and more befitting of an association's chairman, but this place was simple, quaint.

The front door opened as he approached, and Arthur's grinning face popped out through the opening. "Jerry! I'm so glad you decided to join me." He stepped outside, clad in a red cooking apron, and extended a hand. They shook.

Jerry motioned back to his car. "I brought your pressure washer. Thanks for letting me use it."

"No problem at all, my friend. Least I could do. Follow me, I'll give you the dime tour."

Jerry followed him into the garage with the pressure washer. The two-car space was a more recent addition to the home, its walls lined with shelves and storage totes, a deep freezer, and a modest workbench. All the tools hanging on the pegboard were immaculate, had probably never even been used, but Jerry found himself in awe anyway. His father always told him he could judge a man by how he took care of his tools. Based on this, Jerry suspected Arthur was the meticulous sort, with a penchant for appearances.

"Hell of a collection you got there," he said.

Arthur waved off the comment. "I guess so. Don't have much reason to play with these toys anymore, I'm afraid. Now, over here..."

He opened a side door and stepped into the backyard. It gave way to a steep slope, and a dense thicket stood at the bottom. Jerry remembered the house he'd glimpsed from the park, its roof poking out above the trees. *So this is your castle, Arthur, overlooking your kingdom.*

A massive wooden deck adjoined the backside of the house, underneath which Jerry saw floor-to-ceiling windows and a den beyond them. A bar, fireplace, and pool table were the focal points, but then again, so was the jacuzzi underneath the deck. A path of flagstone steps carved their way downhill to a small gravel pavilion, an old barn, and smaller outbuildings off to the side.

"What's down there?"

"Come on," Arthur said, grinning. "I'll show ya."

He led the way down the path toward the pavilion. The backyard was as immaculate as the front, with manicured flowerbeds and shrubbery dotting the property.

At the first outbuilding, Arthur flipped on the lights. A series of halogen bulbs lit up the pavilion and the vehicles parked underneath. A pair of ATVs, a golf cart, and a small Kubota tractor took up the space. The nose of a snowmobile jutted from beneath a large blue tarp.

"This is where I keep my big toys."

"I see that," Jerry said, admittedly impressed by the display. "I didn't expect..." He gestured to the equipment. "From the road, I mean, it all looks so unassuming."

Arthur nodded, beaming. "Yeah, it's my little slice of paradise. Business has been good to me over the years, and I'm grateful for it, praise the goddess."

Jerry smiled. "What sort of business?"

"Real estate, mostly. Before that, land development and excavation."

"No kidding." He turned his attention to the barn. "What do you keep in there? A small Cessna? Hot air balloon? Personal tank?"

"Hell, I wish. Nah, that's nothing nearly as exciting. Just a remnant of the old farm that used to be here. At one point, I was thinking about starting up a community farm down there." He motioned down the hill toward the park. "I still may, to be honest. Maybe next year, if I can find the right partner. It's why I have the tractor. Hell, I even went so far as to stock up on fertilizer. I'm a sucker for a good deal, you know."

Arthur walked over to the barn and motioned for Jerry to join him. There was no lock on the doors, Jerry noticed; only a metal pin held them shut. Arthur removed the pin, opened the doors, and flipped a switch inside the entrance. He waved his hand like a parlor magician when a series of fluorescent lights flickered to life overhead.

Inside was a gas-powered tiller, a wall of assorted gardening tools, and a few stacked bags of potting soil. At the back, a grid of pallets was piled chest-high with full white bags. He gave it all a once-over, then glanced at his host.

"You could call this my *Green Acres* phase." He looked at Jerry with a knowing smile like he'd read his mind. "Yeah, I know, you can't picture me as a farmer. To be honest, I'm not sure I can, either, but I really want to make this place self-sufficient. Now, if my insurance company knew I had a powder keg in my backyard..."

Jerry blinked. "Wait, are you serious?"

"Oh yeah. Those bags are full of ammonium nitrate. Good for crops, but if you set that shit on fire, you'd best be running after you do. We used something like it when I worked in land development. ANFO, we called it. Ammonium nitrate fuel oil. Remember Oklahoma City? Same shit."

"Shouldn't you keep this place locked then? Just in case. . ."

Arthur laughed, clapped his hand on Jerry's shoulder. The gesture rang hollow, though, and Jerry chuckled nervously. "No, my friend. I'm not worried about that. Fairview is a safe place. We're all neighbors here. Friends. *Family.*" Arthur turned back toward the house. "Man, I'm starving. Those steaks are calling my name. I hope you're hungry!"

On their way back up the slope, Jerry glimpsed a figure standing on the deck, watching. A woman, by the look of it. Tall, slender, dressed in a white robe. A nurse?

"Is that your wife?"

"Hmm?" Arthur looked back. "What's that?"

Jerry raised his hand to point but faltered when he looked again. The woman was gone.

"Never mind," he said, and followed his host back to the house.

◐

Arthur's dining room was an antique dream, from original wood floors to cherry-stained table, hutch, and sideboard. A gallery of framed photographs adorned the walls, a lifetime of cherished moments, family and success and pride.

He served up the meal with a proud smile. Everything Arthur had prepared for dinner was purine-rich, but after three weeks of eating garbage, Jerry craved a home-cooked meal. T-bone steaks, buttered potatoes, fried corn, fresh bread—Arthur prepared a feast for the two of them, and together they ate like kings.

"How's that steak, huh?"

"Delicious. Compliments to the chef."

Throughout the dinner, Arthur kept up the small talk and seemed pleasant and easygoing, but there was something behind his questions that set Jerry on edge. Being so introverted for most of his life had afforded him a different set of social skills, like the ability to recognize when something was off—and when it came to Arthur, something was very off, but Jerry couldn't put his finger on what. Then again, maybe it was just the clash of their personalities. Maybe the problem was Jerry being Jerry, as Abby was fond of saying.

Jerry pushed away his empty plate and finished the last of his beer, glad the swelling in his foot had eased up since yesterday.

"Want another beer?"

"No, thank you. I—"

(don't want you to drug me again)

"—need to take it easy. Gotta drive home, you know."

"I get it, man. I'll drink for both of us."

After Arthur left the room, Jerry went to the photo wall to look at his family photos. There was a photo of the Moon Pool and its obelisks; one of Arthur in fishing gear, grinning like an idiot while holding a massive bass; a wedding photo of a young Arthur and his bride, a slender brunette woman. Adjacent to that was a more recent photo with the happy couple in the twilight years of middle age. They stood proudly before an empty lot with hard hats atop their heads and shovels pointed to the earth.

"We broke ground that day." Arthur stood in the doorway with a beer in hand. He popped the cap and took a drink. "This place was Gladys's dream, you know."

"Your wife?"

"Married forty-three years last March. She left us the year before."

Jerry considered asking about the woman he'd seen but decided not to pry. "My condolences."

"I appreciate that, friend, but it isn't necessary. We had a good run, and when it was time for her to be with the goddess, my happiness for her trumped any sadness I felt. Besides, we'll be together again someday soon, by the moon's eye." Arthur raised his beer to the photograph and took another gulp, and they both returned to their seats.

"You said this place was her dream?"

Arthur nodded. "This land was in her family for generations. She always wanted to turn the family farm into a community of some kind, to pay reverence to the goddess. A way to give back and share our prosperity with others. I was still working in development back then, and so when we'd finally saved up enough to get started, we went into business ourselves. Invested everything we had into what is now Fairview Acres."

He stared off into space, a twinkle in his eye, smiling. "None of this would be here if not for her. It's funny, you know, how we're all just specks of dust flying through the universe, molded by gravity into planets. And then, sometimes, we fall into the orbit of a great star. Brighter than we've ever seen. Eventually that star will burn out, leaving us in the dark, but while it's here, while we're caught in its orbit, it's the center of our universe. And we spin and spin in this great cosmic dance. That was my Gladys. My star."

Jerry's thoughts turned to Abby. He'd been trapped in her orbit since the day they met in college. That beautiful girl sitting in the commons, sipping tea and reading a textbook, oblivious to everything around her, especially to the lonely awkward boy watching from across the courtyard. Took him half the semester to work up the courage to approach her, and another two weeks to ask her out. Abby possessed a gravity about her that he couldn't resist. Young Jerry had never had a chance.

He smiled. Maybe he and Arthur had something in common after all. "That was lovely. You should write it down."

"Ah, no, I'm no poet. . ." Arthur straightened in his chair, his demeanor no longer laid back but acute, alert. "But you didn't come here to listen to me get all romantic and sappy." Arthur took a gulp of his beer, wiped his mouth with a grimace. "You've got questions, and I suppose I owe you some answers, don't I? What is going on in this weird community? Sound about right?"

The switch was so sudden, so effortless, that Jerry wondered which man was the real Arthur: this hyper-aware salesman, or the romantic hippie who'd let his guard down and allowed himself to be vulnerable for a moment. He wanted so badly to believe the latter, but the glint in Arthur's eye sent a chill down his spine.

"Something like that."

Arthur stood, pushed his chair from the table, and gestured to the back door. "It's a beautiful night tonight. How about we move this party to the deck?"

Jerry swallowed air. The conversation had turned so quickly he'd been caught off guard. A silly idea crawled through the shadows of his mind: Maybe this was Arthur's plan all along. Wasn't this what cult leaders did to their followers? Put them in a fragile, unstable mental state for easier manipulation?

Hardly a cult leader, Jerry thought. *He's more like Jim Buffet than Jim Jones.*

He followed Arthur outside, breathed deep of the night air, and looked out from the deck railing. Arthur's property was lined with a privacy fence, and beyond it, another pathway of flagstones trailed down the slope toward the park. Someone had lit the torches between the bandstand and the Moon Pool. Even at this distance, he saw glimpses of sparkling light reflecting off the stone.

"That's incredible," Jerry said. "Is it always like that at night?"

"Sure is. Gladys used to call it a conduit to the heavens."

Jerry stared at him, waiting for him to break and reveal all this mystic talk as a joke, but he didn't. Instead, his eyes lit up like a child in a toy store, and he kept on talking. "And you know what? I did some research on the property, and it turns out the stone really is from the heavens. Notice how the park sits in a bowl of sorts, and the whole neighborhood is on the rim?"

Jerry nodded. "Seems like an odd place to build a development—"

"The whole area is an impact crater. That stone is the remains of a meteorite."

Jerry pictured the stone's eerie shape and cage-like pattern. *To commemorate when our goddess touched the earth.* Thinking about it gave him a chill. He'd lived nearby his whole life and had never heard of an impact crater in the area. *Something else to look into,* he thought. "That's amazing," he said, almost wincing when his tone failed to match Arthur's enthusiasm. "So... your wife thought the stone was special?"

"It *is* special, Jerry. Incredibly special, but. . ." Arthur trailed off, tracing his finger along neck of his beer bottle. "I don't know if you're ready for that yet."

"Is this the surprise you mentioned the other night?"

"One thing at a time, my friend. First, I believe an apology is in order."

"I'm not looking for an apology," Jerry said, trying to keep his tone in check. Understanding and friendly, but firm. "Just an explanation."

"Fair enough. Where would you like to begin?"

"We can begin with the drink you gave me. There was something else in there besides booze. I just want to know why."

Arthur sighed. "By all accounts, an accident. I looked into it personally. Your drink was supposed to be virgin; it wasn't supposed to have the potion—a little something exclusive to Fairview. You know, a private concoction brewed right here in the community. We enjoy it at every gathering. Hell, most of us partake every night. Newbies like yourself. . ." Arthur gave him a side-eyed smile that set Jerry on edge. "We usually go slow, make sure you're comfortable in the community first. One thing at a time, you know?"

Jerry nodded, less in agreement and more to keep Arthur talking. His comfort around the man had lessened in the last five minutes. He wanted to like Arthur, but all this talk of goddesses, meteorites, and weird potions was more than Jerry could take. *All this hippie-dippie bullshit. I told that cocky realtor I wasn't interested in this. Maybe I'll let him have a piece of my mind.*

"The Fairview Community Association likes to make sure all its residents are. . . compatible. No, wait, that's not the right word. Amenable is better."

"Right. Amenable." Jerry thought of all the times he'd been asked to fit in just to make the herd comfortable. He came by his introversion naturally, but sometimes it just made things easier. "So. . . what's in the formula?"

"Ah, the million-dollar question! Trade secrets, my friend. All that matters is the effect. And was that effect really so bad, Jerry?"

The effect. All those hideous visions of bodily mutation at the park that night played like a highlight reel in his head. He'd felt the effect, all right. Now he wondered if the drink was what sent Katherine to his doorstep that first night. An unintended side effect on a weakened mind. Mumbling and broken one day, radiant and lively the next. *Sundowner, my ass.*

Arthur stared with an expectant smile, a desperate need for reassurance that Jerry was on board and ready to sail, captain.

Jerry waited for his racing heart to slow as the anger subsided. "I just wish I'd been warned and prepared for it, Arthur. What I saw that night was a hell of a shock, and. . ." He paused, measuring his words, at once eager and yet hesitant to speak. "I appreciate the gesture of wanting to include me, but that's not why I moved here."

A shadow passed over Arthur's eyes. There and gone in a blink. Jerry did a double take, lingering on the man's gaze longer than he liked, but he couldn't look away now. He needed Arthur to know he was serious—and the man's smile suggested otherwise.

"Of course, Jerry. I get that. You moved here to get away from your old life. To start over, learn to live outside the shadow of your late wife. Believe me, I get it. Let me give you some advice, friend. Over time, you'll find you need this community more than you think. We take care of each other. Of our own."

Our own. What the hell did that mean?

"I just want to be left alone."

"I can appreciate that. I really can. But you need to understand that this is a community. As long as you live in Fairview Acres, you're a part of that community."

Flashbacks of a dozen one-on-one conversations he'd had with various managers over the years played through his mind. Every one of them attempting to reign in his introversion, mold him into something more social and acceptable, something more easily controlled. A better attitude about his neighbors in that desert of cubicles. A team player. Amenable.

You make your coworkers uncomfortable, one manager had said. *I need you to be a little more social.*

We're a team here.

We're family.

Anger flared, a thick wave of heat crawling through him, over him.

"Your neighbors need to know you're on board with the community, Jerry. I need to know you're on board with the community. There's so much we have planned, and—"

"What if I'm not?"

"What if you're not what?"

"On board, Arthur. With whatever it is you're selling here." Jerry took a breath, exhaled slowly. "I moved here for a change of scenery, for the solitude. To mourn. You want me to return a smile and wave when I see you? I can do that. But you want me to participate in all your neighborhood activities? Wear the Fairview Acres T-shirt? You've got the wrong guy, so let's make something clear here: I'm just a guy who lives in this neighborhood. A *neighbor*. I can be friendly—and I will be—but if you want me to be a *friend*, this isn't the way to do it."

Arthur shook his head. "Come on now, you don't expect me to believe that. We ran a background check on you when you submitted your application. You worked for the same company for nearly thirty years. You were married to the same woman almost as long. You're absolutely the sort of guy who'd wear the T-shirt."

Two words stopped Jerry in his tracks. "Background check?"

"Yeah, don't you remember? Stewart had you fill out the paperwork when you made your offer on the house."

He couldn't remember consenting to a background check. But there had been so much paperwork, a blur of warm toner, forms, signatures, and boxes to check. Every time he'd filled out one sheet, there was Stewart with another one, all smiles, all teeth. The heat clouding his face dissipated in the span of a breath, his mouth suddenly dry, and a slow tendril of ice uncoiled in his gut.

"Am I wrong?"

Jerry said nothing, every word that came to mind inadequate to convey what he felt in that moment. Coming here was a mistake. He'd underestimated this man. Arthur Peterson wasn't the carefree, unassuming hippie grandpa. That side of Arthur he'd seen inside, talking romantically about planets and stars and the love of his life, was a facade, a mask worn to make Jerry feel more comfortable. *See?* that mask had said, *We're alike, you and me. We feel the same feelings. We share common ground.*

But that couldn't be further from the truth. Jerry had been wrong. Jim Jones *was* a more accurate likeness.

"I. . ." Jerry shifted his weight from one foot to the other. His legs shook like jelly. "I said what I said, Arthur. I'm not going to partake in whatever it is that's going on here."

Arthur stared at him, his smile dropping by the second. Finally, he blinked, cleared his throat. "I see. Well, Jerry, I sure am sorry to hear that. You seem like a perfect addition to our little circle. Perhaps you'll come around, in time. When you're more amenable."

"Perhaps." Jerry forced himself to smile once again. He looked at his watch. "I do need to get going, though. Thank you for having me over tonight, and for dinner."

"Sure. I'll walk you out."

As he followed Arthur back through the house, Jerry considered what he'd said to his host and the way he'd said it. His mind swam, every step twice as heavy as the last. He'd come here hoping for a pleasant evening, one in which Arthur gave simple and rational explanations for all that had happened so they could laugh it off as a misunderstanding. Instead, he was walking away disappointed, confused, and concerned that he'd poked a bear in its den. Worse, all the weirdness wasn't just in his head; this place was truly weird, and in ways he did not understand.

Arthur opened the front door. "Have a good night, Jerry. The invitation to regular festivities still stands."

Jerry nodded. "Good night, Arthur."

He walked along the sidewalk to his car, and Arthur called out to him.

"Oh, before I forget to ask, how are those aches and pains you've been having? I bet they're a real doozy during the day."

Jerry turned, but Arthur had closed the door. *How'd you know?*

He felt the heat of Arthur's gaze every step of the way to his car. A single word followed him all the way back home.
Amenable.

14

"I wondered when you'd be back."

Jerry froze halfway up his porch steps. He'd forgotten to leave the porch light on and was so lost in his own head that he hadn't noticed the figure sitting in the dark.

Katherine leaned forward into the moonlight and smiled. His heart slowly receded from his throat.

"Sorry, Kat. Didn't see you." He dug his keys from his pocket and walked toward his door. "You're welcome to come in."

She placed her hand on her chest and feigned shock. "Why, Mr. Campbell! I'm but a lonely old widow. What would the neighbors think?"

They shared a laugh, and Jerry unlocked the door. "Want something to drink? I think I've got a bottle of merlot."

"That would be lovely."

Katherine took a seat on the sofa and surveyed his living room. Jerry watched her for a moment, and then did his own sweep of the room, still self-conscious about the state of his house. Everything was still in order, for the most part, save a few boxes he hadn't yet unpacked.

She caught him looking and smiled. "Still moving in?"

He blushed. "You could say that."

A few minutes later, after he'd escaped to the kitchen in embarrassment, Jerry returned to the living room with an open bottle and a pair of glasses. They toasted to new friends and drank.

Jerry couldn't help but stare at her, trying to reconcile this vibrant figure with the one who'd visited just a couple of days ago. No need of a walker tonight, and when she moved, there was no slight hunch to her gait. She seemed more relaxed, the air of nervousness all but gone, and he wondered why.

She asked, "Penny for your thoughts?"

"You still owe me pennies for last time."

"I may have a few in my coin purse. What's on your mind, Jerry?"

"It's. . ." *Nothing,* he wanted to say. Anything to change the direction of the conversation. But the nagging voice in the back of his head wouldn't allow it. Something was wrong here in Fairview, and no amount of rationalizing would bury that notion. God knows, he'd tried. *It's everything, Katherine. It's what happened at the park. It's you dying on my porch—or almost dying, or whatever you want to call it. It's those things walking on my roof. It's all this talk of a goddess. And Arthur making vague threats tonight is just the cherry on a cake of shit.*

He didn't want to dump this all on her shoulders tonight, but he had no one else he could turn to. Now, more than any other time in his life, Jerry needed a friend to help him make sense of everything.

She reminded him of Abby in the way she carried herself, the look of playful mischief in her eyes, her smile so big it could break hearts and stitch them back together with a simple expression. That happiness radiating off her like a lighthouse beacon, the same essence that had been snuffed out of his life when he'd lost Abby. He felt himself drawn to it, ready to break upon its shores. This sort of happiness almost made him forget the first time they had met, when it was so absent, and she was muttering gibberish and maiming herself.

"How long are you going to rehearse this in your head? Go on, Jerry Campbell. Out with it."

He shrugged. "Still feeling okay?"

"Wonderful. And thank you for dropping by earlier. My daughter told me you came by. I wasn't myself, or else I would've greeted you."

Wasn't myself. He filed that away for later. "No problem. What's that old saying? 'You're responsible for the life you save.'"

Katherine smiled and sipped her wine. "A true gentleman. My hero."

"So, that was your daughter, huh?"

"Uh huh. Lisa's been overprotective with me ever since Reggie passed on."

"I'm sorry. How long, if you don't mind me asking?"

"Let's see. . . almost two years this winter. Miss him every day."

"About as long as my Abby then. . ." Jerry leaned back in his seat, relishing the warmth of the wine pooling in his belly. "Sorry, didn't mean to make things morbid."

"Hard not to think about things like that when you get to be our age, old man. But you're right, let's change the subject. What brought you to Fairview, Jerry? Everyone's been gossiping about it. They say you're the mysterious type."

He smirked. "Is that what you think?"

"No, not me. I think you're just quiet, want to be left alone. But the ladies down the street, especially Ida and Bethany, enjoy their speculating. Next week you'll probably be a secret agent or something."

He held up his hands. "You got me."

They shared a laugh, and he welcomed the levity. The wine was working its magic, but he suspected the company also had something to do with it.

"No," he said, "I'm just a retired accountant. Worked in finance for thirty years and retired after Abby passed on. Probably a bad call, in hindsight, but I've made it work." He sipped his wine, thinking. "I've always kept to myself. Abby was the outgoing one. If not for her, I'd be living in a cave somewhere."

"You sound like my Reggie. He ran his own security business, didn't have much to do with the public, and would've been happy just to stay inside all day every day. I wouldn't let him, though. I used to work in customer service. Always have, really. I love meeting people. Reggie had to put up with me and my socializing." She leaned forward and whispered, "To tell the truth, I think he enjoyed being around people too, but he'd never admit it."

Jerry smiled. Abby would probably have said the same thing. "I just like to keep things close to my chest. Always been that way."

"There's nothing wrong with it. You do you. That's what my Lisa always says." Katherine smiled and finished off her wine in a single gulp. "So, you retired and moved to Fairview Acres. Who moved you here? Your kids?"

"No, no kids. They weren't in the plan for me and Abby. I moved here on my own. Wanted a smaller place and a fresh start. Something—"

"Free of all the memories, right?"

He nodded, happy that he wasn't alone in that sentiment. A bittersweet thought, knowing others felt the same way.

"That's something I wish I'd done when I had the chance." The cheeriness slowly faded from her smile. "Memories... well, you know. They're the ghosts that haunt us, and it's always so hard to free ourselves from them."

"I'll drink to that." He finished his glass of wine, and his face flushed with heat. *Enough chit-chat, man. Get to it.* Jerry lowered his gaze to the floor, absently dug the toe of his shoe into the carpet. "I haven't made up my mind on Fairview yet."

Katherine's eyes lit up with curiosity. "Do tell."

He felt like he could trust her and spill his guts about anything, but a part of him was still hesitant. Beneath all his reservations and desires was a series of faded images from that night on his porch. The distressed old woman not long for this world who saw fit to visit the newcomer and warn him of something

(the worms are dancing)

before it was too late. He liked this Katherine, but a terrible thought had taken root in his mind and was slowly beginning to sprout. *Which one is the real Katherine? And what happened to her?* The implications of those two questions terrified him.

"Come on, Jerry, you can't leave an old woman hanging like this."

Jerry cleared his throat, forced a smile. "All right. If I offend you, let's blame the wine, yeah?"

"Hit me with it."

"Things have been weird ever since I got here. Seems like no one goes outside until sundown. Well, except for Gary. He's the only neighbor I've seen during the day. On this block, anyway."

"Here's the thing..." Katherine lowered her voice, leaned forward, serious. "Jerry, we're vampires."

Silence.

For three whole seconds.

Her expression cracked, and an avalanche of laughter belted from her tiny frame.

Jerry chuckled with her, at once relieved and embarrassed. He'd almost believed her. "Yeah, yeah, laugh it up."

"I'm sorry... the look on your face... Worth it!"

He waited until her laughter slowed to a trickle: "There are other things," he said. "It's all the parties at night. It's the way Brad and Matilda and Gary all interrogate me about what you say to me." Katherine's expression faded at that, but Jerry kept on. "It's Arthur slipping me a mickey at the party, and how he's got this whole place wrapped around his finger, and the way he dropped threats tonight. And it's what happened to you. I watched you die, Kat."

Tears blurred the edge of his vision, and beads of sweat clung to his forehead, the back of his neck. He rubbed his face and shook his head. "It's your vague warnings. All the goddess bullshit. A giant meteorite in the park. It's whatever the hell is walking on my roof every night..."

Her eyes narrowed. "What do you mean?"

"Which part?"

"Whatever the hell is walking on your roof."

Jerry didn't answer with words. He rose from his seat, walked to his kitchen counter, and returned with the strip of denim he'd found on the hedge.

Katherine took it from him, turned it over in her hand. "What's this?"

He told her about the thing in his yard, how it had chased him back into the house. "I thought I was losing my goddamn mind, and then I found this in the hedgerow. It's what started..."

My depression, he wanted to say, but couldn't bring himself to utter the words. Such a silly thing, this piece of torn fabric, the way it could trigger such a decline of emotional acuity and deafen the outside world.

Katherine read his face, knew exactly what he was talking about. She reached out and gave his hand a squeeze. "I'm sorry," she said.

"For what?"

"For not being more clear. I can't..." Her face blushed bright red. She blinked away tears. "My nurse will hurt me if I tell you everything. Before you're ready."

That familiar cold seeped into his gut. "You mean your daughter?"

"No, not Lisa. My nurse. You... haven't met her. But you will. I tried to warn you, before it was too late, but since that night in the park, I don't know if you can leave Fairview..."

"Leave? All my finances are tied up in this place now. I couldn't leave even if I wanted to."

But part of him did want to pick up stakes and go, despite the financial chaos that would descend upon his life. He'd been putting off paying the realtor a visit, confronting the smug prick about his sales pitch about this place. Maybe he'd call his attorney, too.

"This place has some odd customs," Katherine said. "Things they don't tell you up front. Things they didn't tell me and Reggie when we moved in."

He thought of Arthur's obsession with a so-called goddess and that cute little saying, *By the moon's eye.* "That's one way of putting it. But I wouldn't call them odd; I'd call them creepy, or maybe batshit crazy. I'd call it brainwashing."

And being amenable, he thought of saying, but the word was tainted, sour.

She laughed, humorless. "I was trying to be polite."

"Don't be. I don't mind if you want to be blunt. Anyway, tonight I told Arthur I didn't want to be part of whatever operation he's got going on here."

Katherine's smile slipped away. "You *said* that to him? What did he say?"

Jerry shrugged. "He threatened me, I think. In his friendly way, if that makes any sense."

"It does... More than you know." She glanced toward the door and said in a low voice, "Arthur can be... persuasive. There's the Arthur you met when you moved here, and the Arthur you met tonight. Just please be caref—" She flinched. An instant later, her fingers bent into claws, clutching the air. Her mouth contorted, and she uttered a drawn consonant of guttural noise.

Jerry gasped, terrified that she was seizing again, and reached for the phone to call for help.

Katherine's hand shot outward and clutched his arm. "Don't. I'm—I'll be fine." She spoke mechanically, each word wrenched free of her throat. "They're awake." Slowly, she freed herself of the ensnaring rictus. Within a minute, she was back to her normal self—or seemed to be. She closed her eyes and sighed. "I'm sorry, Jerry."

"I can still call for help," he said. "If you need me to."

Katherine opened her eyes. There was a wild quality to them now, and her dilated pupils were asymmetric to one another. A thin blue vein at the edge of her hairline caught his attention. He thought he saw it pulse.

"I'm okay. . . it's the emissaries. They get feisty when I speak out. . ." She trailed off again, fixing her gaze on the front window. Her jaw tightened. She spoke again through clenched teeth, each forced word a dry and breathless rasp, wind through a dozen dying trees: "Those things. . . you saw in your yard. . . that night." Her hands balled into fists, every syllable a marathon. "They're real. And. . . they're watching."

"Watching?"

Katherine nodded stiffly, robotic.

Jerry eyed the phone once more, but he was afraid to call for help. Who would come to collect her this time? Those two paramedics creeping through the neighborhood like undertakers on the way to the morgue. No lights, no sirens, just two ghouls looking for their next corpse. He was sure Arthur would be right behind them, smiling the whole way, and nothing but teeth.

Finally, her fingers uncurled, and a wave of relaxation flowed slowly over her body. When she looked at him, Jerry saw she was herself again. Her pupils had returned to normal. The blue vein in her forehead was gone.

She sank back into the sofa cushions, skin pale and damp with sweat. Whatever had happened had drained every bit of her strength, and when she looked up at him, he saw the thin and frail thing from his porch all over again.

"Kat, are you all right? Can I get you anything?"

"Water," she whispered.

He shot to his feet and hurried to the kitchen. When he returned, she took the glass from him and drank greedily. Water dripped down her chin with each gulp. Jerry stared at her, afraid to say anything, afraid to move for fear she might seize again. He'd never felt so helpless.

Give her space, Abby whispered. *Let her rest.*

He moved from his chair and sat beside her. Took her hand in his own and waited. They remained there like that for what might have been an hour—he didn't know, didn't care. His focus remained on his friend, her breathing, every subtle twitch of the muscles in her hand. He counted the liver spots on her arm, the light freckles from bygone days spent in the sun, a pair of chicken pox scars along her forearm, one aged crater of a vaccine scar. All those tiny superficial flaws that made a person who they are. Points of interest on a cross-country atlas, destination Katherine Dunnally.

Abby's final days seeped into his thoughts. She'd been out of her mind with pain and morphine and whatever else the hospice workers gave her to keep her comfortable. There were moments of lucidity among wide gulfs of rambling dialogue spoken mostly to herself. The erratic nature of her words and statements were similar to Katherine tonight.

They're awake. Emissaries. Those things in your yard. They're watching.

But Katherine believed what she was saying. In Abby's quiet moments of calm rationality, she knew most of what she'd said was gibberish, fragments of knowledge plucked from a dying brain the way a drowning swimmer will gasp for air underwater. But Katherine's conviction in her words, the struggle to loose them from her lips when her whole body seemed opposed to the idea, troubled him greatly.

"I'm sorry if I worried you," she said, finally. "I should be getting home. I'm sure you're tired from a long day."

You can stay here, he wanted to say. *I can sleep on the sofa. You can have my bed.*

But fear held his tongue. Spending the night here was a step too far. Wasn't it?

She peeled herself from the cushions and shakily climbed to her feet. "I'm sorry. . . I know you had more to say, but I. . ."

"Don't apologize." He walked her to the door. "Are you all right? Can I walk you home?"

She smiled. "No, I'll be all right, hon. My strength is coming back. I'll be fine."

"Okay. . ."

"You're cute when you're worried, Mr. Campbell. I'll call you when I get home. Fair?"

"Fair. But I'll be worried the whole time."

"And cute, too."

Outside on the porch, she stood on her toes and kissed him on the cheek. "Thanks for caring about me."

Jerry said goodnight, his head buzzing from the wine, the worry, and the kiss.

But after he'd locked up and turned off the lights, after she'd called to tell him she was home safe and goodnight, one thought kept on running through his head. It joined up with all the rest, and together, they raced along in an unending marathon of anxiety and fear.

Her lips were cold. God, why were her lips so cold?

◉

The cold followed Jerry into his dreams—

The chilly air takes his breath away, and he sees a hazy blue light in the distance. A thick mist obscures the earth up to his knees.

Something moves under the mist, thin shapes slithering away into the murk. They sound wet—gelatinous and heavy.

He imagines worms, plump and ropey and covered in wet earth. From somewhere in the distance, Katherine screams, begging for the worms in her head to be set free.

This isn't me, *she screams.* They're dancing again.

He rushes forward into the dark, toward her voice, toward the ominous light. The ground is uneven, slippery, and he stumbles to his knees, planting a hand on something wet below the mist. He gets up and pushes on, testing his footing with each step, determined not to touch whatever the hell he is walking on.

He walks for miles, until the light grows brighter. Katherine is still screaming, and now he hears her thrashing about, fighting whatever is inside her head. Her voice has changed—hollow now, scratchy and dry like breaking twigs. Jerry knows the sound all too well. A voice forced through brittle lungs. Air through a rotting husk.

No, *he screams,* it can't be you. Anyone but you. Please, God...

The light dims, revealing its source. Gnarled ridges form a rough lattice around a sparkling, porous surface, a cage to keep whatever lay inside from escaping, but its integrity had failed long ago. Small holes dot its landscape, each the testament of a tiny escape, a portal to a world in which they did not belong.

I can't breathe, *Abby says.*

Something lurches across his foot, and he looks down to see the mist has receded. For as far as he can see, the ground is a mass of pale flesh, irregular like the folds in a brain—but it's all moving. *Coiling, slithering, a knotted mass of sickly gray matter. He thinks of cooked pasta, hears Abby laugh in his ear because he can't stand the sight or texture of these writhing things, and he realizes they're squirming their way across the world one viscid inch at a time. A worm coils around his ankle. Rows of sharp teeth emerge from its fleshy nub and sink into his exposed skin.*

He feels the pain but does not scream. What is the point? These things have engulfed the world, and he is the last one left. Of course he is. Always the outsider, the antisocial hermit whose distrust of people has clutched him in its awkward grip, squeezing until he can no longer breathe. Abby did her best to free him, but he doesn't want to be free. He was content to remain in his cave and wait out his days in obscurity. And he was, until the world was swallowed in this nest of worms.

Abby's voice resonates from within the meteorite, urging him to accept the goddess and bask in her splendor, while more ravenous worms latch on to his legs. Bright light swallows them all in a ring of pestilent brilliance, and when he looks up, he sees the moon.

A clipped voice—pieces of Abby and Katherine joined together in a poor facsimile of both women, human and inhuman alike—booms across the rocky landscape of his mind, its timbre echoing in deep canyons and across unknown plateaus.

You will kneel before your goddess.

He trembles with fear, and a frigid cold rises through his body.

Worship us beneath the eye of the moon.

He watches, transfixed by a full moon that isn't a moon at all. A seam opens across its surface, peeling back nictitating folds of tissue, and revealing conjoined pupils that dilate and focus upon him. Finally, as his mind catches fire and the worms devour him from below, Jerry screams into oblivion.

👁

The loss of gravity is what woke him. Jerry hit the floor with a dull thud, the impact forcing a pained cry from his lungs, and he lay there for a few minutes staring at the ceiling. Drab morning light illuminated the room, but just barely. The sky was overcast, and rain pelted the window.

Once he regained his composure, he sat up, wincing at the pain in his back. An ever-present knot of muscles sang chorus in an opera of cracking bones. He gritted his teeth and pulled himself off the floor. Phantoms of the dream still swirled at the edges of his vision, and his legs tingled from the prickly sensation of teeth biting down. The clipped voice echoed in his mind.

You will kneel before your goddess.

"Joke's on you," he grunted, shuffling his way to the bathroom. "I've got two bad knees. I ain't kneeling for anybody..."

15

The ache in his joints hadn't passed like he'd hoped. Coupled with his fall from bed, every movement Jerry made was signaled by an exuberant jolt of pain. Instead, he popped some ibuprofen, found a semi-comfortable position on the sofa, and resolved not to move unless he had to. He spent the rest of Saturday camped out in his living room, cycling through a variety of channels on TV, sitcom reruns, infomercials, the news.

The Facts of Life. The Golden Girls. Family Matters.
Click.
Viagra. Paxil. CBD oils. Hair loss.
Click.
Arthur's grinning face in frame. "Are you looking for a great place to settle down after retirement? Want your parents to enjoy the rest of their years in complete comfort? Look no further than Fairv—"
Click.
Unemployment on the rise. Wages bottoming out. A local interest story about a kid raising money for his sister's cancer treatment. Where to be for the best view of next weekend's

lunar eclipse. The latest investigation update about a Kentucky town that burned down last year. Film at 11.

Click.

"—in the market for a new home? The experts here at Stewart Realty have you cov—"

Jerry turned off the TV, picked up his phone, and called Katherine. No answer. No voicemail, either. He wondered when her nurse visited, and how costly that care must be. Medicare had its limits. Private insurance, maybe. *God, that must cost her a fortune.*

His thoughts wandered back to his dinner with Arthur. Things he'd said, things he wished he'd asked. Especially about that meteorite. He opened the browser on his phone and searched. Plenty of results about meteorites, but nothing about the village.

Jerry put down the phone, closed his eyes, and tried to ignore the throbbing ache in his hip.

The rooftop visitors returned that night, in greater numbers by the sound, and made his efforts to rest even more difficult. Their nocturnal sojourns usually lasted until dawn, just in time for the birds to begin their incessant chirping. He lay awake, delirious from the lack of sleep and the pain, wondering about Katherine's warning.

They're watching.

For what purpose? He was the most boring man on the planet, so what about him did they find so interesting? Why his house? Besides, he wasn't entirely ready to accept that they were real, despite Katherine's claim.

He recalled the dark figure in his yard. Its proportions and appendages that didn't make sense, its menacing croak—and the jeans. Why the hell was it wearing jeans?

Did Arthur know about these creatures?

These questions followed him into sleep and troubled him there amidst a planet entangled in worms.

He awoke early Sunday afternoon, groggy and irritable, his body one giant toothache that would not relent. Every joint sang, every movement accompanied by a wooden pop.

He returned to his place on the sofa, surrounded by blankets and a trio of pillows to ensure as much comfort as possible, but this grew harder to achieve no matter what position he tried. Abby would've grown tired of his misery and sent him to the doctor at the first sign of a prolonged joint flare, but she wasn't around now, and he felt guilt for being a smidge grateful. She was the sweetest person he'd ever known, but when she'd had enough of his shit, she would be on his case nonstop. She meant well, of course, and he always appreciated her caring after the fact.

Call the damn doctor, you old fool.

"Okay, you win."

He'd call Dr. Rapino first thing in the morning, if the pain didn't kill him first. Driving back to Stroudsburg wasn't something he was keen to do, the mere thought of sitting in a car for any length of time seemed to amplify his aches, but his only other option was an ambulance, no thank you.

He couldn't shake the feeling that this was just a bad confluence of little things piling up into One Big Thing. First the achy joints, then a low-grade fever, and with his lack of sleep and poor diet, he was due for something like this.

I just need some time to rest. I'll be fine. I've felt worse, and for longer.

He nestled his head into the pillows and tried not to move. Better to lie still, slip into a state of sleepy delirium, and let the days bleed into one another.

But his mind wouldn't leave him alone. Something Arthur had said started to nag at him. *How are those aches and pains you've been having?*

A lucky guess, had to be. In a community full of retirees and the elderly, Arthur's odds of hitting a bullseye were better than average. But there was something in the way he'd said it that nibbled at Jerry's certainty. Something that suggested he *did* know about Jerry's ailments.

But how? He had no idea, only a gut feeling that wouldn't go away and was made worse by Katherine's cryptic warnings.

This place has some odd customs, things they don't tell you up front.

"No shit," he said aloud. His voice echoed in the dreary room, tiny and weak. There wasn't much about Fairview Acres that he could take at face value anymore.

◉

"Good morning, Mr. Campbell. How are you today?"

Jerry looked up from his phone as Dr. Rapino closed the door behind him. He was a young fellow, only a few years out of his residency, with long black hair pulled back in a ponytail. Dark circles framed his eyes, betraying the fresh and friendly smile he flashed at his patient.

"Still not sleeping much, I see."

Jerry smiled in return. "You're one to talk."

The doctor sat at a corner workstation and pulled up Jerry's chart. "Says here you're having bad body aches?"

"Started off like the normal joint pains. Thought it might be gout, you know. My diet's been lousy these last few weeks."

"You're still taking your medication?"

"Every day."

"Huh." Dr. Rapino turned, looked him over. "Your allopurinol dosage is optimal, but we can't rule out elevated uric acid levels without some blood work."

"Well, that's the thing. . ." Jerry hesitated. What could he say? How was this any different from any other ache he suffered on a daily basis? *Could be stress. Been under a heap of it lately.*

He shoved those thoughts away. Even now he was trying to talk himself out of being here while his body told him something was wrong with every movement he made.

"What's the thing, Jerry?"

"Sorry, doc." He sighed, shook his head. "I don't think it's gout. I mean, I fell out of bed this weekend, but it's been getting worse long before that, and in weird places. Not just my joints. It's like I've got toothaches in my bones, all over. It just throbs and throbs."

The doctor raised his eyebrows and gave Jerry a look. "Remember what I told you about self-diagnosing? You trying to put me out of a job here? I got student loans to pay."

They shared a laugh, but Jerry immediately regretted it when a lightning bolt shot from his toes to his forehead. The pain was so deep it took his breath away. He winced, leaned forward, tried to compress himself as much as he could from the exam table.

"Sorry, doc. I . . . sometimes compression is the only relief I can get."

"That's all right. I want to hear about it. That's why you came here, remember? Now, let me have a look at you. . ."

The exam took less than five minutes. Dr. Rapino worked him over, applying pressure in his usual problem points, asking if it hurt. How about here? Or this? Yes, on all counts.

When he was finished, the doctor returned to his seat and typed something in Jerry's chart. "So. . . this is an odd one. Physically, I can't see any reason why you'd be hurting like you are, other than that shiner on your hip. What'd I tell you about gymnastics for a man your age?"

Jerry managed something halfway between a smile and a grimace. "I guess I'm no Mary Lou Retton."

"True enough. Well, first thing's first, my friend. I'm going to order some lab work. I know you hate needles, but we need to see what's going on in there. And I'll call in a prescription for something to help with the pain in the meantime."

He sighed. "If it's what needs to be done..."

"It's the first step."

"What's the second?"

"If your blood work looks normal? Probably an MRI."

"Wonderful," Jerry muttered. "Another win for the insurance company."

Dr. Rapino stood, shook his hand, and made for the door. "Look at it this way, Jerry. It's for a good cause."

"Right." Jerry grunted and eased himself off the exam table. "Good for whom?"

"Remember what I said about those student loans?" Dr. Rapino winked and smiled. "Try to have a good day, Mr. Campbell."

◐

The next day, a receptionist from Dr. Rapino's office called with Jerry's lab results. Normal across the board, except for his uric acid levels, which were lower than normal.

"Dr. Rapino recommends you add a little more purine-rich foods to your diet. But not *too* much. We'd like to have you back in a few weeks for more blood work."

"Eat more...? But I take medication to keep the levels low— Is Dr. Rapino available? May I speak to him?"

"I'm afraid he's with a patient," the receptionist said. Her young, chirpy voice grated on his nerves. "But I can take a message and have him call you back when he's free."

Jerry sighed. "No, forget it."

He ended the call before she could reply. At least he had painkillers now.

◐

On Wednesday afternoon, the doorbell rang just as he was drifting off to sleep. He considered lying still in hopes the unexpected visitor would give up and go away, but after the third ring, they began pounding on the door.

He slowly eased himself upright. The medication Dr. Rapino had prescribed wasn't working exactly as advertised. The pain was still there, but it had been dulled to a smooth edge, just enough to keep him somewhat comfortable.

"Answer the door, Mr. Campbell. Please. I know you're home."

He didn't recognize the voice, though the tone sounded familiar, commanding. A dozen faces scrolled through his mind, many of them schoolteachers from his youth. He clenched his teeth until the next dull shock of pain subsided, then called out, "Who is it?"

"Lisa Dunnally. We met last week at my mother's house."

His heart sank. Had something happened to Katherine? He'd been so caught up in his own ailments that he hadn't tried calling her again. "Just a minute." He took a deep breath, preparing himself for the short walk to the door.

By the time he'd walked the six feet or so, sweat dotted his forehead and the back of his neck. He opened the door, and the woman's cold stare softened into something resembling concern. "Is everything okay?"

He forced himself to smile. "Yeah, just some bad joints and a fall out of bed. I'll be fine."

"You fell? Bad dreams?"

"Something like that. What can I do for you, Ms. Dunnally?"

"It's about my mother." She looked over her shoulder, surveyed the street. It was early enough in the day that no one was outside. "May I come in?"

"Sure." Jerry pulled the door wider. "Is Katherine all right?"

"It's... well, it's complicated. Are you sure you're okay?"

He blushed. Did he look that frail?

"I'll be fine." he said, hobbling to the couch. Once he'd settled himself into a position that didn't cause his body to sing, Jerry turned his attention to Katherine's daughter. "So, what's on your mind? If this is about me dropping by the other day, I—"

"No, it's not that. Well, yes and no." She rubbed her eyes, shook her head. "It's just that you're the first person here who's shown any concern for my mother."

His gut reaction was to stop her there, reassure her that couldn't possibly be the case, but held his tongue, because the allegation tracked. He offered her a sympathetic smile. "Tell me what's happening."

Lisa wiped her eyes again, and he realized she was crying. "I began noticing mom's dementia earlier this year. Forgetting where she left her keys, getting her dates mixed up. One day, I stopped by for lunch, and she'd forgotten my name. Watching her struggle to say the right word and the loss wash over her face when she couldn't. . . That was enough for me, y'know? One of the doctors I work with made a referral. She got her diagnosis."

Jerry nodded, remembering the woman who showed up at his doorstep, the gibberish and confusion, the utter terror in her eyes. A horrible disease, yes. But what about the woman she'd become afterward? He wasn't sure how to bring that up, or if now was even the best time to do so. "It's tough. My grandmother suffered from Alzheimer's, and we understood far less of it then. I'm sure your mother is in good hands—"

"She is, or at least *was*, I guess. Her insurance paid for a nurse to tend to her a few days a week. I planned my schedule at the hospital around those dates, and for a while, everything was going about as good as to be expected."

"What happened?"

"It was little things. We started keeping a bedpan in the bedroom in case she couldn't make it to the bathroom. One of the nurse's duties is to empty it in the morning before she leaves. It's fine, you know, maybe the nurse just forgot—but then it happened again and again. When you showed up last week, I'd just discovered Mom hadn't been taking all her meds. She had way more pills than she should, and they refill next week."

"Yes, you did seem upset."

Lisa blushed. "I'm sorry, Jerry, it wasn't personal. I'd expected it to be that fucking Arthur guy at the door or something, so I was ready for a fight. Pardon my French."

"It's quite all right. I know that fucking guy, and I don't fucking blame you." He gave her a wink.

Lisa laughed and relaxed a bit, which made him feel less on edge himself.

"So what happened with the nurse?" he asked. "Did she quit?"

"That's the thing, I'm not sure. Mom says a new woman has been visiting her instead, but when I called the caregiver agency, they told me there was no reassignment for Mom's case and they hadn't heard from the original caregiver in a few days, either."

"Shit... So you have no idea who is sitting with her?"

Lisa shook her head. "And that's not even all of it. I can account for the few nights I'm with her, but beyond that... I think she's leaving the house. The sheets on her bed are always filthy with dirt and blades of grass, and sometimes her ankles are swollen like she's been dancing all night. A month ago, it looked like she'd walked over broken glass or something, but the wounds were already healing."

He thought of how Katherine had looked Friday night, sitting where her daughter sat now, with bright eyes and rosy cheeks from the wine they'd shared. His face grew warm, and a ball of cotton climbed up his throat. "Lisa, I don't know what's happening with your mom, but there is something strange happening here."

"What do you mean?"

He steeled himself, leaned forward to look her in the eye, and began to tell Lisa about everything he'd experienced since moving into the community—all except for the things on his roof. No sense in scaring the poor girl when he didn't even understand the phenomena himself.

Lisa listened with rapt attention. There were times he expected her to stop him, tell him this was all fucking crazy, but she didn't. That made him wonder what she'd seen or heard but hadn't mentioned because it seemed too weird. Giving voice to something so strange meant making it real, tangible, something that had to be dealt with in the confines of reality, even if the subject itself did not belong there.

At one point during his revelations, she gave him a peculiar smile. "You sweet on my mom?"

Jerry's cheeks burned. "What? That's not— I don't—"

"It's okay," she said. "I just haven't heard someone talk about her like that since my dad."

Flustered, he cleared his throat and offered a timid smile. "Like what?"

"Like you care about her."

"I—I'm just a concerned friend, that's all."

"I know. I appreciate that."

When he had finished telling her everything, she looked away, studying the room as if seeing it all for the first time. "I don't know what's happening here, Jerry. I heard nothing about my mom going to the hospital, and I fucking work there, you know? I'd like to think I would've been told if she'd hurt herself. And everything else, the park, the spiked drink, this shit about a neighborhood cult..." She sighed and rubbed her temples. "I'm not saying I don't believe you, but..."

"It's a lot to swallow. Trust me, I've been wrestling with it for weeks, but every time I convince myself it's all in my head, something else happens that says otherwise."

"That big rock in the park... I've lived in this area my whole life and don't remember ever hearing about a meteorite. But that's not even the weirdest part to me."

He shrugged. "What is?"

"The night Mom showed up at your door, what she said to you... It's just that my dad said the same thing to her. Several times." She paused, thinking. "And I remember him saying he didn't trust Arthur."

"That makes two of us."

Lisa checked her watch. "Shit, I'm going to be late for my shift." She took his hand. "Thank you for this, Jerry. It's nice to know there's someone here who's looking out for Mom."

"It's the least I can do. I hope this was helpful."

She forced a smile. "You've given me a lot to think about. Please get in touch if anything else happens with Mom."

They exchanged numbers. Against his better judgment, Jerry forced himself to his feet and saw his guest to the door. Lisa was halfway down the porch steps before she paused, looked back.

"How long have you been having that kind of pain? Not just your joints, but all over?"

"Really, it's just the damp air, and I fell out of bed. Bad dreams, I guess."

She looked him over, studying. "Sorry, it's the nurse in me, I guess. It's just... Nah, forget it."

"It's okay, you can tell me. I'll take free medical advice any day." He'd hoped for a laugh out of her, but Lisa remained serious and grim.

"My mom complained of severe body aches before the dementia really took hold. Dad, too."

"Are body aches early symptoms of dementia?"

"No. It's probably unrelated, but..." She shrugged. "Promise me you'll let me know if it gets worse?"

Jerry smiled and held up two fingers. "Scout's honor, Nurse Dunnally. Have a good day at work, friend."

Lisa waved to him as she drove away, and he returned the gesture. Across the street, Gary Olson watched from behind the hedge. Jerry raised his hand to say hello, but Gary didn't reciprocate. Instead, he remained still, expressionless.

Jerry returned to the living room and closed the door. Next, he closed the front window's curtains, but before he returned to the couch, he took a final peek outside.

Gary still stood in place.

Staring.

16

The ache in Jerry's muscles and joints eased up after Lisa's visit, but the experience left him exhausted. He had no appetite but choked down some toast anyway. Afterward, he resigned himself to spending the evening on the sofa once again, reading another one of Abby's crime thrillers. He'd had his fill of television over the weekend, and though reading hadn't always been his go-to method of passing the time, he found a connection to his late wife through her books. She loved crime and mysteries, even a little science fiction and horror on occasion, but the bulk of her library was filled with the likes of Cosby, Flynn, Leonard, and Lansdale. If nothing else, he figured he'd spend his free time working through her favorites.

But after an hour, Jerry had trouble focusing with so many unanswered questions rattling around in his head. What was going on with Katherine? And what happened to her caregiver? Jerry had no problem connecting them to the community in some way, but the *how* and *why* of it all eluded him. What was he missing?

Lisa's last question also hung over his head, ominous, a glaring reminder of his mortality. He'd fallen and injured himself before, and in worse ways, but the pain was half of what he was experiencing now.

Too proud to admit it, old man, and too scared to think what you're feeling is connected to this place somehow. You'd rather pull the blinds down, lock the door, and shut out the world, but that's not how things work. You're a resident here in Strangeville, and whatever's going on here is your problem, whether you like it or not.

Fairview had seemed so nice and quiet that day he toured the property with the realtor, but even then, little things had stuck in his brain. The price was almost too low considering the market, which should have been a red flag. But the inspector he'd hired to look over everything gave it a clean bill, even remarked this place was a steal for the price and its condition. And then the offer on his old home had conveniently preceded this place going under contract. A series of pieces falling into place at just the right time. Red flag after red flag, so huge and waving in the breeze that they should've smacked him in the face. But he'd been so intent on moving out

(running)

and away from his old life, and so fatigued by house hunting, that when this place finally landed on his radar, he couldn't let it pass him by.

He clenched his jaw, recalling Stewart Taylor's smug expression, so sure it was all a done deal before the ink was even dry on Jerry's good faith payment. The way he'd given Jerry a hard sell on not just the property but the community itself. And that stupid pamphlet!

The association likes me to give this out to prospective buyers.

Jerry had known at that moment Stewart was lying about the place, had felt it deep in his bones, but he hadn't listened. This place *was* too good to be true, only it wasn't a matter of sub-par materials, bad wiring, or faulty architecture; the community itself was rotten. Jerry's original assessment had been correct: it *did* look like Heaven's Gate. No sneakers, no matching track suits, no need for an official uniform, but everyone was hooked on the personality of one charismatic leader.

Arthur's a cult of personality, and they're all drinking his Kool-Aid.

Angry, weak, he reached for his water on the end table—and paused. Stared at it.

A Solo cup. Innocuous. Unassuming.

"Son of a bitch."

A searing jolt shot through his brain, connecting memories to facts, and he sat up so fast the pain took his breath away. Abby's voice spoke up, warning him of the danger of conspiracy theories. *What if you're wrong? What if there's a reasonable and innocent explanation? What if—*

"What if I'm right." The sound of his voice startled him. "The drink. The goddamn drink."

He remembered the gritty taste of dirt on his tongue, and the overripe sweetness that followed. They'd had kegs of the stuff at the party and were doling it out as fast as the pump would allow. Pure love, Arthur called it. Jerry scoffed. "More like pure bullshit."

Everything Katherine had said to him that night at the park clicked together. *You don't have to do anything you don't want to do.*

His mind raced. Was everyone here hooked on that drink? What the hell was in it? Could it be the cause of this sudden onset of body aches—and Katherine's episodes?

Did her husband know? Didn't Lisa say he didn't trust Arthur?

Jerry mustered his strength and slowly climbed to his feet. He thought about calling Lisa but he didn't want to jump the gun. There was more he needed to understand first. The last thing he wanted was to find himself wrapped up in a defamation lawsuit.

Instead, he dialed Katherine's number. Maybe she would answer this time. Maybe—

Two rings. Three.

A click as she answered.

"Kat, it's me." The words tumbled from his tongue faster than he could catch them. "I've been thinking about what you said, and I think I get it now. It's the drink, right? Everything that's happening to you, to me, to everyone in this goddamn neighborhood. It's Arthur's potion, isn't it?"

Silence.

"Hello? Kat?"

A reedy hiss seeped into his ear. Thin, drawn from the bottomless pit of a deep darkness he'd only seen—no, *felt*—in his dreams. The world around him shimmered, the air itself thickened, and he heard the wrenching whine of machinations churning away, massive gears locking into place and grinding together to pull back a dense, impenetrable curtain in his mind.

"Jeeeeeerrheeeeeeee."

His joints locked. He couldn't move, couldn't breathe, could only listen to the hiss of vowels forced from a cold vast nothing.

A weak voice in the background broke the spell, a terrified, muffled plea: "Leave him alone, *please—*"

The call ended.

Jerry crumpled back into the sofa with a sharp cry. He gripped the phone tight in his hand, the joints still locked and fingers drawn into claws, but he could not bring himself to look at the screen. An irrational fear had taken root in his core, the same trepidations he'd felt as a child alone in his dark room, convinced—no, *certain*—that something horrible waited just beyond the threshold of his closet to devour him in one bloody bite. If he could only stay up all night, never take his eyes off the opening, maybe he could outsmart the fathomless beast. And he had, many times, until the rooster crowed and sleep finally claimed him.

There had been no monster back then, or so he'd thought. Only clothes and jackets hung up in the closet above a pile of old shoes and toys. That fear had left him with age, once the world had begun to make sense and its rules were understood, and he'd lived decades under that umbrella of safety: there were no monsters, no reasons to feel such fear ever again.

But growing older was really just the act of regressing back to infancy. Like everyone else, he would spend his final years on this earth the same way he'd spent his first few: swaddled in blankets, wearing a diaper and covered in his own shit, petrified by the notion that everything could and would hurt him if given the chance. Tonight he'd learned the monster was still there on the threshold, waiting to take him when he wasn't ready. Maybe it had always been waiting for him in the dark, biding its time until he was too frail to fight back.

Until he was too tired to keep his eyes open anymore.

Jerry unfurled his fingers and dropped the phone on the floor. He let it stay there, terrified that if he picked it up, that horrid voice would still be on the line, calling his name from the void. All his questions, his indignant rage about the community and Arthur and Stewart, snuffed out in a single hiss of air.

He clutched his pillow, buried himself under a blanket, and fell asleep with the lights on.

He awoke in the night with a cry, fighting off unseen attackers with a flurry of kicks against the blanket in which he'd woven himself, body aches be damned. The dreamy haze lifted like a fog and reality seeped back into his perception. He was on the sofa. The lights were still on. And there was something scratching against the exterior of the house.

His skin was cold, sheathed in sweat, and a chill worked its way through his limbs as he planted his feet on the floor. Fear clung to his heart, even though the phone call felt like a lifetime ago. What time was it? Late. Everything felt late.

A dog barked outside. One of those small breeds, by the sound of it, shrill and yappy and full of nervous energy.

He picked up his phone. Another chill crawled down his neck as the screen brightened to life. After midnight. One of his neighbors must be out walking their dog. The realization set his mind at ease.

Another bark. More scratching.

"Always something." Jerry sighed, imagining the mess of dog shit he'd have to clean up in the morning. He slowly climbed to his feet, wincing at every dull pop of wooden bones, switched on the porch light, and hobbled outside. The street was empty, quiet but for the chirp of crickets and distant music from one of the late-night parties.

A faint whimper and rustling of leaves nearby stole his attention. He leaned on the railing and whistled down at the shrubbery. A brown Pomeranian lay stretched on the grass with half its body obscured by the shrub. "Hey, pup. Come on out of— What the hell?"

Strange pale lumps clung to its body. Cysts of some kind? He stepped to the side, allowing the porch light to shine on the dog.

They weren't cysts. They were huge worms.

Or what *looked* like worms. Big and plump and shiny in the light.

One of them had lodged itself between the dog's lips, its bloated tail wiggling and slapping as it forced its way in. The dog whined again, then accented its distress with a growl. An image from his dreams flashed in Jerry's mind: He was nude, covered in leeches, and floating endlessly in space. His skin prickled.

The dog struggled to move, clawing its way out from beneath the shrubbery, and he told himself to help it, but something held him there. Fear, maybe, or the inability to comprehend what he witnessed. And buried behind all the confusion was a memory, a voice nagging from the back of his mind.

The Pomeranian's legs twitched erratically, its body seizing, and within moments the animal fell still.

My God, is it dead?

He waited, expecting it to get up, shake itself off, and realized the worms were gone.

Nothing moved. Darkened wet patches of fur marked where they'd been, but he couldn't see them anywhere on his lawn. He stepped away from the railing, and grimaced as something sticky pulled at his bare foot. The three streaks he couldn't erase with the pressure washer glistened in the light like slug trails. Sparkled, almost.

The worms, they dance at nightfall.

Revulsion crawled up from his gut. He took another step back, disgusted by the sensation, and terrified the remains were toxic somehow—and nearly screamed when a woman said, "There you are!"

Heart in throat, Jerry spun around and watched a short woman in a polka-dotted muumuu cross the street toward his house. Large rollers decorated her hair and gave her head a bulbous quality in the low light.

"I'm so sorry, Mr. Campbell. Queenie slipped her leash again. I hope she didn't use your yard for a toilet."

"No, but..." He watched her cross the lawn. How could he tell her the dog was dead? That it was attacked by weird poisonous worms?

"Queenie, what did I tell you about nosing around?"

She picked her up and offered Jerry a kind smile. "You have a good night, now."

"Wait."

Ms. Muumuu turned, clutching the dog to her breast. Queenie's body appeared to be moving, but Jerry couldn't tell for sure in the light. Parts were moving, independent of one another, not as a whole.

"Is there something wrong?"

Yes, he wanted to scream, *I watched that dog die,* but he couldn't bring himself to say so. Instead, his calmer self spoke for him. He almost felt Abby's hand slipping the mask over his face, muffling the dissonant terror echoing deeper in his mind. "N-Nothing's wrong. Just didn't catch your name, ma'am."

"Oh, I'm so sorry! Bethany Miles. We haven't had a chance to meet. I live one street over." She lifted the dog's paw to imitate a wave. "And this is Queenie, but you two have already met."

The dog's head hung limp against the crook of her arm.

Jerry forced himself to smile and wave. "Nice to meet you. Have a good night."

He waited until Bethany crossed the street before retreating inside. Was it even possible for a yard to be infested with worms? He wondered if Arthur had called pest control like he said he would. Unlikely, considering their last conversation.

The sticky residue on his porch left a red outline on his sole, but there was no discomfort, no itchiness or pain. He went to the bathroom and sat on the edge of the tub to wash it off, clenching his teeth to hold back the rising tide of aches.

"What the hell. . ." He buried his face in his hands. "What the hell is happening here?"

The room was silent. Abby did not answer. Whatever was happening, there was no one who would give him the truth. Everyone in the neighborhood was either deliberately oblivious or had been brainwashed. He felt like the new kid in school, singled out, and kept out of the joke.

No, Jerry decided, if he wanted the truth, he'd have to go find it himself.

Tomorrow, he vowed. Pain or no pain, he would do what he should've done weeks ago.

👁

He was up and moving again at dawn, watched the sunrise from his back porch while drinking a cup of coffee. When he was finished, he fetched his newspaper and gave it a cursory glance. A headline caught his eye: "STUDENTS PREPARE FOR WEEKEND ECLIPSE." He made to open the paper and read further, but the ache in his arms stopped him.

"Shit," he hissed, and tossed the paper on the patio table. He'd have to read it later.

His muscles and joints sang every time he moved, but he refused to spend another day on his couch feeling useless. He'd passed the night staring at the ceiling, listening to his nighttime visitors walk along his roof, unable to shake the growing dread that no matter how bad everything seemed, things were likely even worse beneath the veneer of a friendly retirement community.

In his pre-retirement days, Jerry had built a career out of investigating fraud, tracing money trails, and determining how funds were allocated. It wasn't exciting, nothing that would change the world, but he was good at it, and he would've admitted to enjoying it way back when. But as time wore on, the thrill of auditing financial records lost its luster. Abby once told her girlfriends that his job was like a game of cat and mouse but with numbers. By the time he retired, Jerry felt like there was no mouse; there was only the cat chasing its tail.

The instinct to look for a thread was something he'd always had, though, and now it urged him to start picking away at the knot that was Fairview Acres. He'd ignored it for too long and was ashamed he hadn't acted sooner. There was a thread here somewhere, and he intended to find it, pull it, and unravel this whole damn thing.

He locked up the house and was on his way to the car when he spotted movement across the street. A brown powder puff trotted along the sidewalk in front of Gary's house. Queenie.

Jerry watched the dog sniff around Gary's rose bushes until it found a good spot to do its business.

The dog is dead. Long live the dog.

Gary emerged from his house just as Jerry backed his car out of the driveway. Jerry dropped the car into drive and raised his hand to wave at the man, wondering what the hell he was doing up so early. His neighbor did not wave back.

Instead, Gary stared at him with tacit contempt, just as he'd done the day before, standing guard over his small patch of property, its shrubbery, and all the beautiful flowers. Jerry wondered what would happen if he got out of his car and walked onto the man's property, imagined himself scrapping with the guy over nothing more than a dirty look and a bad attitude.

Maybe forty years ago, old man. Not now when you can barely walk.

He smiled and stepped on the gas.

In the rearview, Gary reached into his pocket and lifted a phone to his ear.

17

Jerry arrived at the office of Stewart Realty a few minutes after eight. He couldn't remember how he'd heard of the business. Probably one of his coworkers at the time, not that it mattered now. The damage was done, and he doubted there was ill intent there. How could anyone know the sick truth of Fairview Acres's bizarre goings on unless they lived there, saw it for themselves?

But he had a feeling Stewart knew. Jerry had replayed their first meeting several times during his drive toward town. Stewart had been all too eager to recommend the community, trying to steer Jerry toward the place before they had even discussed the area, his budget, and more. Like money didn't matter here as long as they had a warm body to occupy another house.

He'd never given much thought to the village of Fairview. It was a random exit he passed by during his commutes between Scranton and Stroudsburg, another name on a road sign between mile markers, with no featured services and no reason to stop. Always a throughway and never a destination. The sort of place to which no one had cause to go unless they lived there—and who the hell would live all the way out here in the unincorporated wilds of the Poconos, anyway?

People who wanted to be left alone. People who were looking to settle down.

People with something to hide.

He'd known nothing of the place before he'd moved there, a fact which concerned him now that he'd witnessed its greatest landmark: that damn meteorite. Jerry had lived in the general area for most of his life. *Someone would've said something. There'd be studies, a national park, tourism. Every school in range of the Poconos would have their kids out there once a year, easily.* "Come see the big space rock! Exit through the gift shop!" The local municipality would've been all over it. And yet Jerry couldn't think of a single time it had ever come up. It might as well not even exist.

A silver Jaguar zipped into a parking space near the corner of the block. Stewart Taylor emerged with coffee in his hand and a laptop bag slung over his shoulder. Jerry opened the door and stepped outside.

"Stewart. Hey, Stewart. Over here."

The young man slowed his pace and stared blankly for a moment until recognition struck him. "Hey there, mister. . ." Stewart snapped his fingers. "John, right? John Campbell?"

"Jerry."

"Jerry! Of course. I'm sorry, I can remember a face, but names always give me trouble. How's your house working out for ya?"

Jerry forced a smile, told himself to look pleasant, but deep down he was already quaking with rage. He wanted to slap the cup from Stewart's hand, maybe even slap that smug grin off his face, but he reminded himself that going to jail for assault wouldn't help anyone. Instead, he shuffled across the parking lot and stuck out his hand. They shook.

"The house is good. Already feels like home."

They shared a chuckle, but Jerry saw the look in Stewart's eye. It was the same look the teenagers at the grocery store gave him when he decided to count out correct change. The look that said, *Get on with it, old man.* "I was wondering if we could sit down and chat. I have some... questions about the neighborhood."

Stewart shuffled uncomfortably from one foot to the other. He maintained the smile, but the rest of his face didn't share the pleasantry. "Well, it's a bit short notice, Jerry. Maybe we can set something up—"

"Oh, this won't take but just a few minutes of your time." Jerry clapped a hand on the young man's shoulder so hard that coffee sloshed out of the cup. He grinned, showed his teeth—mostly to hold back the ache vibrating down his arm. "Come on, help out an old man. I promise we'll be done before you finish your breakfast."

A slideshow of emotions played across Stewart's gaze, from anger and frustration to resignation and acceptance. This old man wasn't going away, and the longer he stood here trying to wiggle his way out of a meeting, the longer this would take. Better to go ahead and get this over with.

His smile widened. "You know what? You're right. I've got a meeting at nine, but until then, I'm all yours."

Jerry followed him into the building, through an empty lobby, and down a hallway decorated with various awards. Platinum Achievement 2019, Best Realtor 2015, Great Neighbors Award 2008—all gold-plated plaques indistinct from the others except for the wording. Stewart unlocked his office at the end of the hall and gestured for Jerry to enter, but something caught Jerry's eye. A familiar symbol on the last plaque. An eye eclipsed by a crescent moon. Award for Excellence in Service 2022, presented by the Fairview Acres Community Association.

"Something wrong, Jerry?"

"No, nothing wrong at all."

He followed Stewart into a lavish office and took a seat. A built-in bookcase adorned one wall, its shelves filled with books on real estate, architecture, and sales coaching. A few framed photographs accented the shelves here and there, including one of Stewart and a curly brunette standing by a pool with a massive Tudor-style house behind them. Another: The two of them on a beach somewhere. Twin palm trees in the background. Tropical.

"That's my fiancée. We go down to Cabo twice a year."

Jerry nodded and did the mental math on something like that. A trip down to Mexico twice a year. A Jag in the parking lot. A house that was less a house and more like a mansion, no doubt located in one of the ritzy neighborhoods outside of Scranton, with property taxes that would make the average salary scream "Uncle."

How many houses are you selling to keep up with that lifestyle, I wonder.

"All right, Jerry." Stewart unfolded the wrapper around his breakfast sandwich. The smell of bacon made Jerry's stomach grumble. "What can I do for you? You aren't looking to sell already, are you?"

"No, not just yet. I was wondering if you could tell me a little more about Fairview."

"Oh." Stewart swallowed a bite of his food and opened a desk drawer. "I thought I gave you one of the pamphlets..."

"I have the pamphlet, Stewart. I want to know other things about Fairview."

"Other things?"

Jerry leaned forward and stared hard at the young man. "Yes. About the community association, specifically. Things you didn't tell me."

Stewart cleared his throat. "I'm not sure I..."

"About how it's not a community association at all, but a cult of some kind. Or something. I'm still not sure what to call it exactly. It's certainly not normal."

"I think 'cult' is a strong word—"

Jerry slammed his fist on the desk. "It fits."

"Now, Mr. Campbell, there's no need for that. I think you just need to take a breath and calm down. Maybe there's someone I can call—"

"A meteorite in the park. A goddess they all keep talking about. They drugged me at one of their parties. And then there's Arthur with his vague threats..." Jerry trailed off.

Stewart's expression hadn't changed. He hadn't crumbled, hadn't spilled his guts when confronted. What the hell had Jerry expected would happen? He realized now what he sounded like: a crazy old man. Might as well toss him in a padded room and throw away the key.

He took a deep breath and exhaled slowly, hoping for a moment of clarity, and remembered Lisa. The missing caregiver, Katherine's nightly sojourns in the neighborhood—there was more going on there than mere dementia. *You aren't alone in this, old man. Don't gaslight yourself.*

The realtor's cell phone lit up and began to vibrate on the desk. A familiar face appeared on the screen, and though it was upside down for Jerry, he'd recognize it anywhere. Stewart's gaze dropped to the phone, and then back to Jerry.

"You going to answer that, Stewart?" The phone kept on ringing. "Didn't know you were so chummy with Arthur Peterson."

"Arthur's... well, you know how it is. We keep in touch for... when..."

He reached for the phone. Jerry smacked it out of his hand, sent the device flying across the room. It struck the wall and fell to the floor with a heavy thud. The steady vibration stopped, and silence seeped into the space between them. Stewart slowly leaned back in his seat, his eyes wide, his mouth still agape.

Jerry was shocked, too—at his speed, the jolt of pain shooting through his arm, the audacity of his action—but he wasn't about to let Stewart see it. Instead, he rose from his seat and leaned over the desk.

"I suppose every monster needs a Renfield. What did he promise you, Stewart? What kind of price tag does a retiree carry these days?" Jerry shook his head in disgust. "Here's some free advice, son. Keep away from that man and whatever the hell it is he's got going on in his little fiefdom."

Stewart began to laugh. "I'm afraid that ship has already sailed, Mr. Campbell. For both of us."

"How do you figure that?"

"Sooner or later, the goddess gets what she wants." The young man's laughter intensified, until tears streamed down his cheeks. A thin tendril of shadow crossed his pupils. "It's the will of her emissaries. By the moon's eye, Jerry."

Jerry stepped back, his mind buzzing with alarm bells that would not be silenced, unable to process what was happening. Stewart rose from his seat, his face locked in a rictus of pained amusement. Bubbles of skin flared in spots on his cheeks and forehead. One of them began to bleed.

"I'm afraid we have to sever our business relationship, Mr. Campbell."

Jerry backpedaled with clenched teeth. His muscles and joints were on fire. Darkness ebbed at the edges of his vision. From somewhere far away, he thought he heard Abby shouting, *Get the hell out of there, you old fool.*

One of the lumps on Stewart's face burst open, freeing a slender tendril of pale flesh. It swirled and writhed before him, tasting the air before going rigid, focusing on Jerry's direction.

Another swell of agony crashed over him, his vision layering over itself as the whole world shifted and vibrated. He recognized the drone filling his ears and humming through his head. *The engine of the cosmos. Gears slowly grinding down. Turning toward me. Eyes opening. So many eyes, inside and throughout. Measuring the gulf of space between us. A vast canyon of emptiness, deeper than the oceans, deeper than my soul.* Terror crystalized in his mind, freezing his blood and filling his gut with mortar. *It sees me.* He felt the weight of the universe bearing down, focusing on him. *It. Sees. Me.*

"Let her in, Jerry. You've already invited her, now let her in."

He gasped for breath, struggling against the violent undertow of fear eager to drag him down. Tendrils of shadow writhed in his periphery. A dissonant voice broke and reassembled itself in his head, and he heard Abby and Katherine whisper together: *It's the worm. Get away from the worm.*

He backed against the door and slipped out into the hallway. Once the worm was out of sight, the pain eased off and his bones no longer felt as though they might vibrate out of his skin. Jerry leaned against the wall, shuffled away from Stewart's office, knocking several of the awards off the wall. They clattered across the floor, and the sound of their impact hammered in his head.

From behind, Stewart cried out, "Go home, Jerry! What's done is done! Take your place in her court!"

Jerry opened his mouth to respond but all he could muster was a dry hiss. The pain lessened with every step, but it was still wrecking his body. Getting the last word with Stewart didn't seem so important now. All he wanted was to get back to his car, collect himself, and get away from here. He needed to call Lisa. He needed to check on Katherine.

He needed

(worms dancing)

to move as far away from Fairview Acres as possible and never look back.

Jerry made it as far as his car before nausea caught up to him. He sat on the front seat and puked onto the pavement until there was nothing left inside.

Tired and dehydrated, he leaned back against the car's frame and wiped the sweat from his forehead. *Get a grip on yourself, old man. This isn't over. You need—*

Movement caught his eye. He looked down. Something stirred in the pile of vomit.

Oh God, no.

A thin gelatinous string of angel hair pasta twitched and slowly inched its way through the bile. Pasta was the only thing that made sense, the only thing that should have been in his stomach, but he knew better.

The worm rose like a snake ready to strike. Its fleshy nub twisted in the air, turning, sensing his presence. Tiny pinpricks of teeth emerged from its eyeless head like the tips of a regal crown.

Jerry stomped down, crushing the invertebrate into the pavement. He stomped a few more times just to be sure, until the worm was indiscernible from the vomit. Satisfied, he slammed the door and started the car, but before he dropped the transmission into gear, he caught a look at himself in the rearview. His skin was yellow, waxen, and the circles under his eyes were so dark he could've passed for a boxer on the wrong side of a fight. He'd aged a decade in a span of ten minutes. God knows, he certainly felt like it.

Arthur's voice piped up in his head: *You look like a retiree, grandpa!*

A chill worked its way through him. He turned up the heat and made a U-turn back toward the highway. The sun beat down on everything, the warmth of the day already taking hold, but the cold followed him like a shadow.

PART THREE
EMISSARIES

18

Lisa's phone rang and vibrated itself off the nightstand. She cracked one eye open and stared at a sliver of morning light seeping out the side of her blackout curtains. Red digits on her alarm clock read 9:43. She'd been asleep for less than an hour, had been home less than two since her shift had ended, and had forgotten to silence her phone.

Everyone knew better than to call her after a night shift. Sleep was at a premium these days since her mom's condition had worsened. Whoever was calling did so at their own peril, and she was set on letting them know it—until she sat up and retrieved the phone from the floor. "JERRY CAMPBELL" lit up the screen. Her anger slipped away in moments, displaced by a cold spike of fear driven through her chest.

Is Mom okay? She answered the call. "Jerry, what's—"

"Get your mother out of that neighborhood." He sounded out of breath, panicked.

Lisa climbed out of bed, walked to the closet for her clothes. "Okay, but I need you to calm down. Is Mom all right? What happened?"

Jerry began to say something but was stopped short by a coughing fit. She frowned, listening to him hack up a lung, and remembered how ill he'd seemed during her visit. *Body aches, just like Mom before...*

"Sorry, Lisa. I—it's been a rough morning."

"No, it's okay, Jerry. What's going on?"

"It's the worms. They get inside your head somehow, and... hold on—"

Another coughing fit. Retching.

She half-listened, wondering if she was experiencing a man's fevered ravings, if her mom was in any real danger. Jerry seemed endearing enough, a kind soul in mourning who'd taken a liking to her mother, but these weren't the concerns of a friend. They were the paranoid ramblings of a confused man.

Sure, there was something weird about the neighborhood, especially with Arthur, but Jerry's suspicions of cult-like activity and a conspiracy to drug the residents drifted into unhinged territory. She'd even made a few inquiries last night about the ER intake last month. There was no record of a call to Jerry's place, no evidence that her mother had been treated.

Lisa wanted to write off his claims as delusions of persecution and a desire for attention. The man was a widower, was probably lonely and wanted companionship, and she wanted nothing more than to believe as much—except she wasn't a psychiatrist and was ill-equipped to make such a diagnosis. Besides, there was something else that unsettled her and set off alarms in her mind.

Daddy mumbled about worms off and on just before he died. Body aches, too.

"—she's not safe, Lisa. You've gotta get her out of there."

She leaned her head against the wall, closed her eyes. Hints of a stress headache bloomed in her temples. "Jerry, I need you to calm down, okay? Just take a breath for me. Can you do that?"

A pause, followed by words mumbled under his breath. There was fear in his voice. Fear and hopelessness. "I'm sorry, I just... I need to pull myself together here."

"I have to visit Mom this afternoon anyway. I can stop by—"

"No, no, I'm not there. I'm at a hotel in Stroudsburg. Don't go to Fairview yet. Please, Lisa, promise me you won't go before we've had a chance to figure this out."

Lisa opened her eyes and stared at the wall. *Figure what out, Jerry?*

She remembered how her father had gotten lost on the way to the mailbox, walked two miles toward town before her mother caught up to him. He'd insisted someone was watching him and that he kept hearing a weird slithering sound in his head whenever he tried to sleep.

She sees me, he'd said. *In my head. Can't get away. Not when the worms are dancing.*

Putting him to sleep every night had been a chore. Lisa and their caregiver had struggled to settle him into bed, so her mother was usually the one to do it. She was their secret weapon to his nightly excursions, often taking his hand and leading him in a slow dance around the bedroom. *The sundowner's dance,* she called it, with a thin smile on her face. The caregiver thought it was the sweetest thing, but Lisa knew her mother too well. The smile was a bandage to hide the pain she felt watching her husband drift further away.

Jerry reminded her of her father. His sincerity, his certainty, his concern. She couldn't bring herself to dismiss him, not when he needed help the most.

"Okay," she said. "I promise I won't go to Fairview yet. Where are you staying? I'll be there as soon as I can."

He told her, and they said their goodbyes. She muttered "shit" under her breath and went about getting dressed. The least she could do was to set his mind at ease, hear him out. *When he's finished, I'll make sure he gets home, and then I'll try to get him some help. It's what Mom would want me to do.*

👁

Morning traffic was hell, a sluggish stop-and-go death march, and her headache was in full swing by the time she parked her car. The hotel was of the fancier variety, with its own conference center and café, and she passed a group of men and women in business attire on her way into the lobby. *Not too shabby,* she thought.

She found Jerry sitting off to the side of the lobby in a quiet alcove, away from the morning business bustle, with a folded newspaper on his lap. Lisa studied him for a moment before approaching. His face was drawn, eyes sunken in dark circles. Even with his physical ailments, he'd appeared healthier yesterday, even handsome for his age, but now he looked old. Not just elderly, but *old*-old, a walking husk of papery skin that might topple in the wind.

Jerry looked up from the newspaper and smiled weakly. "You look so much like your mother, standing there in the light."

And you look like you're one day away from the morgue.

Lisa smiled, forced the morbid thought to the back of her mind. "Thank you," she said. "Do you want to get some coffee? I think we could both use some."

"I like the way you think."

Most of the tables in the café were occupied by conference attendees, many of them buzzing with caffeine-induced frivolity, but they found a small corner table at the back. After Lisa returned with their drinks, she studied his face, expecting to see signs of confusion or fear. Instead, she found the same wide-eyed intelligence and cognition that met her at the door yesterday—traits that should have been cause for relief, even celebration, but left her feeling puzzled given everything he'd said to her in the last twenty-four hours.

God, none of this makes sense.

Lisa rubbed her eyes, wincing from the pangs of the headache. Maybe the caffeine would help.

"You must think me a lunatic. Hell, I would."

"I'm not sure what to think at this point. I... Look, why don't you tell me what happened?"

Jerry sipped his coffee and began explaining what had happened to him after their meeting. He rambled about a dead dog, worms, things walking on his roof. "I left that part out yesterday," he said. "Didn't want you to think... well, you know." He told her about how Arthur had some kind of connection with a realtor named Stewart Taylor, but when he began describing how the realtor had physically transformed, Lisa watched him closely, looking for a joke, or for anything else that confirmed he wasn't in his right mind.

What he'd said about Arthur Peterson tracked with her impression of the man, even if the allegations seemed outlandish—drugging people in the neighborhood, running the place like a cult, and so on. With everything else he'd told her yesterday, she had plenty of reasons to believe Jerry was delusional. These latest revelations merely confirmed her suspicion, even if she could hear her father in the back of her mind, screaming for her to listen.

She waited for him to finish before asking, "Do you have any family history with dementia?"

The question sounded worse than she'd intended, a callous reminder of her clinical training, but it was out now. If Jerry was insulted, he made no sign.

He shrugged. "Just my grandma, that I can remember. Mom's side."

"Did she?"

"No, Lisa. Neither did my dad."

She nodded. "Sorry, I had to ask. It's the first thing I asked my parents, too."

"Let me guess. No history, right?"

"Right."

"No history..." he trailed off.

She watched the gears turning behind his eyes. He was focused and concerned, and he remembered specific details of his encounters—unusual for a dementia patient, and yet she couldn't say for sure without a battery of tests. All she had to go on was experience with both her parents. Hadn't her father experienced the same fluctuations of cognition in the beginning? And her mother, for that matter? Her symptoms began the same way not even a year ago: paranoia, delusions of conspiracy, a mistrust of her neighbors, physical aches and pains. The confusion and memory loss came later. Same as her father.

But unlike his symptoms, her mother's ebbed and flowed, terrible for weeks at a time and then the complete opposite for even longer. The fluctuations had made attaining an official diagnosis from her neurologist a damn nightmare.

Lisa wanted so badly to dismiss everything Jerry told her, but in the back of her mind, a persistent thought repeated in alarm: *This can't be a coincidence. All three in the same neighborhood, all with matching symptoms of* something *that* looks *like* dementia.

Her gut and her training were at odds here. Any doctor would take this at face value, look at the symptoms, run some tests, make a diagnosis, and call it a day. The other facts were circumstantial and couldn't possibly have any correlation.

Right?

She didn't have an answer. She was exhausted from her shift, nauseous from the lack of sleep, and the damned headache would not relent. She gulped her coffee, hopeful that the caffeine would ease the pressure in her head. The group of conference registrants made their exit together, allowing a peaceful quiet to blanket the room, and she made a silent prayer of gratitude to the universe.

"No history," he repeated.

"What are you thinking?"

"Nothing important. Besides, if I'm you," Jerry said, leaning carefully back in his seat, "then I'm thinking 'dementia' or 'Alzheimer's' or maybe 'temporary derangement.'" He sipped his coffee and frowned. "You seem like a no-nonsense sort of person, Lisa. Tell me I'm wrong."

She shook her head. "I *am* thinking dementia, but at the same time. . . You sound so much like my dad right now, it's scary. You still have your faculties, you're lucid, you're here"—she knocked on the table for emphasis—"and so did Dad, until the end. The difference is, when he was going through it, I was hearing this crazy shit for the first time."

"Even the part about the worms?"

She ignored his question. "I'm talking about the paranoia with the neighborhood, the weird cult-like behavior, the suspicion of Arthur. Mom's symptoms began the same way, but I wrote it off because she'd been there when Dad went through it all. I thought memories of his delusions were resurfacing and playing out through her. For you to be exhibiting the same symptoms—I mean, *identical* symptoms, with the same delusions—that's a hard pill to swallow."

"So, you believe me?"

Lisa sighed. "I don't know what to believe. I rely on facts, not conjecture, but if this didn't involve my mother. . ." She looked away from him. *I'd tell you to talk to your doctor, and my involvement would end there.* But those words were too heavy, even for her, and she suspected they were candy-coated lies anyway. The truth was, she would care, and she would try to get him help, because that's why she got into nursing in the first place. "Well, the point is that it does involve Mom somehow. I still don't know who's caring for her when I'm not there. I know she's wandering outside her house at night. It's a matter of time until she hurts herself—or worse."

She shook her head in frustration. Jerry reached across the table, placed a hand on hers for comfort, but his skin was ice cold. Lisa wanted to recoil but kept her composure *(oh God it's like he's dead)* despite the unsettling feeling. Instead, she offered him a tired smile while screaming on the inside.

"I want to help," Jerry said. A tremor rippled through his hand, and he removed it from hers. His cheeks flushed red, the first sign of color she'd seen on his pallid face since yesterday. "If I can. However I can. She tried to warn me that first night. It's the least I can do."

"You sure you're not sweet on my mom?"

She said it to get a rise out of him, maybe even a smile, something to bring more color to his face. But Jerry's pale complexion remained, and so did his mask of gloom.

"She reminds me of Abby, so if I am sweet on her, maybe that's why."

"I had a feeling. Thank you for caring about Mom."

"Of course. *Is* there anything I can do?"

"You aren't going to like this, but. . . I want you to go to the ER. Check yourself into Lehigh Valley Hospital."

"Lisa—"

"Please don't take this the wrong way, but you look like a sneeze could knock you down, and you're freezing to touch." She watched as he considered her words, absently flexing his fingers in both hands. "Trust me, please? I'm a nurse, remember?"

"I've already talked to my doctor. Gave some blood. Everything came back normal."

"I'm sure it did, but. . . look, what you're going through, this isn't the first time I've seen it. This is how things started with my dad. With my mom, too." He said nothing, but judging by the look on his face, something finally clicked. Relieved, she went on, "Both of their stubborn asses refused to go to the hospital. Please don't be like them."

Deflated, he nodded quietly. "Promise me you'll text as soon as you get to your mom's. At least tell me she's okay."

Lisa smiled. "Of course. You'll be the first one I call. But that works both ways, man. Text me if they admit you. Text me even if they don't."

"I will."

"Are you okay to drive yourself? I can take you—"

"My pride is already bruised, Nurse Dunnally. Don't take my dignity, too."

She held up her hands. "Fair point. I won't push my luck."

"Thank you. Will you at least tell me what you're going to do?"

"Promise you won't follow me?"

He crossed his heart. "Stick a needle in my eye."

"I'm going to the caregiving agency on my way to check on Mom. It's right outside of Fairview."

"I think I know it. At the corner before the highway ramp?"

"That's the one. They keep giving me the runaround on the phone. It'll be a different story when I'm standing in the room with 'em."

His eyes brightened. "That's more like it. Give 'em hell, lady."

She smiled. There was still some life in the old man after all, and she couldn't stand to see his light go out so quickly. A mask had slipped over his face at some point since yesterday, the same sort that had smothered her father's flame. The same sort that her mother now wore, too. She knew that mask, knew it held secrets a person didn't want to share, truths they didn't want to confront.

The death mask, she thought, as they made their way out of the café and back to the hotel parking lot. *The face people wear when they know their time is almost up. The resignation. Acceptance.*

Lisa walked him to his car, and when he was safely seated behind the wheel, she said, "Straight to the ER, okay?"

Jerry nodded. "Yes, ma'am."

"Good. Thank you. I'll be in touch."

Before she sat in her car, Lisa turned and watched Jerry's sedan pause at a stop sign, then make a right. Toward the hospital, as promised.

She started the engine and drove to the same stop sign. She flipped on her blinker. A right turn. Toward the hospital. Toward Fairview.

Nah, she thought, making the turn. *Even he knows he's in terrible shape to play a hero.*

Didn't he?

◎

Thoughts of Jerry haunted Lisa all the way back to Fairview.

What were you thinking? He's frail, something could happen, what if he has an episode or something—

She smacked her hand against the steering wheel. "Stop it. He'll be fine."

Her voice rang hollow inside the empty car, with a tired inflection that reminded her of just how little sleep she'd had in the last forty-eight hours. She had one more shift tonight and then two days off. Not the first time she'd worked a shift on so little sleep, and with enough coffee, she could do it again.

But the stress, girl. It's gonna amplify all that fatigue and fry your nerves to a crisp. This is how you put yourself into an early grave.

Maybe so, but she had to find out what was going on with the caregiver. She couldn't do that with Jerry there and his bizarre conspiracies hovering over her head. Sending him to the hospital was the best thing to do given the shape he was in. She didn't need to be a doctor to see he was in bad shape.

But old men love to feel needed and useful.

Something her daddy had told her on several occasions when she was in school and needed money, her car fixed, or some other trifle with which she was too proud to ask for help.

"He'll be fine," she said once more. But in the back of her mind, a little voice questioned her reasoning, needling and prodding at her resolve. *What if you just don't want to hear his insane bullshit anymore? What if his delusions are clouding your head when you should really be focusing on the real problem: you can't take care of your ailing mom? You're a nurse, for fuck's sake. What kind of nurse can't take care of their most important patient? But let's not stop there, Lisa. You thought you could count on him to keep an eye on her, you thought his crush on her was cute and endearing, and you wanted his help. But now you've discovered he's suffering with early signs of dementia—*

A car cut her off and she slammed on the brakes. She leaned on the horn, gave the driver her middle finger. She caught a glimpse of her reflection in the rearview, saw the dark circles below her eyes, and wondered when she'd become so callous, so cold.

When your daddy didn't recognize you anymore.

When you reached for his hand and his skin

(oh God it's like he's dead)

was so cold and you realized he wouldn't be there to offer you his warmth anymore. That's when your flame withered and died, kiddo. Dementia went from being a word in a textbook to being a thief in the night, stealing the essence of someone you loved and leaving a living corpse behind, like an insidious worm inching its way around his brain, boring holes into the tissue, eating all the good parts and turning him into someone else.

That word again. Worms.

And something else. Something that *looks* like dementia.

She sees me. In my head. Can't get away. Not when the worms are dancing. Her daddy's words replayed in her head with aching clarity. There were times she'd thought her father lucid despite what he was saying. There was coherence in his eyes, a pleading sort of certainty, absolute conviction. And she had suspected he was still himself, even when the symptoms and the doctors insisted otherwise. Her daddy was still in there, screaming to be heard, and no one was listening.

Get your mom out of here, he'd plead, while a nurse strapped him to his bed because he'd been roaming the house and might hurt himself.

Don't let them in here, he'd warned her.

Poisoning me, he'd screamed, while they made him take his medicine.

Now, as she neared the agency, she wondered what medication they'd given him. What might have happened if they'd refused the medication? Or if they'd left the neighborhood before his symptoms got worse? Her daddy was a fighter—rarely got sick when she was a child, always went to work no matter how he felt—and now she wondered if he would've recovered somehow.

"You're being ridiculous, Lisa."

She slowed the car and took the exit ramp, following the road to Fairview's outskirts where an office building sat at the corner. She parked out front. A large sign read "CELESTIAL COMFORTS HOME CARE." Lisa stared up at the bright friendly lettering and noticed for the first time some smaller text on the bottom right. There was a logo depicting an eye partially obscured by a crescent moon, followed by the words "A PROUD MEMBER OF THE FAIRVIEW ACRES COMMUNITY ASSOCIATION."

"Son of a bitch."

Jerry had ranted about Arthur Peterson's connection to Stewart Realty. She'd only been half-paying attention, but seeing this now made her wonder. Had this place always been part of Arthur's network of businesses? She raised her phone, snapped a photo, and hesitated. Sending this to Jerry would only fuel his delusions, but one fact helped her swallow back all the skepticism: This same agency had helped take care of her father.

She pressed 'Send.'

19

Jerry sat in his car and waited for the ache in his joints to subside. *Stupid old fool,* he told himself. *You should've been honest with her.* Of course, driving anywhere was a bad idea. Keeping his joints locked in any one position for too long caused a creeping inflammation that radiated through his bones. He massaged his wrists, then his knees, and tried to take his mind off the agony.

Did she believe me? Doubt it.

He looked out the window at Lehigh Valley Hospital, watching the ill and infirm cross the parking lot, each of them making their own kind of death march toward the inevitable. He'd be one of them, sooner or later. But not yet. No, something else nagged at his brain, more pressing than any guilt he might feel about lying to Katherine's daughter.

No history.

The village of Fairview, sure, that was public record. Anyone could look up the history of that small town. But the lack of history about its surroundings was something else. He'd never heard anything about it in all his years, and he'd found nothing about a meteorite online.

He retrieved his phone, opened its browser, and tried some more specific keywords. But the results were all the same as before. Articles about a fireball over Erie, Pennsylvania, when to view the Perseids, studies by the American Meteor Society. Nothing about Fairview in relation to a meteorite.

Jerry stared off into middle distance. *How could Fairview keep something like an impact crater and a sizeable meteorite a secret from Google?*

Outside, a young woman walked beside an elderly man as he hobbled his way toward the hospital's sliding doors. A pang of guilt blossomed in Jerry's belly. Lisa meant well, and he knew walking through those doors was the best thing for him to do, but it wouldn't be the best thing for Katherine. Not if Lisa hadn't believed him—and he had no reason to think she had.

"Kat was there for me when it mattered."

He chewed his lip, started the car—and paused when his phone chimed.

A text. No message, just a photo. Took him a moment to make sense of it, but when he finally did, a raging heat filled his belly, and he wanted to breathe fire: "A PROUD MEMBER OF THE FAIRVIEW ACRES COMMUNITY ASSOCIATION."

The agency in charge of Katherine's care was affiliated with Arthur's operation. Of course it was.

He thought of what Katherine said about her so-called nurse, and that pissed him off even more.

"Son of a bitch."

Jerry dropped the car into gear, gunned the engine, and peeled out of the hospital parking lot.

👁

A redheaded woman looked up from her monitor and smiled. "Welcome to Celestial Comforts."

Lisa ignored the greeting, surveyed the room. The lobby sat empty, its sterile white walls adorned with framed landscapes painted with neutral greens, yellows, and browns. A muted pop song from a Top 40 station filled the air. She focused on the receptionist and forced herself to smile.

"Hi. I'm Lisa Dunnally. I'm here about my mother's care."

"Certainly. Do you have an appointment?"

"No. I just need to know who is currently providing her care." She showed the receptionist her driver's license. "My mother is Katherine Dunnally. Two *n's*, two *l's*."

The receptionist's fingers clacked across the keyboard. "Ah, one of our Fairview residents. Let's see. . ." Her smile slowly fell. "Looks like we had someone assigned to her, but they've since left the agency."

Lisa sighed. "I know. That's why I'm here. Who is assigned to her now?"

More typing. The receptionist shook her head. "I'm sorry, but there doesn't appear to be anyone assigned to her at this moment in time."

"That's not right." Lisa pulled back a chair and sat. "This has to be a misunderstanding."

"I'm afraid not, Ms. Dunnally. At least, not according to my system here."

"Mom said. . ." Her words failed. Could she trust anything her mother said at this point? The dementia had a firm grip on the poor woman. What if her mysterious visitor was nothing but a phantom conjured by her failing mind? But didn't Jerry mention seeing someone helping her indoors a week or so ago?

Lisa sighed. "Never mind. Why wasn't someone assigned to my mother after the last nurse quit?"

A puzzled look crossed the receptionist's face. "By request, ma'am."

Her words sparked a fire in Lisa's mind, accenting the interminable pressure throbbing in her forehead. "What do you mean?"

"There's a note here that says you authorized cancellation of care."

"That's ridiculous. My mother suffers from dementia. There's no way in hell I'd cancel her care."

"I understand that, ma'am, but our records say otherwise."

Lisa slammed her fist on the desk. "*My* records say this is bullshit. I did *not* authorize any cancellation—"

The desk phone rang, and the receptionist held up her index finger, mouthed "one moment," and answered the call.

Lisa leaned back in her seat and rubbed her eyes, wondering how much was too much and if this would be what finally broke her. She'd forsaken any semblance of a personal life when her mom fell ill. Other than her job, there was nowhere else for her to turn, except maybe to a psychiatrist. *God, if I could just take a vacation and sleep for a week. No phone, no drama, no ailing mother, and no worries—just the simple pleasure of going to bed without setting an alarm.*

"I understand, sir. I'll tell her. Thank you." The receptionist hung up and smiled. "That was our director. He'll be out to speak with you momentarily."

Lisa opened her eyes. "Good. Maybe he can explain how you let someone fraudulently cancel my mother's service."

The receptionist ignored the comment and excused herself. She collected her coffee mug and retreated down the hallway to the staff lounge.

Lisa looked around the room. She tapped her foot absently to the beat of a song from the radio, and when one minute turned into five, she checked her phone.

No replies from Jerry, but he'd seen the message. She imagined him sitting in the waiting room of the ER, scrolling his phone like she was. Safe. In the best place he could be, regardless of whatever his condition happened to be.

And bored out of his mind. Feeling abandoned. Forgotten. Ignored. Oh, stop it, Lisa. He's fine. He will be *fine.*

The receptionist returned with her coffee and resumed typing. After another five minutes, Lisa cleared her throat. "Excuse me, how much longer?"

"The director will be with you momentarily."

"I know, you said that ten minutes ago."

She smiled, a big grin full of pearly whites. "He's in a meeting and will be with you—"

"Momentarily. Got it."

Lisa sighed and pulled up a word game on her phone to kill time.

Another twenty minutes passed. Three pop songs, several triple-word scores, and too many commercials to count.

Finally: footsteps and jangling keys.

Lisa looked up, and her heart plunged into her gut. Arthur Peterson stood before her, his car keys in hand, wearing the same dubious smile her father had hated so much. "Good morning, Lisa! How are you?"

"I'm... I didn't realize you worked here."

"Oh, yes. Celestial Comforts is practically the right hand of Fairview Acres. Speaking of which, I understand there's been a mix-up concerning your mother's care?"

She'd been ready for a confrontation. Her blood was up, fists clenched, teeth bared and ready to strike—but Arthur's appearance here was a wild card despite her discovery of Fairview's connection. The fire in her mind and heart was extinguished to cinders, leaving her feeling cold, hollow.

"Hardly a mix-up, Arthur. Someone canceled my mother's care using my name."

"Oh, dear. That is a shame."

"It will be when my attorney gets involved."

Arthur's smile grew wider and lost some of its cheeriness. "I'm sure that won't be necessary, Lisa. We're all neighbors here. There must be something that we can do to resolve this."

"Reinstate my mother's care."

"Done."

She smiled, felt the flames inside grow hotter. "Five nights a week. On your dime."

"Not a problem at all."

"I want this in writing."

Arthur nodded. "As agreements always should be." He clapped his hands together. "Well, that settles the matter. I'm just on my way over to Fairview Acres right now, as a matter of fact. Would you care to join me? I'll drive."

The idea of getting into a car with him made her skin crawl. So did the smile on his face. His eyes, too. They were wide open, almost cartoon-like, and she couldn't recall if he'd blinked during their exchange.

"Sure," she said, producing her keys. "I'll follow you. I need to check on Mom anyway."

"Just perfect. We can check on her together."

Once back inside the safety of her car, she thought about dialing Jerry's number, but decided against it. He'd only want to tag along, make sure her mom was okay.

Arthur waited in his car for her to leave. He lowered his windows and waved to her. Lisa resisted the urge to give him the finger.

Instead, she picked up her phone and dialed Jerry's phone. Four rings and no answer. Voicemail. She canceled the call. *Probably in triage,* she thought. Maybe he was being admitted. *I'll try him later.*

When she was ready, Lisa drove out of the parking lot. She wanted to feel victorious about getting free care for her mother, but whenever she looked into the rearview and saw Arthur's car close behind, that familiar cold crept back into her gut. Was she being selfish, knowing now that Fairview Acres was so closely tied to her mother's homecare? Or was she making the right call?

For five days a week, completely paid for by the agency? You're damn right, woman. Maybe she'd get to take that vacation after all. Nothing selfish in looking after her own sanity.

And yet there was something else, deep down below this sense of relief, screaming for attention she was too exhausted to give. Who forged the authorization?

A question to which she would seek out the answer in due time. For now, her mother would receive the care she needed. That was priority one.

◉

Jerry slowed as he drove past Celestial Comforts. Only one car sat in the small parking lot, and it wasn't Lisa's. She'd called while he was on the road, but he wasn't ready to talk to her just yet. The last thing he wanted was a lecture, but more than that, he didn't want to listen to her disappointment or frustration. Better to go into that conversation armed with evidence to support his choice.

He drove to the library at the opposite end of town. A series of granite obelisks decorated the walkway leading up to the building. The words he'd read on the plaque at the Moon Pool sprang to mind. *To commemorate when our goddess touched the earth.*

Jerry looked in the rearview, studied the dark circles beneath his eyes. *No wonder Lisa didn't believe me.* He slicked back his hair and rubbed his face, tried to make himself look somewhat presentable. No use, though. The wide-eyed feral appearance remained intact. He sighed, looked back toward the library and the pathway of obelisks. "I've never been a gambling man, Abby, but I'd bet my retirement fund that Arthur's on the board of trustees here..."

There's only one way to find out, old man. Get out of the car and be useful.

Jerry sucked air through his teeth as he forced himself to move, awakening dormant fires in his bones, and opened the door. One breath, one step, one inch at a time—he crossed the parking lot toward the library. If this was the hardest thing he had to do today, then maybe life wasn't so terrible in the scheme of things. Maybe this was the universe's idea of respite.

He approached the first pair of obelisks. A small plaque affixed to one of them read:

TO ARTHUR PETERSON
CHAIRMAN OF THE FAIRVIEW ACRES
COMMUNITY ASSOCIATION
FOR HIS GENEROUS DONATION AND SUPPORT

He smirked, glanced skyward. "If only I were a betting man..."

◉

Lisa parked outside her mother's home and took out her phone to try Jerry again. As she scrolled for his name, she glanced up at the house—the front door stood open. She fumbled the phone, dropping it on the front seat in her panic, and scrambled out to the door. *Oh my God, no. Please, no, tell me she's okay.*

She darted up the porch steps, images of her mom wandering through the neighborhood filling her head, and she thought of the way her father had done the same before he got worse.

"Mom?" Her voice echoed dryly in the open house. The emptiness of the place weighed on her, was nearly suffocating with its silence. What she imagined a tomb must feel like from the inside. "Mama, can you hear me?"

"Lisa?"

She closed her eyes and took a breath. *Thank God.*

She climbed the stairs, laughing out of relief. "I thought something was wrong, Mom. Did you know your front door is standing wide open?"

"Lisa, baby, don't come up here. I—I'm fine, honey. Just... stay downstairs. I don't—"

Her skin prickled at the distress in her mother's voice. "Mom, what's wrong? You can—" The door stood open, but the curtains were closed. A bedside lamp coated the room in yellow warmth. *Why are they closed? Mom loves the light.*

Cold pangs of anxiety settled into her gut. Everything was wrong. Nothing was wrong.

She crossed the threshold and saw her mother sitting upright in bed. An orange thermos sat on the bedside table next to a French press filled with a dark frothy brew. Did she own a French press? Lisa couldn't remember ever seeing one in the kitchen.

"What are you doing here so early?" her mother said. "You weren't supposed to come until later..."

The sadness in her voice gave Lisa pause. Sadness and resignation. She crossed the room to the bed, was about to sit at her mother's side when a ripe smell hit her nose. Rotting fruit. Fresh soil. Something metallic.

Her mother took her hand. "I'm sorry, honey..."

"For what, Mama?" Lisa glanced at the French press. "What's all this? Taking your morning coffee in bed now?"

Tears welled in her eyes. "I'm sorry."

"I'm not upset. I'm just glad you're okay..." She picked up the coffee pot. More of that sickly sweet stench invaded her nostrils, twisted her stomach, prompting her to retch.

"Please don't..."

"What did you put in this, Mom?" Visions of her mother flashed across her mind: she saw her staggering around the kitchen in a demented fugue, adding random ingredients to her brew, thinking she was just making her morning coffee like she'd always done. *God, it's worse than I thought.*

She returned the press to the table, frowning. Something caught the corner of her eye.

Movement. The bedroom door slowly closing.

"Gladys, don't hurt her. I'm begging you, don't hurt my daugh—"

A thin shape emerged from the shadows behind the door and shot across the room toward her. Lisa had no time to react. Leathery fingers clutched her neck and pinned her to the wall, held her in place with an impossible strength. The world fell away in an instant as the thing's grip constricted. Bursts of color and shadow teased the edges of her vision. What she saw standing before her made no sense: a mannequin wrapped in dead skin and draped in a fluffy white robe.

The creature had a face that wasn't a face at all but a plate of flesh riddled with holes. Eyes, nose, mouth—they were larger hollow pits in the surface of pallid skin, accented by smaller portals to a dark emptiness beyond. Fleshy nubs protruded from where her teeth should have been. Something thin and slimy poked its head out from one of the openings in her forehead. Another slipped from the hollow of her nose and inched into a hole in her cheek.

A worm. It's a fucking worm.

The desiccated figure raised its other arm, but it held no weapon, didn't even have a hand. Pockmarked skin stretched out from the bicep like taffy, mottled with dark spots and ribbed segments, a thin tendril of flesh curling and writhing in the air. Jagged barbs protruded from the tip, and when Lisa gasped, the tentacle reared back like a snake ready to strike.

Warm, stagnant air seeped from the open holes in Gladys's face. Something like a voice escaped the creature's maw, the remains of a sigh stretched so thin it might snap.

"Lisssaaa..."

Her stomach lurched. Everything was wrong. Nothing made sense.

Katherine cried out for her, pleaded with the creature to leave her alone, let her go. Behind them, heavy footfalls echoed from the hallway. A moment later, the bedroom door creaked open.

"Ah!" Arthur said, "I see you've met my wife, Gladys!"

Lisa's world slowly went dark as fingers cinched her throat. She gasped, clutching to free herself, but the creature's arm refused to move. Plumes of fire blossomed in her chest, every heartbeat a desperate cry trapped in an inferno, the pressure building behind her eyes so tight and heavy they might burst. Darkness seeped beyond her vision and into her mind, its presence celebrated by a chorus of droning bells.

20

A young woman with glasses, green hair, and a nose ring walked Jerry to a table of computers at the back of the library. As he'd approached her, he'd braced himself for dismissal— just another boomer who couldn't keep up with the times—but to his surprise, the young lady smiled and offered to help. Now, as she navigated the web browser to the library's cataloging system, he felt ashamed of himself for passing judgment.

You really are an old man now, he heard Abby say. *Was it the green hair? Or the piercing? Did you forget about the earring you wore for a week before your father found out?*

"Here you go, sir. Any local records should come up in your search."

"Thank you," he said. "I admit, I expected one of those giant microfiche machines."

The librarian laughed, a soft chirping like a bird's morning call. "You're just a few years too late. The community association's last grant enabled us to digitize everything."

Jerry forced a smile. "That Arthur Peterson sure is charitable, huh?"

"He truly is. If there's anything else I can help you with..."

"You'll be the first to know."

"I'll hold you to it," she said, smiling.

Once Jerry was alone with the computer, he stared at the blinking cursor in the search bar, thoughts of Arthur clouding his mind. *Bastard sure does get around.* He wondered how much of this community support was actual goodwill and how much was for the association's benefit.

Fingers on the keys, Jerry slowly typed out his first search query: "FAIRVIEW WORMS."

Several results appeared. Most of them involved advertisements for the local bait and tackle shop; the rest were about types of worms in the greater Poconos region. He shook his head and returned to the search bar.

Another query: "FAIRVIEW ACRES."

Multiple results this time, mostly newspaper articles highlighting various sponsorships and charity drives. "Fairview Provides Fair View," read one article; another, "Peterson Persists in Face of Zoning Challenges," referring to Arthur's real estate company; "New Company Improves Local Economy," about all the good Arthur's company had done for Fairview; and "Top Ten Retirement Communities of the Poconos," in which Fairview was ranked number one.

Jerry cycled through several pages of results, skimming for anything that might stand out. To be honest, he wasn't sure what he was looking for, but he suspected he'd know it when he saw it. Something about worms, maybe, or possibly an article or op-ed to cast doubt on what's happening in Fairview Acres.

Article after article offered more praise for Arthur and his goddamned community association. The results ended with an article about Arthur and Gladys Peterson breaking ground on their new development. Its centerpiece was the photo he'd seen in Arthur's home, with the two of them grinning while holding shovels.

"Not a single bad word said about them," he muttered, rubbing the scruff on his chin. "Hard to believe."

He stared at the photo. Gladys beamed for the camera. The whole development had been her idea. What was it Arthur had said? A way of paying reverence to their "goddess."

His stomach cramped as if on command, and he winced from the sharp pain resonating through his abdomen. He thought of the squirming things reaching out for him from the holes in Stewart's face. Of the slender gray thing writhing around in his vomit. In his guts. Was their intention to infect him with some kind of parasite? And for what purpose?

To make me more amenable, *as he put it.*

Jerry looked at the photo again, hovered the mouse cursor over the search bar, and stopped. Other than this first article, everything had been about Arthur up to this point. Not even an obituary for Gladys Peterson.

"Huh."

He searched "GLADYS PETERSON OBITUARY" and frowned. Zero results. He tried other word combinations and met the same outcome. Gladys, like Arthur, was a cornerstone of the community. For someone so prominent to not have an obituary seemed unlikely. Even less likely considering Arthur was fond of erecting monuments everywhere—here at the library and the park. Hell, a case could be made that Fairview itself was a monument to Gladys Peterson. And yet no obituary to mark her death.

Either the record of her passing had been scrubbed from the database, or an obituary didn't exist. But Jerry couldn't reconcile that with everything else he knew.

What if she's still alive?

He thought of the robed figure he'd glimpsed that night at Arthur's house. Could that have been her? After what he'd witnessed at the realtor's office, the idea wasn't all that farfetched. The only person who had even mentioned her passing was Arthur, and he'd already proven himself to be shady.

And hadn't Arthur ignored his question about the figure that night? Smoothly, too. Like he'd anticipated the question.

Jerry sighed. A new piece of the puzzle, but one that didn't seem to fit anywhere.

You're sick with a parasite and you're grasping at shadows. Maybe you should've listened to Lisa and gone into the hospital after all. You are out of your depth, old man.

His phone vibrated in his pocket. Jerry sat up and winced from the sudden pain in his elbows. He checked his messages. An alert from his pharmacy about prescription refills, but nothing else from Lisa. He looked at the photo she'd sent earlier.

Fairview Acres being associated with the agency wasn't all that surprising—it was a retirement community, after all—but knowing Arthur was involved added to the growing knot of tension in his mind. Lisa's words echoed in his ears. *I still don't know who's caring for her when I'm not there.*

And something else Katherine had told him a while back: *My nurse will be here any minute. She doesn't like it when I take phone calls.*

Someone was visiting Katherine, and he was sure that this someone had been handpicked by Arthur. He thought of Katherine's reluctance to be candid when others were present, her suggestion that he leave while he still could. She'd tried to tell him something without coming right out and saying it—not to be cryptic or coy, but because she was afraid. Was she being threatened? Held hostage out in the open?

He looked at the image again. The sign stirred something in the back of his head. Something he'd forgotten on his way here when he was too caught up in his pain and terror. Something

(out of this world)

that linked everything together.

Celestial Comforts. Arthur's words from their dinner: *Gladys used to call it a conduit to the heavens.*

He chewed his lip and searched "FAIRVIEW+METE-ORITE." Zero results.

"Fuck." Jerry slammed the computer mouse down hard on the desk. The impact echoed throughout the library and vibrated up his arm. When he realized what he'd done, he looked up from the monitor. The few other patrons there were too engaged with their books to give him notice, but then he locked eyes with the librarian. She sat at her desk, staring in his direction, unsmiling. An icy shard of fear drilled into his gut. That look on her face reminded him too much of his neighbor, Gary.

He raised his hand, waved. The librarian blinked and smiled. She left her desk, and when she approached, he noticed her name tag for the first time. "I'm so sorry, Lydia. My frustration got the better of me. Won't happen again."

She nodded. "I appreciate that, sir. Is there anything I can do for you? You seem stressed."

"I hope so," he said. "I'm not having much luck in my search here. Does the library still have hard copies of local records, or is—"

"I'm so sorry, I forgot to mention the digitization is ongoing. We do have paper archives, yes, but they aren't available to the public."

"Oh, come on now. . ." He gave her a timid smile, hoping his frail grandpa appearance might sway her. "I'm just doing a little research for my granddaughter. She's doing a project on our town's history, you see. I'd hate to let her down. I'm sure you understand."

"I do," Lydia said, "but I'm afraid I don't make the rules, sir. I can give you the director's contact information if you'd like to make a special request. . ."

He waved her off. "No, that's quite all right. Can't blame a guy for trying, huh?"

"Couldn't find what you were looking for on Google? There's plenty of town history online—"

A bell rang from behind them, and they both turned to see an older woman standing at the front desk. Lydia gave him a sympathetic smile before hurrying back.

Google, he thought, watching her go. *You'd think Google would have what I'm looking for, unless—*

He peered at the small placard beside the terminal, where the instructions for using the Wi-Fi were printed. At the bottom was the same crescent moon logo with a computer mouse tethered to it, and the words "FairviewNet."

No wonder he couldn't find anything. It was likely all being filtered out through the ISP. Arthur was a most enterprising individual, after all, and what better way to stop others from digging up dirt than by removing all the shovels.

But he hadn't been connected to FairviewNet when he searched earlier that morning, parked in front of Lehigh Valley Hospital. What, then? He grasped for something logical, something that made sense. *Suppose what I'm looking for is so old, it's never been online...*

Frustrated, Jerry slowly climbed from his seat and made his way down the hall to the library's restroom—but he stopped short when he saw a flickering light from the corner of his eye. The fluorescent fixture at the end of hall was dying, blinking erratically, drawing his attention toward the door just below it.

He looked over his shoulder. Lydia's desk was obscured by several rows of bookshelves, and he could hear her talking to the elderly woman. His mind suddenly alight with an innocent sort of mischief he'd not felt in years, Jerry hurried to the door, cracked it open, and slipped into the room beyond.

◐

The makeshift filing room was lined with shelves and stacks of books. Morning light seeped through a single window and pierced the gloom. As his eyes adjusted to the dim light, he could make out a pair of tables off to the side, both filled with more books in need of sorting. Employment notices and posters adorned a far wall, below which stood a water cooler and a mini fridge. He shuffled past the rows of filing cabinets that divided the back room into an office. A desk drowning in paperwork sat in the corner, its computer monitor covered in sticky notes. Two copy machines sat on the right side of the room, adjacent to a hallway with a small placard above it that read "ARCHIVES."

Bingo.

Jerry hobbled down the short hall, which opened into a room of tall bookshelves filled with large folios. Dust and the smell of old paper tickled his nose. He flipped on the light and went to work.

Each folio, some of them containing multiple volumes, was labeled with a year, dating as far back as 1875. He followed the nineteenth century to the end of the row, then turned the corner into the twentieth, and found what he was looking for. Folio #1903, Volumes One and Two. *To commemorate when their goddess fell to the earth,* he thought.

His joints screamed as he pulled the first volume off the shelf. Doing so unseated a cloud of dust that irritated his nose and stirred a sneeze so deep he felt its force from his toes. He sucked in his breath afterward, terrified the noise might alert the librarian, but no one came. Relieved, he placed the folio on a small table at the back of the room.

Pages of newspaper clippings, legal notices, and business notices greeted him, their brown and brittle paper sheathed in protective plastic bags. Some headlines caught his eye— the premiere of *The Great Train Robbery,* the founding of the US Census Bureau—but he found nothing related to the fallen meteorite. Jerry wasn't discouraged. He retrieved the second volume, gasping as the ache in his bones flared up once more, and waited for his shaking hands to steady before carrying it back to the table.

Volume two gave up its secrets immediately:

SCIENTISTS TO STUDY BAILEY'S ROCK

Dr. Emmet P. Robinson, professor of geological studies, and Dr. Elliot M. Trask, professor emeritus of helminthology, will arrive from the state university on Wednesday to examine the strange rock formation on Harlan Bailey's cattle farm. Their arrival comes at the request of Mr. Bailey, whose cattle stock has suffered in recent weeks due to an unknown "worm" plague.

"I saw them," Bailey told the *Herald*. "Every evening after sunset, they crawl out of the rock. They've been feeding on my livestock, eating them from the inside out. Started just after that eclipse. They all just woke up."

Deputies were called to Bailey's farm earlier this month to investigate a series of cattle deaths which occurred overnight. They concluded the cattle mutilations were not committed by a nefarious party but were instead the result of an infestation of worm-like parasites which have thus far defied classification by local enthusiasts.

"Bailey's Rock," as locals have come to call it, has been the source of many rumors and legends over the years. Stories of queer lights at night and strange behavior by those in the vicinity of the rock have been reported as far back as the township's incorporation. The area was undeveloped until Mr. Bailey purchased the land two years ago.

Jerry read the article a second time. "Worm plague," he whispered. "No shit." He flipped through the pages until another article caught his eye. Half the page was torn, leaving only a short quotation:

> —binson reported to the *Herald*. "The results so far have been inconclusive, and I am returning to the university with samples for further study. What I can say, however, is the meteorite itself is quite old. The basin in which Mr. Bailey's farm sits is an impact crater from some time ago, easily ten thousand years or perhaps more, and bears some resemblance to other impact sites scattered across the Appalachian, Allegheny, and Poconos regions, most notably the one in Moon Hill, Pennsylvania. We believe them to be fragments from a much larger whole."
>
> When asked if the area surrounding Bailey's Rock is no longer safe, Dr. Robinson declined further comment.

He flipped ahead, and paused to read another article:

SEARCH CONTINUES FOR MISSING SCIENTIST

> County authorities continued their search for Dr. Elliot M. Trask on Monday. Efforts to locate the missing scientist were halted late last week due to inclement weather. Dr. Trask was last seen at the Bailey Farm one week ago, having elected to remain after his colleague, Dr. Emmet P. Robinson, returned to the state university for further study. Harlan

Bailey reported Dr. Trask missing when he failed to return that evening for supper.

"He was behaving in a queer manner," Bailey told the *Herald*. "I wished him a good day before setting out for my chores, and then he never came back. He was awfully pale. Looked ill, like he hadn't slept in days. All I can do is pray for his safe return. By the moon's eye."

He took out his phone and snapped photos of the three articles. His suspicions were correct. Everything led back to the meteorite in the park. He finally had something to corroborate his claims.

There was more to the article, but the paper had disintegrated over time and the print was no longer legible. Not that it mattered; Jerry had read enough, even though he wished he hadn't. There was comfort in believing this was all in his head, but with the hard facts staring back at him, he felt lost in a wasteland of pure reality.

He thought of Katherine, suffering the debilitating effects of dementia by day only to emerge rejuvenated at night. She'd been so alive, the opposite of a sundowner, her jubilant mood like

(Abby used to be)

a young woman without a care in the world. When they'd danced, he'd felt like a young man again, alive without worry for the future, no concern for his physical being, a spirit untouched and untested. Pure.

Was this sudden onset of youth in the evening a side effect of a parasitic infection? He wanted desperately to believe otherwise, but Katherine's warnings remained in his mind like a haunting spirit. All of his neighbors were so curious about what she'd said to him, too. Christ, were they *all* part of this? Was everyone in Fairview infected with worms?

They'd wanted him to drink Arthur's potion that night at the party, and like a nervous frat boy, he'd done it just to please them. He'd felt so great after drinking it, too. So great that he'd danced—

Oh shit. Kat!

Jerry sucked air as the world opened up and swallowed him. Trembling, he gripped his phone and dialed Lisa's number.

"Come on, pick up... please, pick up." One ring. Two. His heart slowly wedged itself into his throat. A tear of sweat dripped down his forehead and collected on the tip of his nose. He wiped it away. Four rings. Five.

Finally, she picked up. "Hi—"

"Lisa, it's Jerry. Don't go to your mom's. I've got proof now and—"

"—you've reached Lisa Dunnally. I'm not here right now..."

His heart sank back into the pit of his gut. He canceled the call, mustered his strength, and hobbled his way back toward the main library. The pain in his joints was exquisite, each movement another hot nail driven deeper into his bones, and the tightness in his belly grew loose, gurgling. Something twisted inside his abdomen, a wrenching pain so sudden he cried out, followed by an interminable itch at the back of his throat.

He pushed his way into the hall and nearly knocked the librarian off her feet.

"Oh my goodness." She steadied herself against the wall. "Sir, you aren't allowed back here. I could have you banned from the... hey, are you okay?"

Jerry's knees buckled as something rose from his gorge. He reached out for the wall to catch himself, but gravity held dominion, and he collapsed hard on the floor. From somewhere else, somewhere far away, he heard Lydia scream and shout something about an ambulance.

He wanted to tell her he was fine, he'd just remain here for a few minutes, maybe even take a nap—but when he opened his mouth, all he managed was a violent expulsion of vomit. His belly churned and knotted into itself, and that damned itch in his throat grew worse. He began to cough, spittle and bile spraying across the floor beside him, and a droning of bells filled his ears. Dark bursts of color slowly clouded his vision.

Jerry gagged. There was something in his mouth. He coughed hard and spat out a fleshy lump, long and thin, half-coiled like a snake or piece of yarn. Part of it was still in his mouth. As he lost consciousness, the grit of sandpaper dragged slowly across his lower lip.

21

Stars and darkness. A void of pinprick eyes seeing all, seeing through.
    Jerry drifted.
    Jerry was alone.
    Jerry was.
    A less corporeal being. The essence of a person. Soul. Anima. An isolated consciousness adrift in space and under the scrutiny of an unseen goddess.
    Jerry, the goddess said, *why do you resist us?*
    He had no lips, no voice with which to reply. No matter. The goddess saw through him and knew all.
    To taste our gift is to accept our gift. To refuse is to become a prisoner in your body. All you are will wither away until your mind is but dust. Accept us—
    "—vitals are stable—"
    —or dissolve—
    "—can you hear me—"
    —into nothing.

👁

"—hear me, sir?"

Jerry opened his eyes, squinted at the harsh light above. His mind was a slurry of ice, cold-started from a low-energy state, all the neurons firing in slow succession. There was someone with him, wherever this was, another disembodied voice demanding his failing attention.

"You had an episode, Mr. Campbell."

Another voice, female: "Blood pressure looks good."

"Sir, can you tell me your name?"

My name. My name...

He licked his lips. Dry parchment. Cracked, with a hint of something sour. Bile.

"Jerry," he said. "Campbell. Jerry Campbell. Where. . ." The world slowly lost its fuzziness, fell into focus. He was on his back. White room, white walls with strange instruments everywhere. "The hell am I?"

"Can you tell me your date of birth?"

Not strange instruments—medical equipment. But that didn't make sense. He'd been in the library doing research for his granddaughter. Wait, that didn't make sense either. He and Abby didn't have kids. No, that's just what he'd told the librarian, because he needed to see records, actual records, since all the good stuff was missing, and then—

"Oh God. *Lisa!*"

He tried to sit up, but a gloved hand slowly eased him back. The paramedic wore a blue face mask, but his eyes seemed to be smiling.

"Slow down, Mr. Campbell. Take it easy. You've had an episode."

"What. . . what do you mean? I—"

"You fainted, Mr. Campbell." The other paramedic this time. She had her hair tied back in a bun. "Can you tell us your birthday?"

"Jan-January twenty-first, 1950. Born on a Monday, christened on a Tuesday. . ."

The paramedics exchanged glances.

Jerry smiled. "Old nursery rhyme. But that's my birthday."

"Sit up for me," the male paramedic said. "You took a pretty big spill, so go slow. That's it, easy does it. Good."

Jerry winced as he put his feet on the floor. A bolt of pain shot up his spine. Everything hurt, most of all his knees and hip from the collapse. His throat, too. Every swallow felt charred, raw, and he remembered the sensation on his tongue. He shivered.

"I need to go," he said. "My friend, she needs me, she—"

The woman put a gloved hand upon his shoulder in reassurance. "One thing at a time, sir. You'll be able to go shortly, as soon as your caregiver arrives."

Jerry looked up at her, confused. "What? My caregiver?"

A series of heavy knocks stole their attention. The young man opened the ambulance door, and Jerry's heart sank. Arthur Peterson greeted the paramedic, and then put his hands on his hips like a scolding parent.

"Jerry Campbell, what did I tell you? You've got to be more careful with yourself!"

"No," Jerry whispered, looking to the paramedics for support. "No, he isn't... I don't have a caretaker, goddammit."

"Now, Jerry, there's no need for that kind of language. Let's get you out of there and take you home. Whaddya say?"

The paramedics took him by the arms and helped him to his feet. His head swam. Was this even happening? He was dreaming, still unconscious on the library floor, suffering this interminable nightmare while worms ate him from the inside. Had to be.

One step. Another. Arthur reached out to help Jerry down from the ambulance. "I know how confused you get sometimes, Jerry, but that's all right. We're going to take care of you, like we always do." And then, to the paramedics: "Thank you both. I'll take it from here."

"You got it, Mr. Peterson." The paramedic lowered his voice. "He's stable, but I'm not sure if he's aware of what happened. If his disposition changes…"

"Understood, young man. We'll take good care of him. By the moon's eye."

He gripped Jerry's arm so tight it hurt, one more pain in a symphony of agony, and Jerry tried to pull away. No good. Arthur wasn't about to let him go.

Arthur waited until the paramedics closed the door and started the engine before turning away. "Come along, Jerry. We need to have a talk."

"You've got some nerve," Jerry said. "I don't need a fucking caregiver, and I don't need—"

Arthur squeezed his arm. The pain was stark and blinding, a white-hot iron drilled into the bone, and Jerry gasped. "See, that's what I'm talking about. If you'd just been a good resident, you wouldn't be feeling this right now." He nudged Jerry forward. "Come on, let's take you home."

"I'm not going anywhere with you, Arthur." Jerry raised his voice, hopeful someone would hear and come to his aid, but a scan of the parking lot revealed they were alone. All the library's patrons were inside, insulated from this broad-daylight kidnapping. Jerry felt helpless; worse, he was scared. He swallowed back a hint of bile, grimaced. "I don't understand why you're doing this. Just let me go."

"Believe me, Jerry, I really want to. But I also can't let an initiate like yourself run wild without taking more of the potion. It would be irresponsible of me."

Potion. Initiate. The words swirled in Jerry's head. *Amenable.*

Arthur led him around the side of a pickup truck, opened the door. "Go on, get in."

Defeated and weak, Jerry did as he was told.

◉

"I suppose this is all my fault. I misjudged you, thought you'd welcome our goddess's gift. Normally we wait a little while before sharing the potion with newcomers, but you just seemed. . ." Arthur drummed his fingers across the steering wheel, thinking. "Lost. Like you needed others in your life. Like you needed a *purpose*."

Jerry watched the library grow smaller in the side view mirror. "You don't know anything about me."

"Well, now, that's not true. We vet all of our residents. Remember your application to join the community?" Arthur held out his hand, counted off one finger at a time. "You retired after your wife passed away. No kids. No friends. No hobbies. Prone to anxiety, depression, gout, arthritis." He held out his thumb. "That just leaves you, buckaroo. With a whole lot of nothing in your life. See, I don't believe you're naturally antisocial. I think you just need the right environment to really come out of your shell."

"So, drugging me was the solution?"

"What? No. Goddess, no." Arthur scoffed, but with a smile. "It's. . . look, it's complicated, okay? We didn't expect Katherine to. . . *rebel* the way she did. She'd been doing so well, like all the other residents in fact, but when you showed up, well. . ."

"She tried to warn me about you, about the whole damn development. Tell me the truth. Katherine died that night, didn't she?"

Arthur sighed, measured his words. "In a manner of speaking—but that's the power the goddess provides. And that's all we tried to give you, man. A way of ending your aging, of giving you back the strength of your youth. Something to fill that void in your life."

"By infecting me with a parasite."

"Semantics," Arthur said. "We call it symbiosis with a celestial emissary. She came from the stars, and we give ourselves willingly to her as vessels in exchange for her cosmic gift. It's a win-win, here. Or it would be if you would've just kept drinking the potion."

Jerry's gut churned at the thought of the gray frothy liquid he'd imbibed that night. There had been all those crunchy bits in the mixture, something that tasted of blood and dirt. "That how it works, huh? You grind up those worms and drink 'em?"

Arthur shrugged. "Trust me, mixing it with booze is better than the way we used to do it. That feeling of something crawling in your skull is like an itch you can't scratch, man, and it *never* goes away. But that's beside the point. How you're feeling now, like you're aging faster, all those aches and pains getting worse—it's in withdrawal. The emissary, I mean, and your body is too, by proxy. They wake up when they're hungry, start leeching on you from the inside, and it's always worse at night."

"So the potion—"

"Keeps them satiated. They like to feed on themselves. Keeps 'em happy. A scientist buddy of mine from a long time ago called it a 'autosarcophagic ouroboros.' Mouthful, isn't it?"

Arthur slowed the truck at a stop sign, let his words resonate in the silence between them while a car crossed the lane ahead. Jerry leaned his head against the window and closed his eyes, relished the brief silence.

It's always worse at night. He thought of Katherine again. *Sundowning. Bless her.*

Even now, as the pieces fell into place, he had trouble focusing on the singular thread linking them all together. The pain was too much, little slices of light piercing his skull with every movement, every breath. He thought of Abby, tried to conjure her reassuring voice to ease him into a sleeping oblivion free of pain, but all he found waiting for him in the dark was an unrelenting itch on the inside. A crawling sensation around his bones. He imagined his skeleton covered in those leech-like things, every bone wrapped in gray tissue like cancer, only this cancer was sentient. Worse, it was hungry.

"Hey, hey, stay with me, man. We're not done."

Jerry snapped his eyes open and tried to consolidate what little strength he had left. Ten years ago—hell, ten days ago—he might've opened the door and rolled out of the truck despite the costs. A dislocated shoulder, maybe a broken hip, but at least then he'd be free of this man he'd grown to despise.

He lifted his hand, and a searing pain shot from his wrist to his shoulder, one so sudden he gasped in shock.

Arthur glanced over, nodded. "The goddess gives, and the goddess takes away. Taste the gift and refuse, you get this. First your body, then your mind. Trust me, I've seen it happen, and it ain't pretty."

"The dementia..." Jerry stopped at the sound of his voice. Weak. Forced air through brittle pipes. *Just like Abby's. God, no.* He grunted, braced a hand against his stomach, and waited for another spike of pain to rip through him.

"An unfortunate side effect, I'm afraid, but far worse if you don't take the potion regularly. Katherine's late husband fell victim to it. Hell, we almost lost Katherine, too, but the emissaries were still active when we got to her, thank the goddess. You really did save her life."

Silence fell over them again, and Jerry returned his attention to the window and the passing landscape. Fairview Acres wasn't far now. He hoped Lisa had heard the brief message he'd left for her, that she was smart enough to stay away and hadn't just dismissed him outright as a lunatic.

Maybe you are, old man.

"Anyway... all of this to say, you should really, *really* reconsider the potion, Jerry."

"It's not much of a choice, is it?"

"Come on, now. Why's it gotta be like that? You're so focused on the negatives all the time. Think about the positives! It'll be good for you in the long run, man. You'll be in good company. Parties every night. I hear Katherine even has a thing for you, so it's not like you'll be alone. Me and Gladys, you and Katherine..." Arthur stuck out his elbow as if to poke Jerry in the ribs. "Double date? What do you say?"

Jerry forced a quiet laugh.

Arthur's face lit up with a huge grin. "That's what I like to hear, my man. Music for the soul, Gladys always says."

"You... you told me Gladys is dead. A couple years now."

Arthur's smile slowly faded.

"And I bet you are, too. Dead. Just like Katherine. All of you are dead. Nothing but... worm food." A hearty laugh escaped his dry lips, one so deep and heavy it filled the cabin like a roar, and though his body cried out in pain, he hadn't felt so alive in days. "And when the rest of the world finds out—"

"The rest of the world? Oh dear." Arthur shook his head, flipped on the turn signal, and pulled into the community entrance. "Is that why you were at the library digging up all those old records? To 'expose' us to the world? Goddess, your withdrawal really has gone to your head, hasn't it?"

"Why else would you hide records, if you didn't want to be exposed? Or filter out everything through your internet service?" Jerry's words were coated in venom. "And then there's the real estate office, Katherine's caregiver..."

Arthur offered a slow clap. "Well done. I applaud your efforts. But you left out the land developer."

Jerry's focus sharpened as the gravity of Arthur's words bore down on him. "*You* made the offer on my old place?"

"The moment I saw your application, I knew we had to have you. You looked lost even on paper before the background check came back. But Stewart's office? Celestial Comforts? Just facets of our business, man. You're welcome to be a stakeholder in the association if you want. You used to be a finance guy, right? We have need of someone with your expertise, if you're interested, but we can talk about all that later. Let's get you home. I need to see how Lisa is doing."

"What about Lisa?"

Arthur guided the truck along the neighborhood's outer rim before turning down Jerry's street. "Well, that's a tricky situation. Not quite as tricky as yours, but similar. She showed up at Celestial Comforts earlier this morning, made a huge fuss, and... Well, let's just say I have to make a tough decision now. Not looking forward to it, but that's life sometimes. Anyway... looks like your neighbors are here to welcome you home. Hey, the Getty folks are moving in! Old *and* new neighbors!"

He slowed the truck and waved to an elderly couple standing in their yard. A box truck was parked in the driveway, and a trio of movers struggled to ease a giant sofa onto the sidewalk. The house next door had finally sold. Jerry wanted to call out to them, warn them, but the strength simply wasn't there.

Arthur pulled into Jerry's driveway. Gary Olson stood on the porch alongside Bradley and Matilda Scott. Bethany Miles stood in the yard, a plastic baggie on her hand, while Queenie nosed in the grass for a place to squat.

"Why are they here?"

Arthur smiled. "To make sure you don't try to interfere. All of this is important to us, Jerry. And I get it, it's a lot to swallow, but please think about it. Just... not too long, okay? We're having a special get-together in the park for the eclipse tomorrow night, and I'd love for you to be there."

He lowered the window, waved Gary, Bradley, and Matilda over to the truck.

Jerry said, "After all of this, you really think we can be friends? Or even good neighbors? Like I'll forget everything, and suddenly we're happy and tossing back drinks together? You're crazier than I thought."

Arthur closed his eyes and sighed. "I just don't get it, Jerry. We offer you a community, new friends, a new start. Practically a new life. It's safe here. We've taken all these measures to make sure of that. All that we ask in return is submission to the goddess and her emissaries. That's all. And you're spitting it back in my face."

"Believe me, I would if I had the spit."

"See, that's what I mean. I really thought you were better than that. But I'm not giving up." Arthur reached down to the floorboard and produced a plastic shopping bag. "I even got this for you. A little gift from a friend."

Jerry eyed the bag but didn't move. Everything hurt. Arthur pulled a T-shirt out of the bag. White fabric and bold, black lettering: "PROUD MEMBER OF THE FAIRVIEW ACRES COMMUNITY ASSOCIATION." Below the text was the community logo.

"You're a real fuckin' comedian, Arthur."

"I think you'll come around. I really do. Now get some rest, okay? See you soon."

Jerry sucked in his breath and heard a strange rattle in his lungs. He'd grown accustomed to listening to his body like a mechanic listening to an engine, and this was a new noise. A cold fist tightened around his abdomen, squeezed. How soon before the dementia set in? Not long, he figured. Helping Lisa and Katherine was out of the question now. He couldn't even help himself.

This was all his fault. If he hadn't called Lisa this morning, if he'd only kept his mouth shut, she wouldn't be in this predicament.

Arthur's words replayed in his head: *I have a tough decision to make now.*

As his neighbors appeared at his side of the truck, Jerry realized Arthur wasn't alone in that regard.

22

They led him inside, an inmate being marched to his cell, two escorts in front and one behind. Jerry wasn't surprised to see Gary had a key to the front door. Of course he did. Arthur probably did, too.

"Such a lovely home," Matilda said, fluttering about the room like a moth.

Jerry resisted the urge to tell her to get out. He would've, if this were still his house, but now the writing was on the wall: this was never his house. The Goddess of Fairview Acres owned this place. Always had, always would.

Matilda stepped into the kitchen, opened the cabinets and then the refrigerator, taking an inventory of their contents. "Is there anything you need at the moment, Jerry?"

For you to get the fuck out of here, he wanted to say. He chose to say nothing instead.

Bradley nudged him. "Best answer her, Jerry. Don't make this more unpleasant than it has to be."

"I don't need anything," Jerry said.

"Not true." Gary removed his straw hat and took a seat at the kitchen table. "Arthur says you need more of the potion."

"Not what I meant, Gary." Matilda walked back into the living room and patted Gary on the shoulder. "But Bradley's right. Things really don't have to be this way." And then, to her husband: "Stop treating him like a prisoner. Look at him, for Goddess's sake. He can barely stand up."

Jerry showed no emotion, gratitude being the last thing he wanted to extend them, but secretly he was relieved to get off his feet.

Matilda led him to the sofa, and he resumed his careful pose on the cushions to achieve as much comfort as he could. His condition had worsened significantly since yesterday, and the aches which had once been isolated in his joints were everywhere now, his whole body a screaming wound. How long since he'd consumed the drink? At least a month, but the pain made his head fuzzy, every thought an effort.

Matilda knelt beside him. "Want some water, Jer?"

"Please," he rasped, leaning his head back against a cushion.

She looked to her husband. "I saw some bottles of water in the fridge. Would you?"

Jerry watched a silent conversation pass between Bradley and Matilda, told in expressions. It was the sort of language only a married couple would understand, the hidden gestures of careful social maneuvering, a wink here, an arched eyebrow there, the slightest hint of movement in the corners of the mouth. He and Abby had their own coded language, a necessity for his social anxieties, and seeing the similarities on display warmed his heart, if only for a moment.

Bradley rolled his eyes and left the living room in a huff.

"Was this Mrs. Campbell?" Matilda got up to take a closer look at his and Abby's twenty-fifth anniversary portrait. "My, look at that dress... She was a looker, Jerry. Very classy."

He tried to muster enough strength to raise his middle finger. No good.

Bradley returned with an open bottle of water, tilted it back so Jerry could take a few sips. "You wouldn't have this problem if you'd just take more of the potion. One cup and you'll be as good as new in the morning. Not even that long, really. Just a few hours."

Matilda slid her hand within Jerry's, and alarms went off inside his head. *Cold, so cold, she's dead, all of them dead, stop touching me, stop—*

"He's right, Jerry. It's. . . honestly, it's the miracle cure to end all miracle cures. We were both in a bad way when we moved here, me with diabetes and Brad with a bad heart."

"Three quadruple bypass surgeries in as many years. Doctors had no idea how I was still alive. And then. . ." He looked to his wife and smiled. "Then Arthur and Gladys introduced us to the goddess. We opened our souls to her, and she healed our bodies in return."

"I just turned ninety-four," Matilda said. "And Brad will be ninety-one in December."

Gary stood up from the table, crossed his arms. "One hundred and six here. We are all of us blessed."

They smiled proudly at one another, a gesture of solidarity that they'd all beaten the system somehow under the guise of divine intervention. Jerry stared in awe. Not of their happiness or age, but of their pride in playing host to a cosmic parasite. Their "goddess" was a trick of nerve signals and puppetry, a pluck of the strings by the worms growing within, these tiny creatures with such intimate knowledge of our inner workings they knew how to placate us; worse, how to make us believe their consumption was of divine right.

It's the human way, he thought. *Clinging to something so we feel less alone.*

Jerry shivered, his body quaking so terribly that Matilda gasped, lifted a crumpled blanket from her side of the sofa, and draped it over him. "Please," she said, "now is not the time to be stubborn about this. If you don't drink more of the potion, the emissary is going to kill you, and it won't be pretty."

"She's right," Gary said, jingling his keys in his hand. He crossed the living room toward the front door. "You don't want to end up like Reggie Dunnally. Poor guy had so many holes in his brain by the end. Horrible way to go."

Dunnally. Jerry closed his eyes. *Katherine and Lisa. . . how am I going to help them when I'm in a state like this?*

Gary opened the front door and gestured to Matilda. "Go on, give it to him."

Jerry watched as Matilda produced a jar of gray fluid with a thick frothy head. Particles floated in the mixture. She set the jar on the coffee table in front of him, and the contents within churned and swirled, the shapes like clouds in a hurricane, disintegrating and reforming in a never-ending chaos. It reminded him of the jar of tadpoles he'd collected from the creek near his home when he was a boy. That jar had sat on his dresser, full to the brim with murky liquid dark as chocolate milk. Sometimes tadpoles would swim to the glass.

A jar full of bubble tea, he thought, staring at the drink.

"Not that you're in any state to do so, but. . ." Gary gestured to his house across the street. "Don't try to leave. We're all watching you, Jerry. Take our advice, drink the potion. I promise you'll thank us for it."

"Please," Matilda said. "It's really for the best. For all of us. For a stronger you and a stronger Fairview."

Jerry mustered a smile. "That's good. How long did you rehearse that line?"

Matilda scoffed, her cheeks blossoming deep red, and stormed out of the house. Bradley scowled, followed after her.

Gary was the last to go, but he stopped short of the entrance and placed his straw hat back on his balding dome.

"You know, that wasn't very nice, Jerry."

"Go fuck off to your garden, Gary."

He did.

When Jerry was finally alone in the house that was now his prison, he forced himself upright on the sofa and glared at the jar placed before him. *So much trouble in such a tiny container,* he thought. Hadn't his grandpa said something similar about the radioactive isotope in the A-bomb? Maybe, but his memory was hazy, certain nodes of his brain flickering off and on like dying bulbs, shorting out when he needed them most. The worms at work, eating him alive from inside out.

They want more of themselves, to be more them *so I can be less* me.

Something bubbled up inside the jar. A thin dark shape brushed the side of the glass for an instant, there and gone again, swallowed up by the murky liquid.

As if on cue, a blade of pain sliced through his chest so sharp it stole his breath. In the aftermath, he listened to his racing heart. Arrhythmic, struggling to keep in time.

Can it sense its brothers and sisters are close?

Another pain, this time in his gut, not as heavy as the last but still powerful enough to carve through his thoughts.

When a semblance of clarity returned, he thought of how Katherine went as long as she could, until she couldn't stand the agony any longer and came up for air at the last possible moment. No wonder they had someone watching over her during the day. She was likely enjoying the side effects of her infestation—but he struggled to accept that this was by choice. *No, she's been fighting them for a while.*

Something sloshed in the jar, but when he focused on the glass, all he saw was the same cloudy murk. *It knows I'm here.* Was it mocking him?

Because it knows this isn't a real choice at all, Abby whispered. *And you know it too, old man. You know what needs to be done.*

He blinked away tears, welcomed them on his cheeks.

Means you're still alive, that you're still you. Question is, how long can you hang on to yourself before they start pulling your strings?

Jerry reached forward, gripped the jar in his hand. To the empty room, he said weakly, "Long enough."

23

I can't believe they stuck me in the goddamn basement.
Lisa lay on her side with her hands bound behind her back. Layers of silver duct tape held her ankles together. Her head swam and her guts lurched. The act of breathing felt like inhaling smoke. When she tried to move, bright splotches of light burst before her in a kaleidoscopic pattern, dazzling sparkles, the ever-changing color of agony. For a span of seconds, she was nothing more than a raw mind exposed to sensation, a slave to her nerves and synapses, trapped inside a wounded vessel.

Footsteps overhead. Creaking boards. Thin rails of dust fell from the ceiling, caught in the sickly yellow light of a single bare bulb. Shadows clung to stacks of boxes, storage totes, and her father's dusty tools. A low hiss gave her a start. Lisa slowly turned her head and saw the source: the water heater, refilling its tank.

She tried piecing together what came before: *Gladys Peterson*—her face full of holes and worms. Lisa's skin prickled with gooseflesh as a chill crawled down her back.

"Are you awake over there, baby girl?" A figure shuffled into view from around a stack of boxes.

She'd recognize her mother's silhouette anywhere, but her voice was different—stronger. More alive. Her mother drew closer, no longer walking with that slight hunch or with arms held out ready to catch herself if she fell. There was a shimmer to her hair and a light in her eyes.

Lisa looked up at her mother's smiling face with a mixture of awe and terror. She spoke with a throat full of gravel. "Mama?"

"How's that head of yours, honey? You hit it on the nightstand when you passed out."

Lisa blinked back tears, tried to be brave, but there was no use. Her head hurt like a motherfucker. "Not great, Mom." The irritation in her throat spurred her to cough. Fire and razorblades. "Throat's not any better."

"I imagine not." Her mother pushed aside a stack of boxes labeled "Christmas" and retrieved a metal folding chair. She took a seat in front of her daughter. "Gladys got you pretty good. There are bruises on your neck, and you've got a nice goose egg from the fall."

Lisa slowly pulled herself upright, leaned back against the wall. "I'd feel a lot better if I wasn't tied up."

"I know, baby. I know. We need to talk about that." More footsteps overhead. Muffled voices. Her mother looked up, and then back at Lisa. God, she was trembling. "But before I tell you anything, I need you to promise not to be mad."

Lisa wanted to scream, *Mad? I'm fucking furious, Mother.* But that wouldn't solve anything. She merely smiled, nodded for her mother to go on.

"Arthur and the others here in Fairview. . . well, I got to know them better. Your father never wanted much to do with them, but after he passed—"

"You made new friends."

"Yes, and I wish I hadn't. I gave everyone a second chance,

and. . . how can I put this? I met their goddess, and she gave me a gift."

Lisa stared at her, recalling the rank liquid in the French press. Cloudy, a frothy head, just like what Jerry had described to her. A yawning pit opened in her stomach. Hands of regret reached up, tried to pull her down inside herself. She felt so foolish dismissing everything Jerry had told her as the ramblings of another dementia patient. And if Jerry was right, what about her father?

She said, "It's not dementia."

"Not exactly, honey. It just looks like dementia if I don't drink enough of the potion."

"So, Daddy, he. . ." The tears surged, and this time she let them free. All those times he had pleaded with her to take him away from Fairview, he had been in his right mind after all. *Poisoning me,* he'd told her, and the weight of this realization was a sucker punch.

Her mother reached out and wiped the tears from Lisa's cheek. "I know. I didn't understand it either. Not at the time."

"Why did you do it, Mom? Why drink that awful shit?"

She sighed. "I didn't know what was in it until it was too late. One cup, that's all it took. I didn't realize I'd have to keep taking it, and I avoided it as much as I could, but that's why the symptoms started. . ."

Lisa clenched her teeth, forced words through them, every breath like broken glass in her throat. "You tried to warn Jerry. And then you. . . you had a seizure. He said you died on his porch."

"But the important thing is the goddess wouldn't let me go. And I'm grateful for that, I really am, because now I can think clearly again." She wiped away tears of her own. "The drink keeps me stable during the day, and at night, I feel like myself again. I feel young, I have energy, I can dance every night if I want—"

(legs covered in grass and dirt)

"—but the cost, Lisa. Goddammit, *the cost.* I tried to go without it, I really did. This last time, though, they sent Arthur's bitch to make sure I take it. Wouldn't let me check on Jerry or call you. Gary told me I talk too much..."

"All your episodes," Lisa said, more to herself than her mother. "Every time you got better for a while, only to get really bad again. Just like Dad..."

"Every day I risk slipping back into that awful fog, forgetting your face, forgetting myself. And if I keep taking their 'miracle drug' long enough..."

All the missing pieces came together in Lisa's head: the canceled caregiver, no record of her mother's intake by the EMT, everything tied back to the Fairview Acres Community Association—and the Petersons. *They killed my daddy,* she realized. *And they're killing my mama.*

"They've been watching me ever since I tried to warn Jerry," her mother said. "And when you showed up this morning, you really threw everyone for a loop. We weren't expecting you until this afternoon, and I guess you'd upset Arthur at the agency, so when you arrived..." Katherine gestured to Lisa's bindings. "Here we are. Now they have to figure out what to do with you."

"What to *do* with me?"

"They go to great lengths to make sure no outsiders know about the potion. Arthur's got his hands in a lot of pockets..."

"It's the fucking elderly mafia." Lisa struggled against her restraints, tried to pull her legs free, but they wouldn't budge. Empty cardboard rolls laid on the floor nearby. They had used every inch of duct tape on her. "Were you even going to tell me what happened to you?"

Katherine looked away. "Well... no. Fairview promised they would take care of everything. A car accident, I think. They were going to tell you I wandered into traffic. A closed casket funeral. I'd move into a different house, take on another name, and..."

"And never see or speak to me again. Unbelievable."

"That's not— You promised you wouldn't get mad."

"Do you have any idea how fucking worried I've been about you? How much I've sacrificed just to be there for you? And then you hide all this from me. Do you even understand how selfish this is? *Fuck.*"

She wanted to tear herself free of the restraints in a fit of rage and go find Arthur Peterson. Maybe even that thing he called a wife. *And do what? You should be worried about what he's going to do to you. What that* thing *will do to you.*

"Honey, please try to stay calm. I don't want them to hear you." Her mother's voice was barely there, a hushed whisper in the vast basement.

Lisa raised her gaze to the ceiling. *Them.* "Is it Arthur?" Lisa raised her voice to a sharp growl: *"Tell that motherf—"*

Her mother clapped a hand over Lisa's mouth. Her skin was cold, clammy. "He's here, and so is Gladys. They're pissed about you showing up here. They want to give you to the goddess tomorrow night during the eclipse."

Lisa pulled away from her mother's hand, studied her face. "Give me. . . what? Are you hearing yourself right now?"

"Sacrifice you," Katherine hissed, wide-eyed with fear. "They want to *kill* you, Lisa. They might kill *both* of us."

The words sank in slowly, their severity driven home by the look on her mother's face. She couldn't remember the last time she'd seen her mother so afraid. Not even when her dad passed away. Not like this.

Lisa wanted to reach out and embrace her, but the impulse was soured by what she'd been told. Her mother had kept all this from her, had even been willing to fake her own death and cut off contact. She hadn't even cut Lisa free of her restraints.

"What do *you* want?"

Her mother frowned, and Lisa glimpsed the woman she'd known all her life. The real Katherine, tired and battle-weary from the stress of modern life but eager for a reason to smile, the dancer who'd lulled their ailing father to a calmer state. Was she still in there, that version of her mom? Lisa wanted to think so. *Hoped* so.

"Lisa, I didn't ask for this. Believe me, honey, if there were any other way, I would—"

"I would rather have you forget me, Mom, than watch you just give up like this."

Her mother flinched from the bite of Lisa's words, and a deep sadness slipped over her face. Lisa immediately regretted it. They hadn't always seen eye to eye, especially since her father had died so horribly, and all the awful things she'd said to her mother came crawling out of the memory sludge where she'd buried them.

You never listen to me,
you're the reason I don't have a life,
Dad deserved better,
you're incapable,
you can't,
you won't,
I can't,
I won't—

Lose you too. If only she could muster those words now, when they mattered. How long since she'd told her mother she loved her? How long since she'd meant it?

The slats overhead creaked as footsteps crossed the room. A moment later, three knocks sounded at the top of the basement steps. The door creaked open.

"Kat? Everything going okay?"

The blood in Lisa's veins chilled to ice, and she listened to her racing heartbeat. Her mother held up her finger to silence her. She twisted in her seat and called back toward the stairs, "Everything is fine, Arthur, but she's not all with us yet. She hit her head pretty hard, you know."

"Perhaps Gladys can—"

"No, I think she just needs rest. I'll be up in a moment."
"All right then..."

The basement door closed.

Lisa slowly exhaled. She stared hard at her mother. "Aren't you going to cut me free?"

"I have to go." She kissed Lisa's forehead and whispered, "Keep quiet for me. We'll figure this out. Promise."

"Mom?" Lisa struggled to pull her hands free, but the duct tape held firm. *"Are you fucking kidding me right now?"*

Lisa watched her mother go, waited until the basement door opened and closed before freeing the panicked horror built up inside her. She wanted to scream until her lungs fried, but all she could manage was a pitiful whimper.

◉

Katherine thought of Reggie's words the day he received his diagnosis. *We'll figure this out.*

He'd smiled through the appointment even as the neurologist outlined a road map of the rest of his life. Afterward, he'd joked that she was more upset about it than he was, which might have been true at one point. But she knew her husband, and she knew he was putting on an act so she wouldn't worry. He'd thrown his arm around her on their way back to the car, kissed her cheek and said, "Don't worry, Kat. We'll figure this out. What do you want for dinner?"

He drove her to their favorite Italian restaurant. She even remembered their meals: chicken parmesan for him, a Caesar salad for her, because she had no appetite after his appointment. Other details: the horrendous music playing in the restaurant, too upbeat and poppy to suit her mood; the damned waiter returning every few minutes, just when she'd worked up the courage to address the elephant in the room; the way the woman at the next table scraped her fork tines across her plate; and how Katherine wanted nothing more than to scream until her lungs were dust.

While Reggie enjoyed his meal, she'd pushed lettuce around her salad bowl and made a frantic list in her head. *Update our will, call Beckett's office and sort out power of attorney, talk to Lisa about our options for in-home care—oh God, how do I tell Lisa?*

"Easy," Katherine muttered, her voice a hushed phantom in the lonely hallway. "Just lie and tell her we'll figure this out."

She felt stupid for thinking their conversation could have gone any other way. Lisa was Reggie's daughter through and through, headstrong to a fault, always refusing to admit defeat. Nothing like Katherine, who had let herself accept her fate without so much as an argument.

Reggie spoke up in her head. *You knew there was something in that drink, and still you drank it when Arthur offered it to you. For what, Kat? To belong? To fit in? I tried everything I could to warn you, told you every day to pack up and leave, but when the time came...*

Another memory from the same day: Stopping alongside the highway on their way back to Fairview. Reggie had forgotten the way, had panicked when he couldn't recognize their surroundings. Then the slow crawl of minutes as she held him, shaking and sobbing, *The way's just not there. Where did it go? Why can't I see it anymore?*

She'd lost her way in his absence, been duped by a master manipulator, and that misstep had cost her life, her faculties, her daughter.

Katherine's emotions overtook her. She sank to the floor, hugging herself as deep, earthshaking sobs racked her body, and she bit down on her fist to stifle the noise. She didn't want them to know she was crying. She didn't want Lisa to hear, either.

Reggie had worn a brave face as long as he could, until it grew so bad he couldn't stand on his own anymore. Every day, he forgot who he was, who she was; and every night he begged for her to take him away from this place. She'd been strong then, or considered herself to have been; now she wasn't so sure. Maybe her focus was merely a redirection of anxious energy, a way to channel her fear into something productive. She could read the writing on the wall better than anyone, but why spell it out when the bed sheets needed to be changed, his bedpan needed emptying, his pills counted and divided by the day.

So what if Arthur came by to visit one day—a neighbor wanting to pay his respects. Sure, Reggie didn't care much for the man, but Arthur had seemed nice enough, and she thought her husband could benefit from a visitor or two. Anything to brighten his spirits, which grew considerably darker with each day.

Katherine lifted the hem of her shirt and wiped her face. Fragments of that visit flashed before her with harsh clarity.

The guttural scream erupting from Reggie's mouth.

Her panic as she ran upstairs to the bedroom.

Arthur's face contorted in a portrait of rage.

Pieces of the shattered jar on the floor, and the thick trails of gray foam leaking down the bedroom wall.

The rest was a blur: Arthur mumbling something about trying to help as he escaped from the room, Reggie's groans and the tears slipping down his cheeks, and the overripe sludge staining their floor. She hadn't understood then, and she wouldn't until long after Reggie was gone.

Arthur called out from the kitchen. "Everything okay?"

She wiped her eyes once more, shot to her feet. "I'm coming," she said.

Gladys stood at the kitchen counter, waiting.

"Okay, Kat," Arthur began. "What did she—"

"My daughter is out of the question," she said flatly. "Leave her alone."

A dry croak of air escaped the holes in Gladys's face. Arthur put his hand on his wife's shoulder. "Now, now, honey. She's just protecting her child. You'd do the same." To Katherine, he said, "I can appreciate your position—mama bear, and all that—but you know the rules here. No outsiders. It's too risky."

Katherine shook her head. "You can't punish her like this."

"Please, Kat, don't phrase it like that. This isn't punishment. It's..." He shrugged. "It's ordinance. From the goddess Herself."

Fuck your goddess.

The words were on the tip of her tongue, targeted and ready to fire, but a whisper from the back of her mind held them at bay. *Play along. Buy yourself some time. They need to trust you.*

"What if... what if I can convince her to drink the potion?"

Arthur glanced to his wife, but Gladys remained silent and still. A plump worm inched its way out of her nasal cavity and plopped onto the floor below.

"I suppose that would change things," he said. "I'm sure the community would have need of another nurse. What do you think, love?"

A crackling hiss erupted from Gladys's maw, filling the room with the stench of rotting fruit. Arthur seemed not to notice. Katherine swallowed back the rise in her gorge.

"We'll think it over," he said. "Now, would you mind checking on our dear friend Mr. Campbell? Make sure he doesn't get himself into more trouble. I would go myself, but I've got a celebration to plan. Tomorrow's a big day."

He didn't wait for her to answer. She watched as his golem of a wife escorted him outside. On his way out the kitchen door, Arthur turned and said, "Remember what I told you, Kat. Step out of line, and I'll have no choice but to cut you loose. I don't have to explain what that means, do I?"

She said nothing, just held his stare until he finally turned away again.

When she was finally alone, Katherine braced herself against the kitchen sink and stared out the window with glassy eyes. *I won't let them hurt you, Lisa. I'll make this up to you somehow. We'll figure it out.*

Outside, dark clouds brewed on the horizon, burying the late afternoon sun in an early grave.

24

Jerry staggered through his bedroom and into the bathroom, collapsed on the floor beside the toilet, and tried to expel the coagulated drink from his belly. His stomach churned in waves, a motion that awakened the muscles in his abdomen and set them screaming through his weakened frame. He retched once, twice, and nothing came up but a few drops of spittle. What he'd consumed was there to stay.

Stop fighting it, old man. That's what makes it worse.

But he couldn't help himself. His every natural impulse was to resist the ingestion of this foreign matter, and with every involuntary flex of muscle and spray of bile at the back of his throat, he prayed he might undo this mistake. What the hell had he been thinking, drinking this awful shit again? To regain his strength just enough to fight back against his captors?

No, his body told him, that had been a bad idea. A massively *stupid* idea. Only Jerry Campbell would be dumb enough to think he could fight fire with fire, worms with worms. He'd witnessed what the potion had done to the others, how it had changed them. Now Lisa was in danger because he'd dragged her into this conspiracy, Katherine was probably lost forever, and he was about to join her.

He stuck two fingers down his throat to trigger his gag reflex. Nothing. Not even his breakfast.

Exhausted, he slumped away from the toilet and braced himself against the bathtub. He listened to his heart, the rattle in his lungs, and lay helpless as the pain resonated through his body, through his skin and deep into his bones.

What if it's too late? Maybe I'm too far gone and this potion isn't going to do a damn thing and I'm suffering for nothing. So long, Jerry Campbell, husband of Abigail, killer of worms and conspirator of suburbia. We hardly knew you. Hell, you hardly knew yourself.

The truth in that last sentiment hurt him the most. It was the cold, stark reality of his life that he was less himself without someone else. So little of him remained that he was hardly a whole person without his mate, something he hadn't truly understood until he'd met Abby. The comfort of her presence had brought him out of his shell to experience the world, but without her shadow to stand in, he withered under the sun.

Death had always been something he feared, although maybe it wasn't so much death as it was being alone. Dying was just the action that brought about this change of states, and so he feared it by proxy, a cloud hanging over every moment of every day he spent with Abby at his side. Lying there on the cold tile of the bathroom floor, listening to muffled gurgling of something otherworldly rooting around his gut, Jerry realized how selfish he had been to fear Abby's death.

Losing her had meant he'd have to stand alone. She'd given him purpose, a means of being, a role to play as her husband and not as a blank person.

Who am I without you?

He'd spent every moment of their marriage terrified she would be the one to die first. Not only because it would break his heart, but because her death meant resetting himself back to zero. Starting over with a new life. Waking up to an empty bed. Coming home to an empty house. Staring at himself in the mirror every morning and every night, trying to remember how to talk to people, how to smile, how to exist in a social environment. Jerry hadn't merely stood in her shadow; he *was* her shadow. Her passing had freed the sun to erase his definition.

Now, facing the possibility of his own death, Jerry welcomed the release. Maybe he would see her again, maybe he wouldn't. Maybe there was only the bliss of nothingness waiting for him beyond the mortal coil. In any case, he would be free of the agony crashing over his body.

He listened to the slow drip of the faucet count off the seconds as time slowed. Whenever he opened his eyes and stared at the humming light overhead, the world shifted somehow, separating from its layers like sheets of misaligned vellum. These thin slivers of reality fell out of sync just enough that he could see they were there.

Staring, fascinated, Jerry felt the bathtub, the tile, the whole room slip away from him. His surroundings fell away like stage props, one after the other, until he was floating, alone, amidst a vast expanse of stars. A low growling hum droned through his ears and mind, filling him with the image of a vast machine, its parts not of cogs or metal but of a slimy film of skin. A machine of flesh and blood, its pistons made of bone, the fueling fluids piped through arteries and veins, some pieces so massive they dwarfed a hundred million suns.

The engine of the cosmos.

A familiar image, one he'd glimpsed that night in the park and in his dreams thereafter, and yet not with such clarity. Now he was seeing it all in a layer of reality separate from the expanse of stars, the gelatinous machine running full steam ahead behind the scenes, with its many networks of tendrils all reaching out and crisscrossing themselves, tasting their destinations, feeding from them—

Jerry.

His name, spoken by the voices of a thousand unnamed gods in a unified tone so powerful he let go of himself. His mind, his faculties, all of him, melting into a slow vibration of matter and energy, stretched into an unseen band of fluctuating hyperbolas tuned to a singular sound.

The engine.

The goddess.

The voice.

A dark canvas of eyes so vast and far he mistook them for stars. They watched and they studied, sizing up this morsel of meat that had slipped between the layers of reality and into the dimension beyond. Jerry craned his neck, tried to turn away from their stares, but they surrounded him, their pupils converging and dividing and tracking his weightless ascent into their plane of existence.

There came guttural noises he could understand, their translation second nature in his mind, interpreted in a pattern of vibration. He operated on a higher frequency now, the dial turned as far as it would go, and the roiling churn of the cosmos transformed into a language.

Jerry Campbell. At last, you have opened a window.

Gears of bone twisted, snapping sinew deep within the gargantuan mass. Something tugged at his extremities, pulling, stretching. Gravity contracted, and he felt himself pulled forward into the shadows. His mind was an exposed nerve of experience, every sensation at once overwhelming and numbing, and soon he could not feel the wrenching distortions his body suffered. Jerry was merely an observer now, unable to move or resist, an individual consciousness locked inside a prison of meat that was no longer his own.

The goddess owned his body now.

Now.

Now you see. Now you believe. Now you are ours.

A reward for you, a promise. A gift of time for your fragile corpse. You will be our emissary—

He watched as his fingers distorted, elongated into thinning strings of putty wrung pale and cold. His blood seeped from his pores in chains of red pearls, each globule floating away in the clutch of inertia. And still he stretched, until his bones cracked beneath the weight of this vast alien machine, less a goddess than the unknown nature of the universe itself.

—and you will become one of many, child, beneath our eyes—

Fingers, then hands, followed by his arms. Jerry could not struggle, could not even scream, as every tendon was slowly wrenched apart.

"Jerry?"

—to serve us in our eternal reign—

A rift opened into the machine, lined by jagged and broken pieces of bone the size of mountains, and he was drawn to the black hole within.

"Jerry, honey."

He tried to open his mouth and scream, but here there was no sound and no life, no senses but for the gibbering thoughts in his head, the caress of a soft hand on his face, and a warm voice drifting from beyond the sea of starless eyes, through the teeth of the maw of time—

◉

"Abby!"

Jerry's eyes shot open to a dark room. The sensations of bodily contortion were thankfully gone, but the visions of teeth and bone and skin lingered for what felt like eternity. Slowly, the phantoms in his eyes slipped away, along with the sense of looming doom, and he grew aware of a figure kneeling beside him.

"Shh," Katherine said. She held her hand against his cheek. "You're okay. I'm here."

He sighed with relief, wasn't sure his heart could take another scare, and raised his hand to hers. The movement was swift, natural, and absent of pain. Jerry raised his other arm, tested the muscles, and balled his hand into a fist. Nothing but a slight pop of bone in his joint. Less wooden by the sound.

"It... it doesn't hurt."

Katherine nodded. "I know, my friend. That's the emissaries at work."

Jerry took a breath, braced his hands against the floor, and slowly sat up. No pain. Even the wrenching agony in his belly was gone. The rattle in his chest had quieted as well.

"How..." He turned to her, finally realizing they sat in the dark. "Why's the light off?"

"Power's off," she said, climbing to her feet. "Big storm's blowing through."

He watched her stand, and then did so himself, still waiting for a sudden shock of pain somewhere, anywhere. But there was none. Not even a stiffness in his neck. He followed her back to the living room. Everything was as he'd left it. The jar of infernal gunk sat empty on the coffee table.

"Where is Lisa? Arthur said—"

"She's in my basement. Tied up and uncomfortable, but okay. How am I going to get her out of there?"

"*What?* Why didn't you let her go?"

Katherine closed her eyes. "They're guarding her. I wanted to help her escape, but then we'd have had to deal with Arthur and Gladys. Maybe we could've taken care of Arthur—he's too far up his own ass to think little Kat Dunnally and her daughter could pose a threat—but Gladys is a different story. I bought Lisa some time though—told them I'm going to convince her to drink the potion. It was the only thing I could think of. They want to sacrifice her to their goddess tomorrow night."

The wind rushed out of him. "*Sacrifice?* Jesus H. Christ."

She told him what had happened and finished on the verge of tears. "That stunt they pulled in the park wasn't an accident, Jerry. They did the same thing to me. Reggie, too. I can't let them do it to Lisa. My God, what am I going to do?"

"It's my fault she got involved. I never should've called her. If not for her, I'd still be. . ." He glanced at the empty jar on the floor. "Never mind. What's done is done."

"I know your heart's in the right place, hon."

"You're right, though. We can't let them infect Lisa. There's gotta be something we can do."

"But what? They know I'm here. They sent me to check on you, make sure you drank the potion." Katherine looked down at the jar and trembled. "I'm so sorry, Jerry. For all of this."

He took her hands in his own. "It's like I said. What's done is done. And I did it to help get us out of this nightmare."

Katherine shuddered. He gave her hand a squeeze and motioned to the sofa. "Here, sit down. Please? We need to focus, figure this out."

She did as he asked, then broke down into quiet sobs. Jerry put his arm around her, held her close. They sat there for a while in the dark, listening to the steady rain overhead, and he tried to forget their predicament, if only for a moment. There was no parasite, no Fairview, no goddess, and no worries. He and Katherine were the center of the universe in that span of silence, two fading stars in a tenuous orbit and surrounded by unknowable chaos. Jerry held her until her cries dwindled to whimpers, the hitching in her chest nothing more than a faint rattle, and after a time she rested her head on his shoulder.

"I wondered if you would drink the potion again," she said finally, easing herself back on the sofa. A flash of lightning lit up the room and her tear-stained face, followed quickly by the rumble of thunder. "To be honest, Jerry, I'd hoped you would. Sorry, I know that's selfish."

"Hah. Why's that?"

She squeezed his hand. "Because. . . well, *because*. I like you. I appreciate your friendship. With everything that's happening, I'm glad I don't have to go through it alone. And I'm glad it's you. I just wish we could've met under different circumstances."

A silence slipped between them as rain battered the world outside. He felt heat flood his cheeks and was grateful for the darkness now. The last thing he wanted was for her to see him reduced to the awkward shyness of a teenage boy. Besides, this setting felt too hazy and dreamlike, a conjuration of his hopes and desires, and he expected to awaken under the hum of the bathroom light, alone and terrified and changed.

He recalled the agony washing over his body in terrible riptides, each one stronger than the last. To think he'd felt that way just a few short hours ago was like a bad dream. Old pains that were present long before his first taste of the potion had been silenced by the presence of the parasites, and he felt twenty years younger. *No wonder everyone is so eager to be part of this thing. A fountain of youth is hard to resist.*

He cleared his throat, flexed his fingers. "How is this possible, Katherine? I thought I was going to die."

"Maybe a part of you did. A piece of us dies every time we drink the potion. We are all part of *it* now, or maybe it's a part of us. I don't know—I don't understand it fully myself. I'm just happy I can talk openly with you now. I really expected you to throw me out of your house."

"No, I wouldn't. . ." But then he remembered all that had transpired earlier in the day. How the others had threatened him, given him their ultimatum. Was she one of them? Was he? "This is all so much."

"I know," Katherine said. "I fought them for so long, Jerry, but I just couldn't take the pain anymore. I don't know of anyone who could." She touched his cheek. "I'm grateful you're here, because I don't feel so alone anymore."

"I would've kept fighting them too, if not for you and Lisa. I wasn't of much help to anyone before. . ."

She smiled. Another flash of lightning revealed the glint of tears in her eyes. "You're a good man, Jerry Campbell. And I—"

Jerry kissed her. They connected in a pleasant cataclysm, as the world crashed and fell around them. He feared he would feel guilt or, worse, hear the voice of his beloved Abby in his head, but there was only silence in his mind. Silence, and the storm raging outside.

Katherine leaned into him, kissed him deeply. When they separated for a breath, he saw that she was crying. "I'm sorry if I—"

"No, it's not that." She wiped her eyes, and then took hold of his hand. "It's just been so long since I've felt something like this. I'm happy, I'm sad, I feel guilty because I feel this way..."

"We don't have to," he said. "I mean, if it's too much."

"No, it's okay," she said, and kissed him again. "I want to."

◉

They lay in his bed, her head on his chest, and listened to the rain pattering overhead. Jerry stared at the ceiling, still trying to wrap his mind around this sudden rush of emotion and virility, the reckless abandon of a teenager too young and dumb to understand what love is. They'd taken their time, their lovemaking tender and careful, both unsure of how far their newfound youth would carry them. *How long has it been for you, old man? At least fifteen years, maybe twenty.* He couldn't remember the last time he and Abby had made love, and that realization saddened him.

"Penny for your thoughts?" Katherine's voice hummed against his chest.

"You'll need a whole lot of pennies."

"I've got a whole jar of them at home..." She sat up in panic. "What am I doing here with you while Lisa's still tied up. I should've stayed, figured out a way to free her. God, I'm a terrible mother—"

"Hey, now. Don't talk like that."

"It's true. I shouldn't have left her. Hell, what are we going to *do*, Jerry?"

"I don't know, but we've got until tomorrow night to figure it out. How long before that potion stuff wears off?"

"The jar was full when you drank it?"

"Uh huh."

"Then you should be good for a while. It doesn't take much. Just enough to keep the emissaries happy. . ." She sat up, began reaching for her clothes. "I—I'm sorry. I need to get my daughter."

"She will be okay, Kat." He took her hand and gave it a squeeze for comfort. "Take a breath. It's not going to do her any good if you panic."

Katherine sank back against the headboard. She clutched her dress, wringing it absently in worry. "You're right. . . Goddammit, I hate this."

"I know. But we're going to figure this out. Together."

He'd hoped for a smile, but her brow remained furrowed with concern. *Change the subject,* he told himself. *Get her talking about something else.*

"Tell me something," he began.

"Anything."

"Did you ever think about what you'd do if Lisa found out about all this?"

She laughed, humorless. "Is this your idea of pillow talk?"

"Go easy on me, I'm out of practice. But seriously, she was going to find out sooner or later, wasn't she?"

She told him about Arthur's plan to make her disappear. When she was finished, he lay silently, rolling her words over in his head.

"You were just going to leave her without saying goodbye?"

"You sound just like her. Of course not. I'd say goodbye in my own way, on my own terms, before any of that would happen. She didn't give me a chance to explain it to her, but I truly thought I'd be doing her some good. Relieving her of me, you know? Between nursing and taking care of me, she doesn't have much of a life to speak of. Freeing her of my burden seemed like the best thing I could do for her."

Something wet and warm touched his chest, and Jerry realized she was crying again. He nudged her. "None of that."

"She was right, though. I was being selfish. I still am, if I'm honest. By being here with you, I mean, instead of being there with her."

"You had to keep up appearances, Kat. You're no good to her if they suspect you too."

"I know. I just hate feeling helpless. I hate that I'm in this position, that I even went along with everything. It's that goddamn potion, this place, that rock in the park—it changes the way you see things. Changes your perspective on life and relationships."

"Changes the way you see reality."

"Yeah," she whispered. "That most of all. Sometimes the voice I hear in my head doesn't belong to me, and I wonder if the next time I drink the potion, will that be where I stop being me? Will that be when I turn into Arthur or, worse, Gladys?"

"Arthur's wife? The one who's dead?"

Katherine sighed. "She's not dead. Or maybe she is. I don't know what to think anymore. She's less a person and more of a... *nest* for those things."

"Jesus..."

They fell silent, and a chill ran through them both as though they were of one mind and body. Finally, Jerry spoke up. "Why the eclipse?"

"Arthur mentioned something about a convergence with the goddess. He says a doorway will open."

"A doorway?"

"To the goddess. Something about the position of the moon, and some kind of power being channeled through the stone."

He thought of the voice in his dream and shivered. "This is all too much."

"Mmhmm. It's happened before, a couple of years ago. Right after me and Reggie moved here. The goddess chose someone."

"What does that mean?"

"I'm not sure, but it sounds awful. I don't think I want to know."

The rain tapered off, the constant hiss receding into an occasional pattering. Jerry's thoughts wandered back to Bailey's Rock.

Not really a rock at all. A long-dormant nest of extraterrestrial worms. If only we could get rid of the damn thing—

He tripped over a memory. Something Arthur had said, locked up in an old barn at the back of his mind. A *Green Acres* moment.

"A-N-F-O." Jerry mouthed the letters to himself. "We close the door."

"Close it, lock it, throw away the key. If it were up to me, I'd blow it all sky high so it couldn't open ever again."

He brayed laughter, couldn't help himself.

She jabbed him in the ribs. "What's so funny, old man?"

"You're right," he said. "That's exactly what we need to do."

And then he told her how they were going to do it.

PART FOUR
ECLIPSE

25

Jerry opened the back door, eager to greet the night and terrified of what dangers it held. Damp air chilled his skin, a quality he would've avoided a mere day before, but his joints had yet to complain. He was grateful, even if the cost was high, yet he feared the strength he enjoyed now would fade before his task was done.

Get moving, old man. Don't dally.

The sky was still choked with clouds from the storm, and for as far as he could see, the power was still out. Darkness blanketed Fairview Acres. Now was the perfect time to put his insane plan into action, whether he was ready or not.

Katherine stuck her head through the opening and handed him a flashlight. She whispered, "Be careful, Jerry. Stick to the shadows, or they'll see you before you see them. Don't use your flashlight unless you have to."

They listened to the stillness. Soft thumping in the distance, followed by a series of rattling croaks. Further down the block, another croak answered in quick succession. *No telling how many of those roof-walking things are out there tonight.*

"What are they, Kat?"

She hesitated. "You... really don't want to know."

"Try me, lady."

"They're Arthur's watchdogs. His most devout. They were on your roof because they've been keeping an eye on you. Making sure you don't go snooping around." She closed her eyes and shook her head. "Making sure you don't try to run."

He watched her expressions, noted the fear and disgust, and questioned if he really wanted to do this—to go out there in the open with those things on the prowl, stumbling around in the dark and praying they didn't catch him. One of Abby's favorite movies came to mind. Don Knotts. *The Ghost and Mr. Chicken.* He sure as hell felt like Mr. Chicken right now.

"I'll try not to use the flashlight," he said. "But what *are* they? They're sure as hell not human."

"They're more human than you think."

Her words lingered in the silence. Ridiculous, impossible, terrifying—Jerry's mind refused to accept their implication. No wonder she didn't want to tell him.

All right, old man. You got yourself into this mess. Too late to back out now.

He sucked in the cool air. Brisk and invigorating, a welcome change. "I'm terrified," he said, "but I feel like I could run a marathon and fight an army. Like the air I'm breathing is electric."

"Great sex will do that," she said. "Now kiss me and go, before I change my mind."

His fear and trepidation melted away in an instant. He kissed her eagerly and with a smile upon his face. How long had it been since he'd felt such a charge of happiness, of purpose? So long that he'd forgotten what joy felt like. He'd been coasting along on autopilot since Abby's death, a robot conditioned to live until all functions ceased.

No longer.

Now he had a purpose. Katherine's daughter needed his help; so did the people of Fairview, whether they realized it or not. He hadn't a clue what might happen to them during the eclipse, but if he had any say—if he could put this newfound strength to use—it wouldn't matter. Come the sunrise, Arthur's grip on the community would cease, and Bailey's Rock would be little more than dust.

Katherine closed the door behind him, and he journeyed forward into the shadows with a spring in his step.

◐

He'd barely left his property and crossed into the Scotts' yard when he heard movement. Scraping—*scritch, scritch, scritch*—and something wet like meat slapped on a cutting board. Not from anywhere around him, but above. Jerry skulked from the corner of his neighbor's storage shed toward an adjacent trio of evergreens, braving the needles and sap for a vantage point. All he heard was the hush of wind in the pines and his heart thundering away in his chest. He sank to his knees and crawled forward across a bed of dead pine needles. Far enough that he could see the back side of the Scotts' home. All was dark except for a trail of solar lights along the back patio.

All in your head, old man. What makes you think you can make a difference when you're jumping at shadows—

The clouds parted overhead, allowing a sliver of moonlight to illuminate the street, and Jerry saw them. He stared for several moments, unsure at first what he was seeing, perplexed and horrified by their movements, their sounds. The shapes didn't make sense.

Uhk-uhk-uhk.

He had no illusions about the horrible things they might do to him if he was caught.

A dry scrape of skin across the rooftop shingling.

The sickening smack of wet flesh as one arm wrapped around another.

A stretched silhouette against a darkened sky, reaching for the heavens with erratic wriggling motion.

Now he understood Katherine's ominous statement. They *were* more human than he thought.

There were two of them, half human and half worm, writhing upon one another, upper extremities coiling and uncoiling like snakes while their legs dangled in the air at awkward angles. One of them reared back and uttered a wet guttural cry, freeing the slick remnants of a tattered tank top. The shirt landed in a clump on the stone patio.

Jerry stared until colors danced before his eyes, and then he made himself look away. Memories of that night in his backyard. The thing had rushed from the shadows so fast, he hadn't caught a good look at it—but now the ripped denim made sense. *Brad and Matilda.* Other memories from that night in the park intermingled with the horrific dreams he'd experienced in recent days. Everything he'd dismissed as the effect of powerful hallucinogens was now laid bare before him in startling, disgusting clarity.

My God, is that what's going to happen to me? To Katherine? Nothing was free. One of life's truest axioms. Forsake the potion and suffer; indulge and lose one's humanity. *Not much of a choice at all.*

Jerry rose from his knees, using a branch to steady himself, and the limb snapped loose in his hand. He fell backward on his ass with a soft thud and a short cry, and immediately sucked in his breath, waiting.

One of the Scott creatures straightened and turned in his direction. An ululating trill filled the air. Damp and dull—*uhk-uhk-uhk*—a rattling croak more akin to falling river stones than birdsong. The creature's tendrilled torso flopped forward and reared up, supported by its human legs, with withered arms that were little more than useless remnants of evolution.

He covered his mouth, terrified it would hear him breathing.

The worm-headed thing, what he imagined used to be Bradley Scott, held its flattened nub of a head aloft in the air, seeking, tasting. It remained at the roof's edge, peering into the backyard, and then the clouds sealed the rift in the sky and reduced the world to darkness once more. Jerry couldn't see it in the shadows, but he heard it, shuffling along the rooftop with its awkward gait.

The creature croaked out another trilling call and was joined this time by Matilda. Or maybe Jerry had them switched. Either way, they weren't human anymore, not the parts that mattered.

Another one called out from across the street. And then another, further down the block. Across Fairview Acres, the warning cry was echoed by others.

Nightcrawlers, he thought. He and his old man used to go night fishing when he was a kid, over at the lake near his grandpa's property. His pops always had a Styrofoam container of those things, eight or nine inches long, purple and plump. The fish went nuts for them.

A slow, cold fear lurched into his belly. *And now they're fishing for me.*

Jerry collected his wits, what little was left, and waited until the alarm call faded into the distance. Then he slipped out of cover from the trees and began to creep through his neighbors' backyards, heading toward the park. *Navigating your neighborhood in the dark isn't the best idea you've ever had, old man.*

He used to pride himself on his sense of direction, a skill he'd honed during his time in the Boy Scouts, and it had served him well on many road trips in his youth. Abby was fond of telling her girlfriends, *"I can't find my way out of a paper bag, but if you drop Jerry in the Amazon with bubblegum and a paperclip, he'll make it out in time for dinner."* But he was no MacGyver, and after getting turned around twice in the dark, he was ready to hand over his merit badge.

And yet he carried on, an old man bumbling around with neither streetlights nor stars to guide his way, creeping through shrubbery, shuffling along fences and hedgerows, and pausing only to listen to the awful things waiting in the dark.

◉

Katherine looked at her watch. Jerry had been gone half an hour already. She'd waited by the back door until he was out of sight and then heard one of those awful things crying out into the night, chilling her blood. Another erratic croak had joined in chorus, and then another from a few houses away. She'd lingered at the door until the night fell mercifully silent, then closed her eyes and made a silent prayer for his safety.

Maybe it was a false alarm. Maybe he got away. Or maybe...

"You worry too much, darling." Reggie's words weighed heavily on her lips. She pictured him sitting at the kitchen table, one eyebrow cocked, smirking.

You warned me, and I didn't listen. God, I'm so sorry I didn't listen.

When she'd walked into Jerry's home and found him on the bathroom floor, her heart had nearly given out. Because it wasn't Jerry she'd seen slumped against the bathtub. It was Reggie, pale and bloated and dead for days—and then he was gone again in the flash of lightning that knocked out the power.

You can be with him forever, Katherine. All we require is your tribute.

She buried her face in her hands, tried to force the goddess's presence from her mind. But the entity wouldn't let go; their bond was growing whether she liked it or not, and soon she would begin to face the changes. "The Great Metamorphosis" Arthur called it during his many speeches of grandeur. She'd seen firsthand what those changes meant. Watched in terror at the Moon Pool when they shed their clothing and contorted their bodies, a bizarre orgy of skin and bone and transformation.

Every time was more horrific than the last, but the goddess always had a way of soothing her mind, assuring her it was for a greater purpose, that she would live forever like the beautiful butterfly she'd dreamed of being as a child. Still, she kept resisting for as long as she could, always reaching a critical point before giving in once more.

Even now, she felt the emissaries stirring in her belly and chest, felt them slithering through her brain and wriggling behind her eyes. They were awake, and they were hungry. Soon, she would feed them. And then?

By then, Jerry will have done what he needs to do, and maybe we'll be free. Maybe we'll still be the same. Who knows. But we have to try to escape. For you, Reggie. For Lisa. For us.

Her hopes weren't enough to resuscitate Reggie in her mind and conjure his presence. There was only the chill breeze and stillness of the neighborhood.

She paced through the living room, eyeing the photographs on the walls. Jerry in happier times, beside his beautiful bride. Next to it, another one taken much later, when they were older and graying. An anniversary, maybe, or some other special occasion. She studied Jerry's face in the photograph, wondering if he would ever smile like that again.

Probably not. You know as well as anybody that you can't catch that kind of lightning in a bottle more than once.

In the time since Reggie's death, Katherine grew to realize the love she shared with him was as unique as their personalities. What they shared would never be replicated, and if a new love could be nurtured in the aftermath, it would be wholly its own thing. She supposed the same was true for anyone who had found—and lost—their partner in life.

She'd resigned herself to living the rest of her life alone, but ever since she'd met Jerry, her outlook had changed. He was funny, charming in his shy and grumpy way, and he had heart. No wonder she'd become smitten with him over the last several weeks. In another lifetime, she might have thought of herself as moving too fast, but at her age, dancing around the obvious was just a huge waste of time. *Better to be forthright,* Reggie might say. *Go after what you want. Skip the Brontë bullshit.*

Was this a new chapter in the life of Katherine Dunnally? She hoped so, but goddamn these circumstances.

The house's silence pulled her from her thoughts. There were no other calls of alarm, nothing to signal that Jerry might be in trouble. She had faith in him. He'd proven himself resilient, even when he was in withdrawal, but that awful phantom still lingered in her mind. Reggie's lifeless corpse transposed over Jerry's unconscious body. An image she couldn't shake, one that filled her with immense guilt.

Why not go to him, Katherine? Reach him before he commits to his foolish actions. Tell him the alternative is so much worse.

"No. No, no, no, you evil bitch, get out of my head."

But the goddess had a point. She didn't want to see Jerry end up like Reggie. Couldn't bear it, in fact, but if she stopped him now, somehow convinced him to return with her, then—

"Goddammit, *stop.*"

She stamped her foot, realized the last time she'd done so, she'd been trying to break the glass bottles so she could slit her wrists. The goddess was in her head then, too, and had pulled

(there is no death for you)

her back from the abyss. Katherine had finally surrendered after that, because why not? Not even death could free her of the infernal voice crawling through her brain.

Do you even understand how selfish this is? Lisa, a voice of reason in all this madness. Everything had fallen apart the moment she spoke those words, every syllable a sledgehammer to Katherine's resolve. That wall of promises and certainty built in part by the goddess residing in her head and part by the Petersons, always cajoling and urging in her ear. Katherine had been so resigned to her future, and to the Petersons' plan for explaining her disappearance, that Lisa's true feelings hadn't entered the equation.

We do this all the time, Kat. For years now, and it's never gone wrong. She's better off without having to worry about you. We're all a burden after a certain age. You're doing her a favor.

And that may have been true too, but deep down, Katherine wasn't ready to say goodbye to her daughter, and Lisa wasn't ready to say goodbye to her. Reggie's passing had strained their relationship—the distance between parent and child widened and distorted, the roles reversed—but if they lost each other now without repairing their connection, they'd both be haunted for the rest of their lives. She couldn't bear the thought of Lisa living out the rest of her years in the dark, unaware that her mother was still alive in the community that had taken her father.

And that was assuming Gladys Peterson's plans for her daughter could be stopped. Katherine couldn't allow those plans to come to fruition.

You'll know when it happens, Jerry had said. *I'll meet you back at your place. Be ready to leave. But if I don't come back, promise me you won't wait. Promise me you'll both get the hell out of this place.*

Of course she'd promised. He wouldn't have accepted anything less.

She crossed the living room and opened the front door again. No movement on the street or the rooftops. Crickets and the soft hiss of grass caught in a breeze.

"He's okay," she told herself. "He'll be okay."

She remained on the threshold, a widow at her watch.

26

The journey felt endless—one dark street after another, the infernal labyrinth of a nightmare—but after doubling back and changing course a second time, he finally arrived at Arthur's cul-de-sac. A strange pale glow came from beyond the row of houses, one that appeared to condense and expand.

Something in the park, breathing in light.

He used it as a guide, orienting himself to the park's rim, and before long he felt the steady incline of the hillside where Arthur lived—the one that was just a bit higher than the rest, enough for Arthur to overlook the kingdom he'd built.

A chill breeze swept over him, cooling the sweat on his forehead. Even with the potion's benefits, the incline was a challenge, enough to get his heart pumping.

When he reached the summit, he crouched beside a neighbor's fence to catch his breath. Arthur's house was dark like all the rest. He'd expected a backup generator, considering Arthur's love of heavy-duty toys. Jerry cracked a smile, indulged in his snide satisfaction. *No power here, not even for the chairman himself.*

He waited, listening for movement or another croaking call announcing his arrival, but all he heard was the calming thump of his heartbeat. Wind in the bushes and trees. And a low bassline hum. He hadn't noticed it before, wasn't even sure it was real until he steadied himself with a hand on the ground and felt the vibration.

The engine of the cosmos. Gears of bone and teeth like mountains. A galaxy of eyes watching me from the inside.

Jerry pulled his hand away. His palm tingled with pins and needles, the fingertips hot like he'd touched a live copper wire. What had Arthur said? A conduit to the heavens?

Jerry listened to the hum, frowning. He was no electrician, but there was a definite energy coursing through the earth below.

Like it's charging up. A big battery. For what?

He shook off another chill. "Don't want to find out," he muttered, and forced himself to action. He crept across the driveway, then around the side of the house, and waited at the corner to be certain no one had seen him. When there was no movement but the wind, he darted down the hill toward the barn—and his foot slipped on the gravel. He pinwheeled his arms, overcorrected, and fell backward at an angle, digging himself into the gravel like he was sliding in for home plate. Stones scattered everywhere, ripping through the silence with the gracefulness of a buzzsaw.

He lay there on his back in that fading gulf of time before his nerves woke to a screaming chorus.

Haven't seen you move like that since our wedding night, honey.

Jerry sat up and sucked in air. Jagged edges of stone punctuated his every movement, but worse was the dawning realization that he'd made a lot of noise. And that he'd lost the flashlight.

Shit!

How far had it gone? He reached out, pawing the surrounding area, and nearly cried out in relief when his hand fell upon its metal handle. With his heart firmly lodged in his gullet, he climbed to his feet and limped around the side of the barn, out of view from the house. He pressed himself against the wall and listened for voices or footsteps, but none came.

Only then did he chance turning on the flashlight to survey the damage. Scrapes and a torn sleeve, some chips of stone embedded in his skin, and a small gash on his leg were the worst of it. At his age, in his state, a fall like this should have crippled him. From what he could see, some stitches and ibuprofen might be all he needed when he was done.

He held his breath and listened once more. Nothing but the breeze through the trees, a distant car or truck passing through the neighborhood, and the infernal hum—even more present now. From where he stood, the light emanating from the park was brighter. A thicket of trees stood in the way, and beyond them, the bandstand, but there was no mistaking that it originated from Bailey's Rock.

He watched for a time, mesmerized by the light's slow, steady pulse.

The engine breathes, Jerry. It is a living machine, churning and conducting and connecting, and tomorrow it will open the moon's eye. You will gaze upon your goddess and rejoice.

Something cold and wet fell upon his face. He raised his hand to his cheek. Tears.

"We'll see about that," he said, and half-expected something in the dark to reply, but nothing did. He wiped his face and shook off the trance.

He checked the barn doors—still unlocked—and swung one open. Inside, he clicked on the flashlight and looked over the stacks of fertilizer bags near the back. A large yellow label read:

"CAUTION: KEEP AWAY FROM FIRE, HEAT, AND OPEN FLAMES. DO NOT DROP."

The rest was chemistry jargon, but he'd read all he needed to. Fifty pounds of inert pellet-sized explosives. Just add fire. All of Fairview would be in for a rude awakening come dawn.

Jerry clutched the first bag, sucked in his breath, and heaved it carefully up to his shoulder. He stepped back out into the night, toward the fence gate, and the trail leading down to the park.

◉

Bailey's Rock shimmered, a pulsing beacon in the dark, guiding his way down the slope. He stopped to catch his breath when he reached the edge of the thicket. The meteorite was sheathed in an eerie brilliance, its glow rising and falling as if breathing for the worms within. At this distance from town, without light pollution to obscure the glow, it really did look like a small moon.

The hum below his feet
(the engine breathes)
intensified as he descended the hill, vibrating in time with the light. His mind ran wild with conjecture and possibility, imagining all the alien things that might reside inside. One massive egg waiting to hatch. An interstellar version of the Mexican jumping bean. Hell, maybe it was trying to phone home.

But he knew the reality. They were slaves, hosts to parasites that were part of a much larger organism. A being so large it dwarfed planets and stars. And all of Fairview served as a walking, talking antenna for the horrible thing.

Not for long.

Jerry reached the Moon Pool and dropped the bag at his feet. He tore open the plastic, scooped out a handful of pellets, and waded over to the stone. Standing this close, the rumbling hum emanating from within filled him with dread. When he made to pack the first pellets into its crevasses, the eerie glow slowly dimmed in response, as though it sensed his intentions. He hesitated, realized his hand was shaking. *Now's not the time to chicken out, old man.*

He began packing the ANFO into the porous surface, taking fresh handfuls from the bag and working his way around the stone. He made it halfway before he'd emptied the bag, and welcomed the short break. The incessant hum had spurred on a headache, the sort that resonated behind his eyes and felt like something boring into the back of his skull.

What are you doing, Jerry?

He sloshed through the shallow water and stumbled back toward the hillside path. The ache in his head eased up, waiting for an answer. Jerry pushed on, piercing the night with his flashlight, a stubborn old man on a mission to defy the gods. Another jolt surged between his eyes. He cried out in the dark.

You'd best answer me, hon.

Jerry reached out, steadied himself against a tree. Through clenched teeth, he said, "That's real low, talking like Kat." He raised the flashlight, studied the path. Not far to go now. "But if you're so powerful, why don't you already know? Maybe you can't know. Maybe all you're good at is turning people into monsters. Some 'goddess' you are."

He continued his ascent. So did the worms inside his head, boring deeper and building pressure. Something warm trickled out of his nose. He wiped it away and kept on. A dissonant chorus of voices churned in his head.

We are what you make of us. God or goddess, titles of your limited language, we care not.

We were old when your planet was dust.

You are a speck. A crumb. Mere atoms of a greater morsel we will devour.

Nothing will prevent the consumption of your mind, your home, your world.

Jerry reached the gate to Arthur's backyard. He waited a beat, caught his breath. "You still didn't answer my question, but that's okay. I don't think you can." His headache eased off, the pressure released, and he opened the gate. "Don't have a comeback for that, do you?"

Silence but for the wind through the trees and the droning chirp of crickets in the underbrush.

Didn't think so. But stay focused, old man. One more bag should do it, and then kaboom.

He returned to the barn, heaved another bag up over his shoulder, and froze when the outdoor lights flickered on. The utility company had done its job after all, and with the worst goddamn timing. No matter. He stepped outside once more, doubled his pace across the pavilion toward the gate—

Crunch.

Footsteps behind him. Raspy breathing made shrill by congested lungs. Something wet, slapping, warbling the air.

And despite what his instincts told him, when every alarm in his head sounded for him to drop the bag and run, Jerry turned slowly to the source of those awful noises.

A woman stood near the outbuildings, clad in a furry bathrobe and bunny slippers, silhouetted against the floodlights. The harsh lighting gave her a diffuse, pink aura. Her face was partially obscured by the shadows, but Jerry wasn't as concerned about who she was so much as *what* she was. Thick tendrils protruded from her face, writhing and slithering through the air like violent jump ropes, a vision so absurd that he felt an empty laugh crawl into his gullet. He would've let the humor take over if not for the terror flooding his mind.

After what he'd seen crawling along the rooftops, the woman's appearance shouldn't have terrified him as much as it did. And though he wanted to run, his legs were jelly, his knees weak, and the sharp headache had returned. Flashes of light filled his mind. Colorful stars burst before his eyes. *Go,* he told himself, *get the fuck out of here.*

His muscles did not cooperate.

The gorgon-like creature approached, her visage even worse as she stepped into the light, and Jerry felt something release in his mind. A flood of adrenaline, maybe, or a quart of his sanity swirling down the drain. *God, her face!*

Holes riddled her skin, slimy with a gray luminescent fluid accenting each wound—and the *things* crawling inside them. Thick stalks of striped skin and muscle protruded from her eyes and mouth, each slithering rope frayed at the ends with strips of teeth-lined sinew. No, not teeth, but barbs of some kind, sharp enough to pierce skin.

One of the appendages shot toward him and latched on to his arm. He gasped as the barbs sank into his flesh, and the gorgon closed in. Darkness pierced his vision, made to swallow him whole from the inside out, and all he saw when he hit the ground was all those stars above. Twinkling. Watching. Judging.

There was no thought, no time. Only the bliss of nothingness, a warm blanket pulled over the world, alone in the emptiness of the vast cosmos. And in the distance, a rattling alien cry of alarm.

27

Movement overhead. A heavy thump, followed by the pattering of feet across the rooftop.

Katherine snapped to attention. She'd taken a seat on Jerry's sofa, closed her eyes for just a minute, but now—

Another set of footsteps. Running.

Had she missed her moment to act? She shot to her feet in panic, tried to ignore the racing pulse in her throat, and returned to the front door. Gary's lights were on across the street. The streetlights flickered on as she watched, one after another, filling the block with pallid halos. She caught sight of silhouettes in the street and across the neighboring rooftops.

Dry, clattering cries filled the night. *Uhk-uhk-uhk.*

Katherine stepped back from the door and hid herself in the gloom, watching. Distorted figures all ran in the same direction, drawn to an unseen point. *Oh God. Jerry!* Why else would they be so frenzied?

She remembered the first time she'd seen them. Reggie, confused with what they thought was dementia, had left the house one evening while she was in the shower, and for two hours had wandered the neighborhood looking for a way out. She'd set off on foot, calling his name in the dark. When she found him, he was huddled next to someone's trash can three blocks away, just outside one of the nightly parties, terrified and sobbing. *I wanted to leave, Kat, to get us help. I can feel them chewing on my brain.*

Something had rustled in a tree nearby. She'd looked up just in time to witness a dark shape leap to a nearby rooftop. *Uhk-uhk-uhk.* A scramble of footsteps shadowed them all the way home. She'd told herself it was just her imagination, a figment drawn out of panic and adrenaline. God, if only that were true.

You will join them in time. Our emissary, remade in our image.

She ignored the goddess in her head. If Jerry had been caught, she wouldn't have much time to reach Lisa and escape.

Promise me you won't wait.

She regretted promising him anything of the sort, but seeing the horde of creatures rampaging through the night put things in perspective. They were only two people against an entire neighborhood. Three, if she counted Lisa. Even with the benefit of the parasites, Katherine was no action hero. Everything had seemed so fool-proof when Jerry explained his plan. Sure, they could meet back at her house—but that still meant going outside where those things were lurking.

They would catch her, overwhelm her.

They would likely kill her, and then—

Lisa. I'm coming, baby girl.

Katherine took a breath, waited for her heart to slow, and stepped outside. The night air had cooled following the storm. Any other time she would've been concerned about the damp—it always made her arthritis worse—but tonight she moved briskly and without concern for herself. Lisa was her focus now. Lisa, and getting the hell out of Fairview for good.

She clung to the shadows as much as possible, darting across the street toward Gary's front yard, and peeked around the corner of the house. Her home was two blocks away, a straight shot from here, with plenty of darkness to hide her passage.

A double-edged sword, this darkness. She hadn't given her eyes enough time to adjust to the low light, and when she turned the corner, she tripped over something on the ground. Metal clanged against the house, joined with a shrill cry escaping her lips when she hit the earth. Pain shot through her ankle and knees from the heavy landing.

She looked back, caught the gleam of metal. A cluster of yard tools—rakes, a shovel, some kind of tilling tool. Gary and his damn gardening hobby. She pulled herself off the ground and winced when she put weight on her ankle.

Dammit. You're such a klutz, Kat.

She limped forward alongside the house. Each step was another jolt of pain filling her head with white light. Those two blocks to her home might as well be a hundred miles. Panic threatened to take hold, but she remained focused on her destination, determined to reach her daughter.

Her father came to mind as she limped through the dark. A distant memory from a lifetime ago when she was still a child and the world was a simpler place. She remembered falling at the playground while playing a game of tag with the other neighborhood children. Crying, she'd presented her skinned hands and knees to her father. *Walk it off,* he'd told her. *It'll go away in a few minutes.* Somehow, magically, it *did* go away after a while, and she had thought her daddy was a wizard for years after.

A sprained ankle wasn't so different. If she kept her goal in sight, kept moving, she would reach her house in no time—

Uhhhhk-uhk-uhk-uhk!

The sound took her by surprise, silencing every thought in her head. She froze, slowly looked up.

One of her neighbors—she couldn't say who, their features were too distorted—stood on the roof of the next house, peering down at her. Their segmented body glistened in the moonlight, wet with slime and something darker, maybe blood. Remnants of clothing stuck to its deformed body, but what caught her eye was the pair of loafers on its feet.

I bet their wardrobe budget is nuts.

The absurdity of this thought eked a laugh up her throat and into the night. It was a sound she couldn't halt, not that it would've mattered. This thing, whomever it had been, had her in its sights now. Time hadn't been on her side before; now it was actively against her.

No more walking it off, Kat. Time to run.

She clenched her teeth and darted for the sidewalk. The creature trilled its horrid noise from behind, followed by heavy footfalls on shingling. A moment later, she heard the monstrosity's impact on the ground, but she didn't dare look back. The pain in her ankle was nearly blinding, each step a bright phosphorous flash in her brain, but her daughter needed her. She limped along as fast as she could, her lungs ablaze and heart a heavy piston hammering away in her chest.

One block down.

Her neighbor's footsteps trotted along the asphalt somewhere behind her, accompanied by an erratic swishing which could only be its noodle-like head. The thought called an image to mind, one that both amused and repulsed her. *If I make it out of this, I'm never eating pasta again.*

Half a block to go. Her ankle screamed, joining a chorus of bodily protest. The muscles in her legs were on fire. She couldn't remember the last time she'd moved this fast.

And the thing giving chase would catch her at any second.

Go, Reggie chanted in her head. *You can do this, honey. I know you can.*

Katherine grunted in pain as her ankle gave way. She staggered forward, reached out for something to help break her fall, but there was only empty air and sidewalk. Her hip popped, a twinge like a snapped guitar string, but the pain wasn't there. Not yet.

"No," she whispered. "Lisa, I'm sorry, baby. I'm so sorry."

Silence. Crickets and a series of trilling croaks in the distance. No footsteps.

She raised her head and looked back. No sign of Noodlehead. Had it lost interest in its prey? Unlikely. Something else had stolen its attention, something more pressing than chasing her down.

Promise me you won't wait.

Wincing, Katherine pulled herself off the sidewalk and limped forward to her home.

◉

A door opened somewhere above. The front entrance, maybe? Lisa couldn't tell.

She flexed her arms, twiddled her fingers, and realized she couldn't feel them. As the blood began to circulate, she braced for the discomfort of pins and needles. Her limbs grew sensitive and fuzzy—filled with static, she used to say—and she waited until the sensation finally passed before trying to move again.

She listened, afraid to call out for fear that the visitor wasn't her mother. Only silence and the emptiness of the house, the hum of its mechanics and the occasional pop of a settling foundation. Had Arthur and Gladys returned to deal with her?

Lisa struggled to hold back a sob. No, now wasn't the time for crying. That came later, after she was safe, after she got her mother out of this place. Jerry, too, if he was still alive.

And that wouldn't happen so long as she was tied up in this goddamn basement.

She'd already searched the room for something sharp, had even hopped over to her father's old toolbox and rummaged through it, but all she'd found was a box cutter missing its blade. This stolen victory had cinched the air from her lungs, deflated her resolve, and she'd sunk back to the floor in defeat.

But if someone was coming for her, she couldn't give up now, not if she wanted to survive.

She scanned the room again. What about the shelving unit along the wall?

Its metal frame had a strange yellow sheen from the bare bulb hanging overhead. Maybe she could cut herself free on the frame's edge.

Maybe. One way to find out.

She braced herself against the wall, tried wriggling herself into a standing position again. No good. Her legs still tingled with paresthesia. Applying pressure to them hurt like hell. She sat down hard and winced. Stiff muscles shot a jolt through her arms and into both shoulders. A flash of light filled her head, signaling the return of her headache.

I'd fucking kill for some Tylenol—

Footsteps creaked overhead. The steps were light, quick. Not heavy like Arthur's footfalls from earlier.

Gladys, then. Returned to take care of me. Lisa's heart sank. She couldn't defend herself like this. All she had was her teeth to fight back. *So be it. I won't make this easy, you holey bitch.*

The basement door opened, revealing a woman's silhouette.

"Lisa? Honey, it's Mom."

"You scared the shit out of me," she said, gulping back the lump in her throat. All the adrenaline fled her system, washed out with a tide of relief. "You've gotta get me out of here, Mom—"

"I will, but we have to hurry."

"Where's Jerry? What did they do to him?"

Her mother ignored her question. "You—you're right. I was being selfish, and I know saying I'm sorry doesn't mean much right now, but I am." She stepped into the light, a kitchen knife in her hand. "Let me cut you loose."

Lisa recoiled against the wall. "Answer my question, Mom."

"He left to deal with Arthur, but he should've been back by now." She held out the knife. "May I? Please?"

Katherine cut her free and helped her to her feet. Pins pricked her fingers and toes. Lisa asked, "Have you been with Jerry this whole time?"

Her mother looked away.

"Are you... Mom, are you blushing?"

"What? No."

A taste of acid rose in the back of Lisa's throat. She clenched her jaw, reminded herself a screaming match wouldn't help them now. "We'll talk about this later."

Her mother nodded. "I'll explain on the way." She turned and limped up the stairs.

Lisa followed, thought of asking what she'd done to herself, but decided one thing, one lecture at a time. "Mom, where are we going?"

"Away from here," was all Katherine said.

They hurried down the hallway to the front door. Her mother grabbed the handle and began to pull it open when headlights flashed through the window. They froze, exchanged glances.

"Is it Jerry?"

Katherine peeked outside, slammed the door, and shook her head. Lisa's heart leaped into her throat.

"Mom, where's your phone?" She snatched her car keys from the table and began looking for her purse, but didn't see it anywhere. "I'll call the cops—"

Her mother stepped back from the front door just as the frame splintered under the weight of Gary Olson's boot. He stepped over the threshold and leveled the barrel of his hunting rifle at her mother's chest.

Katherine slowly raised her hands in the air, dropped the knife. The blade clattered at Gary's feet, and he kicked it away.

Arthur strolled in through the doorway behind Gary, his face flushed and splotchy, wearing that too-wide smile. He tapped Gary on the shoulder and pointed in her direction. "Keep an eye on that one. She's a little feisty."

"You smug prick." Lisa took a step toward the bastard, ready to knock the smile off his face, but Gary swiveled and held her in the rifle's sights.

"I wouldn't do that, little lady. Can't be feisty when you don't have a fuckin' head."

Lisa froze and held up her hands. "Mom?"

Her mother held Arthur's stare. "It's okay, honey. It's all going to be okay. Just do what they say."

"That's right," Arthur said. "You always were a smart one. Was it you who put Jerry up to. . . whatever the hell he was doing? Not that it matters now." He looked at Lisa. "I'm sorry your mama lied to you, kiddo."

Lisa glanced at her mother. "Lied about what?"

Arthur motioned to the door. "About everything being okay. That's just simply not true. Not for you two, anyway."

28

Footsteps crunched through gravel somewhere nearby. Jerry stirred, wincing from the sting of his wounds, and took in his surroundings. Dusty tools, farm equipment, a few musty bales of hay—Arthur's barn. Morning sunlight shone through gaps in the old barn's roof. He gazed dreamily into the light, questioning how he came to be here. He couldn't recall much following the attack. Everything had gone dark, fuzzy, and now his head throbbed in protest.

The attack. Memories of the gorgon's face ushered a sliver of ice through his gut. He shot to his feet in a panic. *Katherine, I hope you had the good sense to get the hell out of here.* God, he wanted to believe she did.

He checked his arm. A series of puncture wounds in a circular shape, tacky with dried blood, like he'd been bitten by a leech. Rivulets of deep blue seeped from a couple of the wounds, burning his skin like acid. *Or poison*, he thought. He snatched a dirty rag from the floor and wiped away the fluid from his skin. *Bitch stung me.*

The doors shuddered, then swung open. Jerry squinted against the sunlight. A figure stood in the opening. Human, judging by the blurry shape, but that was no guarantee.

Arthur stood with his hands in his pockets and a blank expression. He'd expected a half-worm monstrosity without a face, but Fairview's chairman appeared outwardly normal, wearing his usual baggy khaki shorts and a red Hawaiian shirt open at the chest. Jerry studied the man, tried to decide if the look on his face was born from anger or concern, or maybe a bit of both.

"Somehow," Jerry grunted, "you look even more like a monster than the rest."

Arthur shook his head. "That reminds me of a line from a book I read in school. 'In the country of the blind, the one-eyed man is king.' H.G. Wells. Do you know it?"

"Been a while, but yeah, I've read it."

"That's me, Jerry. I'm no one special. Just a guy running a business, trying to help others." He paused for effect. "Did I ever tell you about my pops?"

Jerry crossed his arms. "No." *And I don't give a shit,* he wanted to add, but kept his mouth shut. Arthur's demeanor set him on edge, and he wasn't sure how the man would react.

"Come on out of there. Let's take a walk. I'll tell you a little story."

He left the barn and waved for Jerry to join him.

Jerry followed him outside. Little had changed about Arthur's backyard, except for one thing: the woman standing on the deck. She looked even more out of place in the daylight.

Arthur followed Jerry's gaze and waved to her. "Hi, honey! Just having a chat, that's all."

Gladys Peterson did not wave back. Even at this distance, Jerry recognized her shape, the general wrongness of her face. He couldn't put the swirling tentacles out of his mind.

"I see you two met last night." Arthur pointed to Jerry's wounds. "Looks worse than it really is, right? She just wanted to keep an eye on you, make sure you didn't hurt yourself wandering alone in the dark."

Jerry only nodded, didn't trust himself not to let his anger take over and spew insults he might later regret. Instead, he followed Arthur to the back gate and out toward the hillside trail.

They stopped there as Arthur surveyed the neighborhood. "My pops, he suffered from dementia. The early onset kind. I was in college when it took hold of him. Horrible way to die, if you ask me." He set off down the hill toward the park. Jerry followed.

"He lingered in that state for almost a decade," Arthur continued. "One day he was his old self, the next he was a stranger, and you couldn't tell which one he'd be until you talked to him. Was I getting my father, or was I getting his shadow? A crapshoot. My mother took it all in stride, of course—she lived through the Great Depression, part of the Greatest Generation. Just made of sterner stuff than folks nowadays.

"But me, well, I couldn't deal with it. Just couldn't stand the thought of my old man forgetting my face. That was the worst, you know, when he thought I was a stranger in his house. One time he thought I was a Bible salesman. Another time, when I was home for a weekend, he pulled a gun on me because he thought I'd broken in to steal his coin collection."

Arthur looked over his shoulder, but Jerry gave no sign of sympathy, remained balanced between fight and flight. He focused on his breathing, measuring the seconds before each exhale. Any sign of emotion would be more than enough ammunition for Arthur to use against him. Jerry knew the type and had sparred with his fair share in his corporate days—the type who sought an emotional connection for later exploitation. Sociopaths.

"My pops pulled me aside one day and said my mama was trying to poison him," Arthur said as they crossed into the thicket. "I brushed this off, told myself it was the dementia talking, but it planted a little seed of doubt, you know? Later that night, I spied my mother trying to give him his medicine—only it wasn't pills or anything. It was some weird drink she kept in a jar. And my pops, he fought her with everything he had and slapped the jar from her hand. It shattered on the floor, and I remember seeing gray foam bubbling and twitching in a puddle.

"The next day, I confronted Mama, told her what Pops said and what I'd seen her doing. I expected she'd tear me a new one. No talking back to Mama in those days, you see. But she didn't scold me. Instead, we went on a walk and she told me a story about my grandpa. Mama said he 'passed through' before I was born, and no one ever talked about him, so I was all ears, you know? She told me he used to be a professor for the state university, and one day he was called upon to investigate a farm upstate. Would you believe there's a specific science for the study of worms?"

Jerry slowed to a stop. "Helminthology," he said.

Arthur was several strides further down the path before he turned back. "What was that?"

"Elliot Trask. Your grandpa was the missing scientist, wasn't he?"

A thin smile spread across Arthur's face. "You really *did* do your homework yesterday. I am impressed, sir."

"Is that why you hid the old articles? To keep your family's connection a secret?"

"When you're responsible for a community, Jerry, you'll do whatever you can to keep it safe. 'Keep a degree of separation,' Mama told me that day. 'If anyone finds out about this place, it could jeopardize the integrity of the nest.'"

"Don't tell me you built this place to protect the worms."

"The roots of Fairview began when my grandpa saw the glory of the goddess for himself. He gave up everything to be her acolyte, and Mr. Bailey helped him do it. They raised their families here. How do you think I met Gladys?" Arthur turned on his heels and resumed his walk down the hill.

Jerry chewed his lip, piecing together his guide's revelation. *They're all drones, protecting their queen.*

"You coming?"

"Do I have a choice?"

The smile was gone from Arthur's face. A soft breeze swept over them, rustling the tree limbs overhead, and though the morning was mildly warm, Jerry's arms broke out in goosebumps.

He studied the thicket, wondering how much the underbrush would slow him down if he decided to run. Would running even matter? Fairview Acres was huge, and his new-found boost of energy might not carry him far. And there was Katherine and Lisa to think about.

This is all on you, hon. Just stay and listen to the man. Maybe he'll show you a way out of this. Maybe he'll change your mind. Maybe...

Jerry pushed those thoughts away. The goddess's emissaries had compromised Abby's voice and were using it against him. He'd already lost her once; now some alien intelligence was stealing her from him again. He cleared his head, ignored the sour feeling roiling in his gut.

"Run if you want," Arthur said, "but I wouldn't. Your neighbors are on the lookout all around the park rim."

Overhead, a crow cawed in agreement. Bile burned at the back of Jerry's throat. *Be calm. Keep yourself together for Katherine and Lisa.* No one else was coming to save them. He was their only cavalry, and without a horse.

"All right, then." He carried on in Arthur's shadow. "So, your whole family has served this goddess?"

"Of course not." Arthur cleared his throat. "My daddy refused his responsibility, decided he didn't want to be part of our goddess's glory. A bit like you, in a way. That's why Mama told me all about our family that day. Our responsibility. Said it was time I learned the truth, and my purpose, since Daddy wanted no part of it."

They reached the edge of the thicket. Below them, several men and women were decorating the bandstand for the ceremony. Streamers, banners, bouquets of flowers adorned the stage. Amplifiers and other audio equipment stood off to one side. The same DJ, sporting a red bandana and a mane of flowing white hair, busied himself with his setup.

"Back then, my daddy's refusal was a problem. There wasn't a neighborhood from which others could be brought into the fold. You can't cultivate the same field over and over every year. It must be cycled, or else it goes fallow. That's why I bought this land from Gladys's father, so we'd never have to worry about finding others. Quite proud of the idea, actually."

The DJ plugged in the amplifiers. A huge whine of feedback ripped through the air, followed by a gravelly voice saying, "Check, check." A moment later, music. Johnny Cash.

"From time to time, the most devout of us will pass through to be with the goddess. My grandpa did, and my mama after that. It is a great moment of ascension, to be chosen by the goddess and ushered through into her dreaming. Gladys was the last to be chosen, and she returned to us a divine being."

Jerry thought of the holes in her face, and the slimy wriggling ropes protruding from them. Wet slapping sounds in the dark. Barbed tips cutting the air with whipcrack speed. *Yeah, she's a real angel, that one.*

"Tonight, when we pass between the moon and the sun, the moon's eye will open and the goddess will see us, and I will be the next to receive her blessing."

"And leave Fairview behind? Whatever will we do without you?"

If Arthur sensed his sarcasm, he made no sign of it. He was too caught up in his own speech, so high on his own supply there was no pulling him down.

"Gladys and I weren't blessed with children. Goddess knows, we tried, but these flawed vessels of ours. . ." He looked down, dug his heel into the grass. "So, we poured ourselves into our work. The people of Fairview Acres became our children."

"And you became the one-eyed man," Jerry said.

Excitement lit up Arthur's face. "Yes, exactly! You get it. I knew you would."

Johnny Cash transitioned to Bobby Darin, a big band welcome for the procession of Fairview residents arriving from the opposite side of the park. They carried coolers, camping chairs, parasols. A pair of men began setting up a volleyball net. Jerry heard the clank of a horseshoes game nearby.

An ordinary Friday in appearance only. This slice of mundane Americana was little more than a charade to make its residents feel normal, a veil pulled over their eyes to mask the truth. They were all victims here, all sheep, all blind. Willfully, he suspected. They were so eager to reap the potion's benefits, the side effects be damned.

"I don't know what Katherine had you doing out here last night, Jerry—I can't imagine it was good, whatever it was—but I choose to believe you will rise above it. You've tasted the potion, enjoyed its effects for a day. I mean, look at you." He gave Jerry a once-over. "You're a new man. A complete one-eighty from the guy I picked up at the library yesterday. And you're compassionate, caring. I knew the moment you tried to help Katherine that I'd found the right guy."

Jerry blinked, shook his head. "What do you mean by that?"

"It's simple, really." Arthur clapped a hand on his shoulder and grinned. "Once I pass through, someone's gotta take my place. It can't be Gladys. The outside world wouldn't understand her ascension. And Gary. . . he's loyal, but too reactive. The Scotts, they're too eager. Most of the longtimers here are too, if I'm being honest. I want someone who *doesn't* want the burden. Someone with good financial sense to run the day-to-day operations, who's tenacious enough to see things through. There are lots of business dealings under the Fairview umbrella, my man. Lots of irons in the fire. I *need* someone who can listen, who cares about his work, who *understands* the delicate balance at work here. So, I choose you, Jerry Campbell. You're the new one-eyed man, and you will be king."

The world dropped away from him, and his knees grew weak, gelatinous. His head hummed with the groan of the great cosmic machine and its gnashing teeth. He steadied himself, took a breath. Was this another panic attack? Or worse, a heart attack? There was no pain in his left arm, only the suffocating hold of gravity squeezing his insides like a tube of toothpaste.

"This is why you wouldn't leave me alone," Jerry said. "Why you looked into my background, bought my old place so I'd move here—"

"I knew from the moment I saw your application that you were the perfect fit. Fairview was made for you, friend, and I believe it will flourish under your care."

He wanted to scream; he wanted to clock Arthur in the jaw. But a voice—his voice this time—reminded him of Katherine and Lisa. They were more important, and if he played along, maybe he could still save them.

"You okay there, bud? Looking a little pale."

"Yeah," Jerry grunted. "It's just... been a while since I had the potion."

The words were heavy, sour. He needed the strength, and he also needed to wear the mask of a faithful convert, if only until the evening. Whatever he could do to save Katherine and Lisa, he would do it—even if it meant wearing the stupid T-shirt.

"Oh, that's no problem at all, Jerry." He beckoned to one of the men working at the bandstand. "Hey, Bob, are those kegs set up yet? We got someone who needs a little pick-me-up."

"Not yet," Bob called out, "but I've got some in a cooler. Come on over."

Arthur turned back. "See? We've got you covered, man. Bob will take care of you. Just, uh, one thing..." He leaned next to Jerry's ear and whispered. "Gladys doesn't trust you—many don't—and that's why you'll be part of the ceremony tonight."

Jerry's face flushed with heat. "Part of the ceremony?"

He wanted to scream, but kept a smile fixed to his face the whole time. It was the only way he could hold back the rage burning him on the inside.

"Yeah, it's just a small thing. Come on, let's get you that drink. I'll explain everything. . ."

29

Lisa sat on Arthur's huge sectional sofa and stared at the "LIVE LAUGH LOVE" sign on the mantle, just below the widescreen TV. Her hands were bound again—zip ties this time—but not her feet, which felt like a small blessing. Arthur and Gary had left her and her mother free to roam the confines of Arthur's den. The door to the upstairs was locked with a key, and the sliding doors to the backyard were barred with a chain and padlock. Across the room was a small bar surrounded by awful décor. Framed photos of athletes, pennants, and a football jersey for the Philadelphia Eagles adorned the walls. A huge print of *Dogs Playing Poker* served as a centerpiece. In all, the den was decorated like something out of a furniture catalog to give the impression that someone lived there.

A model home. Like a fucking dollhouse.

They'd explored the entire space, but anything useful had been removed. The utility closet, laundry room, and bathroom were open, but sparse. Lisa had considered shattering the mirror to cut herself free, but she feared accidentally slitting her wrists. They were both tired, sore, hungry and thirsty, and in desperate need of coffee.

Her mother drew her knees to her chest. Red rings lined her wrists from the plastic ties. "I'm worried about Jerry."

"I knew you were sweet on him."

"Lisa, please—"

She forced herself to laugh, because if she didn't, she might explode with rage. *You left me alone in that fucking basement so you could go sleep with your new boyfriend. Goddammit, Mother.* But it could wait until they weren't held captive in someone's basement. A raging fit would help no one. She took a deep breath, counted to ten, and changed the subject.

"What's going to happen to us, Mom?"

But she already knew what they had planned for her, as crazy and horrifying as it was. *I guess human sacrifice has come back in style. Look at me, behind on the latest trends once again.*

She used to pride herself on keeping cool under pressure, a trait that had served her well as an RN, but this? Knowing her life's expiration date was currently being measured in hours and minutes had undermined what composure she had left. Even back in her mother's basement, she'd had hope, but after being captured a second time, and now watching the way her mother avoided eye contact, she was finally beginning to lose her cool.

I never should have answered my phone yesterday. Should've muted the goddamn thing and gone back to sleep. But no, I had to answer, because something might've happened to Mom. Now I'm counting down my final hours. I swear to God, if I live through this, I'm trashing my phone and going to live in a fucking cave—

Two shadows stretched across the room as a pair of figures appeared at the glass doors.

"Jerry!" Her mother was on her feet in an instant. She met them at the door, beaming with relief, and wearing a smile Lisa hadn't seen in what felt like years. *Definitely sweet on him,* she thought, and rolled her eyes. *We're going to have a long talk when this is over, Mom. If we make it out of this alive.*

Arthur unlocked the doors and followed Jerry inside with a bounce in his step, like he'd won the lottery or something. Lisa wanted to knock his teeth in.

Her mother took Jerry's hands in her own. "I thought you were..." She glanced at Arthur, lowered her voice. "I'm glad you're okay."

Arthur said, "I'll leave you three to chat." He nudged Jerry's arm. "Just remember what we talked about, huh?"

Lisa watched their exchange, felt that familiar lump climbing up her throat. Arthur was his usual faux-friendly self, but Jerry's pale skin and grim demeanor set off alarm bells in her head. Sure, the old man looked better than he had yesterday, but he also looked worse somehow, like a guy who'd been given a death sentence. The wounds on his arm didn't look too good, either.

They were silent, listening to Arthur's heavy footsteps up the stairs. The basement door opened and closed, and then his voice carried down as he greeted his wife.

Lisa shot to her feet and held out her wrists. "I don't know what happened to you, but you can tell us after we're far away from here. Can you cut us free—"

Jerry shook his head. "Lisa, you need to listen to me very carefully—"

"—so we can get the fuck out... Wait, what?" She swallowed the rest of her syllables.

Jerry put his hand on her shoulder. "I need you both to sit down." He glanced to the ceiling, tracing footsteps overhead with his eyes, and lowered his voice to a whisper. "I'm supposed to be saying goodbye right now. That's the only reason he allowed me to see you before tonight..."

Lisa sank back into the sectional. "What are you talking about, Jerry?"

"Tell me you didn't make some kind of deal with that man," her mother said. "What's going on?"

She listened to the old man's story about what happened the night before—his description of the Scotts turned her stomach—and his exchange with Arthur this morning.

"He wants me to be a part of the ceremony tonight. Both of you are to be sacrificed, and he wants me to be the one to do it."

"You're shitting me," Lisa snapped. "What the hell for?"

"He believes it's the only way the rest of the community will trust me."

Her mother took Lisa's hand in her own and squeezed. "Jerry, what do you intend to do?"

"The plan remains the same. I was almost finished when they caught me last night." He looked at Katherine, and then Lisa. Tears filled his eyes, and his chin trembled. "Whatever I have to do, I'll keep you both safe. I promise."

Footsteps creaked above.

Her mother's breath hitched in her throat, and her words came out in a sputter. "And who's going to look after you, old man?"

Jerry answered her with a kiss. Happiness lit up her mother's face, the sort of joy that had been absent for far too long. Seeing this quelled the flames burning away inside Lisa's mind. *We're still gonna have that talk, though.*

Her mother kissed Jerry back, and a tear slid down her cheek. She whispered, "You come back to me, Jerry Campbell. You still owe me a dance."

The basement door opened above, and Arthur called out, "I'm heading back to the park, hon. See you tonight."

Jerry smiled at her mother, but there was sadness in his eyes. "I guess I do, don't I?" And then, to Lisa: "When the time comes, get your mother out of there."

"Enough of this macho bullshit," Lisa said. "Just tell me—"

"How are things going down here?" Arthur turned the corner and stared at them. He held half of a peeled banana in his hand. The other half he chewed with his mouth open, smacking his lips. "We all good?"

Jerry kissed Katherine's hand and then faced Fairview's chairman. "Yeah. We're good."

"Great." Arthur shoved the rest of the banana into his mouth. "Katherine, sweetheart, I hate that things have come down to this, but—"

"Go fuck yourself, Arthur. It's because of you my husband is dead. And now..." She tried to say more, but the floodgates were open now, and all she managed was a bitter cry of anger and sorrow.

"Now, Katherine, that's no way to be. Think of the good you'll be doing for the community."

"You heard her," Lisa spat. "Go fuck yourself, Arthur." She thought for a moment, then added: "With a cactus."

He went quiet and forced a smile, a look that would kill if only he had the ability. Instead, he turned to Jerry and nodded. "We're done here, then. Come along."

Jerry gave them both a timid glance before following Arthur into the backyard. The sliding door closed, and Arthur locked it behind them.

Lisa held her mother's hand until the woman's tears faded into quiet sobs, and then finally to sleep. Lisa eased her mother down on the cushions, lifted her feet so she'd be more comfortable. While Katherine slept, Lisa paced the room like a trapped animal, seeking any means of escape—but there were none she could find. She envied her mother then, sleeping away the hours until their execution, as Lisa's mind was on manic overdrive.

Whether Jerry had a plan worked out or not, she couldn't deny his loyalty. And seeing him kiss her mother, how careful he was, holding her face in his hands, and the way her eyes lit up... Six months ago, Katherine would've yelled at him for being too close, or she would've called him Reggie. *And now that she's found someone who brings out the best in her again, everything's going to hell. What a fucking nightmare.*

A nightmare would make sense, in an ironic sort of way. Perhaps she was still dreaming, still back in her apartment, still enjoying a deep slumber after an endless night shift at the hospital. Because that was the only way an entire community's desire to sacrifice them to some impossible moon goddess could compute.

She sat and stared at the backyard while the shadows slowly thinned, watching the morning give way to the afternoon. Maybe a moon goddess wasn't out of the question after all. And if that was true, then all bets were off. What could someone like Jerry do to stop such a force?

Or worse, what if he did? What would happen to all the people in Fairview?

Gooseflesh spread up her arms and down her back. She looked at her mother, still in a deep sleep, and frowned.

The possibility terrified her.

◐

Jerry spent the afternoon watching his neighbors toil in the park, setting up decorations and tables and chairs for the gathering. Most of them gave him a wide berth, leaving him to find a quiet place to sit and work things out in his head. He sat in the shade, reclining against a tree, and observed the lords and ladies of Arthur's kingdom. Their king remained on the bandstand, issuing directives to the rabble, and Jerry was never far from the man's watchful eye.

All of this, he mused, *for a rock and some worms. Arthur's leading the blind, indeed.*

His head was trapped in an anxious fog he couldn't shake. Would the ANFO he'd packed into the meteorite be enough? Could he pull this off without any harm to Katherine or Lisa? He feared the day was slipping through his fingers like fine sand. He would spend the minutes counting its grains if he could, anything to postpone the inevitable.

Had he lied to them?

He wanted to believe he hadn't, that his plan was solid, but deep down he knew the truth: a million things could go wrong, probably *would* go wrong. His anxiety-riddled mind conjured a hundred different possibilities, each with an outcome more disastrous than the last. He knew nothing about explosives, other than to be far away from them when they ignited. What if the rock exploded into tiny bits of shrapnel, killing everyone near it? Worse: what if the ANFO was too old, a dud, and the explosion didn't happen? Or if the rock was destroyed, but nothing changed: the goddess stayed in their heads, everyone was still a drone, and he was forced to execute—

Stop it, you foolish old man. You haven't been this bad since the layoffs in your office years ago.

The real Abby this time, or at least as real as she was going to get. His thoughts in her voice, and not distorted by the goddess lurking in the darker corners of his mind. Abby was right, of course—he'd worked himself to the edge of a breakdown. *I got through it, though. Abby intervened, made me keep that appointment with my doctor. Hell of a thing, learning you have an anxiety disorder in your fifties.*

Somehow, for all their positive effects, the supposed divine emissaries at work in his body hadn't cured his anxiety. Perhaps a state of constant worry was something even a cosmic being couldn't defeat.

He had coping mechanisms on which to fall, some he'd spent his entire life perfecting, and there was one he could use just now. A mask he'd made to look like an ever-smiling version of himself. It was the one he'd worn to work every day so others would be comfortable, though he was always reluctant to put it on and hide who he was inside. A mask so heavy he sometimes cried in relief when he removed it in the evenings.

Only Abby knew his real face. He didn't have to wear the mask around her, and goddamn, he loved her for that.

But that wasn't true, was it? Abby wasn't the only one anymore. Kat knew his real face, had seen it in the intimate spaces of the dark, and this realization made his heart ache.

He glared across the lawn at Arthur, who stood facing the Moon Pool, hands on his hips, his bright Hawaiian shirt a second sun for them all.

You think I'd kill the only people here who are real to me. You think I'm that easy, so addicted to your drug that I'll do anything for more, that I'll just throw away the life I want for the life you want me to have. But that's where you're wrong, bud. And I can't wait to show you tonight.

Arthur slowly turned, peered over his shoulder at Jerry, and waved. Had Jerry thought so loudly that Arthur heard him somehow? Perhaps the worms held some psychic link and all of Fairview was a huge Wi-Fi network of invertebrates. But if that were true, he'd be dead already, and so would Katherine and Lisa.

Jerry forced a smile, raised his hand in return.

Arthur nodded, satisfied, and turned his attention back to the community.

No, you don't know what I'm thinking. If you did, you'd have locked me up along with Kat and Lisa. Your drones would be combing Bailey's Rock, pulling out pellets.

He wondered how many of them knew Arthur's intentions for tonight, wondered if even his new neighbors, the Gettys, would be there. Hell of a way to make an introduction. *Hi, I'm Jerry, I live next door, nice to meet you. Hold my drink while I kill my friends.*

Or would the Gettys even care come nightfall. His faith in people—which, admittedly, hadn't been so great in the first place—had diminished over the last month. These people, all of them, wore masks of their own, except their eyes were shrouded too, willfully blind. Here they crawled, toiling at the sound of their one-eyed king.

Perhaps it's fitting they're all infested with worms.

Thinking on it now, Jerry realized he'd seen this before. He'd glimpsed this compulsion to follow the herd during his corporate days, when words like "family" and "team" were tossed around so haphazardly, and their meaning was reduced to the number of hours one was willing to commit for the profit of a few. His resistance to this mentality hadn't made him popular in the office, but he'd remained out of a fear of change, calculating numbers and extinguishing fires, crawling in the dirt with the rest of them.

Maybe Fairview Acres wasn't so different. He'd had plenty of opportunities to leave, but the weight anchoring him here was always the fear of change. Sure, he'd dressed it up as something more palatable—a mystery, a rivalry, a love—but beneath all that glamour was the same old stone pulling him down. A big porous rock out of space, having traveled an immeasurable distance only to crash through the atmosphere, its outer crust burning away in a magnificent blaze searing across the sky, and land here long before a fish dared to walk on land.

That big rock, a key to the engine of the cosmos, held him here in its orbit along with everyone else. Sooner or later, it would pull them all to its surface in a brilliant flash of oblivion.

Sooner, by his estimation. Tonight, even.

"Hey, neighbor. Drink up."

Jerry blinked, startled from his thoughts. Gary Olson stood over him, offering a bottle of water. The sun had crawled across the sky during his reverie, the passage of time once more the cause of anxiety, but he had to mask the worry. He took the bottle and drank. The cool water was a welcome distraction, quenching a thirst he didn't realize he had. Cords of tension slowly unwound in his neck, shoulders. The weight on his mind wasn't any lighter, but he could deal with that. One thing at a time.

Gary watched him with curiosity. He smiled. "Glad you came to your senses. Me and Brad had a bet going, you know."

"How were the odds?"

"I owe him a hundred bucks."

Jerry laughed. He couldn't help it.

Gary seemed surprised. "He laughs! You can be something other than a grumpy old man. I'm impressed."

You have no idea, Jerry thought.

"Things didn't go so great last time, but tonight you'll see just how special this place really is. How beautiful it is when the community truly comes together. Tonight is going to blow your mind."

Jerry finished off the water and wiped his mouth. He looked up at his neighbor, another blind idiot crawling to appease his master for the sake of a shallow reward. No, Fairview Acres wasn't different at all. He smiled and said, "I truly hope so."

The mask was heavy, still a burden, but in that moment, Jerry felt strong enough to wear it through to the end.

30

After sundown.

Friday night's special gathering in the park was in full swing. The DJ faded the Doors into Pink Floyd. Someone lit up a joint, and others followed their lead, until a skunky miasma lingered over the park. Jerry watched the glow of a cherry ember pass from one person to the next. He smirked, wondered how long it had been since he'd last smoked. College, at least, and before Abby entered the picture. It was the smell he couldn't stand, a harsh reminder as the pungent aroma wafted in his direction.

He moved away from the tree and wandered down the slope toward the crowd.

All of Fairview was in attendance—five hundred people, easy. Each one infested with a mess of parasites. He chewed his lip, did the math. *That's a lot of worms.*

He'd watched them transform the park into a proper temple for their goddess. Tiki torches lined the stone path and surrounded the Moon Pool, filling the night air with a hint of citronella. Arched trellises formed an entrance between the obelisks, each wrapped in flowers and illuminated with solar lights. Rows of folding chairs stood on both sides of the path. At a glance, one might think a wedding was about to take place.

A woman Jerry didn't know pulled a cart down the aisle between seats, offering refills of the potion to anyone who wanted it, and there were many who did.

Pink Floyd gave way to Bob Dylan.

Dylan to Elvis Presley.

The minutes crawled by, amplifying the tension in Jerry's skull. How long until showtime? He kicked himself for not following up on the eclipse when he was at the library. God, that felt like a lifetime ago, an eternity since yesterday. He hoped the green-haired librarian wasn't involved in this madness like Stewart was. She seemed like a nice kid.

Elvis to Chuck Berry, "Johnny B. Goode."

Murmurs rose from the crowd. Jerry followed their collective gaze toward the sky. The full moon was visible now, a giant cataract peering over its congregation in silent judgment. Seeing it in this context ushered a chill down Jerry's neck.

By the moon's eye. He understood now and wished he didn't.

A sliver of red shadow lingered at the moon's rim. The lunar eclipse had begun. He stared at the celestial body, his thoughts swirling in a vortex of anxiety and anger, but an argument broke his attention. He turned back toward the bandstand. A quartet of figures walked two by two down the hill.

Katherine and Lisa. Behind them, Arthur and Gladys.

A wad of cotton crawled into Jerry's throat. Cold panic welled in his guts. He touched his fingers to his thumb, an old nervous tick he'd acquired in college while trying to learn piano, warm-up exercises to limber himself. He'd forgotten the muscle memory of chords, but the exercises remained, silent remnants of another life, another world lost to time.

Lisa turned and planted her feet. "I told you to get your fucking hands off me."

"Gladys, honey, be a dear..."

The gorgon's tendrils snaked out of her vacuous skull, reared back like cobras ready to strike.

Arthur said something else, but Jerry couldn't hear. A beat later, Lisa resumed her death march with Katherine close at her side.

Jerry worked his way through the crowd toward them, fighting back against the panic hammering in his heart.

As he reached the edge of the crowd, Katherine saw him and cried out his name. Her cheeks glistened with tears, her face pale, and there was pain in her eyes. Had the bastards withheld her potion? Jerry suspected as much. Why waste a perfectly good drug on the condemned?

He supposed the withdrawal was fortuitous for Arthur and his lackeys. An old woman in pain wouldn't put up much of a fight. Lisa was a different story. A dry riverbed of blood covered the gap between her nostrils and upper lip. She peered through a swollen left eye, the skin already purpling into a nice shiner. Jerry swelled with pride, would've congratulated her if not for the situation. *I hope you gave 'em hell, kid.*

Lisa stumbled toward him, placed her chin on his shoulder, and hissed through clenched teeth. "I hope you know what you're doing, old man."

He pulled away, looked her in the eye. *I haven't the slightest idea,* he wanted to say, but couldn't bring himself to destroy whatever hope the poor girl had left. He steeled himself, hardened his gaze, and gave her a short nod. If this young woman could fight so hard in the face of her mortality, then so could he.

"Mr. Campbell! Did you see?" Fairview's chairman pointed to the sky. "Our goddess is soon with us!" And then, to the crowd: "Rejoice, friends! I told you all she would clear the skies for us this evening! Her eye is opening!"

All of Fairview Acres erupted in jubilation. Jerry ignored their cheers and closed the gap between himself and Katherine. Her knees buckled and she fell into him. He caught her, pulled her close, held her tight.

"I'm so sorry," she said, her breath hot on his cheek.

"Don't. Not your fault."

She pulled back to look at him. A thin string of tears spilled down her face. Words formed and dissolved on her dry lips, words she could not voice. He studied her yearning, a dawning terror slowly enveloping her face as she struggled with what to say, a million possible platitudes that might serve as her final words to him.

Jerry freed her of the indecision. He kissed her forehead, whispered in her ear, "Tell me when this is over."

Gladys Peterson pushed Katherine ahead into the crowd but stopped short of following.

Jerry hadn't seen her this close before. If he survived the night, he wasn't sure he would ever forget her, either. Her skull was far less human than he'd thought, the skin dry and cracked and riddled with holes, a small facsimile of Bailey's Rock rendered in bone and flesh. Whatever had once been Gladys Peterson was long gone, her body a hollow nest for the worms and whatever else that dwelled within.

She faced him. Something thick and sinuous stirred in the darkness of her hollow sockets. Gray worms inched out of their hiding place in her cheek, tasted the air around them. A wheeze of air escaped her throat. Shrill and trilling like a flute.

Jerry swallowed back his fear, energized by the anger building in his chest, a boiling furnace churning with pressure and ready to blow. "Anyone ever tell you ya got a face for radio?"

One of her tendrils crawled from the shadow of her eye socket and flexed a mouth of curved barbs. The jagged maw hovered an inch before his face. A bright blue tear of thick liquid dripped from the center opening. He thought he heard it sizzle on the grass below.

"Come on, honey. Jerry didn't mean that." Arthur put his hands on his wife's shoulders, pursed his lips. "We're gonna have to work on your social skills, Jerry. Enough frowning. This is a celebration!"

The residents nearby cheered, as if on command. The chairman and his prisoners continued their procession toward Bailey's Rock.

Jerry followed.

Chuck Berry faded into Frank Sinatra. "Fly me to the moon," Ol' Blue Eyes sang.

In the distance, the eye of their goddess slowly opened.

👁

Katherine wasn't ready. She wanted to be, just so this would all be over no matter where the chips fell—but that was a big fat lie, and she knew it. Every time she thought she had resigned herself to fate, a hollow ache announced itself in her chest.

Even when Gladys ushered them to the Moon Pool's stony shore, she told herself, *I'm ready.*

A moment later: *Who're you kidding, Kat? You think you're ready to say goodbye to Jerry and Lisa? Were you ready to say goodbye to Reggie? And were you* really *ready to say yes when Arthur offered you some of his drink that one night way back when? No. You were never ready. Will never be ready.*

Who would be? Mortality was sobering enough upon contemplation, one of life's final mysteries and so cruel in its unannounced arrival. But to face it head on, stare right into its hollow face, and defiantly shout "Bring it on!" was an act of foolish pride and destruction. No, she supposed, no one was ever truly ready, not even the dying.

And she was *not* dying. Not yet. Maybe before the night's end, but not now.

Now she still had hope.

Gladys forced Katherine to the ground. The sharp crunch of stones beneath her knees shot daggers into her skin. Lisa followed, yelping in pain.

Katherine mustered her strength, braced herself for the wave of pain crashing over her frail figure, the emissaries within crying out for sustenance. She'd known Arthur was a cold son of a bitch, but the depth of his cruelty this time surprised even her. He knew what it was like to go without the potion. To deprive her of it now, with her death warrant signed, sealed, and delivered, was a new low.

You've gone without it before, lady. You can go without just a little longer. Until Jerry does whatever it is he's going to do.

She snapped her head left, then right. Where was Jerry?

The crowd cheered behind her. She glanced to Lisa, wished she could reach out and take her daughter's hand. Gladys had done a number on the poor girl, and though Katherine hated seeing her in pain, she was proud, too. Lisa had always been a fighter. *You made your daddy proud,* Katherine wanted to say, even opened her mouth to do so, but the cheering of Fairview's residents drowned out such encouragement. Instead, she offered her daughter a meek smile.

Arthur marched between them and sloshed into the water like a minister on his way to a baptism. He turned and surveyed his people with a grin of pride, his cheeks almost as red as his shirt. In another time and place, she might've considered him a jolly old man, but she knew better. He was rotten below this façade of friendship, a selfish prick who cared more about appearances and power than his so-called community. They were all drunk on his promise of long life and prosperous health, too inebriated with the potion's effects to see him for what he really was: a Music Man, come to rob the neighborhood blind.

This band he'd built would play to his beat all the way to hell.

Arthur raised his hands. The DJ faded the music to silence, and the crowd's jubilation slowly dropped to a few dissonant murmurs.

When he was satisfied, Arthur began: "This is a special occasion, Fairview. Many of you already know that, but we've grown so much since the last time, and I see so many fresh faces out there tonight. Before we get started, let me just say thank you, from the bottom of my heart, for making Fairview what it is today. Without you, there is no Fairview. Let's hear it for you all!" He led them in a round of applause that carried on for a full minute.

Katherine watched their false prophet soak it in. She couldn't help but roll her eyes. Reggie used to call him a suburban Napoleon, a memory that struck her funny bone at the worst moment; she fought to stifle laughter as the applause died. Arthur glanced down, clenched his jaw, and the cheeriness slipped from his face in a blink. He stared hard in her direction, just long enough so she'd know he didn't share her amusement. *I'm going to make this so painful for you,* that glare said.

But then his disdain morphed back into a smile, and he was Arthur again, your old pal from a few blocks away. Fairview's friendly chairman and despot, drug dealer and cult leader.

"And now, my friends, the time has come around again. Years ago, when our goddess opened her eye and blessed us with her celestial presence, it was my wonderful wife, Gladys, who passed through the veil. She communed with the divine and returned to us changed,"—he motioned toward the humanoid creature wearing his late wife's skin—"a living conduit and nest for the emissaries which grant us eternal life. And tonight, Fairview, I believe it will be my turn to pass through."

Murmurs rose in the crowd, voicing an uneasiness that hung over the park like a toxic miasma, slowly eating away at their celebratory veneer. Arthur was prepared for this, however, his words already loaded and ready to fire. Katherine had to hand it to him: he was good at stirring a crowd.

He could be a politician if he wanted to be, but that would be much too public. He likes his power consolidated. Easier to control.

"Now, now, I know what y'all must be thinking. If I ascend and return changed, who will become the face of Fairview? Who among us is worthy of such a burden? To grow and strengthen our wonderful community. Who, indeed, my friends? I have given this much thought, and after many sleepless nights, I have settled on a worthy candidate."

Arthur gestured to his congregation.

Jerry emerged from the crowd, his chin held high, staring daggers at Arthur's beaming face. He touched Katherine's shoulder as he walked past, a slight gesture of reassurance, and a butterfly beat its wings inside her belly. She wanted to chastise herself for being childish, but Reggie piped up, told her to be true. *That feeling is valid, honey. And it might be the last time you'll feel something so pure.*

A few upset jeers erupted from the gathered folk behind her.

Arthur maintained his smile with a burning intensity, and she was certain its superficial nature went unnoticed by most. The greater populace of Fairview Acres had no cause to see Arthur's other side, probably wouldn't notice it unless he wanted them to.

The chairman went on, "Now, now, I know what you're all thinking. How can this man, this troublemaker and denier of our goddess's glory, be the one to take over as Fairview's leader? Believe me, I get it, friends. He's a newcomer. He's quiet, likes to keep to himself. In recent days, he's said and done some hurtful things."

Arthur stepped forward, put his hand on Jerry's shoulder, and for a moment they could've been best friends. War buddies, maybe. When Jerry turned back to face the crowd, Katherine saw something she hadn't expected. His smile was too wide, all teeth. She couldn't recall a single time she'd seen him smile like this, and for once, she saw something he and Arthur had in common. The same intensity, the same façade.

"I've searched my heart, friends," Arthur said. "Over the last few weeks, I've grown to understand Jerry Campbell. As we all know, every cold and stony surface hides a core of warmth. The week this man moved in, he was compelled to save the life of one of our own. It wasn't his responsibility, no one had appointed him to such a role, and yet he did it anyway. He did what any good neighbor would. *That* is the kind of compassion this job requires, friends."

Katherine shot a look at her daughter. Lisa glared up at their warden, staring with such rage she wondered if Arthur might catch fire. *Good,* she thought, *let that anger burn hot. She'll need it.*

Behind them, the people of Fairview voiced their discontent.

Arthur was undeterred. "But I do understand, friends. Trust must be earned. Far be it from me to put someone in charge who hasn't met with your approval. And that is why Jerry's first act as chairman will be to prepare tonight's sacrifices for the glory of our goddess. Once her eye is open—and it is very close now, friends—he will deliver their flesh unto her."

He looked to Gladys and held out his hand. "Darling," he said.

Gladys reached into her blouse and produced a short, serrated blade. She placed it in Arthur's palm. He examined the dagger, studied its weight, and then held it up for all to see.

"This ceremonial knife was first used by my grandfather to slit a calf's throat in her honor. The times have changed, and we have grown in number, but the old ways, friends, are always best." He passed the blade to Jerry, who took it without hesitation.

"Our grandparents, our parents, mine and Gladys's both, our families have carried on this tradition for a century. Although they have returned to the glory of the goddess's embrace, I feel them with us in every sip of potion, every glimmer of the stars, every twist and turn of our divine emissaries. And now, as the eclipse closes and her eye opens, I go to follow in their tradition."

He raised his hand to the sky, and every head turned to follow its path. Far above, the earth's shadow slowly consumed the moon, its cratered surface absorbed by the dark of the cosmos. The crowd bristled with uneasy excitement. Even Katherine felt the power of the moment as her arms and neck erupted in gooseflesh.

A steady hum droned from deep in the earth, disturbing the pool's surface with short, jarring ripples that crashed against the shore. The stone trembled and cracked. Bits of sparkling dust rained down to the water below. Light seeped from within, washing over them all, a blinding aura of brilliance tuned to the lungs of something housed within. Something breathing for the first time in years.

Arthur turned, faced the shuddering aura of Bailey's Rock, and cried out with joy. "She comes, friends! Her time is upon us!"

The earth's shadow eclipsed the moon in totality, draping its face in a dark glow of red and purple, old blood and a fresh bruise. Katherine's ears rang as the hum grew from a drone to the steady groan of a voice. Not one, but several voices in dissonance—voices of the cosmos and the infinite, the pitch so immense human senses could only process a fraction of its sound.

She wished she could cover her ears but doubted it would do any good. This voice resonated beyond her hearing and deep into her bones. It was everywhere and nowhere, a phantom screaming from the liminal space of beyond, the volume rising to announce not only its presence but a base impulse universal with even the smallest of creatures: hunger.

Bailey's Rock pulsed with light as arcs of electricity snapped and sizzled across its surface. The world around them breathed and cried out in agony as it gave birth to a foreign entity that pushed its way through a fissure of time and space.

Katherine closed her eyes, but overhead, the moon opened wide.

◐

Jerry thought he was prepared for what came next.

He'd been closer than this last night—had felt the slow inhale and exhale of something he could not see, heard the cogs of the cosmic machine groan and click into place—but despite bearing witness to those sensations, he had not expected Bailey's Rock to move.

Maybe it was a trick of gravity, something to do with the alignment of sun, earth, and moon, but he could not say for sure. He could only trust his eyes, and what they sent back to his brain were ocular recordings of the meteorite slowly wrenching itself free of the earth. The movement disturbed the waters of the reflecting pool, spraying them with a cold mist as the stone began to spin, gaining speed until it rose into the air. Electricity arced across its gnarled surface, and the brilliant white aura faded into the same bruised shade of the moon. Faster, faster the stone spun, gaining height with each rotation until it hovered far above their heads.

Heart racing and still unable to believe his eyes, Jerry took a step back toward the shore. Arthur and the others were oblivious to his movement. They stood transfixed with joy, the sound of their excitement lost in the tumult of wind and crackling energy and the rising drone of organic machinery locking into place.

The stone spun on an unseen axis, held afloat by a gravity of its own making, and gained so much speed its features vanished in a blur. So, too, did the energy coursing over its surface, melding into a singular glow. The meteorite was hardly recognizable now. Its cracked and ridged form flattened into a glowing circle of ruddy light.

Arthur glanced back, read the fear on Jerry's face, and brayed a mule's laugh. *"This isn't even the best part! Behold!"* He raised his hands like a crazed conductor and beckoned to the bloody disc looming over them. The chaotic drone slowly dipped in volume until it was barely audible, and the wind died down in tandem.

An eerie calm fell over the park. Even the congregation was silent, and when Jerry looked back, he wished he hadn't.

Many of his neighbors were changing, their bodies twisting and twitching and seizing, each limb seemingly possessed of a separate sentience. Other folks—perhaps recent converts, newcomers—merely watched in amazement and horror. This was the fate that awaited all of Fairview, sooner or later.

Bones popped and cracked in a dissonant chorus.

Flesh became clay.

Gary Olson's face bled from its orifices as his features distorted and skin stretched apart from itself. Slowly, painfully, the man's head elongated. His fingers fused together. He bent forward violently, every vertebra cracking in protest, and lowered his torso to the grass. Cords of muscle protruded from his neck as the skin reconstituted itself into a thin, fat nub. Patches of gray hair stuck out of its many folds, the skin slick with blood and sweat. Amid the horrid sounds of bones reconfiguring themselves, Jerry thought he heard muffled screams.

Oh my God, he thought. *It's Gary.*

Others joined him: Bradley and Matilda Scott, just a few rows back, were transforming. Bethany Miles, too, alongside so many others he didn't know, didn't *want* to know. Further back, he thought he glimpsed remnants of Stewart's bloody face, but the crowd moved in waves, crashed in upon itself, and an instant later the face was gone. One by one, the people of Fairview Acres were remade in their goddess's image, their blessing and curse for eternal life.

"Mama..." Lisa cried. The impossible transformations taking place around them had reduced her to a frightened child.

Katherine called out to her daughter and pleaded, "Close your eyes, honey. Don't look."

Jerry caught the desperation in her eyes, the sheer terror of her inevitable mortality. Her expression broke through the fear sheathing him from the cold reality of their situation.

He turned, cast his gaze toward Arthur's wife, expecting to see the gorgon monitoring his every move. Instead, she stood beside her husband with her arms raised in supplication to the blood red portal open above.

Now, Abby told him, *while you can.*

Jerry gripped the ceremonial blade and darted toward Katherine, aware of every sound he made, the beat of his heart and crunch of pebbles underfoot. He took hold of her hands and cut through her bindings. When he was done, he did the same for Lisa. She climbed to her feet, wiped the tears from her eyes, and stared at him with wide-eyed fear.

"Go," he hissed. "Take your mother and get the hell out of here. Before..."

Lisa wasn't looking at him; she was staring over his shoulder, up to the sky.

"Jerry..." Katherine began but was silenced by a crack of thunder booming overhead.

He readied himself, turned. A memory from his dinner with Arthur replayed in his head while he tried to make sense of what he was seeing.

A conduit to the heavens.

Bailey's Rock had transformed into a flat circle of reddish light, a mimicry of the eclipsed moon. It was a perfect circular hole carved out of time and space, and from it thundered the sound of the great engine. The gears of bone ground together, clacking into place, while a jagged mountain range of broken teeth gnashed against the palate of a great vast nothing. A nothing so immense it defied calculation, a division of zero on an unfathomable scale.

An immeasurable universe of eyes gazed upon them all, unblinking, the blackened flesh of spaces betwixt. Galaxies of bones swirled in its depth, filled with the rotted carcasses of worlds. The bottomless maw of an entity neither alive nor dead, this virus of existence that always was and will always be. Consuming what it can, when it can, and influencing when it cannot. Its emissaries cast like dice across space to change, mutate, and devour; to disseminate the one into many and deform all into its likeness.

A shape emerged from within the circle—a long appendage, sinuous, composed of winding fibers of glistening muscle—and forced itself through. Patches of ice clung to its skin in jagged crystalline formations. At the front was a fold of skin, its underside lined with curved teeth.

The massive thing hovered from the opening, unsure at first, almost timid in its movements. A moment later, it continued outward, thick as a redwood trunk and jointed like a knuckle. A finger, perhaps, or maybe a leg—it was impossible to tell, and Jerry's mind struggled to give it a definitive shape. It was alive, yet it reeked of decay. The ice affixed to its skin began to melt into a viscous sludge wriggling with worms. Thick rivulets of slime drenched the earth below and sizzled with impossible heat.

The limb planted itself in the Moon Pool, spraying flecks of water into Jerry's face. He flinched from the sudden cold. Freed of his trance, he took hold of Lisa and gave her a shake. Her pupils readjusted, and she returned her focus to him, then to her mother. She rushed to her side, draped Katherine's arm over her shoulder, and began to move them away from the crowd. Katherine called out Jerry's name, but he didn't reply, was too afraid to draw more attention to them.

Uhk-uhk-uhhhk! The nightcrawlers cheered for their goddess.

Jerry tried not to think about the army of worm-headed things lurking mere feet behind him. There was just enough of a cacophony from the rip in space to mask Lisa and Katherine's escape. *Thank the Universe for small favors,* he thought, but felt uncertain after the fact. The Universe was here—or was trying to be, at least—and he wanted no part of it.

"*That's it, my goddess!*" Arthur cheered on the monstrosity as it birthed itself. "*Come through and claim what is yours!*"

Arcs of energy sizzled across the open portal as it widened. Arthur's goddess had more to show of itself, and Jerry glimpsed a multi-lobed eye peering down from beyond. There was curiosity in its gaze, like a child pressing her eye to a window, peering in to see all she could see. But this was no child, and there was no innocence to its stare. Only eagerness. Unyielding hunger. Ravenous.

We see you, Jerry Campbell. A morsel of flesh and bone. Bow before us and submit to the Eater of Worlds.

A flash erupted behind the rift. Something popped. An M80, maybe, or a gunshot. *Pop-pop-pop* like a chain of firecrackers, only these were the size of dynamite. But how could their fuse be lit if—

The energy! Abby screamed in his head, and Jerry realized her meaning an instant too late. Time slowed. He sucked in his breath, spun on his heels to dive for cover.

Arthur dropped his arms, tilted his head in confusion. "What's tha—"

The back half of Bailey's Rock exploded, swallowing the world in a brilliant flash of white.

31

Darkness.
A deep insufferable ringing.
Something heavy moved, slapping across water, beating the earth like a drum.

Jerry wiggled his fingers and curled his toes. He took a breath to make sure he could. Finally, he opened his eyes. He lay on his stomach, his cheek pressed against wet grass. Shapes moved behind a curtain of smoke. Something was on fire. His ears rang, but other sounds slowly penetrated the wall of tinnitus.

Muffled voices.

Screaming.

He heard someone crying out his name, but they were far away, might as well have been in another state. His nose tickled with smoke, and when he opened his mouth, all that came forth was a violent cough. The fog over his mind cleared, his eyes regained their focus, and the world began to make sense again, but not the way it used to. No, Jerry doubted it ever would again.

He braced his hand against the earth and started to pull himself to his feet when a sharp pain exploded in his ribs.

A voice screamed, *"You son of a bitch!"*

Another swift blow followed, and Jerry found his voice. He cried out, sought to shield his ribs, but his attacker wasn't deterred. A rubber sole connected with his fingers, and Jerry heard them crack. The pain hadn't arrived yet—he was still too numb from the blast, his brain still waking up—but it would, and soon. He clenched his teeth and rolled away from his attacker.

The pain announced its presence mid-roll. He tried to flex his left hand and shrieked. Gasping, he collapsed on his back and sucked air through his teeth. His left hand was already swelling, the index, middle, and ring fingers bent back a little too far. Trying to move them was pure agony.

"You goddamn murderer!" Arthur's scream sliced through the ache coating his mind.

The world snapped into focus with harsh clarity.

The explosion had thrown him out of the pond. Curtains of smoke billowed in the wind. The bandstand was ablaze, its roof partially caved in, and a whine of feedback droned from one of the speakers. The Moon Pool was alight, and the portal was no more. A massive slab of Bailey's Rock had splashed down and appeared to be moving.

He strained his eyes against the smoke. No, not moving. *Writhing.*

Worms covered the stone's remains, crawling over one another, panicked by the loss of their nest.

When Jerry looked away, he witnessed a similar sight across the park. The people of Fairview were in the throes of painful reversion. They lay on the ground, convulsing amid the overturned chairs and mess of party favors, their bodies little more than gnarled roots of a felled tree.

Standing between them and the pool was Arthur, blood seeping from a deep gash in his forehead and coating half his face like war paint. His loud Hawaiian shirt hung in tatters at his shoulder, exposing a field of burned skin down his left arm.

He clenched and unclenched his fists. "She's dead because of you! You couldn't just let things be, you selfish monster!"

Jerry scanned the chaos again, unsure who Arthur was talking about. Then he saw movement near the fragment of rock in the pool. A leg lay exposed at one end, twitching.

Ding-dong the bitch is dead.

He took a breath, worked through the pain in his ribs, and forced himself to his feet. The world swam with bursts of color.

"Do you have any idea what you've done?" Arthur stared at the smoking remains of Bailey's Rock. "My legacy—my *family's* legacy—all gone." He turned back to Jerry and staggered forward. Light glinted from blood and sweat coating his face. "I *trusted* you."

Jerry cleared a wad of phlegm from his throat and coughed, wondered how much smoke he'd already inhaled. His lungs were on fire, his words crackling like kindling. "You drugged me and tried to make me one of your slaves, like all of them." He swept his hand through the air, across Fairview's population caught in contorted suffering, but Arthur paid them no mind. "And it never once occurred to you that someone wouldn't want your goddess's 'gifts.' I just wanted to be left alone, Arthur. To mourn. To die. And you *stole* that from me. Goddamn you."

"I took a broken man and gave him new life. Just like I did for all of them. All those broken people clinging to life while it slipped from their hands. They didn't know what they wanted until I gave it to them. I gave you all a reason to go on. A purpose." Arthur stooped down, fished something from the grass, and straightened with a grim smile across his gory face, a crazed desperation in place of his eyes. Patches of his face bulged and broke as worms pierced the skin. "But if you want to die, old man, far be it from me to stop you."

Jerry's heart froze in his throat. The dagger. Now back in the hands of its owner, the old blade looked far more menacing than it ever had in his.

He couldn't face this man, not with a half-broken hand and a few broken ribs. Even breathing hurt. Part of him wanted to turn and run, but the other part wanted to kick Arthur's ass, injuries be damned.

The earth trembled beneath them, and stones rattled and cracked somewhere behind the smoke. A single word filled Jerry's mind in a pulse of psychic transmission.

Hunger.

The crowd quieted, and Arthur froze, his expression dipping from psychotic joy to icy realization. Eyes wide, he turned just as the alien monstrosity pulled itself toward them through the smoke. The bulging limb, once part of a greater beast, had been severed when the portal abruptly closed, and yet it lived on apart from itself, driven by hunger. It crawled along the ground, digging a trench in its wake while thick vines of muscle flexed and contracted in unison.

The creature was more than just tissue. As it drew nearer, Jerry saw other appendages sprouting from its mass. Bones poked through the muscle, forming a million tiny scuttling legs. Together, their movement created a rippling effect along the lower half, aiding the mass in its movement.

Pustules erupted through the creature's trunk and split open, revealing more of the eyes Jerry had glimpsed through the portal. Jaundiced and marred with flecks of brilliant green, the multi-lobed eyes turned erratically in their sockets, observing this brave new world before they focused on the two men. The maw opened wide, revealing its lamprey formation of curved teeth, a ravenous smile eager to devour the world and everything in it.

"Goddess," Arthur said.

The serpentine beast reared back and struck the chairman with whipcrack speed. Arthur screamed only once—a quick, gurgling cry not of pain but of disbelief. A sickening crunch followed, silencing the man forever in the roiling guts of his moon goddess.

Jerry sucked in his breath, terrified of making a move or sound. He hadn't planned for this—how could he?—and there were limits to his bravery he wasn't too proud to admit. Blowing up the stone had been his goal, but now he was at a loss.

God, I hope Kat and Lisa got out of here.

The creature swung around. Gouts of Arthur's blood poured across its rows of fangs. A shred of his Hawaiian shirt hung from the teeth, tattered and bloodstained, all that was left of the man's legacy.

Yellow eyes studied Jerry, sizing him up as a morsel to be indulged or savored later.

He closed his eyes and thought about what he'd said to Arthur, how he'd only wanted to be left alone, to mourn and die. Maybe that had been true months before, but now, as he faced his end, he realized he wanted to go on. Not only for Katherine and Lisa, but for himself. It's what Abby would have wanted for him. To keep on living. To find happiness and love again. Even if he lost his mind in the process, he would do it on his own terms.

"He isn't worthy, goddess. Take us instead!"

Bradley Scott, shirtless and bloody from his transformation, knelt before the monstrosity with arms in the air. Matilda joined him, followed by dozens of others. They threw themselves at the mercy of their goddess, begging to be the next devoured. Was their madness the work of the emissaries or a collective psychosis wrought by years of Arthur's brainwashing?

Jerry would never know.

The goddess swung its body around to face its throng of supplicants, swatting Jerry with its tail like a horse to a fly. The impact sent him flying backward across the park, where he landed in a crumpled heap. The force stole his breath, dulled his senses so deeply he couldn't voice a scream.

No matter. The rest of Fairview Acres screamed for him.

Lisa eased her mother down when they reached the street at the edge of the park. Winded, aching, she fell beside her and gasped for air. *I'll do more miles on the treadmill,* she promised herself. *After a nice long shower and a week's worth of sleep. And that vacation.*

She sat on the asphalt and gazed back at the remains of the park. They had just reached the foot of the slope when Bailey's Rock exploded, and she'd had to fight with her mother to keep going. Now, staring across the crater, Lisa observed the carnage of Jerry's plan. Screams echoed from below. There was something moving down there through the smoke. Something the size of a bus. Maybe two.

Her mind flashed back to the portal in the sky and the massive eye staring through. Fairview's moon goddess. Whatever it was had scrambled something in her brain, filled her with unease whenever she thought about it, and made the hairs on her neck stand at attention. It was something ripped out of a nightmare, and it left her feeling small, insignificant. She feared it would haunt her for years to come.

"Jerry!"

Her mother tried to stand, and, when she couldn't, resolved to crawl her way back down the hill. Her whole body hitched and shuddered as her chest filled with uncontrollable sobs.

"Mom, no. Please." Lisa took hold of her arm and pulled her back. And still her mother fought, tried to push Lisa away. "We can't. Whatever's happening down there isn't finished."

But her mother wouldn't listen. She was a gibbering mess, looked worse in that moment than Lisa had ever seen her before. A thin pale widow crying over another lost love. The realization filled her heart with an ache she hadn't felt since her father died.

"I have to go back for him. Please, Lisa, let me—"

A shape flew out of the smoke and crashed hard into the grass just beyond the obelisks.

Her mother pulled herself to the rim and peered down. "Oh, God, it's him."

Lisa didn't wait for her mother's plea. She raced back down the hill. Leaving him to die down there was something she couldn't live with; worse, her mother would never forgive her.

When she came upon her friend, she approached with caution, afraid that whatever she had glimpsed through the smoke would take notice. Jerry lay sprawled across the grass like a ragdoll, twisted at the waist, one leg curled at the knee, the other pointed straight. His left hand looked bad. She couldn't see any other injuries, but after an impact like this, the worst of it was likely internal. However, his chest rose and fell. Slow, but steady. She could work with that.

"Jerry, can you hear me?"

He made no sound.

Okay, we'll do this the hard way. She glanced back at the hillside. *How the hell am I going to drag you back up there?*

He coughed himself awake, opened his eyes, and looked up in confusion.

"Hey there," she grunted, forcing herself to smile. "You had a big fall, Mr. Campbell."

"Is it—" He tried to sit up and cried out in pain.

"No, hey, hold on. Try not to move—"

"It's still here," he gasped. "Get away from here, Lisa."

She slipped her hands under his armpits, braced against his weight, straightened her back, and began to lift. "Not without you," she said. "Get up. Mom will kill me if I leave you." A beat later: "Do you think those worms are still, you know, active?"

Jerry caught his breath, winced as he put weight on his feet. "I don't know. Maybe?"

"Good, 'cause I'm not carrying you all the way back up that hill."

Lisa waited until he stood on his own to let him go. The earth rumbled beneath them, and a new chorus of cries erupted from what remained of the congregation. She caught a glimpse of something huge and dark curling through the smoke in silhouette against the blaze. Something like a snake—or a giant worm.

Wide-eyed, Jerry turned to her and motioned toward the road. "Get moving," he said, "and don't look back."

"Are you alri—"

He pushed her forward. That was as good an answer as she could expect, and she did as he'd told her. Together, they retreated up the hill.

Below, the last of Fairview's residents screamed into the night while their goddess consumed them.

Above, the eye of the moon closed, and the cosmos turned away from their plight with a full belly.

EPILOGUE
THE DANCE

32

The following days were a blur for Jerry, half of them spent drugged and unconscious in his hospital bed. When he was awake, he whiled away the time staring out the window, trying to piece together all that had happened into an image that made sense—or at the very least, one that didn't follow him into his dreams.

There was pain, of course. Wasn't there always?

Three broken ribs, two broken fingers, and multiple surface-level lesions, burns, and scratches. His whole body felt like a fresh bruise, and no matter how carefully he moved, something inevitably hurt. One of his many doctors had said he was lucky one of the ribs didn't puncture a lung. Jerry had wanted to ask if anything else showed up on his X-rays, something that might look like a nest of worms, but the drugs in his IV dragged him back under the surface into sleep.

His memory of the night at the Moon Pool had fractured since his intake at the hospital. He remembered Lisa had come back to save him, bless her, but he couldn't remember where the car came from. He remembered Katherine and the way she'd held him in the backseat, but he couldn't remember how long the drive had taken or the name of the hospital. Lehigh Valley, maybe, or St. Jude's. Questions for the nurses about Fairview Acres were met with blank stares and sympathetic smiles, suggestions that he get his rest.

Lisa came by to check on him, always dressed in her scrubs, a different color for each day of the week. Today she wore purple, but he forgot to ask which day it was. He was more interested in how Katherine was doing.

"She's good," Lisa said, checking his fluids. Vague and deflective, the sort of reply he'd expected.

"Don't bullshit me, Lisa." He took hold of her hand. "The worms, did they—"

"They're still there. A tech spotted them on your CT scan, so the doctor ordered an MRI. You don't remember?"

He tried to remember. Nothing remained but bits and pieces of that night after the blast.

"You and Mom and other survivors from Fairview are a huge topic in the medical community right now. Specialists are expected to arrive next week to examine you all."

"What's being done about it now?"

"We're treating the survivors like we would sporadic Creutzfeldt-Jakob disease. I know, it's a mouthful. Basically, prion proteins begin eating brain cells. No one knows why."

"Except it's worms."

Lisa nodded. "That's the wild card, hence all the special interest." She tapped one of the plump bags hanging from the IV pole. "So, we're pumping you full of antiparasitics and crossing our fingers they do the job. Otherwise, surgery—"

Jerry let go of her hand. "No need for that. The damage is already done."

Deep down, he'd hoped that destroying the meteorite would somehow magically save them from its deteriorating effects, but that had been a pipe dream, one as haphazard as his plan. *You tried, Jerry, but in the end it didn't matter. You had a good run.*

She took a step back from his bed. "Mom said the same thing."

"Is she okay?"

"As good as she can be. She's comfortable, which is all I can ask for at this point. Are you comfortable? Need anything?"

"A new brain, maybe. Otherwise, I guess I'm as good as I'm gonna get. Thank you."

Lisa gave his good hand a squeeze. "Always." She glanced over her shoulder, made sure no one was watching, and quickly gave him a kiss on his forehead. "For what you did. For me and for Mom. I'll never forget it."

He reached up, wiped away a tear rolling down her cheek. "It's what good neighbors are for."

She smiled. "Duty calls. It's going to be a long night for me. Need anything before I go?"

"Just one thing. What happened to Fairview? After... you know."

Lisa nodded, switched on the TV hanging on the wall. She changed the channel to the news station. "Remote controls are on the panel at your side. Have a good night, my friend."

Jerry gave her a weak thumbs-up as she left the room.

"—an update on a developing story."

His attention snapped back to the screen, yanked free of the sludge in his mind. He focused on the well-manicured newscaster and the red banner stretched across the lower third. "EXPLOSION AT FAIRVIEW," it read.

"It has been four days since emergency channels were swamped with reports of an explosion here at Fairview Acres, a retirement community outside the village of Fairview, Pennsylvania. Since then, investigators continue to be puzzled by their findings, and as of this afternoon, they remain unwilling to provide definite facts as to what truly occurred here Friday night."

Unwilling. Jerry rolled his eyes. *More like unable.*

He imagined the police were having a hell of a time making heads or tails out of what remained. The newscast cut to a clip of the state police commissioner at today's press conference: "—not enough evidence to suggest foul play at this time. Our priority is to locate the missing members of the community. Given the size of Fairview Acres, this will take a considerable amount of time."

Jerry's blood pressure rose a few points. *Not enough evidence? It was a goddamn blood bath.*

The newscast cut to images of the neighborhood. The front gate. The park. Bailey's Rock. At the end, an aerial photo of the park. Recent, too—an angry plume of smoke billowed from the bandstand's remains. What caught Jerry's attention, however, was an enormous ring of bare earth entrenched near the Moon Pool.

Looks like a big hole, he thought, and felt the world give out beneath him. *It went into hiding.*

The image transitioned to a familiar photo. "Among the missing is local philanthropist and community founder Arthur Peterson. Police have requested that anyone with information regarding the disappearance of Fairview's residents please come forward—"

Jerry pressed a button on the side of his bed. The television blinked off.

He closed his eyes, tried to force the implications from his mind, but they remained no matter how hard he pushed. Visions of the goddess crawled through his head, inching their way deeper into his subconscious and entangling with something his nurse had said.

Katherine was already suffering the effects of withdrawal when everything exploded at the park. He would, too, if he wasn't already—the medication in his system softened the edges of everything, obscuring where one ended and the other began—and his thoughts slowly retreated into the shadows.

Had he truly saved them?

He feared transforming into one of those nightcrawler creatures, flailing blindly in the dark at the behest of an alien master. Instead, he was destined to become a different kind of creature, flailing blindly through the darkness of the mind, lost in a funhouse of mirrors where nothing was as it seemed. Would Katherine suffer the same fate? Would what was left of their lives be riddled with debilitating pain and confusion? He had gained nothing, saved them from nothing but Arthur's hubris, only to waste away in the shadow of his own.

"You stupid old man..." he whispered.

His heart sank deeper into a blackened pit of regret. It might have remained there if not for a voice somewhere above, just out of reach from the shadows of his darkened mind.

You're foolish sometimes, Jerry Campbell, and you never see the bigger picture.

Abby. Always Abby, the voice of reason, his guiding light.

How many others did you save from slavery to Arthur's goddess? The ones who would have followed after you in the years to come? Countless. For someone who wants to be left alone so much, you sure do like to put others first.

But now the goddess is loose, he thought, *digging its way into the earth. Hiding from us. What if... what if it...*

He drifted along a warm current of drugs and fatigue, lulled deeper into sleep by a woman's voice. Not Abby this time. Not Katherine's either, though the voice sounded similar. Younger. Confident. What he imagined a daughter might sound like.

For what you did. For me and for Mom. I'll never forget it.

Such a sweet thing to say. He'd have to remember to thank her in the morning. But what was her name? It was there, right on the tip of his tongue, written across the walls of his mind in script he couldn't read, the letters shifting in and out of focus and changing whenever he looked away.

She was a friend. Someone who had helped him, and he had helped her in return.

God, what was her name?

◐

Katherine watched the sunset from her hospital bed. Finally, the medication in her IV bag had kicked in, and she could enjoy her time free of the withdrawals gripping every joint and muscle in her body. The body aches were so bad she hurt to breathe. Even the act of moving her eyes brought her pain. The worms inside were starving.

Soon they would go to work on her mind just like before. The rest of her life would be spent with one foot in the shadows—not closer to death but to erasure. The parts that made her Katherine Dunnally and not a faceless mannequin would slowly, painfully be deleted one piece, one memory at a time.

She wanted to be angry, wanted to rage against this cruel fate, but beneath it all she was grateful. Not for the nightmare they had survived, but for the connection she had made through it all. After Reggie's passing, she'd thought she would spend the rest of her days alone, in the grip of her home's emptiness, haunted by the ghost of what might have been.

Instead, she'd found Jerry.

No doubt he was suffering the same effects as she. Struggling against this forced entropy, anxiously awaiting the moment when everything began to slip away. But somehow, she hoped—she prayed—their connection would survive. Even with one foot in the dark, when their faces were all but vanished, they would still find the other's hand to hold.

A friend.

A love.

A light.

He would regret what he had done, she was certain of that. A terminal thinker, that one, always considering what could have been, what should have been. The maybes and the ifs. Steppingstones to hell, her daddy used to say. She wondered if Jerry's late wife had been his anchor to keep him from drifting too far into his own head.

She hoped so. And she liked to think she could do the same if he'd let her.

The door opened, and a nurse in purple scrubs stepped inside. "Mama? How're you feeling?"

Katherine studied the young woman, thought she looked a bit like Reggie in some ways. She stared in silence for a minute before the nurse's features slowly came into focus. Yes, she knew this face.

"Hi, honey."

Lisa smiled, more from relief than happiness.

Something lit up in Katherine's mind, a bright light that filled her with joy, made her heart sing. "I always loved your smile, baby girl."

"I know, Mama." Lisa pulled up a chair and sat at the bedside. "I saw Jerry a little while ago."

"Oh, did you? How is my love?"

Lisa blushed, chuckled to herself. "He's got a long road ahead of him. He asked about you."

"Did he? He's such a sweet man."

"Mmhmm. How are— Do you remember those exercises we talked about?" She pointed to the book of crosswords on the bedside table. "Did you do any of them?"

"I tried, honey, but I got so tired. And my fingers hurt, too." Katherine held out her hands, tried to clench them into fists, but found she couldn't. "I promise I'll keep trying."

"Good," Lisa said. "Please do, okay? And listen, I probably won't see you tomorrow until after my shift starts. I have a call with your insurance advocate, and I don't know how long that's going to take."

"That's okay, sweetheart. I'll be all right."

Lisa took her hand and flinched. "Your hands are so cold all the time... Maybe if you're feeling up to it tomorrow, I can take you to see Jerry. I think he'd like that."

"I would, too."

Katherine smiled when Lisa kissed her forehead. She watched her daughter leave, waited until the door was closed before freeing the tears welling over her eyes. Would she remember her tomorrow? Would she remember Jerry?

She closed her eyes, and replayed a handful of memories from her life, eager to see them one more time. Just in case it was the last.

◐

Three weeks passed before Jerry and Katherine saw each other again.

Both had setbacks to their recovery, as Lisa had feared they might, related to the ongoing chronic pain affecting their cognitive functions. Others had arrived since the explosion, all suffering from the same symptoms, and their respective scans corroborated what the doctors already knew. Specialists and other medical experts came and went, took samples and scans, each positing a different theory, but their prognoses remained the same: No cure. All they could do was treat the symptoms and keep their patients as comfortable as possible.

Lisa took the treatment in stride as best she could, rising every day with determination, eager to see Jerry and her mother in better spirits, and returning home each morning feeling a little more defeated than the last. She'd known this was coming, knew it couldn't be solved with anything modern medicine had to offer, and there were times she struggled to keep her mouth shut about the cause. But rationality always won out in the end. There was no way to sugarcoat the words "space worms are the problem" that might help her avoid being laughed out of the hospital. She supposed the same truth wouldn't go over well with the detective who'd left her a voicemail that morning either.

Instead, Lisa tried to focus on what mattered: the time she had left with her mother and the man who had saved her.

Everything else was secondary. She'd read the writing on the wall the moment her mother struggled to recognize her. It had happened faster than she expected, but then again, dementia always would happen too fast.

The last time her mother had gone through this, Lisa struggled to make it through her shifts without sobbing. Now she was numb to the experience, choosing instead to enjoy the time with her mother, even if the role she played was less a daughter and more of a caregiver. It allowed her to see a different side to Katherine Dunnally, the dynamic between parent and child having fallen to the wayside, and she discovered that she liked her mother as a person, a friend. Funny, observant, and so sharp-witted despite her maladies. The ladies at the nurse's station on her floor were in love with her too.

Jerry, however, was a different matter.

He had improved enough physically to go for daily assisted walks despite the crippling pain. His medication eased the symptoms, but like he told her, the agony was always there and ready to sing. His and Katherine's daily routines were identical, their doctors having conferred and agreed that physical activity might ease their suffering, but Lisa feared the walks weren't doing much for Jerry's disposition.

Each time Lisa visited him, he seemed a bit more distant, a few degrees more morose. Katherine had her, but Jerry had no one. Depression was a common and insidious visitor for people in his predicament. It was bad enough that he was struggling to remember his surroundings every day, or the staff with whom he interacted; an inherent sadness and loss of meaning only made the situation worse. There were times she struggled to motivate him enough to climb out of bed. Her father had gone through the same thing, and while his deterioration had been heartbreaking to witness, at least she'd had the benefit of ignorance over the cause. Knowing the cause now—and being unable to cure it—seemed worse somehow, made her feel even more helpless than before.

One day she had flowers delivered to Jerry's room, hoping it would spur a smile, but he only gave them a passing glance before zoning out. The next morning she lay in bed, half-delirious from sleep deprivation, trying to figure out a way to preserve Jerry's cognition just a little longer.

There's gotta be something else I can do, she thought. *What did we do for Dad? What can I—*

The answer tumbled upward from the dark of her sleep mask. She'd been so focused on her patient with the careful, pragmatic eye of a nurse that she'd forgotten the matters of heart. The answer was obvious.

That night, she came prepared.

Lisa opened the door to Jerry's room and called his name. "Jerry, it's that time again, my friend."

He looked away from the television with heavy eyes. "I told you people to leave me alone."

"That's no way to talk to me, Mr. Campbell. Come on, we're going on a little trip." She pushed the wheelchair to his bedside. "There's someone who wants to see you."

"Don't have anyone left," he sighed, returning his attention to a game show on the screen.

Lisa reached over and switched off the television. "Yes, you do. You remember her. Katherine Dunnally."

Recognition flashed across his face.

Yes, that's what she was waiting for. Something to trigger the man lost inside. The memories weren't gone; they were just hidden away, and sometimes she had to help with the search.

"Kat," he said.

"Uh huh. She's waiting for you downstairs. Says you owe her a dance."

"I. . ." He trailed off, chewed his lip as he searched his memories. Finally, he nodded. "Yes, I do. Did you bring my dancing shoes?"

Lisa smiled. "They're downstairs waiting for you. Let's get you out of that bed, okay?"

Lisa wheeled Jerry out of the elevator and down the hall toward the nurse's station. Three nurses in blue scrubs and party hats stood outside, sharing a laugh with a white-haired lady in a wheelchair. The station was decorated with balloons and streamers, and an oldies station played from a small desktop radio.

"What's all this?" Jerry asked.

"It's for you," Lisa said, smiling through the tears. "For you and Mama."

The nurses parted, allowing Jerry to see Katherine in full view. His fingers drummed nervously along the arms of his wheelchair.

Lisa parked his chair in front of her mother's. She leaned next to his ear and said, "She's waited so long to see you, Jerry."

But he wasn't listening anymore. He leaned forward and held out a shaky hand. His breathing hitched, sputtered, as he fought against the pain. Recognition beamed across his face, his cheeks rosy red and his eyes alight with a life he hadn't had in weeks.

Lisa stepped back and watched the same life return to her mother. Sallow cheeks flushed with warmth. Her mother was suddenly radiant again, the cheerful woman Lisa had once known and feared she had lost, a beam of hope in a cold universe of chaos.

Katherine took Jerry's hand. "I missed you."

"I've been upstairs this whole time," he said. "I thought I... No, I didn't forget. Not you."

The other nurses sighed a collective "aww," but the couple paid them no mind. Lisa and her coworkers might as well have not been there.

"You'd better not," Katherine said, a mischievous grin spreading across her face. "You still owe me that dance."

"I know, honey, I know."

Katherine braced her weight against the arms of the chair and slowly began to stand. Jerry followed her lead, stepping down from the footrests, pushing himself up from the seat.

Panic rose in Lisa's throat, but she held out her hand to stay the other nurses. *Let's see if they can,* she wanted to say, yet the words were stuck in fear of ruining the moment. The nurses watched in silent awe as Jerry and Katherine stood before one another.

From the radio, a DJ said, "Here's one from way back. Love will tear us apart, folks. Always." His voice faded to a quick guitar riff and steady beat.

Katherine said, "Want me to lead?"

Jerry tapped his feet to the tune. "No. . . I think I can lead this time."

She smiled, took his free hand, and leaned her head close to his shoulder.

Together, they held on, one shuffled step after another, two stars in orbit around the vacuous dark. They shone brighter with each movement, blocking out the emptiness that would consume them in time. Maybe soon, maybe tomorrow, but not now.

Now was all that mattered.

And they danced.

ACKNOWLEDGMENTS

This wasn't supposed to be a book, and it wasn't titled *The Sundowner's Dance*.

What began in 2018 as a short story titled "By the Eye of the Moon" slowly morphed into a potential co-writing opportunity with Chad Lutzke, but I wasn't in the right headspace for a collaboration at that point in time. Unsure of the direction I wanted to take—and uncertain that I was ready for this story—I set "By the Eye of the Moon" aside to work on other projects.

Sometime around 2021, Doug Murano and D. Alexander Ward invited me to submit something for *Shadows Over Main Street: Volume Three*, and that old unfinished short story came to mind. The pandemic and COVID-19 already had me thinking about mortality, and "By the Eye of the Moon" seemed like a good opportunity to work through the issue, so I returned to the story of Jerry and his weird neighbors.

But after dusting off the pages and reacquainting myself with Fairview, I realized this couldn't be a short story. This was a year after the release of *Devil's Creek*, my longest novel to date, and the idea of writing another novel-length work seemed too daunting. *Fine,* I thought, *it could be a novella.*

Obviously, since you're reading this, you know I was wrong. As I often am.

The title changed around the same time I realized I had a novel on my hands. By that point, it was the summer of 2022, and I was still thinking about mortality—just not my own. My wife, Erica, discovered a lump in her breast, which led to several intense weeks of tests and procedures and waiting.

So much waiting. My anxious brain loves to fixate on worst case scenarios, and believe me, I was full of them. There were many sleepless nights spent sitting in the dark, wondering what the hell I would do if I lost her, and how pointless life might feel without her by my side.

I'm happy to say her tests came back negative and the cyst was benign. I was grateful but shaken. How quickly our lives hit the brakes in the face of such a scare. The anxiety was palpable, deep-rooted, insidious.

The aftershocks found their way into this story, in Jerry's tendency for isolation and secret yearning for connection, in the emissaries with their need to burrow, consume, and assimilate. Art is nothing if not a reflection of the artist at their most vulnerable human moment. I guess this is one of mine.

But I digress. Anyway.

I've got some wonderful people to thank for making this book happen.

Alan Lastufka and the team at Shortwave Publishing for taking a chance on this weird, wormy book.

My amazing agent, Becky LeJeune, for her insight, guidance, and early-morning texts.

Marissa van Uden for her sharp editorial eye.

Several early readers gave vital feedback to an earlier draft of this story. Thanks to Laurel Hightower, Anthony J. Rapino, Nikki Nelson-Hicks, and Richard Dansky. Go buy all their books.

Thanks to my sensitivity reader, Kenlyn Elisha Kelly, for making sure I treated the elderly with utmost respect.

Amelia Bennett, for taking my call that night, and listening to me cry in the dark.

David Rockey and Richard B. Wood, for listening to me ramble when I just needed to talk.

Cynthia Pelayo, my sister in publishing, for talking me off a ledge more times than I can count.

Dacia Arnold, for introducing me to her friend, Becky.

For Mom and Dad and Brenda and Kim and Mamaw, and for my friends, my family, my tribe: there are far too many of you to name, but I love you all. Hugs and gratitude to everyone.

For Erica and Gabe, my love and light, forever.

And lastly, for you, dear reader and fellow heathen: Thank you for reading my words, always.

Todd Keisling
Womelsdorf, Pennsylvania
July 2024

ABOUT THE AUTHOR

Todd Keisling is a writer and designer of the horrific and strange. His books include *Devil's Creek*, a 2020 Bram Stoker Award finalist for Superior Achievement in a Novel, *Scanlines, The Final Reconciliation*, and most recently, *Cold, Black & Infinite: Stories of the Horrific & Strange*. A pair of his earlier works were recipients of the University of Kentucky's Oswald Research & Creativity Prize for Creative Writing (2002 and 2005), and his second novel, *The Liminal Man*, was an Indie Book Award finalist in Horror & Suspense (2013). He lives in Pennsylvania with his family.

toddkeisling.com

ALSO BY TODD KEISLING

THE SOUTHLAND MYTHOS
Devil's Creek
Scanlines
The Final Reconciliation

THE MONOCHROME TRILOGY
A Life Transparent
The Liminal Man
Nonentity

COLLECTIONS
Ugly Little Things: Collected Horrors
Cold, Black & Infinite: Stories of the Horrific & Strange

A NOTE FROM SHORTWAVE PUBLISHING

Thank you for reading *The Sundowner's Dance*! If you enjoyed this book, please consider writing a review. Reviews help readers find more titles they may enjoy, and that helps us continue to publish titles like this.

For more Shortwave titles, visit us online...

OUR WEBSITE
Shortwavepublishing.com

SOCIAL MEDIA
@ShortwaveBooks

EMAIL US
contact@shortwavepublishing.com

Content Warnings:

This story contains themes, scenes, and/or depictions of elder abuse, dementia, medical trauma, self-harm, mutilation, mental illness, animal death (and resurrection), death of a spouse, gratuitous wormage, gaslighting, violence, and body horror.